ALL OUR BROKEN VOWS

AN MMF ROMANCE

THE BROKEN SERIES
BOOK 2

MYA MORE

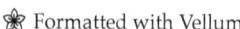 Formatted with Vellum

To anyone who wishes for boyfriends that are boyfriends, I hope you get double the dick and double the Os.

CONTENT WARNINGS

Mentions of anxiety and an on-page panic attack
Bullying (not between the main love interests)
Death of a sibling (off the page)
Elements of homophobia, including internalized homophobic thoughts
Outing of a queer person
Child neglect (implied-not by a main character)
Light Impact play (spanking)
Kink exploration
Hand necklaces
Degradation

You know your limits and triggers. Your mental health is important.

Any scenes with kink depicted in this book are for entertainment purposes and are not intended to be educational or accurate depictions of a BDSM/kink lifestyle. Please do your research before engaging in similar acts to make sure you are your partner(s) are informed and safe.

Author's note:

This series contains a sex club named Pulse. I want to acknowledge that in 2016, a real nightclub named Pulse in Florida was the site of an unspeakable tragedy. While the Pulse in this story in entirely fictional and unrelated, I chose the name with care and intention. My hope is that this imagined space reflects the values the real Pulse came to represent: a place of safety, freedom, and inclusion. In this story, Pulse is a sanctuary where all people are welcome to explore their desires without fear, shame, or discrimination.

DICKTIONARY 🌶

For anyone wondering where the steamy scenes take place—whether you're eager to dive right in or prefer to skip them altogether—you'll find them in the following chapters:

🌶 Chapter 4
🌶 Chapter 5
🌶 Chapter 8
🌶 Chapter 9
🌶 Chapter 16
🌶 Chapter 17
🌶 Chapter 18
🌶 Chapter 19
🌶 Chapter 20
🌶 Chapter 21
🌶 Chapter 23
🌶 Chapter 24
🌶 Chapter 27
🌶 Chapter 30
🌶 Chapter 33

🌶 Bonus Chapter (download)

PLAYLIST ♫

Feels Like Home - Chantal Kreviazuk
A Safe Place to Land - Sara Bareilles & John Legend
The Bones - Maren Morris
Best Friend - Ingrid Michaelson
I'm in Love with My Best Friend - Baggio
I Choose You - Sara Bareilles
Lucky - Jason Mraz & Colbie Caillat
If You Leave Me Now - Charlie Puth & Boyz II Men
Can't Let Go - Anthony Hamilton
I Get to Love You - Lyndsey Elm
my other half - Novulent
Soulmate - Chanin
The Vow - RuthAnne
Still Into You - Paramore
Say You Won't Let Go - James Arthur
This Love (Taylor's Version) - Taylor Swift
Kiss Me - Ed Sheeran
Next to Me - Nicotine Dolls
You Belong With Me - Taylor Swift
We're Going Home - Vance Joy
Lay Me Down - Sam Smith

You Matter To Me - Sara Bareilles & Jason Mraz
The Lucky Ones - Pentatonix
Perfect - Ed Sheeran
sea of lovers - Christina Perri
I Miss You - Sarah Miles
Missing Piece - Vance Joy
Blessings - Hollow Coves
All That Really Matters - ILLENIUM & Teddy Swims
Loved You Before - Natalie Taylor

SPICY SPINE SISTERS

TBR

Because Becka's love of books and book club are important to the story, I wanted to share what's on her book club's TBR. I was inspired by Kristen Proby sharing a TBR in *When We Burn*. Happy reading!

He's Not My Type by Meghan Quinn
When We Burn by Kristen Proby
Give Me More by Sara Cate
The Foul Out by Jenni Bara
Ice Rivals - Kristen Granata
Ignite by Melanie Harlow
Trouble by Britannée Nicole
Reckless on Ice by Adrian R. Hale
The Secrets We Hide by Berlin Wick
So Wrong by Abby Millsaps

CONTENTS

PROLOGUE

ROBERT

Becka is the most beautiful bride in the world. And the most stunning part about her, the thing that knocks me off my feet, is the way this woman loves me. She gets me, truly sees me, and for some unknown reason, wants to marry me anyway. As she walks down the aisle to me, all I can think about is how fucking lucky I am.

Despite the choice of venue and the minister standing behind me, we aren't church people. It was the only compromise I was willing to make with my super religious parents. My family is important to me, but today I'm choosing a new family, a new person to build a life with.

Once she reaches the end of the aisle, her father kisses her before taking his seat, and she joins me on the dais.

"Marriage is a blessing from above. It's forming a union that bonds the whole family. It's a lifelong commitment that, like a garden, requires constant love, work, and attention to thrive. We're here today to join Robert Gardner and Becka Daniels in holy matrimony," the minister starts, but I can't focus on his words as I turn to stare at my bride. She's nodding and smiling as the minister drones on. I take in every inch of her gorgeous features, the plumpness of her full lips, the arch of her cheek, the way her beautiful brown hair is pulled back, curls framing her face. She's a vision, and in a few minutes, I'll get to call her my wife.

"Will you please join hands and face one another?" the minister asks. Becka hands her bouquet to Bridget and then turns, taking my hands in hers.

"Robert, is it your intention to take Becka as your lawfully wedded wife?"

"It is," I say, smiling down into her brilliant green eyes.

"Becka, is it your intention to take Robert as your lawfully wedded husband?"

"It is—or is this where I say I do?" she asks.

"Either is fine," the minister says as a laugh rolls through the crowd. "It's my understanding that the two of you have written your own vows as a testament of the love and devotion you have for one another. Vows are a sacred covenant expressing your feelings for each other and the lifelong commitment you're making. Robert, please read your vows."

I clear my throat. "Becka, I knew I'd marry you the second our eyes connected and you smiled at me. I knew right then I would love you until my last breath. That I'd want to spend every minute of the rest of my life in your light.

"I vow to push you out of your comfort zone.

"I vow to love you, and only you, for the rest of my life.

"I vow to make you laugh, often and thoroughly.

"I vow to always communicate with you, open up to you, and share my feelings with you, even when it's hard for me.

"I vow to provide everything you need to be happy."

"Dammit, you're not supposed to make me cry," she whispers softly so only I can hear as I reach up to catch the tear before it spills over her lashes. "It's a good thing I wore my waterproof mascara today," she jokes loud enough for the crowd to hear.

"Becka, please read your vows," the minister says.

She looks up at me with tears shining in her eyes. "Robert, I love you more than I can begin to express, and trust me, that's saying a lot because I don't have a hard time expressing myself," she says as the crowd laughs. "You are the only person I could imagine as my husband, and the only person I could ever imagine loving for the rest of my life.

"I vow to always tell you the truth, even if it's painful, but to do it in a way that doesn't hurt you.

"I vow to always share my feelings with you, even if they're a lot, because I know you can handle it.

"I vow to always choose you above others, even when life is difficult.

"I vow to be everything you need.

"I vow to love you, who you are, who you will become, and the family we build together."

I pull her forehead to mine, kissing it three times, our secret language for "I love you." The minister clears his throat behind us. If I want to kiss my bride, I will, even if we're not to that part of the ceremony yet.

"The rings?"

Bridget hands Becka a ring, as my best man, my brother Jack, hands me mine. She delicately pushes it onto my finger, struggling slightly to move it past my knuckle before she teasingly wipes her brow, and everyone laughs again.

I carefully thread her ring onto her finger as the minister speaks. "These rings are a symbol of your love and lifelong commitment to each other. Let them serve as a constant reminder of the love you have for one another."

I mouth the words "I love you" to her, and she does the same.

"Having made this declaration in front of friends, family, and God today, and by the power vested in me by the State of Ohio, I now pronounce you man and wife. You may kiss your bride."

I don't even let him finish his sentence before I'm pulling

3

her in and capturing her lips in a passionate kiss, willing her to feel every ounce of love and devotion I have for her, only her.

CHAPTER 1

BECKA

I *will not lose my shit on my sister today.*

"Really, Becka? Another one?"

You'd think my sister would be shaming me for drinking one beer too many, adopting too many cats, or sleeping with too many men based on that comment, but no.

"Aren't there enough people on the planet? And you want to create another one? That's irresponsible," she continues, sipping her drink, blissfully unaware of the effect of her words.

I will not lose my shit on my sister today.

"I was just thinking how great it would be if Hallie had a sister. It's not like we're trying or anything." I say defensively. I'd love for my little girl to have a sister. Maybe she'd have a better relationship with hers than I have with mine.

"Plus, aren't you a little old to be having more kids? You're almost thirty-seven."

Not till July, and you're pushing forty.

That does it. I don't care if we're blood and I'm supposed to love her. It doesn't mean I have to like her. And it doesn't mean I have to put up with the hurtful shit that comes out of her mouth.

"I'm going to head out," I say as I pull some cash out of my wallet and throw it on the table.

"Already? We just got here. I've only had one drink." Miranda pouts, pushing out her bottom lip like a petulant toddler.

And I'm already tired of your bullshit.

"Another time," I say, and while I want it to be an empty promise, we both know I'll come back and deal with her venom. It's what I've always done.

My sister means well—sometimes—but she's often thoughtless when it comes to me. The two of us have never fit together the way we should. It's like someone mixed up two puzzles: her precisely cut pieces and my slightly off-kilter ones. I keep trying to mash them together and make them fit, but I end up damaging my pieces in the process. She's not a bad person; she's just not my person.

She has no clue who I am at my core. She's never gotten to know me, preferring to live in her little bubble in which she is the center. I've tried to get closer to her, to get to know the grown-up version of who she's become, but it's useless.

Maybe if you stood up to her, Becka. You could tell her how much her words hurt you. And risk losing more family? No thanks. I'll take my daily dose of WTF and swallow it down like the placating people-pleaser I am.

I've always wanted a big family since the one I was born into doesn't seem to value family relationships the same way I do.

Today's meetup was one I'd been pulling off for months. I hadn't planned on sharing that I wanted another kid. It's not something Robert and I've even talked about. But I was staring at my sister, hoping that this wouldn't be Hallie in twenty years, and it just kind of came out.

I should've known better than to share my thoughts, let alone my joy, with Miranda. While she was excited about us having our daughter Hallie five years ago, this is the same woman who divorced her husband when she found out that he'd fathered a child, deciding that she'd rather be single than be a stepmom. To be fair, the news that her husband was a father came as a shock, even to him.

My sister was livid. Even though he never broke their vows, she declared him a cheater and a deadbeat and demanded we all cut ties with him. She made Robert and I prove that we had deleted his phone number and blocked him on all social media, despite how much neither of us wanted to do it. Robert was especially close to my brother-in-law. Being an introvert, there aren't many people who get to see his true self, and William was one of the few. His extrovert adopted Robert the same way I nabbed my bestie, Bridget. Like a koala clinging to her back and refusing to let go. She hasn't been able to shake me, no matter how hard she's tried.

I push my way through the doors of the pretentious bar where my sister had insisted we meet and leave her at the table. The May humidity hits me instantly, and a bead of sweat trickles down my back. Spring in Columbus is a fickle bitch. It makes dressing a challenge when you never know if there's going to be snow, tornadoes, or summer heat. I tug at the collar of my blouse, peeling it away from my sweaty body as I try to cool myself.

Once I reach my car, I crank up the AC and type out a text.

ME

Remind me why I keep agreeing to this?

ROBERT

That was quick. Miranda being Miranda?

Yup. You'd be proud, she started up with me and I left her there. Paid for my drink and left.

You stopping at Bridget's or coming straight home?

7

> You and Hallie okay if I hang over there for
> a bit?

I got you.

My husband knows me so well. Of course I was going to stop at Bridget's first. It's the only upside to letting my sister choose our meeting spot; while it's inconvenient for me and usually not my scene, it's almost always some new hotspot downtown that ends up being relatively close to my best friend's place.

Or I should say *their* place, since her boyfriend Ethan recently moved in. Ethan is perfect for Bridget, the golden retriever to her black cat energy, and he brings out parts of her that she hides from everyone. It's so good seeing them happy. He helped her recover after she had her ovary removed, and I witnessed my relationship-phobic friend slowly find her person after that. I'm so glad he didn't give up on her, even when she pushed him away.

Guilt still gnaws at me that I couldn't be there for her after she had surgery—but if I had, they may not have fallen in love since he's the one that took care of her.

And I might not have learned my husband's secret kink.

I'd initially freaked out when I'd discovered it and blew up Bridget's phone with texts once we were stateside again after our anniversary trip to Mexico. When she didn't answer me, I even showed up at her place ready to tell her all about it until I came face-to-face with Ethan. I knew in that moment that she'd found her soulmate, and I expected her to fight him tooth and nail. The way he cared for her is the stuff I read about in romance books, reading her thoughts, meeting her needs, standing by her—he was her real-life book boyfriend, and I didn't want to burst that bubble with my discovery that my quiet, grumpy raincloud of a husband enjoyed getting pegged.

It was an accidental discovery. I'm not sure he was aware it was something he'd like. We'd been in a sexual rut ever since our daughter was born, and she recently turned five, so that should tell you how desperate we were for a kid-free vacation. Our daughter loves to sleep in our bed, often sneaking in every night despite us tucking her into her own. Between that, and my out-of-whack hormones—thank you, breastfeeding—our sex life was practically nonexistent. Gone were the days of romance and chemistry; they were replaced with quickies and planned rendezvous with little foreplay. It felt transactional, and I often wanted to skip it altogether. But I craved that connection we used to have when we could take our time and explore each other. What we'd been doing wasn't sex, it was a race to get off.

Robert surprised me with that trip to Mexico and packed every toy and scrap of lace I owned. It was exactly what we needed to reconnect. On the last day of our trip, we'd opted to stay in bed all day. I was riding him reverse-cowgirl style with one of my vibrators held to my clit. My orgasm built quickly, and the hand holding the vibrator slipped as the intensity of it hit me. Robert started pumping faster as my toy slid down his balls and wedged between his cheeks. It was completely accidental. I was overcome with my orgasm and lost my grip, but he started chanting "yes" as I came down from the high and I pushed the lube-covered tip into his hole. His resulting orgasm was so intense, his fingers left bruises on my hips. I ended up playing with his ass three more times that day, including fucking him from behind while jacking him off. And things have been better since that trip. For the most part.

But I needed to talk about this new kink with someone, and Bridget wasn't available, so I turned to Alyx, Ethan's best friend, whom I met the same night Bridget took Ethan home. Blame it on the mother in me—I wanted to make sure I kept tabs on my girl, even if she is two years older than me, so I made Alyx swear to text me once Ethan got home, and he did.

It was nice having someone else rooting for Bridget and Ethan, and he was quite funny in text, so we kept talking. Alyx is pansexual and a bit of a fuckboy, and my questions about kinks never faze him.

The thing is, I've never told Bridget about my friendship with Alyx. She was in her own little world with Ethan for so long, and the longer I went without fessing up, the worse I felt about it. Nothing inappropriate is happening—we're honestly just friends—but I don't want to upset her thinking I'm hiding something from her. She had an ex that cheated on her, and secrets can be a trigger for her.

Bridget knew I was seeing my sister tonight and how these meetups with Miranda normally end, so she's probably expecting me. I text her as I leave the bar to let her know that she and Ethan have ten minutes to get the humping out of their system before they have company. I'm a good friend like that.

CHAPTER 2

BECKA

"She said *what*?" Bridget asks as she hands me a bowl of boozy ice cream.

"Aww, did you make this for me?"

"You got me hooked on it," she admits. "I always have the ingredients on hand now."

"This is definitely a boozy ice cream conversation," I say as I shovel a scoop in my mouth. "So good," I moan as the peach Moscato and vanilla ice cream flavors hit my tongue.

"Don't mind me, I'm not here," Ethan says from the kitchen. "I'm gonna pop my earbuds in and keep working on meal prep."

Bridget beams at him from her seat on the couch. I sigh wistfully, remembering when Robert and I used to share looks like that, back when our relationship was new and less complicated. We're still in love, don't get me wrong, but I miss that rush of endorphins that hit every time we look at each other. They still hit, but not as often.

"Spill," Bridget demands, snapping me out of my thoughts. "It's been months since I've seen you, and I'm not sure when we'll have time to do this again with you going back to work. You find anything yet?"

"Not yet, but I have a few months before Hallie starts kindergarten."

"My company is always hiring in customer service if you can't find anything," she offers before shifting gears. "Back to the evil sister. You told her you want another kid, and she accuses you of trying to overpopulate the planet?"

"Kind of? I don't even know if I want another baby. The first one killed my sex drive and continues to cockblock my husband."

"Breadcrumbs, Becka. You gotta fill in these gaps for me faster," she complains as I chuckle.

Sometimes my brain is already three thoughts ahead of the words coming out of my mouth. I don't mean to dole out information in small pieces, but once I start sharing a thought, my brain starts down another rabbit hole and I'm moving on before I finish the first.

"You've never mentioned wanting another kid, and now you're telling me that you told your sister you do?"

"I don't know what hit me, but I was sitting there in that bar looking at her and I started disassociating. She was droning on about her coworker and how awful she was, and my brain started picturing her as Hallie—well, not current Hallie, but a grown-up version of Hallie. And I wondered if she'd ever have any sisters and if they would be close or not. Would they meet up every week for drinks, or would her sister constantly blow her off? Would she be a good big sister, or would she make her sister feel like she's too much yet invisible at the same time? The longer she spoke, the more my mind kept thinking up all these scenarios about a grown-up Hallie and her imaginary sibling, and it made me realize that I wanted her to have a sister. I may have blurted it out in the middle of her story."

"That you want another kid?"

"Yeah. She kept prattling on and on, saying the most hurtful things about this woman she works with, and from what I could tell, that lady didn't do anything wrong, but Miranda has a way of making everything all about her and playing the victim. When she wouldn't get to the point quick enough, I wanted to hurry her along and changed the subject. I shouldn't have said anything. I haven't even talked to Robert about it, and it's not like we'd have time to try for one even if we wanted to. Our house is too small, we're barely making ends meet, I miss having sex with my husband, and another kid could complicate all that even more. It's my fault for interrupting her. That's probably why she lashed out and said what she did."

"Why do you make excuses for her? From what you've shared about her, she doesn't know badass Becka."

I sigh. Bridget is an only child, so she wouldn't understand. "She's family. I can't turn my back on her, even if she is awful, she's not as bad as our mom. But I don't have to spend a lot of time with her. I'd much rather spend it with you. You're my friend soulmate, one of a few in my life."

"Who are the others?"

"Jealous?" I tease.

She laughs. "Maybe. I want to know who I'm up against for your attention."

"Says the woman who constantly ghosts me," I accuse, shoving her foot with mine from across the couch.

"Fair, but I'm getting better, I promise. Last year was a lot."

I return to her original question. "When I met you and Robert in college, I realized that there's the family you're born into and the family you choose, and you're both the latter. Of course, Hallie is one of my soulmates. And there was someone else that I'd felt was a soulmate once, but he's not in our life anymore. I wish Miranda was part of the family I've chosen, but she's not really."

"Okay, I want to hear more about the lost soulmate later. I feel like you're breadcrumbing me again."

"Ooh, we're making it a verb now? I'm so here for this."

13

Bridget's blue eyes lock on mine, a stern look crossing her features, "Focus, Becka. We're talking about your shitty sister."

"Got it. She's not as bad as she seems, and I can't blame her for—"

"You can absolutely blame her, she's an adult that's responsible for her own words and actions." Bridget says sternly, crossing her arms.

"True, but remember, my sister isn't the villain in my story. Our mom was." I take another bite as I shift in my seat.

We grew up in the same house, with the same narcissistic mother and absentee father, but we had very different childhoods. Where I expressed how I felt to the point of being labeled dramatic, Miranda preferred to keep it all in and what did come out, often didn't go through a filter. She was hurt repeatedly by our mother and now is unaware of how her words and actions hurt me. And somewhere along the way, I stopped pointing it out and became a people-pleaser instead, which stuck even after I escaped that situation. "I had no problem telling my mother how I felt when she wounded me, but I can't do the same with Miranda."

"Why not? I would," Bridget says, scooping another mouthful of ice cream.

"Of course you would." I laugh. "It's why I love you so much."

"I don't know anything about having a sister. Hell, I wouldn't know anything about having a friend if it weren't for you. But what's the worst that could happen?"

"What if she stops talking to me completely? I've already lost my dad and gone non-contact with my mom. Miranda's the last connection I have to my family, even if she is a jerk sometimes," I admit as I pull a blanket over myself and lean back into the couch. We eat in silence for several minutes.

What's the worst that would happen? I'd lose a sister, something I so desperately want.

Everyone I know who has a sister will talk about how close

they are and how no friendship could ever compare. A sister is a built-in best friend. Not mine.

Where most girls grew up watching Disney and waiting for their true love to find them so they could have their happily ever after, I watched those movies and longed for the loyal animal sidekick that would follow them anywhere and support them on any journey. Somehow, deep down, I knew I'd find love one day—that wasn't something I worried about. But growing up in the house I did, with the family I had, I worried about making friends. The only sister I'd been given didn't like me or want to be my friend, and everything I did as a child to fix that was only misconstrued by said sister.

If I couldn't get my sister to like me, how would anyone else? When I got older, I watched *Friends*, *Sex and the City*, and *How I Met Your Mother*, where those people found each other and created amazing support systems. All I had to do was find the right bar, coffee shop, apartment, and then I'd find the friend group I so desperately wanted.

So when I met Bridget in college, I held on tight. She reminded me of my sister in a way; she was quiet, standoffish, and spoke her mind. Except she didn't spew hatred and hurt at me. I could tell she'd been through a lot in her life. There was something about her that told me she needed a friend, and I was determined to be that for her no matter what. She was the sister I chose, the friend I needed, but it wasn't what those sitcoms depicted. It took a lot to get her to open up to me. There were periods where I questioned if she even liked me, but I realized that she needed me as much as I needed her. She listened to me and was never afraid to offer her opinion, pushing me to be the best version of myself.

From our first interaction, I knew we were soulmates destined to be a part of each other, as if a missing puzzle piece of my heart clicked into place. That's happened three other times in my life: the day I met Robert, the day our daughter was born, and once with the person I thought would be family forever.

I don't believe the term soulmate should only be reserved for romantic love, and I've been lucky to find a few of mine, even if I have trouble letting go of the idea that my sister wasn't one of those.

"What are you going to do?" Bridget asks after we finish our bowls.

"Probably nothing," I admit, swirling the melted ice cream in the bottom of my bowl.

"That's bullshit. Gimme your phone," she says, wiggling her hand at me impatiently.

"You're not texting my sister," I tell her. "Knowing you, you'd tell her to fuck off and then she'd know it wasn't me."

"Fine, how about this? You tell her in your nice Becka way that this isn't working for you and you're moving on."

"Best I can do is just blow her off for a while. Does that work?"

"You're such a people-pleaser," she says, sighing. "When are you going to start pleasing yourself? When do your needs get to come first?"

"Well, you're not getting me to text her. It's not going to work like the last time you made me text someone." I laugh, thinking about when she had me text my husband *I want to sit on your face*. It did work, though, so maybe Bridget bossing me around gets results.

"What if the next time she texts you, instead of ignoring her or telling her you're busy, you tell her how you really feel?"

"If I do that, what are you going to do?" I challenge her. "Last time we made a deal like this, you had to see Ethan again."

"I'll let him move in?"

"He already lives here." My phone lights up, and my eyes flick to hers when I see my sister's name on the screen. "Did you work your black cat magic?" I ask, swiveling the phone to show her.

"Works every time. What does it say?"

Swiping up, I open the text and read it aloud, imitating my sister's whiny voice. "'What the hell, Becka? I haven't seen you in months and you bail after the first drink? I had to sit there alone like a loser after you left.' Ugh, she's exhausting." I drop my head back against the couch.

"Look, I know I ghost you from time to time, and we can easily go months without talking, but I would never pull this shit with you."

"I know you wouldn't. She just can't stand that I didn't give her all the attention she thinks she deserves."

"How are you going to respond?"

I blow out a breath and type out a reply, showing it to Bridget before I hit send.

ME

> You said some hurtful things to me, and I need time and space from you to process my feelings. I couldn't stay and listen to any more. I'm sorry if I wasted your time and cut things short. My family is extremely important to me, and I need to focus on them right now. Maybe we should take some space from each other for a bit.

She nods her approval. Seconds later Miranda's reply comes through.

MIRANDA

> Whatever. Drama queen.

"Do you feel better?"

"No. And you totally owe me. I texted her, now you need to do something with Ethan." My eyes flick to the kitchen where he's nodding his head to his music, chopping something, completely oblivious to our shenanigans.

She looks at him over her shoulder. "There's not much we haven't done at this point."

"Marry him," I tease, knowing it'll get a rise out of her.

"Okay, hold on, let's not get carried away."

"You need to lock that down."

"I'm getting used to living with the man. I let him in, and you know how hard that was for me. I love him, but let's not rush into more just yet."

I know it'll happen for them one day, even if she isn't ready to admit it now. And that's what I love about our friendship, how we push each other to go after what we deserve.

CHAPTER 3

ROBERT

A dollop of neon-yellow mustard stains my finger as I pull my sandwich out of the baggie and cram as much of it in my mouth as I can, wiping the crumbs that fall from my lips into the trash can next to my desk.

My classroom is empty, just how I like it, though you can still catch a faint whiff of Axe body spray. I don't enjoy being around people longer than I have to and small talk annoys me to no end, so I prefer to eat alone in my classroom than in the teachers' lounge. My lunch is always the same, exactly the way I prefer it. Routine calms me. Big changes overwhelm me, causing my anxiety to spiral.

Most people are surprised to learn that I'm a high school teacher. It could be the "don't fuck with me" vibes I give off. Is there a male equivalent to resting bitch face? If so, that would accurately describe the scowl I permanently wear. I'm not a man of many words. The introvert in me doesn't trust easily, and I've been burned too many times in life to give up more information than needed.

How did I become a teacher? My love of film.

I love creating something from nothing, telling a story with images that move on the screen. But I didn't have any desire to run off to Hollywood to create my art, appeasing producers, making decisions based on profits rather than telling the stories I wanted to tell. When a buddy of mine reached out about a job teaching film at a local high school, I leapt at the opportunity and got my certification while I was in the classroom. This fall will be my fifteenth year teaching, and I never thought I'd enjoy my work so much.

The best part about teaching film is that I've cultivated a highly competitive elective, making it easy for me to be selective about who I let in. I have a beginner's course that anyone can sign up for, a large class at forty students, but the majority of my classes have ten to fifteen students, allowing me to really develop my student filmmakers. At least seventy-five percent of my students get accepted to the top film schools in the country, several have gone on to participate in major film festivals, and three have won Golden Globes and even an Oscar.

So, I literally get to pick and choose the students I want to work with. It's an ideal scenario that prevents my social anxiety from overwhelming me. Plus, most of these kids are my kind of weird little film nerds, which makes it easy to talk to them.

It definitely doesn't pay as well as a Hollywood director, but it fulfills me in ways that job never could.

The bell rings, alerting me that my rowdy fifth period group is on the way. Stuffing my lunch bag into my backpack, I stand and brush the crumbs off myself as the first student walks in.

"Yo! Mr. G! You miss me?"

"No," I reply with a slight smirk as I round the desk and head to the door to greet students.

"Harsh, bruh!"

"We've talked about this, Miles. I'm not your bro."

"Yeah, but we tight since I'm your favorite."

With my back to Miles, I let out a small chuckle. He's one of my most promising students, and one of the most troubled.

"There's an apple left in my lunch. You want it?" I offer, turning to him right as he bites into it. "Seriously?" I say with a shake of my head. "You haven't learned your lesson?"

"What? You said I could have it," he says around a mouthful of food.

Miles has a habit of eating my leftovers. It's why I pack extra in my lunch. His home life isn't the best, and he's always hungry despite getting free school lunches. This is his second year in my class, and I've learned a lot about him from our time together. He was raised by a single mom after his father was killed in a motorcycle accident when he was three. His mother did anything she could to get by, and unfortunately that resulted in her getting into drugs and other illegal activities. She went to prison when Miles was nine, and he's bounced around foster homes since. For most of ninth grade, he was in and out of in-school suspension, which made completing projects difficult for him, but we were able to come up with creative solutions. He completed his first film with a camera I let him check out since he didn't have a decent phone to use to film.

It was one of the best student films I've ever seen, poignant and touching while using creative camera angles and shots to tell the story. Freshmen start their journey with a silent film that forces them to tell a story without relying on dialogue, SFX, or music.

Miles's face lights up as he continues crunching on his apple. "You know you love me."

"Am I going to have to teach you a lesson about consent again? It applies in all situations, including this one, *bruh*." I wince as I say the word I chastised him for using. "You don't take things from people without permission. Even if they give you snacks, you can't assume they always will."

"We talkin' about more than snacks, right?" A goofy grin lighting up his boyish features as he takes another bite.

"Right. I'd hate to have to teach you a lesson again," I warn, with a teasing smile.

"You couldn't get me again. That prank was one of a kind. Legendary, Mr. G."

Hakim walks up, throwing an arm over Miles's shoulders and laughing as he joins in. "Are we talking about the time you got Miles to eat cat food?"

"Yup!" Miles smiles, oddly proud of something that would easily embarrass others. Miles would sneak in and steal food out of my lunch every day. At first, I was mad, until I realized he did it because he was hungry. I knew he meant well, but he was still crossing a line that would've landed him in trouble with any other teacher or gotten him arrested if he'd done it in public. I pulled him aside and spoke to him about it, and he got defensive after I explained that there were resources he could use to get the food he needed.

The little shit came back the next day and made a show out of stealing from my lunch, using his charm and humor to get the entire class on his side. I knew there was no reasoning with him, so I needed to meet him on his level. After a couple weeks of playing into his games, I bought a bag of cat treats and mixed them into my Chex Mix.

As expected, he stole it from my lunch and spent the entire class making a big show of eating it, saying how delicious it was. I waited until he went through most of the bag before I let him know what he was eating. I'd made sure it was safe for human consumption, of course. Instead of getting angry, he laughed, finished the bag, and even went so far as to meow for the rest of the class.

I waggle a finger at him. "Don't you underestimate my pranking abilities, Miles. I had three younger siblings."

Once the dismissal bell rings, my room empties quickly,

and I straighten up the chairs so the night janitor doesn't have to spend too long in here. Ten more days until summer break.

The drive home is quick, one of the many blessings of teaching: missing rush hour traffic. Becka's car isn't in the driveway when I pull in and I walk through the house calling out for her and Hallie when I notice a note on the counter.

Daddy,
Went to the park with Hallie. Be back after five.
Love you,
Becka

I smile thinking about the day Becka must have had if Hallie convinced her to go to the park. Becka has a love/hate relationship with the park, so either Hallie guilted her into going, or it was a rough day and this was a "mommy break" for Becka.

Fuck, I miss my wife, like really miss my wife. It hasn't been the same since we had Hallie. I love my daughter with everything in me—she is my world—but my wife is the air I breathe, and I miss connecting with her. When my arms are wrapped around her and her green eyes are peering into my soul, I feel more at home and grounded than anywhere else.

For the first four years of Hallie's life, it was torture having Becka so close and yet so far. Gone was my confident wife, replaced by an anxiety-filled new mother who was constantly worried about the baby, and equally insecure about the body that was left behind. Normally, I'm the one that's filled with anxiety—it runs in my family, along with depression—but motherhood hit Becka hard. While she didn't have postpartum depression, she wasn't her normal bubbly self. It was maybe selfish of me to cling to the person she was before becoming a mother, but I missed that person and worried I'd never find her again.

During that time, we grew as parents and as partners, and I fell in love with her all over again. She's the best mother to our daughter and an amazing wife, and while we got through all the emotional changes that parenthood brings, neither of us realized how big of a cockblock our kid was going to be. We tried to get her to sleep in her own room, and on rare occasions she makes it through the night in there, but most nights she sneaks into our bed within thirty minutes of putting her down. She is so predictable, we can set a timer by her. Between our consistent guest and Becka's ever-changing hormones killing her libido, it's been hard to keep the romance alive.

I'm a man who likes sex—what man doesn't? But more than I need to fuck, I need connection—to feel her soft skin, taste her sweet lips, and hear her sexy moans.

We were able to spend uninterrupted time together when we went away for our anniversary last year in Mexico, and it definitely helped our marriage. But recently something feels off, and I can't figure out what it is.

I vow to provide everything you need to be happy.

Maybe I was young and dumb when I wrote that vow, but lately I feel as though I can't keep that promise I made to her. I can't explain where this is coming from, and she hasn't said anything to make me feel this way, but I can't shake the feeling that something is changing between us, and it scares the shit out of me.

CHAPTER 4

BECKA

Robert is putting Hallie to bed tonight, so I sneak into his office for a quiet moment. It's been stressful with Hallie starting school this fall and me deciding to go back to work. I've applied for a few work-from-home customer service jobs, and I'm hoping one of them will work out. I've spent most of the month making plans so we can cram everything into our last summer of fun together, but I've been falling behind around the house. Robert helps with chores, but I love to prepare our meals and lately I've been slacking. And he's been busy helping his students wrap up their final film projects, often staying late hours after school. Between getting my résumé together while looking for work-from-home jobs, entertaining Hallie all day, and doing all the prep and cooking for dinner, it's been hard to get the timing right. I should get one of those air fryers to save some time.

I flop into his office chair and pull the keyboard and mouse closer to me. Opening Pinterest, I scroll through a few of my boards and remember that we have a crockpot packed away in the garage. I tucked it in there after I watched the second season of *This is Us* and haven't used it since out of fear my whole house would burn down.

It'll be okay; I'll be home all day, so surely I'd smell something if it did catch on fire. Besides, ours isn't quite as old as the one on that show. Isn't it amazing how movies and TV can influence a whole generation's choices? I still can't drive behind a log truck thanks to *Final Destination*.

My fingers drum on the keys as I consider what to make in the crockpot. Robert loves pot roast, but an entirely different site comes up when I start typing "p-o" into the URL. I've watched porn before, but not often; I prefer to get lost in a storyline and wrapped up in the romance of a sex scene when I need to relieve some tension. It's a misconception that married people don't masturbate—I know my husband does, and I definitely do, especially when our schedule and crazy life with Hallie doesn't allow us to sync up to alleviate our needs together.

Curiosity makes me scroll through the site. What is getting my husband off lately? It's not me, that's for sure. After a few clicks through recently watched and saved videos, I come across a theme: Robert is into threesomes, and not just ones with two women. The ones he's watched recently involve two men and one woman.

My thoughts spiral as I click video after video before landing on one with an attractive brunette and two tattooed men. One man is slender with light brown hair and the other is thicker and built, with darker, wavy hair, kind of like Robert's. I watch, fascinated, as the two men dominate the woman, taking turns using her while somehow being incredibly gentle. One is fucking her from behind while the other cradles her face in his hands whispering what I assume are words of encouragement; I can't tell since I muted the video. At one point she's sucking off one while the other rams her from behind, and I find myself shifting in my seat, unable to deny the wetness pooling in my panties.

Then she climbs on top of the bigger man while the slender one comes up behind her. As the dark-haired one pounds into her from below, the other man holds his impressive cock and guides it into her pussy alongside the other one. The look of ecstasy on her face is incredible, and I find myself wondering what it would be like to experience this scene. I had no clue that Robert was into this kind of thing—maybe it's something he would be willing to try?

The trio continues fucking, the one on the bottom stills as the man behind her takes his turn fucking them both while I continue rubbing my thighs together. I'm so engrossed in the scene, I don't recognize that familiar tingle until I'm full-on coming. It's sudden and intense, and I grip the arm of the chair for support as it washes over me.

What the fuck was *that*?

Did I really come without touching myself from only watching porn? Maybe I'm into this scene more than I realized.

Later that night in bed, I replay the images in my head, wondering if it's something Robert would be willing to explore.

Our intimacy has been lacking for years—not because we don't want each other, but life keeps coming between us. No one teaches you how to be married, how to choose love every single day. We made vows to each other that we'd do just that, but sometimes pretty words spoken from a place of love in front of friends and family don't match up with the actual day-to-day of real life. I meant everything I said to him in our vows, but I constantly feel like I let him down.

Sometimes I worry I'm not enough for him. There are parts of himself that he still keeps closely guarded, even after fifteen years together. I've seen glimpses, but he doesn't share them often. My husband grew up in an extremely religious Catholic family.

When Robert was a teenager, his youngest brother came

out to their parents. He's only shared this story with me once when we were dating and he was drunk. I'm not even sure he remembers telling me, but I'll never forget it.

Robert was eighteen at the time, about to graduate and move out for college. His youngest brother Michael was only thirteen. Robert said he was in his room studying when he heard yelling and glass shattering.

The scene he described was heartbreaking; Michael crouched in the corner of the living room surrounded by broken glass. His mom was shouting about how he needed to repent or he was going to hell, while their father stood arms crossed in the kitchen doing nothing to intervene.

It wasn't clear to him what happened, and Robert assumed that his brother had been careless and knocked over a glass or something. It wasn't until he heard the slur that his steps faltered and he realized Michael had come out to them. He said he suspected that Michael was gay, but they'd never talked about it.

I only got bits and pieces of the story as Robert got drunker the more he shared, but the part that broke me was when he said that Michael begged to go with him. Robert had already signed the paperwork for his dorm and couldn't get out of it, and there was no way the university would let his thirteen-year-old brother stay there. He broke down into tears repeating that he'd failed him, that he was a shit brother, and that if he had taken Michael with him, he'd still be alive today. I held him that night as he cried in my arms, something that's never happened before or since.

Thoughts of a scared, younger Michael flood my brain as Robert shifts in his sleep. Robert never mentioned the incident again, but he's not close with his parents or his remaining brother and sister, and I have a feeling a lot of the reason why has to do with Michael.

When we'd started dating, I was excited that he had a large family. I longed for the day I'd have my real life *Everybody*

Loves Raymond family: loud, chaotic, but full of well-intentioned shenanigans and love.

I did not get that family. Between my narcissistic mother and sister, and Robert's homophobic parents and emotionally distant siblings, we came up short on all fronts and ended up clinging to each other harder, vowing not to make the mistakes our families did when we started our own.

The bed dips as Robert rolls over, throwing an arm over my waist and pulling me into him. His breathing evens out as it tickles my ear in shallow pants. My husband isn't a big snuggler, but there's something reassuring about the fact that while he may pretend to not need the comfort, his body craves it from me so much so that he reaches out for me in his sleep.

CHAPTER 5

ROBERT

O ur anniversary is one of the few nights a year when we get any time away. This year, I booked a hotel room for us downtown while Ethan's sister Emma babysits Hallie.

"I was thinking we could try something new tonight," Becka purrs as she rubs her foot against mine under the table.

Raising an eyebrow at her, I take her in, my eyes roving over her luscious curves and full hips. Her tits are spilling over the cups of her bra and poking out the top of her green dress. There's not an inch of her body that isn't beautiful, and tonight, I want to put my mouth on every part of it.

"I'm listening," I say, stretching my leg out so her foot can travel higher.

"We have the hotel room for the night   " she trails off, and so do my thoughts as she brushes her light brown curls off her chest, pushing her tits out more. Those tits are my fucking weakness. She's won many arguments by simply whipping them out. It doesn't happen as often with a kid running around now, but my mind drifts back to the time I fucked her on our kitchen counter after a particularly heated argument. We laughed later when she told me she'd seen it in a TikTok video and wondered if it'd work.

"As soon as the server brings the check, I'll make use of every minute we have tonight," I promise.

We're a mess of limbs, mouths, and groping hands as the elevator door opens.

"I've always wanted to make out in an elevator," she tells me as we walk down the hall toward our room. My hand is glued to her lower back as she walks slightly in front of me.

"What else have you wanted to try?" I ask, curiosity piqued.

"I'll show you once we get to the room," she taunts, tossing a smile at me over her shoulder.

Becka joined a book club a couple years ago, and let's just say I'm not mad about it. It's adorable the way she gets so excited about the stories she's reading. And I'm a big fan of acting out the sex scenes, or "spicy scenes" as she calls them. We've picked up a few new moves that have become a regular part of our repertoire.

I grew up in a household that preached abstinence as the only form of birth control; sex was only for procreation, not something to be enjoyed. "Carnal enjoyment is for heathens," my mom would say. It's a wonder they fucked enough to create the four of us. My life until college was extremely sheltered—which I didn't realize until I lived on my own with roommates that were raised much differently than I was.

When Becka and I met, I was a virgin. She wasn't my first serious girlfriend, and I'd been intimate with others, but she was the only one I've ever truly loved and the only person I've ever slept with.

She fumbles with the keycard as I pepper her neck with kisses.

"Fuck, Robert, I can't concentrate when you do that."

"Who says I need you to concentrate?"

"Well unless you want to fuck me out in the hallway, I need to get this door open."

I lean into her, pressing my erection into her ass as I push her against the door making it impossible for her to use the keycard now sandwiched against her stomach. "I will fuck my wife wherever I want," I say against her ear as her breathing picks up. "Is that clear?"

"Yes, Daddy." Her voice is a whisper as she turns her head, and I capture her lips in a brutal kiss. I'm not gentle as I squeeze her throat and turn her body to face mine, pulling the keycard from her grasp. With the card between two fingers, I drag it down her back, down to her full ass as I grip it with the rest of my hand and she jumps into my arms, wrapping her legs around my waist.

"Fuck, baby, you taste so good," I groan into her mouth. "It's been too long since I've savored your pretty pussy." With my hand still gripping her ass, I feel around for the pad on the door and rub the keycard against it until I hear the beep and turn the handle.

Once inside, I set our bag down, push her against the back of the door, and rub my cock against her warm center. "What does this needy little pussy want first? My fingers or my mouth?"

"Mouth. I need your mouth on me. Please." She wiggles against me, seeking out the friction only I can provide her.

Setting her down, I drop to my knees and push up her dress, running my thumbs up her inner thighs until I get to the tiny scrap of black lace covering the thing I want most. I run a finger along the elastic and dip my thumb underneath.

"Here? There's a perfectly good bed over there," she moans.

But I need my wife to know that I can't wait to walk the five steps to the bed, I need her *now*. We've spent too many years waiting: for a kid to go to sleep, for a kid to leave the room, for a babysitter to have availability. I'm done waiting.

With my nose pressed against her center, I inhale a deep breath.

"Are you sniffing me?" She tries to push me away. "I haven't showered since this morning, and I've been running around all day."

Ever since some asshole ex told my wife that he didn't enjoy going down on her because of the way she smelled, she's been insecure when I linger near her pussy for too long.

"You smell fucking delicious, baby," I say as I inhale again and move her panties to the side.

"No, I don't. I'm sweaty and probably gross. Maybe we should do this in the shower," she offers as she tries to move away.

I grab her thighs and push her back against the door as I look up at her, silently pleading for her to make eye contact with me. She needs to see the sincerity in my eyes, needs to hear my words and know that I'm not placating her.

"I love the way you taste, Becka. It wouldn't matter if you just got out of the shower or a full workout at the gym. I want to taste you so badly that I can't even wait to get you to the bed. This cunt is perfect for me. I want it—no, I *need* it—and I swear to fuck if you don't stop stalling and let me devour it, I will fuck it so hard you won't be able to sit down for a week."

And then I grab her thighs, throw them both over my shoulders, and stand, pinning her against the door so she can't go anywhere. My dad bod may not have the washboard abs she reads about in her books, but my chest and arms are strong enough to throw her around.

"Fuck, Robert! Put me down! I'm going to fall. I'm not a hundred and twenty pounds anymore. Oh my God, don't drop me, I'm too heavy."

I want to argue back and squash every insecurity she's mentioned, but words of affirmation isn't my wife's love language, and my arguments would fall on deaf ears. So, I feast. She yelps as I rip her panties and dive in face first. With one hand on her ass, I use my other hand to hold her pussy lips open, my fingers in a V as I lick between them from her opening to her clit.

"Oh fuck! That's it, right there!" She moans as I make small circles around her clit. My wife needs a lot of pressure on her clit to get off. But I don't want her there yet. I want her to know that I enjoy eating her pussy, enjoy her smell and her taste. Her hips start bucking against me, seeking out more pressure as I pull back.

"This cunt isn't a snack I want to rush through. I want to savor every part of this delicious meal."

My fingers move from holding her open to tease her opening, dipping one in at a time, enough to make her think I'm going to finger-fuck her without giving her the satisfaction of something to grip on to. Her aroma fills my nostrils as I breathe in her scent. I fucking love it.

Becka doesn't know, but I've looked at some of her books when she's not around and it always makes me laugh when the man describes the woman's pussy tasting like honey or fruit or some other nonsense. Pussy tastes like pussy. Maybe some men have more refined palates and can taste things I can't, but most all pussy is the same. While I've only ever fucked my wife, I've eaten a cunt or two. It doesn't taste like flowers or candy; it's usually salty, or tangy. And I love it. Becka tastes a little salty, but every now and then there's a hint of something sweet, probably from something she ate, but it's not overpowering. There's something else about her scent I can't describe, but it calls to me on a base level. It's probably pheromones or some shit, and maybe that's why someone else didn't like the way she smelled. He wasn't her person, and those weren't his pheromones—they're mine.

"Oh my God, are you teasing me? You know how to eat pussy, Robert, please just do that thing you do so I can come."

I was so lost in thought that I hadn't realized I was still teasing her with my fingers and making slow circles with my tongue. But her words hurt, and I pull back so she can hear me.

"Are you uncomfortable?"

Her brows knit in confusion. "Why are you asking me that? Of course I am."

"Am I hurting you?"

"What?"

"Are you in physical pain right now?"

"No, but—" She doesn't finish her thought as I push two fingers into her soaking wet cunt and move my head back against her pussy to pull her clit into my mouth.

"Robert," she moans as she grabs my head. Her fingernails dig into my scalp as she says my name again, this time more frantic as she pushes against my head. "Robert, stop." I pull back as she tilts my head toward her. "Stop. Just stop," she pleads, and I can tell she's in her head about everything.

"What?" I ask with a little more bite than I intended.

"You don't have to do this to prove a point. This is ridiculous. Put me down."

"Do what?" I'm honestly confused, I thought she was into this. I sure as fuck am.

"I know you're trying to make a point. I get it, you like eating me out."

"Fuck yeah, I do, and I want to finish what we started if you'd stop criticizing every move I make."

"Excuse me?" Her face is flushed, but not in the good way, and her shoulders are bunched up to her ears.

Oh fuck. Never in the history of marriage have the words "Excuse me?" said in that tone not ended in a fight.

"First, I'm not allowed to sniff you. Then, I'm not strong enough to lift you. Next, I'm not doing it right because I'm teasing you. What if I *want* to tease you? What if I want you so overcome with need for me that you writhe against me begging me to fuck you?"

"That's not what I said at all. You're not even listening to me. Can we not have this conversation while I'm sitting on your shoulders pinned against a hotel door with your fingers still inside me?"

I'm not even sure how everything went so wrong so fast. One minute I was enjoying my wife's perfect cunt, the next I've set her down and she's pacing around the bed, laying into me about semantics.

"You said I couldn't lift you," I argue. "I can bench over two hundred and fifty pounds, overhead press two fifteen, and squat lift over three hundred. You're nowhere near that, so it's insulting to imply that I can't lift you."

"I'm not talking about your lifting. Ugh, you're infuriating! I'm not comfortable with you lifting me because I'm bigger than I was before I had Hallie."

"You're still significantly less than what I normally lift at the gym."

"Can you stop arguing with me and listen?" I make a key turning motion near my mouth and cross my arms to let her know I'm done talking. "I'm not saying you can't lift me. I know you can lift heavy shit, but I don't *like* being compared to heavy shit. You used to lift me like I weighed nothing. Now you have to work out at the gym to be able to lift me. I know that I never lost all the baby weight, and I know that even before we had Hallie, I gained weight since our wedding day. I'm not the skinny little thing I used to be. I feel like I've let you down because I'm more than anyone needs. My personality is a lot, and I'm too much for most people to handle, physically and emotionally, and what you just did was a reminder of that."

Is that what she really thinks? That's not why I work out, and to me she still weighs nothing. And I love everything about her, even the parts she thinks are too much.

I vow to be everything you need.

She said those words to me, and she is everything I need. In fact, I can't get enough of her.

"Baby, I don't throw you around anymore because I can't take my time with you without a kid interrupting us. I'm not working out more to lift you. I work out more to burn off my sexual frustration. And before you say it, that's not your fault, it's just the season of life we're in right now."

Becka looks down. "When you lifted me just now, you hit every insecurity of mine, and I couldn't get out of my head. I couldn't stop worrying about how I smelled, and I didn't have time to take another shower or even spray perfume, and the position you had me in was gonna force you to be all up in there. If we were on the bed, you could take a breather if it became too much."

"It's not too much. I love the way you taste and smell. It's real and it's you and I want to be covered in it."

"I get it, you love my pussy," she says, rolling her eyes.

"But do you?" I ask, grabbing her hand and pulling her into me. "You don't let me down there a lot, and I know you said that someone made you feel shitty about it once, but you also don't seem to believe me when I say I love it. I'm not just saying it to make you feel better. What is it going to take to prove to you that I love it?"

"I don't know. I know you say that, but it's hard to drown out past criticisms in my head sometimes, even when you say all the right things."

"Then I'm going to keep telling you how much I love this pussy, how I want to devour it every chance I get, how I want to be covered in your juices."

"Ew, can you not say juices? That makes me think of Hallie dumping a Capri-Sun on your face."

I bark out a laugh and wrap my other arm around her, holding her to me. "Since I know you have an opinion on it, given all your reading, what do you want me to call it? Slick? Wetness? Cream? Arousal fluid? Lady arousal? Girly goo? Vazz?"

She shakes in my arm as laughter bubbles out of her. "Goo

sounds disgusting, like I got slime all over you! And what the hell is vazz?"

"The female form of jizz? But it comes from your vag so... vazz."

"That's not a thing."

"Baby, everything is a thing on the internet. I'm sure someone else has called it that."

"Well, they shouldn't, it sounds nasty." She breathes through her laughter and wipes a tear from her eye. "Thank you for making me laugh."

"I vow to make you laugh, often and thoroughly," I say as I kiss her forehead.

"That was one of my favorite vows." She smiles against me as we touch foreheads.

"Well, it's not hard to do. You laugh at all my jokes." Becka laughs with her whole body. Rarely does she ever give someone a small laugh. She throws her head back, there's usually a kick or stomp of her foot, and her hands are always involved, flapping, clapping, or covering her mouth after the snort that inevitably comes out.

"Ugh, I ruined our night," she says. "We got a sitter, and you planned this amazing meal and hotel room, and I spoiled everything."

"You didn't," I promise, moving her hand to the boner still tenting my pants. "I still plan to fuck you and all those stupid thoughts out of your head." She scrunches her brow at me, and I clarify, "The thoughts are stupid, you're not stupid. You know what I mean."

"I do," she reassures as she grips my cock, giving it a quick tug before she drops to her knees. I help her as she slides my pants and boxer briefs down, gripping me by the base, teasing me with her tongue.

"Fuuuck, that's it baby. Fuck, your hot little mouth is so perfect wrapped around my cock," I groan as I cup her cheek, guiding her movements as she bobs on my dick. "That's so fucking good, the way you're sucking Daddy's cock. Such a filthy fucking girl on your knees for me."

I never used to speak to her this way. My sex education was limited and definitely didn't include anything about foreplay, roleplay, kink, or dirty talk. If it wasn't for Becka's books, I wouldn't have known this was something people did during sex. The last year has been a sexual awakening for me, for us. It's a wonder she's stayed with me as long as she has; the sex we had the first few years we were together was nothing like this. I wasn't even sure she had orgasms, and it took several years before we had some difficult conversations.

It's not easy to hear that you aren't pleasing your wife sexually. Even when Becka insisted she shared the blame for not being direct with me about her needs, I still felt like an asshole. What kind of man has sex for years being the only one to get off? A selfish one. Or an incredibly sheltered one who'd never been taught about the female orgasm and was led to believe that sex was only for making babies.

Becka's romance reading transformed our sex life. After reading some of the scenes in her books, I learned that the urges I had were normal and something Becka was open to exploring. Every man wants to let his inner freak out in the bedroom, and having a partner who welcomed and encouraged it was fucking hot.

Her cheeks hollow as my cock slides to the back of her throat, and she sucks hard. She knows I like it rough, and I fight the urge to rut into her mouth. It's the one thing I've never done with her. I always allow her to control the pace when she sucks me off, refusing to lose control.

That familiar pulse builds in my balls, and I pull her off me and watch as a line of spit glistens in the air connecting her lips to my wet cock. "It's been two weeks since I've been inside your perfect cunt, and I plan to come inside it, not your mouth, baby."

She stands up, wiping her lips as she crosses the room to

grab the bag we dropped by the door. "I want to try some-thing," she starts warily. Becka doesn't get nervous often, so this must be something good she's read in her books. My eyes get wide as she pulls out a bag of adult toys.

We've used a lot of different toys in our years together, especially when I discovered that I alone wasn't getting the job done. I've spent hours playing with her cunt with a variety of toys, testing out which ones made her come the fastest and hardest. It used to intimidate me thinking there was something wrong with me that I couldn't get the job done without help, and we fought about it a lot. But once I figured out that toys were allies and not enemies, the real fun began. What does it matter if I get my wife off with my hand, tongue, or dick, or if I get her off with a toy? At the end of the day, I still make her come.

"What ideas are floating around that beautiful brain of yours?" I grin as I cross the room in a few strides and carry the toys to the bed for her as she takes her clothes off.

"Remember last year in Mexico?"

Fuck, do I ever. We spent an entire week in our hotel room fucking like rabbits. Becka even tried out a few toys on me, and I was surprised by how much I enjoyed it.

"I remember," I say as I reach for the lube, but her hand shoots out to stop me.

"Actually, I was thinking you could fuck me with this," she says holding up a realistic-looking dildo.

My excitement dissipates at the thought of fucking my wife with something other than the missile between my legs that's currently ready for action. But I take the toy from her. "If that's what you wa—"

"At the same time you fuck me," she continues. "I want you to fill me up with your cock and that at the same time."

She must notice my cock twitch at the thought, and I catch her looking at it with a smile on her face.

This is one of my fantasies come to life. The thought of two dicks filling her up at the same time is what gets me off when I masturbate. And when I have time to watch porn, lately I've been seeking out threesomes with two men and one woman.

I've never been with a man before and I'm not even sure I'm attracted to them, but what would it feel like to have another dick rubbing against mine as we both pump in and out of her? And who would that dick belong to?

"Looks like someone is into this," she teases, pointing at my cock. I look down to see precum leaking from my tip, so I grab my shaft and swipe at it with my thumb.

"Mine," she demands as she grabs my hand and pops my thumb in her mouth, swirling her tongue around the tip of my finger.

"Fuck, that's hot, such a good fucking girl." I guide her back to the bed, taking the toy and lube from her. Squirting a generous amount onto the tip of the toy, I spread it around until it's coated.

"Why is that so hot?"

"What?"

"You jacking that dildo."

"That's not what I was—" I stop mid-sentence, determined not to derail this moment with another argument about semantics. "I don't know why it's hot. That's how I always lube up our toys."

"Put the toy in first," she commands, "then put yourself inside me." She props herself on her elbows as I push the toy into her wet cunt, and she watches with rapt attention. I notch myself at her entrance and ease the head of my cock inside her, keeping my eyes glued to her face as I make sure she's okay.

"Oh fuck. Fuck." Her head drops back, and I take that as a sign that she's enjoying this.

"Fuck, baby, you're so tight. Goddamn, you feel so good," I grunt as I feed a few more inches into her, moving slowly so she has time to adjust. My hand with the toy shifts, and the toy pushes in deeper, sliding against my cock as it goes. The dildo is a realistic, flesh-colored one with real veins and everything, and even though it's silicone, it almost feels like another dick rubbing against mine. The sensation is overwhelming and confusing. Why do I like this so much? Would it feel better with a real cock? Anything rubbing against me would feel good, regardless of its shape, right? It doesn't mean...fuck, I've gotta get my head in the game.

"Are you okay?" Becka asks, and I groan. My internal battle must be evident on my face.

"I'm good." I nod, reassuring her. "Can you handle more? I don't want to hurt you."

"More," she whines as she moves her hips. "So good. Need more of you."

She looks down to where we're joined, and I scan her face for any signs of distress but come up empty. Pure ecstasy and wonder fill her features as she reaches down to grab my hand that's holding the toy. "I need you both to move," she begs, and I catch on to the fantasy she's playing out. She wants to pretend that there are actually two of us filling her right now.

Brushing up my acting skills, since these days I'm mostly a behind-the-camera-guy, I deepen my voice and growl, "Can you handle both of these cocks filling your tight hole?" I move the dildo in and out, fucking her as it rubs against my shaft. "You need us both to make you come?"

A smile lights up her face when she realizes I'm playing along. "I want you both to fuck me, but he always talks so sweet to me. I want you to treat me like your filthy whore."

Blinking quickly, I can feel my cheeks heat at her words. Where the fuck did this dirty little minx come from?

"I'm his good obedient wife, but I want to be your bad little slut." She lies all the way back on the bed, her hands groping up her stomach before stopping on her nipples and rolling them between her fingers.

Continuing in my deeper voice, I say, "You're my perfect fucking cumslut, and you're gonna take everything we have to give you. Now get on your knees and put your ass up in the air so we can fuck you like a whore should be fucked."

"Yes, Daddy," she moans, and that honorific nearly does me in. She calls me Daddy all the time in front of Hallie, but she slipped one time during sex, and it's stuck ever since.

She's up on her knees, ass in the air before I realize, and I take a second to admire it before I smack one cheek and bite the other at the same time as if there are two of us back here.

"Maybe next time you can take her here," I say in my normal voice, pushing a finger against her other hole, "while I take her here." I feed my cock into her pussy.

"Or next time we can take her ass together," I growl in my deeper voice as Becka moans into the mattress while wiggling her ass in the air.

"I need you both in my pussy now," she begs, so I push the toy in alongside my dick and begin pounding into her hard. My thrusts start with the toy moving with me in tandem but quickly devolve into an opposing rhythm with me thrusting in while I pull the toy out. Her orgasm is quick as she clamps down hard, the feeling even more intense since she's so full. She screams into the bed, and I don't even try to quiet her before I'm coming quickly behind her, grunting with each final thrust as I let go of the toy and grip her hips, pushing my fingers in hard as I grind out the last bit of my release.

"That's going to leave a bruise," she quips.

"Shit, sorry," I apologize, retreating off the bed to find a washcloth.

"You know, not everything's a criticism of your performance, Robert. I wasn't complaining. I like it when you grip my hips."

She always knows where I'm at emotionally, even when I'm not aware of it. I worry all the time about not pleasing her, even when she's given me no indication that she's unhappy. It's probably due to me being a selfish lover with her in the past, and now I'm hypersensitive to everything when it comes to her pleasure. At least now I can tell when she comes, whereas before I was too lost in the feeling of fucking to notice.

I cross the room and hand her the washcloth, knowing she likes to clean herself. In the early days of our marriage, I'd dote on her after sex and take the time to clean her. But after fifteen years together and too many quickies where time was of the essence, she normally takes the towel from me and cleans herself so I can run interference with our child.

My eyes track her hand as she swipes at herself. Seeing all my cum dripping out of her is hot as fuck.

"Hey, big guy, wanna give me a hand?"

"Sure—"

"Use your mouth," she commands, cutting me off. I freeze and stare down at her glistening pussy. Part of me wants to lick her clean, but there's a voice in my head saying this is wrong.

"Isn't that gay?"

"No, it's not gay, Robert," she says gently. "You need to stop listening to the homophobic shit your parents say to you. Besides, you finger-fuck me and then make me taste it. Is that gay?"

"No, that's fucking hot."

"So is this," she counters as she lies there staring up at me waiting for me to lick her clean. In my heart, I'm bending down feasting on her cunt, cleaning every drop of my seed from her until she comes again on my tongue, but there's a small voice in my brain that says this is wrong and I can't get it out of my head. Would I like it if I were licking someone else's cum from her?

"I don't know, I just don't feel comfortable doing it. It doesn't feel right."

I take the washcloth from her and gently clean her up. Even though something wonderful happened tonight, part of my brain is flooded with shame. I toss the cloth in the bathroom and climb into bed next to her, determined to push those intrusive thoughts from my mind.

Becka

I'VE KNOWN THIS MAN FOR ALMOST SEVENTEEN YEARS, AND HAVE been married to him for fifteen. There's not a thought in his head that I can't read on his face, but I wish he could read my thoughts the way I can read his. Occasionally, he picks up on something, but he's so damn conflict-avoidant that even if he is aware of more, he'd never voice it.

Robert grew up in a house full of turmoil and constantly craves peace. He's my worrier and our protector, and he insists on carrying the weight of the world on his shoulders even when it's not necessary, ramping up his anxiety in the process.

While this evening is proof that our rut is fixable, it was on-brand for us. Even when we have a night alone, we don't get lost in the passion anymore. Somehow our insecurities and baggage seem to always creep in.

Marriage is hard. It's a constant string of choices that you've committed to making when love isn't always the answer to the problem you're trying to solve. I love Robert more than any other man on this planet, but my love for him doesn't take away the anger I feel when he leaves his underwear on the bathroom floor or piles his dirty dishes on the coffee table. He's a wonderful husband and an incredible father, but there are things about living with another person that grate on your nerves eventually, no matter how much you love them. And when you make another person with that man, and that tiny human takes on his bad habits? Well, let's just say that I didn't have this eye twitch eighteen years ago.

Is this why people get divorced? As much as his roommate habits annoy me, I can't imagine leaving Robert because he doesn't pick up his dirty clothes. But I wonder if that's what happens for some people: We equate bad habits with bad intentions and make incorrect assumptions about how our partner feels about us. I was guilty of that early in our marriage, but after a year of counseling we realized that my nagging wasn't because Robert wasn't good enough in my eyes, and his refusal to pick up after himself wasn't because he expected me to do it for him. He loved me, but he was just terrible at picking up after himself. And I loved him, and my constant reminders were intended to be helpful. Once we put ourselves in each other's shoes, we stopped taking offense at the other's actions.

Robert tugs me against him, fitting my back against his front. He's been asleep for at least an hour now, while my brain can't seem to power down.

"Can't sleep?" his rough voice croaks from behind me.

"Not yet." I sigh as I wiggle my head into the pillow.

"Am I keeping you up?"

"No, I just can't shut my brain off. Sorry if I woke you."

"You didn't, baby," he says as he pushes his hips against me and his erection presses into the seam of my ass.

"Robert, you're hard," I say in shock as I turn my head toward him.

"Well aware," he groans as he surprises me with a kiss. He pushes his tongue between my lips when I gasp and he explores my mouth, swirling and sucking as arousal overwhelms my body. His hand snakes down my thigh as he grabs it and pulls it over his, opening me up and before I have time to register what's happening, his thick cock is sliding into me.

"Yes, Daddy," I moan against his lips through kisses as he refuses to let go of his hold on me. He's fucking me tenderly as his tongue moves against mine and his hand grips my breast, squeezing my nipple. "Harder. Squeeze it harder," I plead, unsure if he can understand me around the kiss.

"I love you so fucking much, Becka. I need you to know that," he pants, pulling back from the kiss, still hovering close to my lips as he squeezes my nipple harder and twists it between his fingers.

It's in these moments that I wonder if he can read my thoughts, maybe only the ones that really matter. "I love you too, Robert."

We stay like that for several minutes as he fucks me, him whispering declarations of love against my skin as he kisses my lips, cheek, and neck, his hand still working at my nipple. My orgasm builds slowly but burns quick when I rock back against him. A minute later he comes too, filling me up as he holds me close and softly growls in my ear. It's not loud and wild, but tender and heartful, exactly what we needed in this moment.

We're both determined to prove that we still have that passion and need for each other, that we can fuck without interruption after this long. And even though I should clean up, I settle back into his arms and let him hold me as we drift off to sleep together.

CHAPTER 6

ROBERT

I'm not exactly sure why everyone thinks teachers have the summer off, but it couldn't be further from the truth. There's not a week that goes by that I'm not up at the high school at least one day a week between professional development, week-long camps intended to teach us the "latest" technology we're required to use in our classroom, and a variety of different orientations. It's not hard to see why so many teachers count down the years to retirement.

It's nearly the end of June, and I'm bored out of my goddamn mind listening to our district IT coordinator drone on knowing none of this applies to me and the subject matter I teach. My students and I could teach this seminar with our eyes closed.

My phone buzzes in my pocket, and I look around the room and notice that most of my peers are on their devices so I decide it's okay to peek at mine. It's hard to override the part of my oldest child brain that tells me I should follow the rules. Sliding it out of my pocket, I notice several texts from Becka.

BECKA

We ran out of popsicles. Can you grab some
on your way home?

The kind without food dye.

Flavor?

Doesn't matter as long as there's grape.

Got it

Maybe if you're lucky, I'll suck your cock like
a popsicle, licking every drop before it melts.

Holy shit. I shift in my seat, my eyes darting around the room to see if anyone is looking at me. Nope, I'm in the clear.

Baby, you can't send me that when I'm
surrounded by teachers. Now I'm trying to
hide a massive erection and you know how
hard that is for me.

Trust me, I know, big boy ;)

I love when she teases me, but she's rarely able to fulfill her sexts by the time I get home. It's no wonder I'm looking forward to Hallie starting kindergarten this fall. Hopefully, she'll be so worn out from a day at school that she'll fall asleep in her bed at night and stay there. I'd give anything to be able to fuck my wife in our bed, unrushed, every night.

When I pull into the driveway a couple hours later, popsicles in hand, along with several other items Becka added to my list, the house is quiet. We were lucky to buy our house right after the last recession when the housing bubble burst and prices were low. There's no way we'd be able to afford it now on a teacher's salary alone. Becka worked for years in various retail jobs, and we built up a decent savings before we had Hallie so she could stay at home with her on just my income, but that well is running lower than I'm comfortable with. Luckily, Becka recently decided she wanted to start working again once Hallie starts kindergarten.

Our home is a simple three-bedroom, two-story house in a neighborhood with good schools. It wasn't in great shape when we purchased it, but Becka and I put a lot of time into fixing it up. She'd come up with a Pinterest board full of ideas, and I built her what I could to make it happen while she painted and added all the finishing touches. She got into shiplap and grays when they were popular, but don't ask me what color gray. Hell if I could tell the difference between all of them.

The kitchen is the highlight of our house and our most used room, and it makes me smile every time I enter it, thinking about all the memories we've made here. Creating a home. Creating life.

"Did you get the popsicles?"

I hold them up and shake them a little to make my point. "Got 'em. Now what were you promising earlier?" I tease.

Her eyes twinkle as she looks me up and down. "Later." She winks at me, then moves to help me unpack the rest of the groceries.

"What do you want to do for dinner?" The words are out before I realize it, and I cringe internally as she sighs, her back to me as she puts items in the small pantry.

"I hate that question."

I know she does. It's the source of most of our tension.

"Why is it on me to decide what's for dinner? I've made enough decisions today. I don't want to make any more."

"I didn't say you had to decide." But I know if I make something and it's not what she was craving, she'll say something about that too.

"Sometimes I just want you to decide," she says.

"Why is deciding what's for dinner so hard when you get older? It makes me miss the days when you showed up to the table and ate what your parents made you without complaint."

"When has that ever happened in this house?" She laughs as she collects the empty reusable grocery bags and hangs them on the pantry door.

She's right. With two opinionated women, there's always something to comment on, especially when their tastes differ or change on a whim. I love my girls, but I'd rest easier if I knew what they wanted to eat every day. Most of keeping women happy is feeding them exactly what they want at any given moment, even if they aren't aware of what they're craving.

Opening the fridge, I poke around looking for what I need. "I can throw some burgers on the grill. We have cheese and buns."

"I love you and your buns," she says, coming up behind me and squeezing my ass.

"Don't start something you can't finish," I warn as I grab the hamburger meat and move to get the bowl and spices. I need to mix the seasoning before I can start forming patties.

"I can fin—" I turn and glare at her as I raise one eyebrow. "Well, I want to finish, I just can't promise our offspring will let that happen."

"Exactly," I say as I mix the meat together in the bowl, taking my frustration out on it since I can't relieve it the way I really want to.

———

Since it's summer and bedtimes aren't real, we agree to let Hallie watch a movie later than we probably should. It's only twenty minutes into the film before she's fast asleep, her head in my lap as I stroke her hair.

51

Becka motions toward upstairs and sneaks off as I gently ease Hallie off me. She's already covered with a blanket, so I slip a pillow under her to replace my thigh and follow my wife to our room, curious to see if she's going to give me the blow job she promised earlier.

When I enter our room, she's sitting on the bed with her arms crossed and I know the BJ isn't happening. Fuck, what did I do wrong now?

"I'm sorry," I start and notice the puzzled look on my wife's face.

"What are you sorry for?"

"Oh, nothing. I thought you were mad at me."

"And you start apologizing before knowing what I could be mad about?" She laughs, and my heart settles when I realize I'm not in trouble. "You're adorable. You're not in trouble, Robert. Come sit, though. I do have something I want to talk to you about."

"This sounds serious."

"Kinda?"

Fuck, what does that mean?

"I'm not sure how to start this, and I don't want you to freak out, so please remember this is coming from a place of love, okay?"

"Okay," I say, drawing out the word, unsure of where she's going with this but certain I'm going to freak out.

"This isn't working."

My world freezes with those words. Is she ending our marriage? I can't stop the questions clattering around in my head. Her lips are moving, she's still talking, but I'm unable to process anything she's saying.

"Robert, say something."

"I… I can't breathe," I pant as my chest tightens and I drop onto the bed. Am I dying? I feel like I'm dying.

"Oh my God, are you having a panic attack?"

Nodding, I take a deep breath and hold it, silently counting to ten before releasing it and dropping my head between my knees as her nails rake up and down my back.

"Why are you this worked up?" she asks as I gulp in air, trying to calm my racing heart. "Wait, you didn't hear anything after I told you this wasn't working, did you?"

I shake my head and continue to take deep calming breaths as she kneels in front of me to hold my cheeks, forcing me to look at her.

"Robert, I'm so sorry to scare you. I just meant that what we're doing isn't working and I'm frustrated. I'm not divorcing you or anything, if that's what you thought."

She stands, forcing herself between my legs, wrapping her arms around my neck as I cling to her waist, squeezing tighter than I probably should, but feeling as if I let her go, I'd lose my entire world.

"I made a vow to love you, who you are, who you will become, and the family we build together. And I love every version of the man you are, but I feel like something is broken with us, or... missing, maybe? I don't even know if I'm making sense and I'm not sure how to even communicate it, but things haven't been the same between us lately, and I know you feel it too. Hell, we couldn't even enjoy a night alone without picking at each other, and we never used to be that way. I don't know if it's the lack of sex, or intimacy, or connection, or what, and I know I'm rambling, but I can't keep going like this or I'm worried it *will* end. You'll get tired of not getting laid and you'll leave me."

Her words immediately snap me out of my haze, and I pull back so I can look in her eyes as I speak. "I'll never get tired of you, and I'm not going anywhere, ever. It doesn't matter if all I get to do is hold your hand for the rest of our lives. I love you more than I love sex."

"But you love sex."

"Of course I do, but I want you whether or not I could ever

touch you again. I just hope our daughter doesn't intend to cockblock us until she leaves for college."

Becka throws her head back and lets out a full-body laugh at my words. "Oh God, I hope not. Mama needs to bone Daddy!"

"Speaking of, how long do you think we have before she wakes up?" I ask, running my hands up the backs of her thighs.

"Not long. You know she doesn't sleep well on the couch."

So, enough time to talk, but not fuck. I continue stroking her thighs as her earlier words permeate my thoughts. "So, if this isn't working, what do we do?"

"I don't know. Some days I just worry this isn't enough for you," she says, waving a hand between us.

I squirm under her scrutiny. Something *is* missing, but I've never been able to pinpoint what it is. I'm not comfortable talking about it, not even with Becka, when it's something I can't even admit to myself. I've battled with depression and anxiety for most of my life, and nothing I've tried has ever really helped for too long. Medication works until it doesn't. Talking to therapists is difficult with my social anxiety; I have a hard time trusting people I don't know and often give up before I connect with one. Becka does her best to help me, and I can share more with her than anyone else, but she's not responsible for my happiness, and it's not fair to dump my storm on her rainbow.

"I'll always crave your light, even in the darkest corner of my heart," I say as I pull her face to mine and plant three kisses on her forehead.

"I love you too," she says against my lips, our noses still touching from where our foreheads are pressed together. "Maybe we need to keep planning time away for just us, kid-free. We can keep experimenting and see if there's something else you like as much as the stuff we did in Mexico. My friend Alyx told me about this club we could check out."

"What kind of club?" I ask suspiciously.

"It's a private club. Where adults can explore their… interests. Alyx could help us find someone if you're interested in exploring other sides of your sexuality."

I know what she's implying, and it's not something I'm ready to admit, but she keeps pushing. "I'm not gay."

She looks at me, confusion knitting her brow as she cups my jaw in her hand. "Robert."

Her voice is sincere, and she probably thinks she's coming across as understanding, but it's condescending as fuck, and I feel like she's not listening to me. I drop my arms and stand from the bed, crossing to the bathroom to get away from her before leaning over the counter, trying to calm myself so I don't say something I'll regret. I don't know why she's been pushing this so much lately. First there was that comment on our anniversary, and now this.

"I love women. Actually, no, I don't—I love *one* woman. You. I've fucked only one woman. You. And I've owned every single one of your holes, as you have mine. I don't want to be with anyone else or fuck anyone else, least of all men. If letting you fuck me in the ass with a toy has led you to believe I'm gay, then I think that's pretty fucked up."

"There's nothing wrong with being gay. That's not what I was trying to say."

No, there's nothing wrong with homosexuality, but I was raised to think gay people were sinners who go to hell, and it took me years to get over those ingrained thoughts. It's a fucked-up way of thinking, because I'm certain Jesus was more concerned with the way we treated others than what we were shoving in our asses. I still struggle with the guilt, though, and it keeps me from telling her that I have desires that she can't fulfill.

"Then what are you trying to say? You open with 'this isn't working' and then suggest we go to a swingers club like the issue with our lack of a sex life is because you think I'm into men? Even if I was, it wouldn't matter because I couldn't act on it anyway. I made a vow to love you and only you, and I take that seriously."

"I know you love me. And I know you're not gay because clearly, you're into me. Our vows are important to me too. I think we get to decide how we honor them. We make the rules for our marriage. You're important to me, and that will never change, even if our vows do."

"So, what are you saying?"

"There are other parts of the sexual spectrum. It's not that black and white, gay or straight. We get to decide our commitment to each other and who is involved with that, whether that breaks or changes our vows, they can evolve like we do, as long as we both agree. And if you need something in addition to me, I'd like to be a part of it."

"Will you just let it go? This isn't one of your books, and I'm not into swinging," I seethe, letting my anger get the better of me, uncomfortable with how on the nose she is. She always knows what I'm thinking, and being under her microscope feels unwelcome for the first time in our marriage. I need time to process this. I'm still trying to figure out these feelings inside my head, and I don't need her in here pulling at every loose thread she finds.

When I shift my gaze to the bathroom door to look at her, I regret it instantly. She stands there, arms crossed, tears streaming down her cheeks. Fuck, when did she start crying?

"It's not a swingers club, it's a... Never mind, it was only a suggestion. I don't know what I'm saying, I'm sorry, I have no filter when I try to work out these issues out loud instead of in my brain," she says between small sobs. "I just know something is broken with us, and I don't know how to fix it. I don't know if I'm enough for you sometimes. It feels like you're constantly looking for something I can't give you. Pile onto that the massive changes my body's gone through since Hallie, and it's a wonder you're still attracted to me."

I'm so confused. "Hold the fuck on, where is this coming from?"

"You used to not be able to keep your hands off of me, and now…"

"Now you're still sexy as fuck."

"Now my breasts aren't as perky as they used to be," she says, crossing her arms, pushing up her fantastic rack.

"But I've seen them sustain life. They've earned their weight in worth," I say, taking a step toward her. "And these stripes here are my favorite medal of honor. They're proof that you carried our daughter," I add, trailing a finger under her shirt, across her stretch marks. "Baby, you grow more beautiful with each passing day as the proof of your life and love etches itself on your skin." I trace a finger around her mouth. "These lines are faint, but proof of every bad joke you've laughed at to humor me."

"Some of them are actually funny."

"And these lines here were earned from every smile you've given this grumpy asshole, and every ounce of joy Hallie's brought you."

"And the one between my eyebrows is from all the anger I've felt," she says, rolling her eyes.

"It's proof you've lived. It's part of life, and those lines aren't as deep as your smile lines, which tells me how happy your life has been. There's not an inch of your body that I'm not obsessed with. I've seen it transform over the years into this magnificent work of art, and there won't be a moment of my life when I don't look at you in awe of the wonder you are," I promise, pulling her into my arms.

A small, sleepy child interrupts us. "Can I have some water?" Hallie asks, her voice scratchy as she rubs her eyes.

Swiping away her tears quickly, Becka scoops Hallie into her arms as I turn to the sink and fill up a paper cup with water.

"Here you go, Halligator." I offer her the cup, and she downs it quickly.

"I want to snuggle with Mommy tonight."

"Ok, sweet girl, let's get in bed," Becka says, soothing a hand on her back as they move toward the bed and turn out the lights. I climb in behind them for another sexless night and another unresolved argument that will hang between us.

CHAPTER 7

BECKA

"I'm heading out!" I call out as I grab my purse and slip on my shoes. Robert's head pokes around the corner at the top of the stairs.

"Oh my God, you look great," I can barely say through fits of laughter. His dark, wavy hair is gathered into four short ponytails around his face with feathers sticking out of each one. There's bright red lipstick over-lining his lips, making them appear twice their normal size, and his eyes are so smoky they look like a raccoon.

"Where are you going?" he asks, frowning.

"You have to stop making that face," I wheeze out between laughs. "It makes you look like a sad clown."

"Daddy," Hallie calls, drawing out the end of the word, "Princess Pajama Pigeon is lonely without her prince!"

"I can't!" I clutch at my stomach, bending over in laughter.

"Coming," Robert responds.

"Daddy!"

"Coming, my dearest Princess Pajama Pigeon!" he shouts down the hallway before turning back to me. "Where are you going? You can't leave me here. Princess Pigeon is an unruly dictator, and she and all her pigeon minions keep pecking me.

Seriously, why are all the action figures equipped with the pointiest beaks? I'm going to be covered in bruises."

"You'll be fine. I'm headed to book club. I reminded you last night."

"I forgot."

"Well, I reminded you three times and it's on the calendar, so have fun with your pigeon friends!"

"Daddy!" Hallie whines again as she runs over to him and he picks her up.

"Enjoy your tea!" I call as I slip out the door.

"Becka, I'm so glad you could make it," says Amanda, the owner of The Spicy Shelf and leader of our monthly book club.

"Me too. This month's read was one of my favorites," I say, returning the smile.

Amanda's created one of my favorite places in the city, a store dedicated to all types of romance books. The shop is small but spacious, with floor-to-ceiling shelves full of every type of romance you could ever want to read categorized into all the different sub-genres. Every month she holds a book club that's open to everyone.

I take my seat in the circle and pull my copy of this month's read out of my Mary Poppins bag. My purse isn't *that* big, but I swear it can fit everything my child or I could ever need, and anything my husband asks me to hold for him.

There are many faces I recognize and several ones that are new to me. I've been trying to get Bridget to join me here, but she isn't a fan of people she doesn't know, and I couldn't see her opening up to a bunch of strangers. Our group tends to go deep into the books, and every meeting turns into a therapy session where we take turns sharing personal anecdotes inspired by the books we read. It's not Bridget's scene.

Two girls take the seats to my right. I recognize Hannah, a

regular in our circle, but it looks like she's brought a friend with her. A grumpy friend who doesn't want to be here, based on the way she slumps into the chair and immediately crosses her arms.

"I thought book club was code for getting drunk on wine and bitching about our husbands," the friend gripes to Hannah.

"We can do that after," Hannah says, hushing her friend.

Amanda stands up and claps to get everyone's attention. "Welcome to the Spicy Spine Sisters book club. Tonight, we'll be discussing *He's Not My Type* by Meghan Quinn."

"Ugh, we actually have to read the book?" grumbles my grumpy neighbor.

"I love hockey romances! Anyone ever see those hockey warmup videos where they hump the ice?" says a girl across the circle from me, waggling her eyebrows.

"Yes, we have, and you can stop sending them to the group chat," someone retorts.

"Yeah, you're acting like a total puck bunny, and they never get the guy."

"We should go to a Cobras game! Spicy Spine Sisters field trip!" says Hannah next to me.

For the next hour, we talk about the entire Agitators series, digging deep into the themes of each one. Several women share their love for the audiobook version, and we all agree that the narrators nailed their performances. There's a lively discussion about whether people prefer the e-book, audio-book, or paperback version. The vibe is friendly and support-ive, and I love the community of reader friends I've built here.

As the meeting wraps up, I can't help but overhear the women next to me and smile to myself.

"I swear to God, if that man leaves his dirty clothes on the bathroom floor one more time. The hamper is three fucking feet away! How hard is it to pick up your clothes and put them in a bin literally three feet away?"

"My husband is so bad about that sometimes," I jump in. "What made him decide he needed to be barefoot in the kitchen? I've found socks in the most random places in my house."

"Right? Why do they do that?"

"I know! I'm Becka, by the way," I say, offering her my hand.

"Hey, I'm Cate."

"Is this your first time here?"

"What gave it away?" she says sarcastically. She definitely reminds me of Bridget.

"I thought there'd be wine my first time too." I smile and see her shoulders instantly relax.

"So, what do you like so much about book club?" Cate asks.

"I love the community. I love how all it takes is finding out you've read the same book as someone, and you become instant friends. It's like this secret shortcut to friendship. We can say a few sentences about the book and instantly know each other."

"I mean, I guess that's cool."

"Also, romance books saved my marriage. That sounds dramatic, but I promise it's true. I'm kind of a people-pleaser and my husband grew up in a super religious household. He didn't have a lot of experience, and I was so worried about hurting his feelings that I never said anything to him about his... one-sided performance, if you know what I mean."

"That's rough. I can sort of relate, I mean, I get off, but it's not every time, and I'm the one ensuring it happens."

"That was me for about five years. It got to a point where it became a chore for me."

"What did you do?"

"I fell in love through books. I devoured every romance I could get my hands on. Each time I opened a new book, I fell in love with a new MMC, and I got the same rush of endorphins I did when I fell in love with my husband."

"What's an MMC?" Cate asks.

"Oh, sorry, it's the main male character, the hero. Reading made me feel things I hadn't in a while, and it got me in the mood a lot more too. It was the perfect opportunity for me to teach my husband something new too. I'd be like, 'Check this out, babe, doesn't this sound fun?' and then I'd read parts of my book. His sheltered brain about exploded, and then he was excited to try all the things I'd read about. He'd be like, 'What fun thing are we doing tonight?'"

"That's a good idea, but I don't know if mine would be down for that."

"You never know until you try it. I was worried I'd upset him, and we had some difficult conversations throughout the years, especially once he figured out what I actually looked like when I orgasmed. But he had urges and hidden desires he'd locked away because they were things the church frowned upon. If it wasn't for romance, he wouldn't have learned how normal those things are, and we wouldn't have explored kink, or toys, or roleplay. These books are so much more than what society labels them. It's not just porn for women, even though we joke about that. There are stories about people who are struggling, figuring out who they are, overcoming internal and external conflicts all because they fell in love with another person. With most of the books we read, the story would be just as captivating even if the sex wasn't on the page—but the banging is fun to read too." I wink.

"Huh, I've never thought about it like that."

"Take this month's book. There's so much more to Halsey than him being a hot hockey player. He's a broken man struggling with his guilt and grief over the loss of his brother. The disconnect he feels from his family is profound and he creates this amazing found family in the form of his teammates and their girlfriends." I know I'm rambling, but I'm so excited to talk more about it. "My favorite part of the book is the bond he has with his friends. Don't get me wrong, the spicy scenes are top-tier, and the mouth on that man? Phew! But the bromance is what won me over. The way his friends consistently show up for each other throughout the whole series, but especially in this book, is what makes it one of my favorites."

"I guess I'll have to read it, cuz that does sound really good."

"Here, take my copy," I offer, holding it out to her.

"Oh, I couldn't."

"It's okay. I have the e-book, audiobook, and hardback," I say, handing her the book, knowing that if she doesn't have it in hand today, she may put it off and never pick it up. I know, because I was that person once.

"Thanks. It was nice to meet you, Becka. Sorry if I was a jerk earlier."

"You're totally fine! Sorry if I made you uncomfortable. I love talking to new people, especially about books."

"Well, I'm glad you did. Maybe I'll see you at the next meeting, and I'll actually have read the book," she says, and turns to catch up to Hannah.

I sit in my car outside the bookshop thinking through my conversation with Cate. There's a reason these books draw me in, and it's not just the sex or six-foot-five dudes with wash-board abs and large wingspans. It's the little pieces of myself I see in the characters. It's the truth that smacks you in the face when a profound line hits you out of nowhere. And it's the hope I feel knowing that there's a happily ever after out there for everyone, no matter what you look like or who you love.

Even though my life feels unstable right now, I know that something is on the horizon. Call it intuition, or a gut feeling, but something tells me not to give up hope.

CHAPTER 8
ROBERT

I could never forget my wife's birthday. In fact, she made sure of it. She thought it was a sign that we were both born on the seventh of the month, so she insisted that we get married on the seventh as well. Hallie was due on the seventh but came on the eighth. If it's nearing the seventh of any given month, odds are it's a date I should remember.

But what the fuck do I get her for her birthday this year? She insists she's easy to shop for, and for the most part she is, but I still struggle with her gift. I could get something off the standing list she made me, but she always goes out of her way to get me and Hallie the most thoughtful gifts, and I want to return the favor.

Hallie throws open the sliding glass door to the back porch and runs into the kitchen, pulling me out of my thoughts. "Close the door!" I bellow.

"I got it," Becka says, getting up from her chair on the porch to shut the door before returning to her book.

"Hey, Halligator," I say, motioning for her to come closer. "What should we get Mommy for her birthday next week?"

"Books!" she squeals as I gently cover her mouth with my hand.

"Shh, it's a surprise," I warn as I peek to make sure my wife isn't looking. Sure enough, her head is blissfully buried in a book.

"I think she wants the new *Pajama Pigeon* book," she says mischievously.

"I'm pretty sure *you* want that book, not Mommy."

"No, she wants it too. She said that she can't wait to find out what happens in the next one. And she does all the voices and noises when she reads it. She only does that with books she likes," she says, proud of herself.

"Mommy likes reading those with you," I say but trail off. She likes reading those *with* Hallie because it's the experience, not the book. My wife loves quality time. If only there was an activity we could do together, but she'd roll her eyes so hard if I gave her my dick as a gift.

But could I give her my dick as a gift?

No, I can't. Unless... The thought slams into me all at once. *"My friend Alyx told me about this club we could check out."*

"Do you want a popsicle, Daddy?" Hallie asks, looking up at me as a dribble of green popsicle juice slides down her chin.

"No, but I bet Mommy wants one." I wince. Thankfully, my daughter doesn't pick up on my perverted sense of humor.

"Hey, Mommy!" Hallie shouts as she rushes to the door, throwing it open. She tears open the extra popsicle in her hand, practically shoving it in Becka's face. Becka takes it, both to keep it from going to waste and to ensure our sugar demon won't have seconds.

Hallie darts into the yard as Becka sets her book on the table and unwraps the rest of the popsicle. I watch in awe as her tongue darts out to lick the liquid dripping at the base.

It's been almost a month since she's sucked my cock. Why the fuck do I know that? Maybe it's because she's so fucking good at it, I crave it every chance I get. Or maybe it's because we get so little adult time that I remember each encounter in vivid detail.

She must feel my gaze on her, because she turns her head in my direction and, with the popsicle clutched in one hand, slides her mouth all the way down until it disappears entirely. She repeats the motion a few times before she pops off it and winks through the glass.

Fuck. That's my wife.

I reach down and press against the hard-on tenting my athletic shorts, relieving the ache momentarily.

Sliding open the glass door, I tell her, "I'm gonna go take a shower."

"Think of me," she says without turning to me, fully engrossed in her book.

"Always."

I know what I need to do. First, I'm going to fuck my hand in the shower thinking about how fucking perfect my wife is. Then, I'm going to work up the courage to give her exactly what she wants.

Becka

"I can't believe I agreed to this. What if I'm not enough? What if you like it better with other people?" Robert asks from his seat, and I turn to face him.

"Like what better?"

"Sex. Love. Marriage." I can see the anxiety all over his face.

I reach up to palm his cheek. "Okay, hold up. Let's stop that train of thought right there. I love you. I love being your wife. I'm not looking for someone to replace you, just like you aren't looking for someone to replace me."

"Fuck no, I'm not," he says, his hazel eyes finally connecting with mine. His thick eyebrows are furrowed, and I smooth away the crease between them with my thumb as the smell of his cologne washes over me. Wood, spice, bourbon, and vanilla.

"Good. We've established that, then."

"Then what is this? Why is this what you want?" he asks, and I don't miss the hint of anger in his tone. "Sorry, I know I said I'd try this, but I don't know if I can."

"We're here because it's my birthday and you agreed to give this a try," I reply calmly. "I think there are things you need that I can't give you. And there are things I'm interested in exploring *with* you. I'm not naive enough to think that I'm everything you need sexually, and I'm okay with that."

"I told you, I'm not gay." he says gruffly. I know it's the internalized homophobia and Catholic guilt speaking. This isn't him. His parents put these thoughts in his head, and I know that part of him is terrified of ending up like his brother Michael.

I blow out a deep breath. "What if you're bi?"

"I'm…I'm not…" His voice wobbles, and I can hear his uncertainty.

"There's nothing wrong with being attracted to another human. And we don't have to do anything you aren't comfortable doing."

"I know there's not; that's not what I meant, but it doesn't describe who I am. I made a promise to you, and I'd be breaking those vows. And what makes you think I want any of this?"

"Because I've seen the kind of porn you watch." The words are out before I can stop them, and I cover my mouth with my hands. This isn't how I wanted to have this conversation, in the parking lot of a sex club.

His posture stiffens in his seat, his eyes stay trained forward out the windshield, and his voice is almost a whisper. "What?"

"Before our anniversary, I was in your office and your

computer was on. I swear I didn't mean to snoop, but I opened the browser to search for pot roast recipes. After typing 'p-o-' it showed several pages on Pornhub that had been recently viewed, so I clicked on one. I'm sorry if I invaded your privacy."

"I don't care about that, baby. You can use my computer." He drops his head as he speaks, and something colors his words. Remorse? Guilt? "Is that why you wanted to try DVP with that toy on our anniversary?"

"Yeah."

Silence stretches between us for several minutes as I wait for him to say something else. I feel bad for looking at his computer, but I wasn't trying to catch him doing something wrong. Does he feel guilty because I know he watches porn? Or that most of his porn involves two men?

"There's nothing wrong with masturbation, Robert. And there's nothing wrong with the kind of videos you were watching. In fact, it was really hot," I say, my tone soft and comforting. I need him to understand that I have no problem with him watching porn, nor with his interest in watching two men sharing a woman.

"Really?" His eyes flick to mine, and his hazel irises soften as his hand cups my cheek.

"Yeah, I got off without even touching myself while watching it. I was a squirming mess on your office chair. Why do you think I wanted to bring you here?"

"Fuck, that's hot, baby." His free hand pulls at the fabric covering his growing erection as he readjusts himself. "But just because I watch it on my computer doesn't mean I want it in real life."

"True, but it couldn't hurt to watch it here, right? Worst case, we watch a live showing of what you watch online."

"Best case?"

"Best case, we get to try the kind of stuff you watch."

"I don't know." The crease between his brows deepens as worry etches his face, but I can see how hard he is, his erection straining to break free from the confines of his pants. I've known this man for most of my adult life. The emotional war his mind is waging is painted all over his face.

"We don't have to do anything you aren't comfortable doing," I promise, moving his hand from my neck and pressing it against my cheek.

"I don't want to lose you." The vulnerability in his eyes is sincere, and my heart breaks a little.

"You aren't going to lose me, I promise."

"But we made vows to each other." He drops his hand from my face, and I take it in mine.

"And you think this will break them?"

"Won't it?"

"Only we can decide that. And if it does, it does."

"How can you be so nonchalant about this?"

"It's not nonchalance, it's optimism. We get to decide if we're breaking vows, but that doesn't break *us*. I can promise that right now. No matter what we do in there, you're my home, my family. But I know this dry spell we've been experiencing is the universe telling us that we need to make a change. It's clear to me that you need something more, and I'm strong enough to know that while what we have is unbreakable, it also doesn't meet all your needs. And that's okay."

"How do you do that?"

"Do what?"

"Say exactly what I need to hear to calm my anxiety."

"Because I know you better than you know yourself." I recite my part like it's the line I was born to say. I know this man inside and out. "We can always make new vows. This is us. Our marriage. I'm secure in your love for me, but if you need something more, I want to be a part of it. We get to decide what our marriage looks like, what the shape of it is. And if you decide this club isn't for you, that's okay too."

"Okay," he says, blowing out a heavy breath. His eyes drift down to where our hands are clasped over the center console. "Tell me something true."

I vow to always tell you the truth, even if it's painful, but to do it in a way that doesn't hurt you.

"I'm not going to hurt you, I promise," I start, my hand reaching to hold the back of his neck, forcing him to look me in the eyes. "The best orgasm I've ever had was when you fucked me with that vibrator. Having two dicks in me at the same time, even if one was a toy, made me come harder than anything else ever has."

"I don't know if I'm ready for that," he admits.

"That's okay. We can work up to that if you want. Or we can keep that between us and the toy. Keep an open mind and know that I love you, and that will never change."

"An open mind," he repeats.

"And an open asshole," I tease, dropping my hand from his neck as he shifts in his seat.

"Nope." I see the panic rise in his eyes.

"Holy fuck, Robert, I'm kidding! But the look on your face," I wheeze out between laughs. "Remember how long it took us to work up to anal? That's not happening tonight."

"I don't even know if I'd be a top or bottom," he admits, and I see a flash of something in his eyes.

Fuck, if he's thinking about that, he might be willing to actually try this. A rush of heat floods my core, and my panties dampen at the thought of him with another man. "You've thought about it?"

"No, I…I mean, yeah, just now." He shrugs.

Before he can waver any more, I grab his hand and trail it up my thigh and under my skirt, letting him feel how wet I am.

"Fuck, baby. Talking about this has you this wet?" He shifts my panties to the side and slides a finger through my slickness.

I love this taking-what-I-want thing. Bridget was on to something last year. Before our conversation back then, I'd never asked for what I wanted in the bedroom, but she made me sext my husband, telling him I wanted to sit on his face, something way out of my comfort zone for many reasons, and now here I am, coaxing him into fingering me in our car outside of a sex club.

He rubs his palm over my clit as he pushes a thick finger inside me, stroking that spot on my inner walls that makes me fall apart quickly.

"Robert," I breathe his name out in a whisper as he continues his ministrations.

Gripping his forearm, I push my head back against the headrest and feel his breath against my ear.

"Be a good girl and come on my hand, baby. You're close, aren't you?"

"Uh-huh."

"I can tell by the way my wife's perfect little pussy is gripping my finger."

"I love it when you talk to me like that."

"I know. Tell me what you need, wife."

"More."

"More what? More pressure on your clit?" His palm pushes harder against me, increasing the friction. "More fingers?" He pushes another finger inside, curling them against my G-spot. "Does my wife need her husband's mouth to fill her ears with praise? Or my cock to stuff her cunt full? What does my good girl need?"

"All of it," I gasp as my walls start to flutter, my orgasm fast approaching.

"Fuck, I wish I could taste this perfect little pussy right now. I bet it tastes so good, considering the mess you're making all over my hand."

That's all it takes for my orgasm to hit as I cry out, digging my nails into the skin of his forearm.

I ride out each wave as he continues drawing the orgasm from my body. He pulls his hand back, sliding my panties back into place before bringing his two middle fingers to his mouth and sucking on them. I track the movements and clench my thighs together at the sight.

"Fucking delicious," he groans as he releases his fingers with a wet pop.

My eyes track the blood trailing down his forearm. "Shit, I'm sorry, I broke the skin." I apologize, reaching across him to open the glovebox for a napkin to dab against the scratch.

"I'm not sorry, that was hot as fuck. God, I love it when you boss me around."

"Really?"

He grabs the hand that's cleaning his crescent-shaped cuts and places it against his cock.

"Oh my God, you're so hard."

"That was all you. The way you grabbed my hand, put it exactly where you wanted it, and rode it until you came. Fuck, that was hot."

"Truth?" I ask as I look into his eyes. I'm hit with a rush of electricity that I haven't felt in years. Robert has the most penetrative stare, and when I look at him, I feel like he truly sees me.

"It turns me on when you tell me what you want. When you told me you wanted to sit on my face, I had a boner for an hour before you came home and let me taste you. I know how nervous you get about me eating your pussy, and I know we've been in a rut, and things have been a bit…"

"Routine?" I offer.

"Scheduled," he counters. "But nothing turns me on more than you telling me what to do and taking what you want. I know we don't always have time for that, but I need more of that."

Thinking over his words, I shift my body so we're facing each other, one hand still on his cock as I offer my truth. "I want to go inside of this club and watch a man choke on this cock while I tell you both what to do." His cock twitches in my hand at my words before I continue, "And then I want you to lick my cunt clean before you fuck me within an inch of my life."

CHAPTER 9

ROBERT

I t's dark inside Pulse, and my hands are sweating. Why are they so sweaty?

"Relax, baby," Becka says as she squeezes my hand.

We approach a blonde woman at the hostess stand. Her face is inviting as she smiles at us. "Welcome to Pulse. Are you members?"

"They're with me," an attractive man says as he steps through the curtains.

"Alyx, I didn't realize you were here already. Have you gone over the club rules with them?" the hostess asks.

"Nope, but they're my guests tonight. Give them the speech then I'll take them back," he says as he winks at me.

Not hating the rush of blood to my cock that gesture brings.

"I'll need both of your IDs and phones. For the privacy of our guests, we don't allow videos or photos to be taken inside. You'll retrieve them here on your way out. Are you familiar with the club's rules and bracelet system?" the hostess asks as we hand over our phones and licenses.

"Oh! Bridget told me a little about the bracelets, but I can't remember what all the colors mean," Becka says, excitement evident in her tone.

"Not a problem. Here at Pulse, your safety is our primary concern. All our members are thoroughly vetted with extensive background checks. All members pay a yearly fee and must produce regular STI tests for full access to the club. Failure to do so will limit access to parts and perks of the club. Since you're Alyx's guests, your play will be limited to him or each other. If you do decide to become members, you'll need to have negative tests on file. Tonight, you'll have access to the main room of the club and Alyx's private room. We have a full bar with a two-drink maximum for the safety of all patrons and employees. No drug use is permitted in the club. And we have a zero-tolerance policy regarding hate speech, bullying, and violence. There'll be no warnings; you'll be removed from the club and banned."

Pointing to a sign on the wall, she recites the color-coding from memory as we follow along.

"Black means only watching."

"Blue means open to men joining."

"Pink means open to women joining."

"Green means open for anyone to join."

"Yellow means here with someone, not open to adding anyone."

"Red means looking for a sub."

"White means looking for a dom."

"Any questions?" she asks.

"Do we need bracelets if we only go to a private room?" I ask. I'm not opposed to exploring more of the club, but my nerves will allow me one new experience tonight and Alyx's eyes are raking my body like I'm a snack and he's starving.

"Everyone is required to wear a bracelet, even if you're only in a private room. Do you know what color you'd like?"

Becka answers for us, and I'm relieved that my little extrovert is looking out for me. "I would say white, but we're with the man that's joining us and we're not looking for more partners. So black, maybe?"

The hostess hands us our bracelets, and I wonder about the kinds of people she's met here and the stories she could tell. They probably sign NDAs. I wonder if any celebrities come through here?

"I can hear you thinking too hard, Robert," Becka whispers into my ear. "We're here to get you out of your head."

We follow Alyx through the club to his private room. Unlike the other rooms we passed, this door doesn't have a number.

Once inside, my eyes immediately go to the bed. It's large with black satin sheets that I'd love to lay Becka on, but a throat clearing behind me pulls me out of my thoughts, reminding me why we're here.

"This is my private room. Each room is thoroughly cleaned after use. They also come fully stocked with toys and other accessories," he says as he points to the counter with multiple drawers.

Fuck, this is awkward. I shift nervously, unsure of what to do next. Out of instinct, Becka grabs my hand and squeezes it three times. Our silent declaration. She always knows how to calm my nerves, and I return the gesture. "What happens now?"

Becka looks at me, her green eyes comforting. "This is my friend Alyx. We met the night Bridget and Ethan met."

"I remember," I confirm as butterflies dance in my belly. These aren't the same kind of butterflies I got when I first met Becka in college. Those floated in magically, dancing around, causing a spark to shoot through my system. No, these butterflies are crashing into each other in a game of tackle football. There's excitement but also a nervous energy, as though I'm afraid if I make the wrong play, I'll ruin the whole game. And in this scenario, the game is my marriage.

Alyx extends his hand, causing my thoughts to scatter. "It's nice to meet you. Robert, right?" He flashes a boyish grin as his eyes meet mine. They're the color of amber, and I drink him in. He's an attractive man, solidly built with a firm grip. Fuck, I might be into this.

"That's a nice grip you have there," I tease as I pull my hand back.

"I have a lot of practice gripping things," he says with a wink. I've never had a man be this forward with me, and I don't hate it. And apparently, neither does my cock as it twitches to life.

Turning to my wife, Alyx gives her a once-over before asking, "You sure you don't want to join us?"

"It's not that I'm opposed to sharing my husband with another man, but it's you." Becka laughs, wrinkling her nose. "I'll just watch you two play. Two hot men getting off? Yes, please. I trust you to make this good for him."

They both turn to me as if expecting me to say something, but the words won't come. My gaze swivels back and forth between them as my breathing picks up. Before I say something I'll regret, my beautiful wife speaks.

"Pull his dick out and stroke it," she commands Alyx.

Alyx looks at me as if waiting for permission. Giving him a slight nod, I take a small step toward him as he drops to his knees. His hands glide up my thighs as he works to undo my pants. I watch him, fascinated at the eager look in his eyes that widens when he tugs down my boxer briefs and my cock springs free.

"Damn, hoss. You part horse?" He turns to Becka. "I gotta lotta respect for you. Didn't know you were sitting on a flagpole every night."

"Eh, you get used to it." Becka shrugs. That's not true. If we go too long without having sex, it's like fucking a virgin. Her tight little cunt will squeeze the shit out of me. And now I'm fully erect as a bead of precum leaks from my tip.

"Fuck, I think it got bigger," Alyx says as he wraps his

hand around it, just under the head, using his thumb to swipe at my cum.

His tongue starts at the base of my cock and licks all the way up to the tip before circling the ridge of my head. "Fuck," I groan as lust clouds my thoughts, and I close my eyes, lost to the sensation of his hot mouth covering my head. His mouth, not Becka's. Why do I like this so much? I shouldn't like this. I'm married. Does this break our vows, or change them?

"He likes it when you play with his balls," Becka says, her voice soft, almost distant.

When I open my eyes, I notice Becka sitting on a chair in the corner, rubbing her thighs together. Alyx's hand cups my balls and tugs, the pressure causing my hips to shoot forward, forcing my cock deeper into his mouth. "Holy shit."

"You like that, Daddy? His mouth swallowing your cock while I watch?"

"Very fucking much," I grit out as I grab his head, forcing him to take me deeper.

"You can fuck my face as hard as you want. I don't have a gag reflex," Alyx says and then continues bobbing on my cock, his cheeks hollowing out as he applies more suction.

My hips have a mind of their own as they piston into his mouth, thrusting my cock further into his throat. I've never been this rough with Becka; she's feminine and sweet, the mother of my child. The thought of fucking her face feels wrong.

But Alyx? This man's mouth has me coming apart at the seams. I want to drive into it as hard as I can while I watch Becka play with her clit. My fingers press into the back of his head—his brown hair too short to fist—as I rut into him harder. A familiar tingle starts at the base of my spine.

I'm going to come. Someone other than my wife is going to make me come. A man is going to make me come. My movements slow as my mind starts racing.

"Get out of your head, Robert. The only thing you should

be thinking about is Alyx's mouth on your dick and this pretty pussy," Becka says, pulling me out of my thoughts as she shifts her panties to the side showing off her glistening cunt.

"Fuck, baby. I'm gonna come," I groan as Alyx hums around my cock.

"Not yet," Becka tells me as she crosses to the counter, opening a drawer to reveal a bottle of lube. She flicks the cap open and grabs Alyx's hand, drizzling some on his middle finger. "If you really want to drive him crazy—"

She isn't even able to finish her sentence before Alyx slides his finger deep in my ass, while I let loose a string of "fucks."

Leaning down against Alyx's ear, her eyes stay trained on mine. "Swallow every drop."

Pleasure shoots up my spine as I explode in his mouth, jets of hot cum coating his throat. He swallows it all before licking my shaft clean. My knees feel weak as I grab his shoulders for balance.

My mind is racing as I try to process what just happened. I let a man suck my dick, and I liked it. A whole fucking lot. Or maybe it was Becka watching that made it so appealing? What happens now? Do I return the gesture? I'm not sure if I'm ready for a cock in the mouth, but my dick swells at the thought, and I'm at half-mast again.

Stumbling back, I sink onto the bed as Alyx walks to the sink to rinse his hands. Soft hands cup my face and Becka's bright green eyes meet mine. "You okay, Daddy?" she asks, concern evident in her tone.

I nod, and her grip on my face loosens.

"Are you sure? You have that look on your face."

"What look?" I ask annoyed.

"The what-the-fuck-did-I-just-do look."

My thoughts are still loud in my head, and I work to quiet the noise so I can form a coherent thought. I pull her close, the smell of her perfume calming me as I inhale the scent of raspberry, citrus, and some flowery shit. "I can't believe... It's just that I never thought… I'm not…" I trail off, unable to finish my last thought. I'm not gay. Am I? I'm still attracted to my wife. But what just happened was definitely not straight.

Out of my peripheral, I see Alyx drying his hands as he walks toward us. "It's not always black and white, hoss. Think of it as more of a spectrum. There's no need to label it if it's overwhelming. Just do what feels right," Alyx says, placing a hand on my shoulder, squeezing it once before knocking his hip against Becka.

She's still holding my face, and her fingertips scrape along the short hairs on my jaw. "I'm so proud of you," she says as she beams down at me.

"Proud?" I chuckle nervously. "You're probably the only one proud of me after what just happened, because I can think of a couple people who wouldn't be proud of what I just did."

Alyx's head swivels between us, trying to piece together a puzzle he's missing pieces to.

"Religious parents," Becka explains.

"Ah." Alyx smiles. "Gay moms, biracial couple, and an age gap. They didn't give me trauma, but I got teased in school. Do I win?"

Becka laughs, her head tilting back. I can see why they're friends. He's funny and clearly knows how to ease the tension in what could otherwise be an awkward situation.

"This stays between us, right?" Becka asks, looking over her shoulder at Alyx.

He nods. "What happens at Pulse stays at Pulse."

"Thanks," she says, letting go of my face to pull him into a hug. His arms encircle her back, avoiding her waist. The placement isn't lost on me, as it's clear he's making his intentions known.

"Not that there's anything wrong with what we did. I'm not embarrassed by anything that happened here," she says, pulling out of his hug, her hands twisting. "I'm just very protective of Robert and don't want to explain anything to anyone that's not a part of this. We're new to all of this, and I want him to feel safe exploring this side of himself. If our friends knew, they might have questions, and I don't want to think about what answers we'd give them when we're still figuring this out ourselves. I'm rambling, sorry. I process my feelings out loud instead of in my head."

I fucking love this woman and the way she looks after me, and as soon as I have the strength, I'm going to ravish her.

Alyx grabs her shoulders, forcing Becka to look at him. "Your secret is safe with me. When you figure out what you want and are ready to share, just know you have people that'll be supportive."

"Thanks, Alyx. Thank you for suggesting this place, and thank you for your help. I'm not sure I could've asked a stranger to do all that," she says, waving her hand between the two of us.

It's cute that she's suddenly so nervous when, mere minutes ago, she was dominating the hell out of us.

I should contribute to this conversation, but my thoughts are still muddled since Alyx sucked all my brain cells out of my dick.

"I'm going to head out. I'm working a VIP room tonight, and I've got to get things ready. Feel free to stay and play. Hey, hoss, you good?"

Nodding my head, I give him a thumbs-up but don't meet his eyes.

"Keep an eye on him, he might need some aftercare," Alyx says, nodding at me before he walks to the bed and places a hand on my shoulder. "It was nice to meet you, Robert. Thanks for trusting me to be your first."

Our eyes connect, and I can feel his sincerity, but I'm at a loss for what to say. *Thank you for sucking my dick and making me see stars while simultaneously making me question every sexual encounter I've ever had?* Yeah, definitely not vocalizing that.

"And you," he says, turning to Becka. "You have a little domme in you. Might be worth exploring that."

"What? Me? No, I'm not a domme. I wouldn't even know what to do. I just blurt things out. Watching you guys was hot, and I just said whatever thought popped into my head. That's all."

"It starts somewhere." He winks as he closes the door behind him.

Flopping back onto the mattress, I let out the breath I was holding. "Get over here and sit on my face," I demand as I pat the bed beside me. It takes a minute for Becka to undress before she crawls over me.

Becka

I STAND THERE IN AWE OF MY HUSBAND. FOR THE PAST FEW months, Robert and I have made more time for each other, getting sitters when we can and sneaking off to get intimate in the backs of cars like teenagers. When you have a five-year-old who makes regular appearances in your bed, you learn to get creative. You also learn how to make things quick.

Pulse has opened a whole new world for us, and I'm a little annoyed that my friends haven't shared this secret with me sooner. I understand Bridget's reticence—it takes a lot of pestering and questions for me to get her to open up—but Alyx works here. What's his excuse?

Over the past year, I've gotten rather attached to his friendship, even if it's mostly us sending each other videos with the occasional conversation sprinkled in. While I don't have romantic feelings for Alyx at all, I trust him with helping Robert explore this side of himself—and fuck, was it hot to watch. He's one of those hot guys you just want to look at. The hottest part about him sucking Robert off was seeing how into it Robert was. Watching my I-swear-I'm-straight husband go after something he's denied himself, and doing it without fear or shame, was sexy as hell.

"Stop hovering over me, and sit on my fucking face, baby." Robert's command pulls me from my thoughts. "How big a mess did this pretty little cunt make? Did my filthy wife like watching another man suck her cock?"

"Yes," I moan as I tentatively position my center over his face. I'm still self-conscious about this, but my confidence is slowly growing each time I see that hungry look in my husband's eyes.

His hands grab my thighs, pulling me exactly where he wants me. "Right now, this cunt is mine," he says, then proceeds to lick at my opening before pulling my clit into his mouth. His head shakes violently beneath me as he licks, sucks, and nips at my pussy like it's his last meal.

"Robert, I'm going to come," I moan as he sucks harder, pulling the bud into his mouth and alternating between gentle bites and hard sucks. His rhythm is sporadic, and it's the not knowing what sensation is coming next that sends me over the edge as I buck and grind on his face like I'm trying to last the full eight seconds on a bull.

I pitch forward, bracing on my forearms as he slides out from under me, running his hands up my thighs. There's movement behind me, but I can't concentrate as I come down from bliss.

The grip on my legs tightens as he pulls me back, impaling me on his cock. I scream, unable to control the pleasure coursing through me at the feel of his thick cock filling me. "Fuck, warn a girl," I scold as he pushes the last few inches into me and stills.

"I like the screams you make when I first fill you. When it's just us and there's no need to be quiet. No reason to hurry." He grunts as he slowly pulls out of me.

"Please," I whine, ass still in the air. I wiggle it, silently pleading for him to fill me again.

"What does my wife need?" he asks, teasing my clit with his crown.

"I need my husband's cock."

"Beg."

"Please, baby. It's so good. I need it. Put it in."

"Be my good fucking wife and say it."

"I need your cock. Fill me with your fat cock. Please," I beg as I writhe on the bed, fisting the black satiny sheets in my hands.

Pushing back into me, he does what I'd demanded earlier and fucks me within an inch of my life. Am I exaggerating? Maybe? But it was really fucking good.

As we lie on the bed panting in the afterglow, Robert pulls me into his arms and presses three kisses to my forehead.

"So where do we go from here?" I ask as I grip his cheek, forcing him to look at me. His hazel eyes have a storm of emotions floating in them, and if I stare long enough, I'll be able to identify every one of them.

"I don't know. This is all new to me. But I'm open to more of what we did tonight. If you are."

"Does that mean we're getting a membership?" I ask excitedly.

"If it means we have a place we can fuck unhurried and uninterrupted, then yes, I guess it does."

CHAPTER 10

ROBERT

Over the next month, I spend entirely too much time overthinking my encounter at Pulse. What does it mean? Do I want more? While I can't deny how hot it was, I'm not sure I'm comfortable doing more with Alyx. Does one experience change my sexuality? I was surprised how much I enjoyed another person's mouth on my cock, but the part of the experience that lives rent-free in my head, the part that's become a daily rotation in my spank bank, was the sight of my wife with her legs spread touching herself while she told us what to do.

I have exactly twenty-seven minutes of peace before my first group of students arrives. Having planning first period makes for a long day, but I enjoy being able to settle in before I'm thrown into the chaos that high schoolers bring with them.

During my non-break summer break, I reviewed all the candidates for my advanced classes and made some difficult decisions. Although interest in my program has grown, I keep class sizes small so I can continue to nurture real talent.

The students I've selected are the best of the best, but that doesn't mean I'm making a lot of friends along the way. Every year I get calls and emails from parents who want me to make an exception for their child, or even try to bribe their way into my program. Thankfully, my administration is supportive and defends the decisions I make. And if that doesn't work, my grumpy asshole face gets the message across.

Sipping my coffee, I look over my rosters and mentally prepare myself for the inevitable onslaught of drama and Axe body spray that will derail the carefully constructed first-day speech I've planned.

"Mr. G!" a familiar yet unwelcome voice calls. I still have twenty-five minutes of peace before the bell.

"Miles," I say, my tone short and clipped. I love this kid, but I need those minutes alone to recharge. I get up and walk to the door, attempting to corral him back wherever he came from.

"How was your summer break, Mr. G? Do anything fun?"

My thoughts briefly drift to Becka at Pulse, before I school my features. "It was good, but I'm still technically on it for the next" —I look at my watch—"twenty-four minutes, since my first class doesn't start till nine."

"Cool. Cool. Mine was good, thanks for asking," he says, awkwardly swinging his arms as he walks around the room touching things. Why do they always touch everything?

"I didn't ask." I smirk. "Where are you supposed to be right now?"

"Man, I got math first period. How messed up is that? It's too early for all that."

"Get back to class, Miles."

"I need to talk to you."

"No, you don't. You're bored. Where does your teacher think you are right now?"

"Bathroom. It's the first day, we weren't doing anything anyway. But seriously, Mr. G, I need to talk to you about my schedule."

I let out a frustrated sigh, knowing that I'm not going to get out of this. "What about it?"

"You put me in the wrong class."

"You're in the advanced class. That's where you're supposed to be," I say, walking back to my desk. I'm going to need more coffee if I'm going to have to deal with students this early.

"But that class is all seniors. I'm going to be the only junior in there."

"Correction, you and Hakim will be the only juniors. Since when do you care about that? And weren't you telling him that you wanted to be in the advanced class?" I ask, turning to him in confusion. There's something he isn't saying, and my guess is it's going to take the rest of this period to get it out of him.

"I don't know if I'm ready for all that."

"If you're fishing for compliments, cut it out. You know your work is good. You wouldn't have gotten into that class otherwise." Since when does this kid not shout to the world about his skills? If braggadocious had a picture in the dictionary, Miles's picture would be front and center. "Apple?" I ask, offering him one from my bag.

"Sweet," he says, inhaling the fruit.

"Spit it out," I say as my patience thins.

He leans over the trash can and spits apple chunks into it. "Why? Did you do something to it?"

"For fu– for Pete's sake, I didn't do anything to the apple. Spit out your words, not your food."

"I got a new foster family this summer," he says quietly.

Shit. This kid has been through way too many homes. "What number is this?"

"Seven."

"What happened? I thought you had a good thing going with the last one."

"I might have gotten into some spray paint."

"Jesus, Miles."

"It's not my fault. Their bio daughter said it was cool when

I asked if I could use it for a project. I had an idea for a background in a shot I wanted, and I couldn't find an image of it online, so I created it… on their shed. I was gonna paint it back when I was done. The old man freaked out when he saw it and sent me packing that night. It's not like I was out tagging shit. It was for a film."

"Language," I warn, setting my coffee on my desk and crossing my arms over my chest.

"Sorry, Mr. G. Are you mad at me?"

"I'm not mad, I'm d—"

"Disappointed, I know. I tried, but I can't do anything right. They weren't my people anyway."

"Is this new family good?"

"I don't know. They got a lotta rules, kinda uptight. Def not my forever home, but Imma lay low."

"But are they good to you?"

"They made it clear that I'm not part of their family, but it's cool."

"What does that mean?" I ask shifting on my feet, not liking where this is headed.

"They do all sorts of stuff together with their bio kids, and they said that I won't be doing any of it because the state doesn't pay them for that. But if I wanna go on their next vacation, I could pay my way."

And it clicks. That's why he doesn't want to be in my advanced class, despite his obvious talent. The program comes with a five-hundred-dollar fee to cover equipment, field trips, and other expenses, and this new family isn't going to cover the cost.

"Don't worry about the class, Miles. You earned your spot there, and I've got you covered," I reassure him. I should have enough to cover most of his fee from state funds, and I'll end up covering the rest if I need to.

"I ain't a charity case, bruh."

"That's right, you're not. You're an extremely talented

student who deserves an equal shot at doing something you love. And you're also a pain-in-my-butt kid who is stealing the last few minutes of my planning period. Now, go to class before your math teacher thinks you have explosive diarrhea," I say, nodding to the door as I sip my coffee.

By the end of the day, Miles is back in my room fitting in with the class. This is the group of students I feel most at home with. I've had most of them for three or four years by this point, and we all work together well.

After I give a shortened version of my first day speech to the group, they break off into pairs to begin plotting and story-boarding their first project. As expected, Hakim and Miles have paired off and are sitting near my desk animatedly discussing ideas. I do several laps around the room, stopping to help or redirect students that are getting off-task. My class-room management skills are hands-on, and while it may appear chaotic to the outside observer, it's organized chaos I have full control over.

A pair of students on the other side of my desk catch my attention, and I walk over to help a senior named Owen and his partner Reagan. Owen has had a crush on Reagan since his freshman year, and I chuckle as I watch them bicker over which idea they should use. He's normally opinionated and used to getting his way as a director, but so is Reagan, and neither one is backing down.

I make a few suggestions of possible compromises, and I recognize the moment inspiration hits them. There's nothing more gratifying as an artist than when your muse starts talking to you, but no one prepares you for the moments as a teacher when you get to step back and watch an artist you fostered step into their genius. I've witnessed it a handful of times, and it's a truly magical moment.

Once I'm sure Owen and Reagan are making progress, I step back, and Hakim's voice has my ears perking.

"Shit, man, that's rough."

I grab a couple of papers off my desk and pretend to glance through them so the boys don't know I'm eavesdropping.

"Yeah, they've got these dumbass rules with their stuff. Like I'm only allowed to eat stuff they buy with my checks, so they label what's mine and if they catch me eating stuff that's theirs then it's 'three strikes and you're on your ass,'" Miles says the last part in a voice imitating what I assume is his foster dad. "But it's not just food. It's clothing, and school supplies, and even toilet paper. They said they aren't spending a dime of their money on me so once my check runs out, I'm outta luck."

"That's fucked. You should wipe your ass on their shit and see how they like it."

"It's whatever. I swiped some rolls from the bathroom between classes."

What the actual fuck? How could anyone treat another human that way, let alone a child?

The bell rings and the room empties quickly as students head to the buses and parking lot, but Miles's words stay with me the rest of the night.

CHAPTER 11
BECKA

I've spent the entirety of Hallie's first day of kindergarten stuck in Zoom training calls for my new job. Bridget mentioned that the company she works for was looking for remote customer service agents, and I jumped at the opportunity. Luckily, I was able to work my hours around Hallie's school schedule. Once my meeting ends, I shut the laptop and head down the street to the bus stop.

When the bus pulls up, my five-year-old ball of energy clambers down the steps, bursting through the doors like the Kool-Aid Man. She runs to me and jumps into my open arms, and my world feels complete again as my heart settles in my chest. I take a deep inhale, breathing her in. She smells the same but different, as if the remnants of her day are still clinging to her hair and clothing.

"I missed you so much, sweet girl," I declare as I hug her warm little body to mine. "How was your first day?"

She leans back, still clutched in my arms, as her cherubic face lights up. "I made a friend! Her name is Lexie, and she's my best friend."

"Wow, a best friend on the first day?"

"Yup. That's how awesome she is."

"Tell me about her," I say, setting her down and holding her hand as we walk toward the house.

Hallie exaggeratedly swings our arms as she gushes, "She's super nice, and she listens to all my stories. And she never interrupts me or tells me to stop talking."

My little girl is exactly like me. A chatty Cathy who's never met a stranger.

"That's awesome. She sounds like a special friend."

"She is! Like the bestest of the best. But she doesn't talk."

Confused, I probe, "Then how did she tell you her name?"

"She's my desk mate. It's written on her desk," she explains as if it's obvious.

"You're best friends, but she doesn't speak to you? How does that work?" I question with curiosity in my tone. There's more to this than she's telling me.

"She doesn't talk to anyone. She can't. Well, I don't think she can. She might be shy, but she wasn't with me. But we colored together, and her favorite color is purple. I told her mine was blue, and she pointed to the purple crayon, so that's how I know it's her favorite."

We continue the short walk home as she tells me about the rest of her day. Once Robert gets home, we head to the park with Hallie.

"I seriously thought she'd be more exhausted," Robert says from his seat next to me on the bench as we watch Hallie make new friends near the slide.

"Me too, but as you can see, she has no shortage of energy." I roll my eyes. "So how was your first day back? Overwhelming? Are you all peopled out?"

"Nearly. Miles is already keeping me on my toes. He got a new family this summer."

"Oh, that sucks. Maybe this one will be better."

Robert nods as he continues watching Hallie, but I can see the wheels turning in his head.

"What's going on in that handsome head of yours? Are you

working out a way to solve all his problems?" I ask teasingly, knowing that's exactly what he's doing.

"Trying to, but this one's a bit difficult."

He doesn't offer more, and I don't push, knowing he'll share the details once he's ready. My husband is a fixer. If there's a problem, he will look at it from every possible angle before working out the perfect solution. And if things don't go according to plan, he's equipped with extra backup plans in anticipation.

We sit there in the kind of comfortable silence you achieve after years of being married. As Hallie plays, I think back on our summer together and all the fun activities we shared. And then my mind wanders to all the fun her daddy and I had at a certain club this summer. We were able to snag a babysitter here and there; when Bridget wasn't available, Ethan's sister Emma helped some during her summer home from college. Now that she's back in school and we're down a sitter, I wonder when we'll be able to go back to Pulse for our adult time.

I sigh, knowing that for the foreseeable future we're most likely back to quickies once Hallie goes to bed. It was fun while it lasted.

―――――――

"Can Lexie come over?" Hallie asks a week later.

"I don't see why not, Halligator." Robert replies

Shooting my husband a look, I lean closer to him. "Don't make promises you can't keep. It's not that easy."

"What's not easy?" Hallie asks.

"Parenting," Robert huffs at the same time I reply with, "Planning playdates."

He shrugs as I round the counter and sit with Hallie at the table.

"But I wanna see her!" she whines.

"And you can, but it takes some planning. We don't know her parents or where she lives. Do you know her phone number?"

"Shit, you're right. I didn't think about all that," Robert concedes as he plops down into the chair next to me.

"Daddy! No swears," Hallie chides.

"Sorry, Halapeno," he says before turning to wink at me. "You're right, my beautiful wife."

He's charming when he wants to be.

"If you want to do a playdate, I'll need a way to get in touch with her parents. Can you get her phone number so I can text them?"

"Okay!" Hallie chirps as she shoves a too-large bite of pancake into her mouth. I cringe as I survey her outfit and the table. Syrup is a bitch to clean, and she's going to need a new outfit before school. These are the things my husband never considers when agreeing to the whims of a messy eater.

———————

It takes several reminders over the next week, and multiple tantrums before Hallie can procure a phone number for Lexie's parents.

ME

Hi! This is Hallie's mom. She brought your number home so we'd have a way to make plans.

With the girls, I mean. lol

UNKNOWN NUMBER

Hi! I'm Lexie's dad. Sounds like our girls want to do a playdate.

Yes! That would be great. We'd be happy to host. We could even do a sleepover if you want.

LEXIE'S DAD

We'd love to come over, but idk about the sleepover. She's never done one and idk how she'd do with a night away.

Not a problem! I totally understand. We can hang out for a few hours if you're more comfortable with that.

Sounds good. Let me know the details and address and we'll be there.

Will do! Hallie's looking forward to it!

I set the phone down and breathe a sigh of relief. Let's just hope this little girl has cool parents. I could really use another friend who understands girl mom life.

CHAPTER 12

BECKA

The doorbell rings, and before I can get up from the kitchen table, Hallie runs out of the room, the words "I got it!" trailing behind her. It's been a month since she started school, and I'm thrilled that she's so close with her new best friend.

"Wait, I want to meet her parents," I shout after her, rushing toward the door. She flings it open, and my heart races in my chest. "William? Oh my God, is that you?"

I can't believe it. I haven't seen him in nearly three years, but he looks the same.

"Hey, Bex," he says, tugging at the back of his neck, his blue eyes roaming up and down my body as a tiny blonde head peeks out from behind him.

I'm hit with a wave of nostalgia. "No one's called me that in years." I usher them in. "And who is this?" I ask, crouching down to the little girl's level as she slowly comes out from behind his leg.

"This is Lexie, my best friend," Hallie proclaims proudly.

William squats down too, his knees cracking as he winces. "I'm too old to squat that quickly," he bemoans.

"You had a birthday recently, right?" I ask, our eyes meeting.

"I can't believe you remember that. Yeah, the seventh of August, the last one before I turn forty."

The girls look between us, confused.

"Lexie just had a birthday too. Hers is the eighth of September. We had cupcakes in class," Hallie announces.

"Happy belated birthday, Lexie. Hallie's birthday is on an eight too." I offer her a smile, and the corner of her mouth tips up before she drops her head.

William tilts her body toward his and addresses her. "Lexie, I want you to meet one of my best friends. I haven't seen her since we moved back. This is Bex."

"You know my mommy?" Hallie asks.

"And your daddy. And you too. I held you when you were a little baby before I moved away."

"I don't remember you," Hallie says.

"Well, you were just a baby the last time you saw him, and it's been a few years," I tell her.

"Too many years," he adds, his eyes holding mine and warmth spreads through my chest. We stand, and he sweeps me up in a giant bear hug, lifting me off the ground, my feet dangling as he squeezes me with his strong arms. I fling my arms around his neck and inhale his scent. He smells like sandalwood and leather, and I instantly regret ever letting him slip out of our lives. "Fuck, I've missed you guys," he admits in a low whisper, his warm breath tickling my ear as he lowers me back to the ground, when I feel arms wrap around my leg.

When I look down, Lexie is hugging me, her big eyes peering up at me. She looks just like her dad, and I reach down, stroking a hand through her hair. "It's so nice to meet you, Lexie."

"C'mon, Lexie, I wanna show you all my Pajama Pigeons. They're in my room," Hallie says, walking toward the stairs, Lexie following.

"I can't believe I was texting you this whole time," I say, feeling awkward. I never should have gone along with Miranda's request to remove him from my life.

"I got a new number. And I didn't realize it was you until I pulled onto the street."

Robert walks in, his head buried in his phone. "What's all the commotion in here? I thought…" he trails off as he locks eyes with William, and a huge smile emerges. "William? Holy shit! How the hell have you been? It's so good to see you." I smile at his rambling. He is not a rambler by nature so I know how flustered he is. How he feels seeing William again is exactly how I feel too. Surprise, joy, guilt, shame, anger toward my sister, and relief, all rolled into one.

Standing aside so my husband can hug his long-lost friend, I notice a hint of something else on his face. Longing, maybe? He's across the room in a few short strides, and the two men cling to each other in a long embrace.

"Actually, I go by Bennett now. William Bennett Emerson the third was a mouthful, and since my dad and gramps use variations of William, I figured my middle name was the way to go. When I left town, I needed a new start and a new name," he explains as they untangle from the hug.

Robert's hands stay planted on Bennett's shoulders as he takes him in. "Fuck, it's good to see you, man."

"Will—Bennett is Lexie's dad," I tell him.

"Wait, seriously? Our girls became best friends? How is that even possible?" Robert asks, the shock and happiness lighting up his eyes as he pulls Bennett into a side hug.

"We moved back at the beginning of the summer. I would've told you, but…"

"That fucking bitch," Robert spits, releasing Bennett and folding his arms over his chest.

"Robert!" I snap.

"I know, I know, but I'd never use that word for a woman unless absolutely necessary, and I will never use it in front of our daughter, but what else would you call this fucked-up situation?" He gestures at Bennett. "This guy was my best friend, and we had to cut ties with him because your sister couldn't handle his past? I can't think of any other word for her." He turns toward Bennett. "For Christ's sake, she made us delete your phone number from our phones in front of her and block you on socials. I wanted to reach out, man, but I didn't want to pull Becka into more of her sister's drama."

"I get it. It's not your fault. I know how Miranda can be. I can't lie, losing you two hurt more than my marriage ending, and I felt like shit about that for a long time." His words gut me, and I see my feelings echoed on Robert's face. "But I've always loved how fiercely you protect Bex." He turns and locks eyes with me, his gaze intense. "And she deserves that."

"We've heard so many amazing things about Lexie. Hallie cannot stop talking about her best friend. You guys are doing an amazing job raising her," I say.

"Oh, Lexie's mom isn't in the picture. I'm a single dad. You didn't know?"

"Mooooom!" Hallie bursts into the living room, instantly breaking the tension, Lexie not too far behind her. "Can we have popsicles? Pleeeeeease?" she begs, drawing out every syllable of the word for emphasis while bouncing on the balls of her feet.

I glance at Bennett, silently asking if it's okay with him, and he gives me a quick nod of agreement. Sugar may not be the best solution here, but it'll grant us some much-needed adult time to catch up.

"Yes, but please eat them in the kitchen over the counter."

"Thanks!" Hallie chirps as both girls run out of the room toward the freezer.

Robert gestures to the couch and motions for us to sit. I sink into the recliner as the two men sit side by side on the couch, their bodies angled toward each other.

The light from the late afternoon sun streaks across the

room, drawing attention to the natural golden-brown high-lights in Bennett's hair.

He's still as handsome as ever as he sits on the edge of the cushion facing us, elbows propped up on his thighs as he steeples his hands against his chiseled jawline. There's light stubble on his face, and I briefly wonder what it would feel like brushing against the inside of my thighs.

Where the fuck did that thought come from?

I've always thought he was attractive, but I've never pictured him like that before now, as he was off-limits, married to my sister. Is it because of what Robert and I experienced at Pulse? Or maybe I'm just overcome with emotions from seeing him again? That's got to be what it is.

"Sorry, it's hard to have a conversation without an inter-ruption around here," Robert tells him as he leans back against the couch, arms out and hands folded behind his head.

"So…" He blows out a breath. "Lexie's mom was killed in a car accident. That's how I found out Lexie even existed. A police officer visited our house to let us know because my name was on the birth certificate."

Robert leans forward and places a hand on Bennett's knee. "Holy shit, I'm so sorry."

"Bennett, that's awful. I hate that we couldn't be there for you and Lexie. If we would've known—"

"I know you would've been there if you knew."

"But Miranda…" Robert starts.

"Miranda," Bennett agrees.

It's amazing how her name is a full sentence, a full para-graph. That one word explains everything and justifies nothing.

"I only know what she told us, and it wasn't much. She said you cheated, and it wasn't until recently that she told me that wasn't true. But she never told us anything about your little girl or her mom. I never knew either of their names."

"Well, you know Lexie now. Her full name is Alexandra

Marie Emerson, but she prefers Lexie. Her mom, Abby, and I dated for a few weeks a while before I started seeing Miranda; it wasn't serious, and we used protection, but clearly it wasn't effective. She never told me she was pregnant. At first, Miranda accused me of cheating, but once she calmed down and did the math, she labeled me a deadbeat dad instead. She was convinced I must have known about my child and chose to abandon her."

"You'd never do that," I defend him.

"Fuck no. And once I met her, I knew I could never lose her. And I almost did. Abby never told her parents about me so they assumed I didn't want her and were determined to fight me for custody. Abby and Lexie were still living with her parents, and they didn't want to lose their granddaughter to someone they thought wanted nothing to do with her. Thankfully, since Abby listed me on the birth certificate, I had legal grounds to fight for custody."

"That's awful, that poor girl."

"I'm thankful she was so young she didn't remember anything about that time. Unfortunately, she doesn't remember much about her mother either."

"How did you end up back here? You are back, right?" Robert asks, worry etching his brow.

"I am. After the divorce and finding out about Lexie, I moved into an apartment close to Abby's parents. I wanted to show them that I wanted to be in her life and that I didn't intend to take her away from her grandparents. We went to arbitration and were able to agree to a visitation schedule."

"That's great. I'm glad you both have a support system. We just have Hallie, and she's a handful. I couldn't imagine raising her without Robert."

"They were helpful until this past summer. Abby's dad died of a heart attack unexpectedly, and her mom had been battling early-onset dementia for a while, unbeknownst to me. Her dad was able to help her manage it, but she declined quickly once he died. Abby's aunt put her in a nursing home this past July. I got full custody of Lexie and moved back a few weeks ago to be closer to my family. It was hard being ten hours away from my parents and siblings. Plus, being back in Columbus puts us closer to better medical care for Lexie."

"Fuck, man, I'm so glad you're back," Robert exclaims, crossing a leg over the other so their knees are touching.

"I'm glad to be back," Bennett says, making eye contact with me and holding it a second too long. Robert nudges Bennett's thigh with his knee, and the two share a look. It's not jealous or possessive but rather appreciative and familiar.

"And it sounds like we're going to be seeing a lot of each other based on the giggles I hear coming from upstairs," Robert says.

"What kind of medical care does Lexie need?" I ask.

"Lexie hasn't spoken since her mother died. Her grandparents mentioned that she could speak before the accident, but she hasn't said a word since. Her doctors refer to it as selective mutism. It can be caused by traumatic events, and they believe that's what caused it in her. I've heard her laugh, but it's more like a whisper. I've never heard my baby girl speak. She's never called me Dad."

There's an ache in my heart at his words, and I absent-mindedly rub at my chest. "Oh, Bennett, I'm so sorry. Hallie had mentioned that her friend didn't speak when they first met, but I figured she meant that Lexie was shy, and she never mentioned her lack of speech again."

Robert reaches out and squeezes Bennett's thigh and claps a hand on his back, pulling him into a hug. Watching them hug has something stirring in between my thighs. What the hell? I must be reading way too many romance books if I'm picturing the two of them together. Not every wife gets two husbands, even if they really enjoy reading about it.

CHAPTER 13

BENNETT

H oly shit. Can they hear how wildly my heart is beating in my chest? I didn't recognize the address initially, but I knew the moment I pulled onto the street that it was their house. She texted that she was Hallie's mom. How had I not put that together?

We've been here for several hours, yet it feels like minutes. The girls have made themselves at home, and I've never seen Lexie so comfortable somewhere so quickly. It took her weeks to warm up to my parents, but she's interacting with Robert and Bex like they're family, giving them her full attention, handing Bex her popsicle wrapper, and even hugging them both at one point when they said we could stay for dinner.

"Fuck, I missed you guys. I can't believe it's been three years, you look just as hot as you did the day we met," I say after a lull in the conversation. I don't miss the blush on Becka's cheeks at my words, and I smile at her and wink. The answering giggle she emits is music to my ears.

"You're such a flirt," she laughs, and I peek at Robert. He's smiling at his wife, and the look of awe on his face momentarily steals my breath. Fuck, I want that. I want him to look at me like that, or her to look at me like that. Or anyone, really.

I'm not sure if I've ever looked at anyone the way he looks at her. Certainly not my ex-wife. There was a time when I thought I loved her, but it was as short-lived as our marriage.

"Still the same shameless flirt you've always been, I see. It's great to see you, man," Robert says, shifting his gaze to me and nudging me with his knee. I don't miss the warmth that blooms on my skin anytime he's done that this afternoon.

Robert is an extremely handsome man, and I cannot deny that I've always been attracted to him on some level. Hell, Becka is breathtaking, always has been, and I've never been shy about my attraction to her, even when I was with her sister.

"Are you seeing anyone right now? Maybe we could do some double dates. Wouldn't that be fun?" Becka says, and I flinch. It's slight, but she catches it. "Sorry, I totally pulled the whole 'Are you single? When are you planning to have kids?' line of questioning you do with distant relatives. And now I'm rambling. Just tell me to shut up," she says. Shit, she's cute when she's nervous. But why is she nervous?

"Not seeing anyone. I haven't since the divorce," I admit.

"Fuck, I'm sorry," Becka says.

"No, it was a choice. Not because I was hung up on Miranda. Honestly, I was over my marriage long before it ended. I just had a lot on my plate, and I'd moved to a new city to try to win custody of Lexie. I didn't want to bring anyone new into her life when I was still getting to know her, and I wanted to prove to her grandparents I was someone they could rely on."

"Where'd you move? We never heard," Robert asks.

"Just outside of Kansas City, on the Missouri side. When Abby found out she was pregnant, she moved back home to be closer to her parents, so Lexie was born there," I explain as I shift on the couch. It's hard to think about my daughter's life before I met her.

A hand squeezes my thigh, and I look over to see Robert's

concerned face. He taps my knee twice and stands. My eyes have a mind of their own as I shamelessly check out his ass while he walks over to Becka and presses three kisses to her forehead. "I'm going to get the spaghetti started. I'm glad you're joining us."

I flash him a smile. "How did I not know you cook?" I never used to flirt with him so openly, but I can't help the feelings escaping me.

"There's a lot about me you don't know," he says with a wink before leaving the room.

Becka's head falls back against the recliner as she bursts out in laughter. "I've missed this. I swear you're the only person that brings out his playful side."

Was he flirting back? He's never expressed an interest in me like that, or in men for that matter.

The girls finally emerge from Hallie's room when Becka calls them down for dinner. Lexie has a huge grin on her face, and my heart feels full for the first time in a long time. When I was having a bad day, when work was shit, or when I was avoiding going home to get an earful from Miranda, I knew I could come here, and I'd be welcomed with open arms. While the friendship between Robert and I was what started things, Bex and I grew equally close, and I never felt like the third wheel when we were together. They were my safe space to land when I needed to feel grounded.

Of course our girls would be friends. It makes sense considering how quickly the three of us bonded years ago. Like calls to like, and I really fucking like these people.

If I'm being honest, I more than like these two.

For the first time since I've known her, my little girl isn't being a picky eater either. Becka had already made them plates of food before I could point out her distaste for sauce on her noodles. But Lexie is scooping huge bites into her mouth as marinara drips down her chin. I swipe at it as they giggle while Hallie talks about a pigeon princess, and Lexie listens and nods with rapt attention.

"How are your parents doing?" Robert asks, pulling my focus back to him.

"Oh, yes, I need an update on Barbra and William! I bet they're thrilled to have you both so close," Becka adds.

"Ha! I forgot Mom made them that joint Facebook account with his full name. Only my mom calls him that. He prefers Bill," I tell them.

There's a slight blush of embarrassment on her cheeks, and my dick swells at the sight. The way Becka blushes has always affected me. "I only met them that one time during all the wedding festivities, and I was nine months pregnant with Hallie at the time, so I'm blaming it on the pregnancy brain."

Hallie asks Robert if they can be excused, and Lexie hands him her plate before they run off toward the stairs. "I remember how miserable you were," I say, leaning back in my chair.

"Yup," she says, popping the p. "I was convinced Miranda picked that date on purpose to torture me. And Hallie came two days later when you guys were on your honeymoon. I didn't expect her to come back for the birth, but I was hurt that she didn't come meet her niece for a whole two months after."

"We got into a fight about that, actually. I suggested we reschedule and even offered to book a second longer honeymoon if we cut that one short so we could meet Hallie, but she threw a huge fit saying that we only got one honeymoon. I tried to convince her that her niece would only be born once, but she didn't appreciate that argument."

"Sounds like her," Robert grumbles.

"And you were right about the date. I'd fought her on that for months. I wanted a spring wedding, but she insisted we do it as soon as possible. Looking back, I should've recognized it as a red flag. I had no clue why she wanted to do it so quickly until I overheard her talking to one of her bridesmaids about… never mind," I cut myself off.

"About me?" Becka asks, clearly already knowing where I was heading.

"It's in the past. I'm done with her and that chapter of my life, but you still have a relationship with her, and I don't want my baggage to weigh yours down."

"I wouldn't call it a healthy relationship," Robert mutters as he stands and clears plates from the table.

"Bennett, there's nothing you could tell me that would shock me at this point, so lay it on me."

I look at Robert for, what, permission? Some sort of clue that it's okay for me to continue, because hurting this precious woman is the last thing I want to do. Robert nods. "She was complaining about you to one of her bridesmaids. I believe her exact words were, 'How does she still look this pretty? I made sure I got married when she'd look like a whale, and she still manages to look better than me.'" I cringe as the words come out of my mouth and look at her apologetically as I lay a hand on hers. Electricity tingles every place our skin touches.

"I knew it," she says under her breath.

"You were right, babe," Robert says, still loading the dishwasher.

"I always thought she picked that date on purpose because she knew I'd be miserable and uncomfortable. I didn't consider the vanity angle, though. I felt anything but beautiful at that point—"

"You looked fucking gorgeous," Robert interjects.

"You looked stunning," I say, nearly at the same time as him, and we share a smile.

"But it makes sense," she continues. "I was worried I'd go into labor at the wedding and then she'd get mad at me for upstaging her. I know crossing your legs doesn't prevent labor, but I remember my legs being so sore after the wedding from all the clenching I was doing." She laughs, easing the tension.

"I never told her that you were my first stop after we got back from our honeymoon. I told her I had to go into the office, but I came straight here so I could meet Hallie and see you guys," I confess.

"I remember that," Robert says as he starts the dishwasher and leans on the counter to look at us. "Hallie threw up on you and you had to borrow one of my shirts. I felt bad that you were in work clothes and all I had for you were T-shirts."

"And it was kinda big on me," I tease him.

Robert smooths a hand down his torso. "Not all of us have washboard abs," he gripes.

"It was a compliment, B. I could spend months in the gym and never get biceps your size or that barrel of a chest," I say, his old nickname slipping out. "You know the saddest part is that she didn't say a fucking word when she saw me come home in different clothes. I'd have been suspicious if she came home in different clothes."

"You're better off," Robert says, before his eyes flick to Bex. "No offense, babe. I know she's your sister."

Bex sighs. "No, I get it. Miranda is a lot to put up with and sometimes I wonder if she's worth all the time and effort I've put into her. Shit, I didn't mean it like that. She's a person, of course she deserves someone to make an effort with her. I just wonder if *I'm* the person that should be trying so hard. There's got to be someone out there that's better suited to put up with her—"

"High-maintenance requests," I interject.

"Mean-as-fuck comments," Robert adds.

"I was going to say 'unique personality.' I know she's a lot, but maybe she'd be better with the right person or people in her life. Someone to hold her accountable, push her to be better, remind her to be kind."

"She has to *want* to be better first, and I'm pretty sure she thinks she's just peachy already," Robert grumbles.

"I know what you mean," I say to Bex. "I was married to

her for two years, and she wasn't always like that. There were good days, enough that it didn't end sooner. But she'd have her moments too, and that's when I'd escape over here."

"You were over here quite a bit," Robert notes.

"Well, sometimes I just wanted to see you," I say to Robert with a wink, and the way he blushes has butterflies dancing in my stomach. "She'd have these moments of kindness, but she'd almost act as though they were a weakness she couldn't show people. I figured it had something to do with the way she was treated by your mom growing up. I suggested therapy, but she wasn't interested. I know what you mean about her finding the right people for her. She views most of the people in her life as competition, and she was constantly trying to prove herself."

"That doesn't give her permission to treat Becka like shit," Robert says.

"No, it doesn't. But I get where she was coming from. When you constantly feel like people are out to get you, you learn to strike first, and that's what she did. Unfortunately, she'd lash out at people who didn't deserve her wrath," I say, locking Becka's gorgeous green eyes with mine. "I'm not saying it absolves her of her misdoings. But it helped me understand the behavior, which helped me better prepare for the divorce. Can't say I didn't see it coming, but having a secret child was not what I was expecting."

"I actually kinda told her off a little bit recently," Becka says as Robert finishes her thought.

"She did, in her own Becka way."

"Super polite so she doesn't hurt anyone's feelings?" I ask.

"I told her how hurtful I found her behavior and that I needed some space," she says as Robert rolls his eyes.

"Let me guess, she called you a name and you haven't heard from her since?" I ask.

"How'd you know? Never mind. I can't imagine all the hate she spewed at you when she found out about Lexie."

I nod my agreement, not wanting to dampen the mood.

"I don't think she'll be bothering us for a while, at least," Robert adds.

"And now you're here," Bex says with a smile as mine grows.

"Now I'm here. And I don't give a fuck what Miranda says, or if she has a problem with us reconnecting, I'm not going anywhere," I say, grabbing her hand again.

We hold eye contact longer than we probably should, but when she looks at Robert, he's smiling at me too. Could there be something here worth exploring? I've always been flirty with Bex, and it's never bothered Robert. But now Robert's looking at me with something a little more intense than I'd expect.

Bex clears her throat and her cheeks fucking pinken again before she blurts, "I should re-friend your parents on Facebook!"

"Where did that come from?"

"I don't know, we were talking about their joint Facebook account earlier and I remembered that Miranda made me unfriend them too. Oh my gosh, and your brother and sister. Wait, do they have any kids? How are they doing? Are they still in town?" she asks, bouncing from one question to another.

"You're so fucking cute when you're nervous." I smile, pulling my hand back as I lean in my chair. "No, neither of them has kids. They're both doing well, both still in town. My sister Bailey is a veterinarian. She likes animals more than people and keeps teasing my parents that they're going to have more fur-children before they get an actual grandchild from her. And Bryson is having a lot of fun with the puck bunnies at the moment."

"Oh shit, I forgot he was playing hockey. Where is he playing now?" Robert asks.

"He's been traded so many times, it's kinda hard to keep

up, honestly. The Cobras picked him up this summer, so he's hoping this will be his shot," I say proudly. We may have thirteen years between us, but I look up to my younger brother and his drive.

"Damn, how did I miss that?" Robert asks.

Bex chuckles. "I know exactly how you missed that. We did have quite a busy summer," she says, winking at Robert as he smiles. Fuck, the way his face lights up has a rush of blood coursing to my dick. These two are going to be the death of me, especially if I can't do anything about the tension building between us.

CHAPTER 14

ROBERT

"Daddyyyyy! Hurry up, we're going to be late!"

"The park isn't going anywhere, Halligator. How are we going to be late?"

"We just are! Get your shoes on, let's go." She tugs on my hand.

Normally, we have to beg Hallie to put her shoes on. While this is a welcome change of pace, I'm a little unsure what her hurry is. After my sneakers are in place, I grab the "park bag" out of the closet, making sure it's been repacked with extra snacks, water, stickers, and toys. It's a diaper bag for big kids, minus the diapers. My wife thinks of everything. Many outings would've been ruined without this bag.

I load Hallie and her bike into the car and make our way to the park, Hallie insisting I hurry the entire time. She's got something up her sleeve, I'm just not sure what. We're barely in the parking spot before Hallie's leaping from the car and running to the swings. Lexie is swinging high into the air, Bennett pushing her, a massive smile on his face as he spots us.

"Hallie insisted on coming to the park today, and now I know why," I say as I approach them.

"We're here every Saturday morning at eleven."

"Daddy, push me! I need a boost, and then I can do it by myself," Hallie squeals as she hops on the swing next to Lexie. I take my position behind her, giving her a solid push before stepping back. Her little legs pump hard as she flies back and forth, and I notice Lexie copying her movements.

"Hey, B, you think I can push my girl higher than yours?" he asks, raising an eyebrow in challenge. Or is he flirting?

"Why do you call my daddy B?" Hallie asks over her shoulder as she continues to swing.

"Well, Hallie, your daddy hates being called anything other than Robert."

"He likes being called Daddy," she says innocently, and I look away so he doesn't see my smirk.

"True. But I'm bad at names, and when I first met your daddy, I couldn't remember his name and I kept calling him Bobby or Robbie, before I settled on B. I knew he had a B in his name, and it helped me remember it."

"Okay!" she chirps as she jumps from her swing, landing in a superhero crouch, before popping up, spinning toward us with her arms in the air, and loudly proclaiming, "TA-DA!"

Lexie audibly gasps and then claps when she realizes that Hallie is okay. Then she launches off her swing and lands with a grunt before popping up the same way Hallie did. She tilts her head back and lets out an "AH AHH!" They take off for the slide before I can process what happened.

I look at Bennett, and his mouth hangs open. His eyes are watery as they connect with mine. "Did she just speak?" I ask, still in shock.

"Maybe? Kinda? I mean, it was more of a yell. Fuck it, I'm counting it. She tried, even if the consonants didn't stick," he says as he throws an arm over my shoulder.

"I'm not gonna argue with you about it."

There aren't many people here today, but I get nervous when Hallie isn't in my line of sight. Once I clock the girls playing on the slide, I look over at Bennett, scanning his face.

There are faint lines around his eyes and mouth. He's biting his lower lip, and I focus on the movement. Have his lips always been this full? Fuck, why am I staring at his lips?

Bennett turns his face to mine, and I step out from under his arm toward the girls and sit on a bench so I can focus on them. That's where my focus should be, not on my best friend's kissable lips.

"I needed this today. It's been a shitty day," he says, taking the seat next to me.

"Daddy, are you looking?" Hallie yells from the top of the slide.

"I'm looking, Halligator!" I confirm.

We watch for several minutes as Hallie and Lexie take turns going down the massive slide in every position imaginable, Hallie taking the lead every time with Lexie following her cue.

After I'm satisfied that Hallie's moved on from needing my focus, I nudge Bennett's knee with mine. "So, what's going on?"

"I don't want to burden you with it," he hedges.

"It's not a burden. Maybe I can help."

He sucks in a deep breath and exhales before continuing. "My contractor's kicking us out of our house earlier than I expected. I knew this was going to be a fixer-upper, but I wasn't expecting it to put us out right after we moved in. We're knocking down a wall to expand the kitchen, and it'll be unusable for a few weeks. I was hoping they would do it in stages, and we could get by ordering takeout if I couldn't cook, but I'm probably gonna have to get a hotel, and the bus isn't going to pick Lexie up from the hotel. And then I found out that I'm going to have to go into the office while this is happening, so I can't drive her to school or pick her up. I'll probably have to get my mom to help if I get a hotel, but then she'll want us to come stay with her, but their place is too small, and then she'll be offended if we stay at a hotel

115

instead of with her and my dad. Sorry to dump all this on you."

He's babbling like Becka does, and it's cute. Shit, I didn't mean it like that. Or did I?

"You should stay with us." The words are out of my mouth before I can think it through, which is unlike me. I think everything through before I do it. But as I mull it over in my head, I realize it's the best solution. They have a problem, and I solve problems. "My office has a bed in it, and doubles as a guest room. You two can stay, and Lexie can ride the bus with Hallie. She'll be thrilled about a three-week-long sleepover with Lexie."

"Are you sure? I don't wanna put you guys out."

"You're not putting anyone out," I assure him with another nudge to the knee. "Plus, we'll get to hang out. It'll be like old times."

The lines around his eyes crinkle as he smiles and we continue watching the girls.

I vow to push you out of your comfort zone.

Even though I made that vow to my wife, I can't help but feel like Bennett is pushing me out of my comfort zone, making me act in ways I normally wouldn't. Something about him coming back into our lives feels right, like he was always meant to be here.

CHAPTER 15
BECKA

Robert is a problem solver; it's one of the things I love about him. And don't get me wrong, he listens to me when I have a problem, but his signature move always involves a solution, when I often just want a sympathetic ear. If I want someone to let me talk for hours on end and empathize with me over every little detail, he's not the person I go to.

Sometimes I can go to Bridget, but it's not her thing either. Like Robert, she likes to look at a problem logically and find a solution. But emotions aren't logical, and sometimes I want to whine about a shitty situation, throw my pity party, and have a good cry so I can move on.

I wish I had a sister who could fill that role for me, but if I ever vented to Miranda, she'd either interrupt to one-up me with her own story or she'd use my words against me later. Plus, I'm taking a break from her right now, and I haven't heard anything from her since my last text. Not even a birthday greeting.

And why do I need vent? My husband agreed to let his best friend and daughter stay with us for three weeks. Who does that? Shouldn't that be something you run by your wife first?

Don't get me wrong, I adore Bennett and Lexie. I'm thrilled

he's back in our lives, but dammit, I would've loved some warning before having houseguests. This is something men don't think about.

"If you scrub that plate any harder, you're going to break it," comes a voice from behind me as the scent of sandalwood and leather fills the space, breaking my thoughts.

Bennett moves closer to me, grabbing a towel. "What are you doing?" I ask suspiciously.

"You wash, I'll dry," he says, taking the plate from my hands.

"Robert never helps with the dishes," I mutter, then wince. "Sorry, I shouldn't have said that."

"Well, I'm not Robert," he says, bumping his shoulder against mine.

I smile as I return to my task, taking a glass in my hands and jamming the brush inside to clean it.

"Damn, Bex, is that how you treat all your men? Robert's one lucky guy."

"Huh?" I ask, looking up at him in confusion.

He gestures to my hands, and I drop my gaze to them.

"That's a pretty lewd gesture you're making with that glass," he says, bumping my shoulder again as I plunge the brush in and out, swiping the glass in a twisting motion.

"For fuck's sake." I laugh as I slow my movements and rinse off the soap bubbles. Bennett takes it from me and dries it off before putting it away in the cupboard.

"Robert's upstairs making sure the girls take a bath," he offers, taking a plate from my hands.

"Are they taking turns?"

"Nah, they wanted to take a bath together, so Robert insisted they wear their swimsuits. He was shouting about there being too many bubbles, but the girls were giving him a bubble beard and crown before I came down here. I wanted to be sure Lexie was comfortable before I came to help you."

"Thanks," I say as I continue handing him dishes. "She

seems like she's at home here. I'm glad we could help while you're displaced."

"What's wrong?" he asks, taking a pan from me.

"What makes you think something's wrong?"

"I know you. It's been a few years, but I know how you look when you're mad but you don't want anyone to know you're mad, so you stew and suffer in silence. I saw you do it after double dates. I watched Miranda get under your skin, saw how you'd start to say something, only to get shut down by her and give up. You'd have this look on your face after. It's the same face you have now," he says as I blow out a breath. "Are you sure it's okay for us to stay with you?" Bennett asks, his blue eyes full of concern. "I know Robert didn't give you a lot of advance notice about it."

Where Robert is a protector, Bennett's a caretaker. His concern is evident on his face, and in the way his hand wraps around my wrist, halting my movements so my attention is on him.

"It's fine."

"Fuck, we'll be out of your hair tomorrow, I promise," he says, letting go of my wrist.

"Was I that obvious? I was going for nonchalant."

"Your sister used to say that all the time, and trust me, it was never fine. But then she'd launch into a five-minute speech listing all my flaws, so at least you aren't doing that."

"Can you list all those flaws for me now?" I tease, as his gaze sweeps over me, landing on my eyes again.

"I've always loved how green your eyes are, the little hints of gold," he says as his gaze move down to my lips. I can feel my cheeks heating again. "I'm easily distracted, that's one flaw," he huffs.

He's trying to be playful, but the way his eyes have moved to my lips again feels like more than flirting, and I squeeze my thighs together to ease the ache growing there. I look down at the sink and try not to think about the arousal currently soaking my panties.

I plunge my arm into the water, feeling around until I make contact with a few utensils, debating how honest I should be. "I want you guys here, I do. I just wish I'd been included in the initial conversation. I hate being left out of things."

"That's valid," he says, and I instantly feel a weight lift at his words. "And for the record, I'd never intentionally leave you out." He grabs my chin and tilts it toward him. "Of anything." He steps back, dropping his hand and crossing his arms over his chest. "Fuck, I love seeing that blush on your cheeks. Is that the only place you blush?"

"I—um—" I'm all flustered as I drop a spoon back into the soapy water and break eye contact.

"Don't answer that. Sorry, I took it too far. You and Robert are happily married, and I'm chasing things I can't have," he says, taking another step back.

"I want you here," I say, taking a step toward him as I wipe my hands against my jeans. "*We* want you here."

"I don't want to put you out."

"You're not. Seriously, stay."

"At least put me to work. What can I do to pull my weight around here?"

"Always the caretaker," I mumble.

"What was that?"

"Any help with bedtime is appreciated," I say as his arms drop. Considering how worked up I am right now, I'd love to be able to fuck my husband without interruption.

"Done. I'd be happy to take over story time and tuck-in. You know they're going to want to sleep in the same room, right? I tried to tell Lexie that she'd be sharing a room with me, and she kept telling me no."

"She said no? Like out loud?" I ask incredulously.

"I wish. How crazy is that? When is 'no' any parent's

favorite word? But I'd love to hear her say it on repeat if it meant she could verbalize it."

"Be careful what you wish for," I joke. "But seriously, it'll happen one day."

"That's the dream," he says. "Lexie tells me 'no' in other ways. She'll shake her head, or pout and cross her arms, and we have some hand signals we use to communicate. She'll grab my hand and squeeze it once for 'yes' and twice for 'no.'"

"That's good to know. I hope she feels comfortable communicating with us like that too."

"I'm sure she will. She's already made herself at home," he says, moving closer to the sink. "Anything I need to know about bedtime? I don't wanna be hustled by a couple of kindergarteners. I'd never live that down."

"No more than two bedtime stories, or Hallie will have you reading her entire library. And if you can make the characters sound different, she likes that. And no matter what she tells you, no drinks before bed, or she'll be up in an hour to use the potty."

"Got it. Why don't you and B go enjoy yourselves? I've got this." He grabs a dish from the sink as he nods toward the stairs.

"Thanks. I need this more than you know." I hurry up the stairs to take advantage of this moment with my husband.

CHAPTER 16
BENNETT

R obert walks in the bedroom, a girl in each arm as he tosses Hallie on the bed in a fit of giggles. Lexie clings to him tightly, and I can tell she doesn't want the same treatment. He wraps an arm around her rocking her back and forth like he's about to launch her. "Do you want to fly too?"

She shakes her head, and he halts his movements, leaning to set her down gently as she clings even tighter.

"C'mon, Lexie, it's fun, I promise," Hallie pleads.

"You want to?" he asks again, and my heart warms at his treatment of her, as if she's his. She gives a small nod, and he makes a show of swinging her back and forth before tossing her onto the bed more gently than he did with Hallie. "Night, Halligator," he says leaning down to kiss her goodnight.

As he pulls back, Lexie reaches her arms up to him, a silent plea for a hug and something cracks in my chest at the ease in which she's let him into her life. He pulls her into a hug, his big arms encircling her tiny body as he looks over at me and mouths "Thank you" before heading out of the room.

We get settled on the bed, each girl tucked against me as I read them *Pajama Pigeon*, Hallie chirping instructions at me the entire time.

Once upon a time there was a pigeon named Penelope with a broken wing. She longed to live in a palace by the sea, where she could eat gourmet meals and have fancy parties with fancy friends in tuxedos and top hats. Penelope dreamed of finding her forever family, one who would accept her for who she was, broken wing and all. But nobody wanted to adopt a pigeon who couldn't fly.

Hallie stands up on the bed, tucking one arm in as she flaps them both wildly, and I feel Lexie shake with silent laughter next to me as I struggle to control my own. "You have to flap your arms," she commands, and I reluctantly wave my hands in the air. "Not like that! One of them is broken," she explains, and I fold one arm against my side as I continue flapping.

"Better?"

"Yup," she says, plopping down on my lap. I smile at the gesture, thrilled that she's comfortable with me.

And Penelope the pigeon watched her new friends get adopted day after day. She sat atop her perch and watched as people oohed and ahhed over the puppies and kittens. Even the sssnakes were fawned over more than she.

"Lexie, you be the animals, and I'll be the people, okay?" Lexie nods and hops off the bed, acting like a dog, tongue flapping and butt waggling.

"Ooh!" Hallie coos, then Lexie pretends to be a cat washing herself. "Ahh!" she cries. When Lexie rolls onto the ground and wiggles like a snake, I give in to my laughter as I continue reading.

"Ruff! Nobody wants to adopt a pigeon who can't fly," barked Bucky the Bulldog," I say in my most menacing bark, and the girls shake with laughter.

"Don't listen to that grumpy guy," purred Katie the Kitty. "Someone will want you."

"Thanks!" cooed Penelope.

"And if they don't, you can always be my lunch, meow!" said Katie, licking her lips.

123

"Plot twist!" I cry, feigning outrage. "I thought they were her friends!"

"Keep reading!" Hallie giggles.

Penelope sighed. All she wanted was a home and a family. But nobody wants a broken bird.

"I really hope she gets adopted," I say, flipping the pages, pretending to spoil the ending.

"Keep going!" Hallie cries.

Penelope was snuggled in her nest, in her favorite pajamas, when she awoke to a new friend in her cage.

"Hello. Argh! I'm Polly. Argh!" The colorful parrot squawked.

"Hi! I'm Penelope the Pigeon. Want to be my friend?"

"Got a cracker?"

"No, but there's some seed in my dish."

"Okay. Okay." Polly squawked in her too loud voice.

Polly and Penelope quickly became best friends.

"That's a really good parrot voice," Hallie says, moving next to me as she snuggles back into my chest. I take a minute to soak in this moment with these sweet girls before Hallie's poking my leg for me to continue.

Day after day, the two birds watched as other animals were picked.

Little boys and girls came to the shelter looking for new family members.

"Polly wants a home. Argh!" the bird yelled, but no one turned.

Penelope quietly cooed, hoping someone would like her voice.

"You have to make all the voices! You need to coo her song. Read it again!" Hallie demands.

Clearing my throat, I do my best pigeon coo.

Penelope quietly cooed, hoping someone would like her voice.

But nobody wanted a loud parrot or a pigeon who couldn't fly.

None of the other animals liked Polly or Penelope.

The dogs would bark at them all day.

The cats would stare at them like a tasty meal.

The snakes would eye them suspiciously.

But the birds didn't care because they had each other.

Every night they would have pajama parties and during the day they would pretend to be princesses having tea parties.

"That one, Mommy, I want the big bird!" the little boy shouted, pointing at Polly.

"You have to do it in a British voice," Hallie corrects.

"I thought this took place in California. Why are they British?" I ask, confused.

"Cuz that's how Mommy reads it. Oh, and the worker is 'posed to sound like a surfer," she says, and I nod in understanding and start again.

"That one mommy, I want the big bird!" the little boy shouted, pointing at Polly.

"She would make a fine addition to our flock," said the mom.

Penelope was happy for her friend to find her family, but sad that she would be alone.

"Argh! Ack! ARGH!" Polly squawked as the volunteer removed her from the cage and gave her to her new family.

Polly squawked all the way out the door.

Penelope missed her friend so much. She missed her pajama parties. She pictured her friend Polly in a palace by the sea eating fancy foods with fancy people. And it made her happy for her friend.

Two days later the little boy appeared in the shop again with his mom. "We adopted a parrot a few days ago, and it will not stop talking. This may be a weird question, but do you have any pigeons?" the little boy asked.

Penelope's ears perked up. She fluffed her feathers and brushed off her beak, ready to make a good impression.

"We do. But may I ask why?"

"It's the weirdest thing. The only thing this parrot will say is 'Polly wants a pigeon.'" said the mom.

"She has a pigeon friend here," the volunteer said, pointing to Penelope.

This was the moment she'd been waiting for. The mom and little boy took Penelope home and reunited her with Polly. And while their home wasn't a palace, it was near the ocean.

Polly squawked loudly when she saw her pigeon friend.

"Argh! Polly got a pigeon! Argh!"

And Penelope was overjoyed to be with her friend.

"Show you the house! ACK!" Polly squawked.

Polly could have flown, her wings were big and worked great, but she walked next to Penelope as they toured the house.

Penelope felt loved.

Penelope was home.

When they said they had a flock, boy, were they right! There were so many birds. They even had their own room in the house with perches everywhere.

"I'm Carl the Cockatoo! Welcome to our family flock of feathered friends!" called a beautiful white bird. He let out several loud chirps, calling the birds to attention.

"Why—"

"You have to do the chirps!" Hallie whines through a yawn.

"Sorry, I don't know what a cockatoo's chirps sound like," I say.

"Like this," she says, letting out a series of little whistles. "That's how Mommy does it."

"Why don't you join us up here?" he chirped.

"I can't," said Penelope quietly, holding up her broken wing.

"I have just the spot for you," Carl called and flew down from his perch to show her.

It was the perfect height for Penelope to use.

"Argh! Welcome home!" squawked Polly.

Penelope learned that you could find friends in the unlikeliest of places. And sometimes those friends can become family.

I close the book, and Lexie claps as Hallie yawns again. "Can we do another one?"

"It's Lexie's turn to pick," I say as Lexie rifles through the bookshelf.

"Pick another *Pajama Pigeon* one! They go on all kinds of adventures! In the next one, they meet a pair of parakeets. Ooh! Or the one where they take a trip to the zoo for the penguins and puffins. That one's funny."

Lexie's fingers stop on a blue spine. "That's the beach one, it's really good. A pelican saves them from the seagulls," Hallie explains. "But don't do the partridge one. That's a Christmas one, and it's not Christmas. They're all great, except the one where they go back in time and meet the pterodactyl. That one is kinda boring."

"How could dinosaurs be boring?" I ask with a laugh.

She sighs. "There's not enough tea parties and princesses."

After two more bedtime stories, including *Hansel and Gretel* —which Hallie insisted I read—the girls are finally snuggled in as I quietly back out of the room. I know Bex said to limit it to two stories, but I was a sucker for Hallie's puppy dog eyes, and I made sure she knew that three was the limit. There was minimal groaning after that so I'm calling it a win.

Lexie is known to slip out for water, and Robert told me Hallie likes to sneak into their bed, so I lean against the wall outside their room, prepared to catch a rogue child if I need to.

As I scroll through emails on my phone, one from my contractor catches my eye and my heart rate spikes. When I moved back to Columbus, I wanted to be near my family so I'd have support with Lexie and be closer to Nationwide Children's Hospital for her therapy. I found a house for us outside the city that had good bones but needed some work.

According to my contractor, today's inspection uncovered multiple structural issues that will delay project completion for several more weeks. Fuck. I need to get us a hotel. Tonight has been great, and the girls are having a blast, but I can't inconvenience Becka and Robert for six or more weeks. Despite Bex's reassurance earlier, I don't want to put them out, and I'm not convinced she's entirely thrilled to have houseguests.

Soft moans echo around me, and I peek in to check on the girls, worried that one of them is having a nightmare. As I walk over to the bed, the sounds stop, and I notice the girls cuddled up against each other. Warmth fills my chest at the sight. I wonder what it would be like for Lexie to have a sister and if that's something she'd even want.

When your child doesn't speak, it's hard to know pieces of her that other parents take for granted. She's not able to share her deepest desires with me unless I ask her explicitly and she can give me a "yes" or "no" answer. Since she's in kindergarten and still learning to write, she can't express her thoughts that way either.

Yet, Hallie has taught me things about my daughter that I never knew, learning sides of her I don't see at school, asking her questions I've never thought to ask. Having this family back in my life has been a blessing they'll never understand the magnitude of. It's brought me closer to my daughter. It's brought her out of her shell. And it's reconnected me with two people I've never gotten over.

I know it's wrong and probably one-sided, but I've been attracted to Bex since the day we met. I'd connected with Miranda on a dating app, and I mistook Becka for Miranda at the bar. It's the only time I've ever confused the two. Bex was finishing up drinks with her sister when I walked up. I was telling her she was even more beautiful in person than she was in her picture when she reared back and blushed. She pointed at her sister, but thankfully Miranda never heard what I'd said to Bex.

It wasn't until weeks later I'd learned that Bex was married. The beginning of my relationship with Miranda was a whirlwind. I'd craved a love like my parents' for my entire life, and I was hopeful that I'd found it in her. What I thought were acts of love that made me fall for her was actually love-bombing. Robert and I instantly connected when Miranda and I went on a double date with him and Bex. There was something about his quiet strength that intrigued me. In a matter of weeks, I had the love I'd searched for and an instant family in these two friends.

But the closer I got to Miranda, the more she wanted to spend time alone with me. She knew how to stroke my ego, and I fell under her spell, proposing quickly. Nothing felt amiss until much closer to our wedding, and by then it felt too late to speak up.

After the wedding, things started going downhill, and the love I thought we shared quickly shattered. I often found myself turning to Robert and Becka for comfort or a distraction, and their friendship got me through that difficult time. It gutted me when that connection was severed. Especially once I started parenting Lexie. They had only recently become parents too, and I'd often found myself wishing I could've shared that experience with them. Being here now is an opportunity I'm determined not to squander.

Satisfied that the girls are sleeping deeply, I quietly close their door and head to Robert and Becka's room to let them know about our change of plans. They've been so accommodating, but I can't inconvenience them with the rest of this renovation, especially when I just got them back in my life. Though the thought of separating Hallie and Lexie squeezes at my heart. They'll still see each other at school, though. The idea of wearing out our welcome with Becka and Robert makes me uncomfortable; losing them once was unbearable enough.

Grabbing the cold, black doorknob, I knock softly and wait until I hear a quiet "yes" before I crack open the door.

Holy fuck.

That "yes" wasn't meant for me. I'm not even sure Robert and Becka know I'm here. My eyes rake over her curves as I watch her ride him, her arms resting on Robert's chest as her hips move in a mesmerizing rhythm against him. Her skin is flushed as a bead of sweat trickles down her spine, and my eyes fixate on it as it glides down the full, round ass that's gripped in Robert's hands.

I *knew* that flush would cover more than her face.

It takes an excessive amount of self-control to keep myself in place. My grip tightens on the doorknob as my other hand moves to readjust the growing bulge in my pants. I peer down the hall quickly to ensure I'm still alone.

When I look back into the bedroom, Robert's hands have moved to cup Becka's full breasts. I wish I could see what her nipples look like. I bet they're the perfect shade of pink and hard as fucking diamonds. My eyes linger before moving to where their bodies connect. She looks incredible as his thick shaft pistons up into her. Robert is fucking *hung*. I'm overcome with desire, and I grab the doorframe, fighting the urge to join them, to lick his cock and suck one of his balls into my mouth while he continues fucking her. His hand moves down her stomach to her clit as Becka throws her head back in ecstasy.

"That's it, baby. Come for me." Robert's arm vibrates back and forth, making friction against her. I can hear how wet she is as the sounds of slapping skin fill the room. "You love that, don't you? Yeah, your needy pussy loves it when I fill you with this cock and play with your clit. Your greedy little cunt can't get enough of this dick."

"Yes. Fuck, Daddy, right there. Yes!"

Daddy? Shit, that's hot.

"Shhh, don't wake the girls," he says as his other hand grips her throat, pulling her to him in a fierce kiss. But not before his eyes flit to the door. They widen for a split second as they connect with mine while he kisses her. His eyes stay locked on mine as his thrusts get more intense. Is he… Is he into this? He's not looking away, and he's staring at me with what looks like hunger in his eyes. When he comes seconds later—maintaining eye contact the entire time—I reach down and palm my painfully hard dick, unsure which one of them turns me on more.

I've always found Robert attractive, but I've never pictured us together until now. Him being into men wasn't something that was on my radar. I've only had relationships with women, but I've hooked up with a few men for a night or two, nothing serious. I'm suddenly overwhelmed with thoughts of the three of us fucking, snuggling in bed, going on dates, building a life with our girls. Talk about a mindfuck.

Where are all these thoughts coming from?

I can't be with them. I'm not even sure they'd want a relationship with me. Besides, the last thing I need is more drama with Miranda. For fuck's sake, they're my in-laws—well, ex-in-laws.

It takes everything in me to shut the door and head to my room. I should find another place to stay. I'll talk to them about it tomorrow. But not before I fuck my hand in the shower, thinking about my best friends fucking each other. Except in my fantasy, they're fucking me too.

The next day at work is hectic, with one problem after another. I've been focused on commercial real estate at this firm for the past decade. I was fortunate to be able to work remotely when I lived in Missouri, and there was a branch of our firm with an office in Kansas City that I frequented when I needed to.

I made my first few millions in real estate in my early twenties when I bought up a few single-family homes and flipped them. The more I made, the more I bought, until I eventually ventured out into commercial real estate, which has a higher return, nearly double my other properties.

It's nearly five o'clock when I finally look up from the pile of papers on my desk. This is going to take me weeks to fix, and I'll be damned if I lose time with my girl. That means I'm going to have to come in early to get everything done if I want to make it home on time for dinner and bedtime. Which means I may need to rely on Bex and Robert and continue staying with them.

On the drive home, I can't stop thinking about what I walked in on last night. Images of the two of them fucking while Robert's eyes were on me flood my mind as traffic sits at a standstill. I had every intention of finding another temporary living situation after last night. I'm not sure my heart can stand to be that close to them and not be able to act on my feelings. But it looks like I'm going to have to stick this out. At least work will keep me away more than I thought, aside from the evenings. I'll just have to avoid them in order to keep my heart in one piece.

CHAPTER 17

ROBERT

Selfishly, I wish Bennett could stay longer because it's allowed me and Becka time to reconnect while he puts the girls to bed. Every night this week, he's volunteered to tuck the girls in, and every time I've left our bedroom door unlocked, hoping he'd show his face again like he did the first night, but no such luck.

What the fuck? He's my best friend and my ex-brother-in-law. Yet I've been having thoughts of him all week. And not once has it felt wrong. But it should. There are a million reasons why this is a bad idea. But I couldn't give a fuck about any of them right now.

"Okay, we're headed out. Need me to pick up anything while we're out?" Becka asks, pulling me from my thoughts. I should talk to her about Bennett seeing us together the other night. Hell, we all need to talk. "Earth to Robert."

I look up from my coffee. "Where are you going?" I ask in confusion.

"Ugh, I told you last night. I'm taking the girls to that tea house that's only open a few hours in the afternoon. They've been begging all week. Remember? You made a joke about tea-bagging me later?"

I chuckle, that sounds like something I'd say. "Oh yeah."

"Are you okay? You've been distracted all week."

Shrugging, I sip my coffee, trying to buy time.

"Clearly, you're not ready to talk, but something is bothering you. I can sense it," she says as she makes a show of waving her hands before placing them on my head.

Fuck, I love this woman.

"When will you be back?" I ask.

"Missing me already?"

"Always," I promise, grabbing her thigh and pulling her close to place a kiss on her stomach.

"We should be back in a few hours. You and Bennett should go shoot some hoops," she says as she threads her fingers through my hair.

"Really?"

"Yeah, something's bothering him too. I think it's work-related. I can see the stress he's carrying in his shoulders."

"And you think basketball will help?"

"You two became best friends on the court, and you and I both know that's the only place you seem to open up with him. You're both clearly holding on to something, and if you won't talk to me about it, talk to him about it. Don't bottle it up."

"Okay," I acquiesce.

"That's it? Okay? You're not gonna fight me?" she asks, shock evident in her voice.

"Yeah, there's something I want to talk to him about, so I agree that it's a good idea."

"Okay," she says, drawing out the word. "You're not telling me something, but I'm fine with it as long as you talk to someone about it." She plants three quick kisses to my forehead.

"Love you too," I say as she heads out the door with the girls, and I bring my empty mug to the sink, washing it quickly.

I head upstairs and change into a pair of athletic shorts. I notice the hamper is full so I decide to start a load of laundry, knowing I can throw it in the dryer once we get back. After I start the washer, I check the dryer and discover it's full of towels. I forgot to fold them last night. I've been trying to step up my laundry game, knowing it's a bad habit of mine that drives Becka crazy. Happy wife, happy life.

The smell of sandalwood and leather wafts out of the guest bathroom when I walk by with the basket of towels. I inhale, taking in Bennett's masculine scent, as my cock twitches in my shorts. Why is the scent of his body wash turning me on?

Shit, I wonder if he has a towel. Looking down at the basket, I confirm my suspicions—all the guest towels and a few of the girls' are in there. I set down the basket and grab one. I'll leave one on the counter so he sees it, I lie to myself.

When I try the doorknob to the bathroom, it turns easily. Even though I only intended to drop it on the counter and go, my eyes drift to the shower where I can see Bennett clearly through the glass. His back is to me, and he's got one hand against the tiled wall while the other furiously pumps his dick.

I can't look away as he continues fisting his cock, a groan spilling from his lips.

I should leave, but I don't. This should feel wrong, but it doesn't.

"Fuck. Fuck. Fuuuck," he rasps as he stills, his ass clenching as I imagine him painting the wall with his cum. Without turning around, he says, "You gonna just stand there, or do you want to help me clean it up?"

"Uhhhh, shit, sorry…I…" I stutter, still clutching the towel.

"I'm fucking with you, B," he says, turning to face me. My eyes dart around, trying to avoid his dick, softening as it hangs between his legs. "I'd have offered to help you and Bex clean up if I knew this was something you were into," he says with a wink.

"It's not, I'm not—" I try to say, but the words die on my

lips as I realize that I might be into it, especially if he keeps bringing up the night he watched me and Becka fuck. I've never come so hard before, and I'm convinced it was because he was watching us. Maybe that's my kink. I like watching and being watched.

"Kinda seems like you're into it, B." He points to the massive boner tenting my shorts. "You know I'm not judging, and I don't discriminate. Love is love."

"Yeah," I say, unsure what to share. I knew he'd been with men in the past, but I've never thought about him this way before, never wondered how any man has tasted before as I fight the urge to drop to my knees and clean his cum-covered torso with my tongue. Fuck. I didn't even have thoughts like this about Alyx that night in the club. It was easy to disassociate and concentrate on Becka there, and I'm convinced it was more her excitement that got me off that night. But Becka's not here right now, and I'm fully turned on by someone who's not my wife.

"That towel for me?"

"Um, yeah," I say, making no move to give it to him. Instead, my eyes rake over his body as his hands smear his cum up and down the defined muscles of his chest and torso. Why is that so hot? My cock presses against the waistband of my underwear, and I reach down to adjust myself.

"You can always join me in here if you want to take care of that. Promise I'll keep my hands to myself, unless you don't want me to."

I manage to rasp out "Becka," and I cringe at my awkwardness. His face falls.

"Fuck, man. I took it too far. I'm sorry."

"It's cool," I say with all the confidence I can muster, but my heart is racing, my cock is still throbbing, and I can't make sense of all the voices screaming in my head. Am I into men? Or am I into *this* man?

I'm not any less interested in my wife, I know that. For

some reason, I figured if I ever had feelings for a man, it would somehow diminish my feelings for Becka. It's a fucked-up way of thinking, and I know it comes from my upbringing, but if anything, I love her more than ever right now because she knew this part of me existed. She always fucking knows.

"Lemme get rinsed off and dressed and we can go shoot some hoops."

Fuck, does everyone but me know that's code for sharing feelings?

———————

Bennett and I spend twenty minutes playing one-on-one before either of us addresses the real reason we're here. And oddly enough, I didn't expect to be the one to break the silence. Becka and Bennett are both outgoing extroverts who never stop talking, and I love that about them, while I'm a man of few words. The only people I ever find myself opening up to is them.

"How did you know?" I ask timidly, still afraid to voice my full thoughts.

"How did I know what?" he asks, passing me the ball. I can feel his eyes on me and my heart races as I line up my shot and sink it in the hoop.

"That you were…" Fuck, why is this so hard to admit?

"Attracted to men?" He grabs the ball and shoots.

"Yeah."

"I dunno, I think I always was. It wasn't hard for me to figure out when literally everyone had me popping boners in middle school. I take it what happened earlier was a first for you?"

"Yeah. I mean, there was one other time with Becka and a guy at Pulse."

"Shit, you're holding out on me. You guys went to Pulse and had a threesome?"

"Not a threesome. He just..." Fuck, am I doing this? Admitting this out loud? I let out a deep breath, dribbling the ball, before I continue. "He sucked me off, then he left, and Becka and I fucked."

"Did not have that on my bingo card." He chuckles, stealing the ball from me, and taking another shot. "And you're freaking out because you enjoyed it and you're worried about what your family would say?"

"Fuck, man. You and Becka are the only ones that know me well enough to put that together."

"Well, yeah. You may be a grumpy asshole to the rest of the world, but we see the real you."

"You do." I flash him a smile.

"Keep smiling at me like that and I'm gonna fall in love with you," he teases. Or at least I think he's teasing. Is he teasing? "Just joking, B. I know these feelings are new to you, and I'm a shameless flirt. I can stop if it's too much." He passes me the ball.

I palm it in one hand, gripping the bumpy texture as I decide how much to share. "I love Becka."

"I feel like there's a but coming."

"I'd never do anything to hurt her. But I'm confused as fuck. Nothing ever felt right with other girls until her. It's why I never had sex with anyone but her. It wasn't all the abstinence propaganda the church forced on me. I was just never really attracted to anyone else, and I never wanted to be."

We play in silence for a few minutes as my confession hangs in the air, but my game is off. He makes shot after shot, stealing the ball from me easily as I try to block him. The press of his ass against me as he backs me closer to the hoop has my cock springing to life. Do we normally touch this much when we play, or am I more aware of his closeness because I'm starting to crave it?

"I don't know a lot about that world, the LGBTQIA+ community. I grew up being told that it was wrong, and it's been hard to shake that mindset. But my limited encounters haven't felt wrong. Though I'm probably the worst possible judge for that, because my encounters with women felt wrong until Becka. Maybe I'm just broken," I confess.

"You're not broken, and your sexuality isn't broken. There's nothing wrong with exploring it if everyone's on the same page."

"Becka's been pushing me to explore that part of myself more, and I keep lashing out at her like a dick every time she brings it up."

"It's hard to ignore internalized bigotry," he offers.

"Yeah."

"So, what are you saying?"

Fuck, he's going to make me say it.

"I'm not saying I'm into men, cuz I'm not, but I can't explain why you turn me on. Or how the thought of you and Becka together has been a constant rotation in my spank bank."

"I'm not going to lie, your wife is hot. Respectfully, of course. But I also find you incredibly attractive. Have you ever thought about us together, or is it just me and Becka?" He passes me the ball again.

"There might've been a few times with me and you too. Fuck. I can't believe I said that. Forget it, I don't know what I'm talking about," I say, tossing him the ball and walking away, embarrassed for admitting it out loud.

"Robert, wait," he calls, his footsteps pounding behind me as I slowly turn to face him. "I know this is hard for you to say, but I can be a safe space for you, I promise. This is hard for me too."

"Why? You've done this before."

"But never with my best friend," he says, taking a step closer to me. "And it's hard because all I want to do is touch you right now and feel your lips on mine until your cock is so hard that all you want to do is rub it against me for release." His voice drops seductively.

My eyebrows shoot up and I take a step back, scanning our surroundings as my mind plays out that scenario in vivid detail.

"It excites me, now that I know you're thinking about it too, but I know you're not ready, and I know how you hate PDA," he says, putting distance between us in a silent promise to show me he understands what I need. "And if I'm honest, I'm the one with the most to lose in this scenario. I can't deny that I'm attracted to you both, but I just got you guys back, and your friendship means more to me than anything. I don't want to lose it just because I'm horny for my friends."

"We should talk to Becka. I know she's been encouraging me to explore this, but it feels wrong to do it without her. We made vows to each other, and they didn't include any of this," I say, my voice shaking. My rule-following brain is telling me I'm breaking the rules, even though I made them.

"That's fair," he says, patting my shoulder, his touch warming me from the inside out as he grabs his bag and walks toward the car.

Now I'm the one chasing him. "Hold up. Becka's under the impression that you needed to talk as much as I did. Said you had something bothering you that was work-related?"

"I don't want to burden you with it," he starts as he gets behind the wheel.

Folding myself into the passenger seat, I buckle in and shift to get comfortable because most cars don't fit my tall frame. "It's not a burden, Will— sorry, still getting used to calling you Bennett. What's going on?"

"Work shit. My firm has been buying up a lot of businesses and real estate, but apparently not everything has been above board since our financial guy is the founder's son and has no clue what he's doing. It's created a paperwork nightmare, and I've been having to pull extra hours to help clean up the mess.

It's why I've been leaving earlier in the morning. I wanted to make sure I was still home in time for dinner and bedtime with my girl."

"So, you haven't been avoiding us because you walked in on us fucking?"

He chuckles, and something flutters in my belly. "Fuck no. I've been going to bed shortly after the girls since I'm getting up so early and I like to work out before work. But I'd be lying if I didn't admit that I sometimes stand next to your door and listen while patrolling the hallway for little cockblockers. Becka mentioned how your typical sleeping arrangement prevents you two from fucking, so I figured it was the least I could give you while you let us crash with you."

"I was worried I scared you off."

"Quite the opposite. Once I hear you finish, I head to the shower to take care of myself so I can start the cycle all over again. I keep telling myself that I'm going to leave and find a hotel for us, but I don't have it in me to say no to those little girls."

"I know how you feel. Hallie has me wrapped around her finger. It's gonna suck when your house is ready and we have to split them up."

"Yeah, but we'll visit. And I'm sure there will be sleepovers in our future."

"Probably." And damn, does my cock swell at the thought of us having adult sleepovers too.

Becka

"I want to watch you and Bennett," Robert declares as soon as the door shuts.

"I just put our daughter on the bus and that's how you want to greet me this morning?" I ask, pressing a soft kiss to his neck.

His hands rest on my waist as his thumbs stroke idle circles under my shirt. "I've been thinking about it. I can see you two are attracted to each other. And you've seen me with someone else, which was really fucking hot."

"When you say that you want to watch us, what do you mean? There was no penetration involved with you and Alyx, just oral. Is that what you want to watch me and Bennett do?" I clarify to ensure I have a clear picture of his desire and limits.

"Maybe. Maybe more than that? I don't know. I'm not sure how I'll feel, but right now, the mere thought of you two together has my cock pressing against my pants. The fantasies in my brain are hot as fuck. I trust him with you. He's always looked out for you, for both of us. And it excites me more than it scares me."

I glance down at his hard-on as images of Bennett's face between my legs have me clenching my thighs together. I look up to see Robert assessing me, looking for an answer.

"Have you talked to him about this?" I ask.

"A little, when we played basketball. There's something else I haven't told you."

"Is it that you love butt stuff, because I already know that," I tease, knowing he needs me to break the tension.

"He watched us that first night."

"What do you mean?" I ask, confused.

"When he put the girls to bed the first night they were here, he came to our room after and heard you say yes, thinking you were answering his knock, so he opened the door and saw us fucking. I don't know how long he was there, but I made eye contact with him right before we came, and he held my gaze through completion."

"And you liked it?" I ask, running my hand over the head of his cock pressing against the seam of his pants.

"I did. We talked about stuff and I'm open to the idea of the three of us…" he trails off.

"Hooking up?" I offer as he thrusts his cock against my hand.

"Fuck, why does just talking about it make me this hard?"

"Maybe you're not as straight as you think. But we don't have to label anything right now. Let's just explore this with each other and see how we all feel."

"Okay. Do you think Bridget and Ethan would watch Hallie?"

"Probably." Holy shit, is he really agreeing to this? He grabs my throat and pulls me close, capturing my mouth in a searing kiss.

"Let's go upstairs, and I'll take care of this for you before I have to log on to work," I say, rubbing my palm up the length of him. "Then you should text Bennett and we can make plans."

CHAPTER 18

ROBERT

Do you think your parents would watch Lexie this weekend?

BENNETT

If I hand her over to them, I may never get her back.

So that's a yes?

LOL yes. I can check with them

Why?

I was thinking the three of us could hang out.

Kid-free.

Are you asking me out on a date?

What am I doing? This is crazy. I'm a happily married man. I have a wife. We made vows. This isn't something I should be indulging in. Is it? I can't deny how excited I am about the idea of all of us together.

When Bennett and Miranda first started dating, we'd go on double dates regularly. At first it was fun. I loved going out and showing off my hot wife, and she wanted to spend more time with her sister, so it was a win-win for everyone.

But the more we all hung out, the closer Bennett and I got. We always had a lot in common, and even though I'm not a fan of people, he was easy to talk to. And when I was all talked out, he'd carry the conversation. We bonded over our love of film and basketball. He quickly became my best friend, and we started hanging out weekly and talking almost daily that first year.

It's amazing to me that I could feel such a close bond to someone so quickly; the only other time that'd happened to me was when I met Becka in college. But I'd only known Bennett for three years when Miranda removed him from our lives.

Now that he's back, I'm not willing to let him go again, even if I'm confused about my feelings for him.

———

I'm home in record time, having just dropped Hallie off at Bridget and Ethan's. The girls weren't thrilled about being separated, but Ethan had agreed to watch his sisters too, and we didn't want Lexie to feel uncomfortable with new people. I find Becka in the kitchen and pull her into a hug.

"How did it go at Bridget's?" Becka asks. "Did Hallie make some new friends?"

"Yeah, all the girls were giggling when I left. Ethan's dad was there too, which was kinda awkward. But I'm sure it'll be fine."

"Shit, I should text Bridget to see how that went," Becka says, pulling away from me to reach for her phone, but I grab it before she can.

"Later," I say, tucking a loose strand of hair behind her ear and leaning into her. "I'm trying here. I'm really trying."

"Trying what?" Becka shudders as my fingers trail down the side of her neck and she arches it, baring it for me.

My lips are a whisper away from her throat as I speak into her skin. "I'm trying not to drop to my knees and devour this perfect cunt. I'm trying to wait until Bennett gets here because he deserves to hear your moans too. But I never get to take my time with you. I know we have all night, but fuck, I want to spend every last minute worshipping this body tonight."

"I love when you talk to me like that," she moans as I kiss along her collarbone.

"You starting without me?" Bennett asks, coming from behind us and startling me. "Don't stop on my account. I'm enjoying the show."

Shit, this is real. He's here, and we're kid-free all night. There's nothing stopping us from crossing that line. But is that what I want?

My eyes connect with Becka's, green and full of love. She reaches up and rubs the skin between my eyebrows, smoothing the furrow there, and my nerves instantly relax.

"Let's go sit," Becka says, looking between us and motioning to the living room.

I exhale and follow them to the couch. This doesn't have to be weird. We've hung out just the three of us before. Bennett and I would shoot hoops, and then we'd end up back here and Becka would join us. We'd snack and watch movies and chill. That's all this is.

But what if I fuck this up and we lose that?

"So where do you want me? Are you going to paint me like one of your French girls, Jack?" Bennett says, flopping onto the couch.

"That's not the line. And he'd film you before he'd draw you," Becka quips, taking a seat in the recliner.

"Oh, I could get on board with us making a film together,

but I'd better not be the only one getting naked," he says, looking between us as he raises his eyebrows.

Becka dissolves into a fit of laughter as I stare at them with my arms crossed from my spot behind the recliner. "You gotta have better jokes than that if you wanna make this grumpy bear smile," she says, pointing a thumb behind her.

"How do you know I'm not smiling?" I ask, hoping there's a slight tease to my voice, but my nerves are on edge thinking about where this is headed, and I'm having a hard time relaxing or coming across as casual.

"Because I can hear it in your voice, and he used your brother's nickname. And now you're thinking about your brother Jack lying on that couch reenacting that scene in the movie."

How does she do that? It's unnerving how well she knows my thought process.

Bennett throws his head back in a laugh. "Fuck, Bex, you should see the look of disgust and surprise on his face. He's totally thinking that, and he's shocked you figured it out."

"I don't have to look at his face to know that's exactly how he looks," she says.

"Are you two done, or are you going to gang up on me all night?" I ask, a bit of bite to my tone. I know they're trying to ease the tension, but this is a big moment for me, and I flex my hands, hoping to take the edge off.

"Oh, I'd happily *gang* up on you with her," Bennett teases as he locks eyes with me.

"That's not what I meant," I splutter.

"Offer still stands," he says with a shrug.

"Okay, grumpy bear, you can relax. We're only teasing, and we're not going to do anything if you're not okay with it," Becka says reassuringly as she tilts her head back to look up at me. "I promise."

I'm out of my comfort zone. Becka looks completely at ease

and carefree, laughing with Bennett, but I can't get out of my head.

"Here, take my seat," Becka offers, getting up and gesturing at the recliner as she sits next to Bennett on the couch.

I lower myself into the recliner as Bennett sits up and props his elbows on his knees. "Hey, B, look at me," he says as he waits for me to follow his instruction.

Our eyes connect, and I instantly feel insecure. What's he thinking? Is this going to change everything? If this gets weird, am I going to lose my friend or my wife?

A small smile flashes on his face, causing the crinkles around his blue eyes to deepen. "We don't have to do anything tonight. There's no pressure. You know I'm crushing on you both," he says as he looks at Becka. "But we can hang out and watch movies kid-free. Nothing needs to change if you don't want it to. I'm just grateful you guys are letting us stay with you."

"What if we did scratch that itch?" Becka asks, her gaze bouncing back and forth between us. "Do you think we could explore this without it changing things?"

No fucking way. How could this not change everything?

"Whatever you want to do, I'm down. If you want to stay friends, or scratch an itch, I'll follow your lead," Bennett says, but I can see the hope on his face. He wants more with us, even if he's trying to act casual about it.

Becka looks up at me. "Truth," she prompts me, waiting for my response.

"I don't know," I answer honestly. "I've never done casual hookups before. I don't know if I'm built for that."

"That's fair—" Bennett starts, but I cut him off.

"I think this is something I want to try, though. But we need to talk to each other. I don't want anyone feeling left out or betrayed."

"Of course," Bennett says quickly.

Becka nods. "Agreed."

Bennett's eyes are fixed on the pink of Becka's cheeks, and I watch him reach down to readjust himself. I've seen men check out my wife before—how could they not? She's gorgeous. But there's something about the way his eyes openly rake over her body as he checks her out. It should infuriate me, but it's kind of turning me on, and making me feel something else. Pride, maybe?

"So, what happens now?" I ask.

"We communicate our boundaries. You two are in a committed relationship, and I'm just the guest star. I don't want to do anything that makes either of you uncomfortable. Is there anything that's off-limits?"

Becka looks at me and shrugs, waiting for me to answer.

"I don't know," I say, unsure where to begin, feeling overwhelmed with emotion and lust.

"What if I list some things and you tell me if there's anything that stands out to you as a no?"

"Okay," Becka and I answer together.

"Kissing. Touching above clothing. Touching bare skin. Oral sex between any of us."

"I've never done that," I say quickly, rubbing my hands on my legs. Bennett swings his head over to Becka in shock before I clarify. "I've never done that on a man. I told you about that time at Pulse, and I'd live in her cunt if she'd let me, but I've never given oral to a man before."

"It's okay, we don't have to do that tonight. What about sex?" he asks, looking at Becka. "Is that something you'd be comfortable with?"

"Only if he is," she says.

"Are you comfortable sharing Becka?"

"I...I don't know," I repeat. "Sorry, I know I keep saying that. This is all new to me and I'm not sure how I'll feel until it happens."

"And that's totally valid. If anyone is uncomfortable, just

say 'yellow' to let us know that you're nearing a limit. If you want something to stop, say 'red' and we'll stop."

"Got it," I confirm.

"Okay," Becka says. "So, what happens now? Do we get naked and start touching?"

"I appreciate the enthusiasm, Bex, but I was thinking we could put a movie on and let things happen organically. B, you want to come sit with us over here?"

"I want to watch," I say.

"You want to pick the movie? I know Mr. Film Buff will have opinions about what we watch." Bennett reclines on the couch, moving back and patting the space in front of him, motioning Becka to lie with him.

I scroll through our streaming services as they snuggle. I think carefully about what film to put on. Nothing that will suck us into the story and pull focus from where this is headed, but nothing overly emotional either. I'm not sure I can process one more feeling. Once I settle on an action film, I recline back, propping my feet up. I try to concentrate on the screen, but my focus keeps shifting to the couch. Bennett's head is propped on his hand, his light brown hair falling over his forehead as he watches the movie. He's only a year older than me, two years older than Becka, but he looks younger than both of us. There's a light dusting of scruff on his jaw, and I rub at mine absentmindedly. His other hand is resting on Becka's waist with his fingers splayed out over her stomach.

I've never taken the time to look at him like this. And why is checking him out getting me so hard? We spent years hanging out as friends, and I never got turned on. Is it because Becka's part of it?

"Keep wiggling your ass against me, Bex, and you're going to get this party started now," Bennett warns suddenly.

"Sorry, I was getting comfortable," she says innocently, looking over her shoulder at him.

I watch as his grip tightens on her waist, and I see the

smirk on her face as she wiggles again. His hips thrust against her once in a quick movement and her eyes get wide as a blush brightens her cheeks.

"I love when you blush, Bex. It's been my undoing since the moment we met," he groans into her hair as I reach down and squeeze my cock over my shorts, desperate to relieve the pressure.

Bennett's hand skims up her body and pulls her hair back from her neck. "Is this okay?" he asks, his lips hovering over her neck.

Her eyes flick to me, and I nod.

"Yes," she says, arching her neck to give him access.

He shifts slightly and leans over her, kissing down her neck. Once he gets to her collarbone, his tongue darts out and licks a trail up to her ear, and then he blows air along the path as Becka visibly shivers.

"Oh, shit," she moans, pushing her hips back into his.

"Knew you'd taste good," he says against her ear as his hand moves under her shirt. "I can't wait to taste every inch of you."

I see the pained look on Becka's face, and he must feel her stiffen. "Hey, Bex, what is it? Sorry, I can be vocal, does that bother you?"

She shakes her head as her eyes connect with mine. "I vow to always share my feelings with you, even if they're a lot, because I know you can handle it. You can tell him, baby. It's okay," I reassure her, reminding her of her vow to me.

"Bex, look at me. You can talk to me," he says softly, turning her face to his.

"One of my exes said he didn't like going down on me because I smelled bad and he didn't like the way it tasted. He said it was too much, and I have a hard time enjoying it."

"What kind of fuck says that?"

"Thank you," I say. "Just so you know, she tastes just as good as you're thinking she does. Trust me."

"We can solve this right now," he says, flipping her onto her back and pulling his shirt off as he inches down her body. Becka throws an arm over her face, hiding it from view as he pauses. "Can I taste you, Bex?"

She inhales deeply, her tits straining against her shirt as his finger dips into her waistband. "Okay," she says on an exhale.

"Nope, I'm going to need your enthusiastic consent, and that was reluctant at best. We'll start slow," he says crawling back up her until his face is hovering over hers. "Can I kiss—" he starts but is cut off when Becka pulls his face to hers.

Something explodes in the movie as it continues playing in the background, but I can't take my eyes off Bennett and Becka. I watch with rapt fascination as my best friend makes out with my wife. And it's making me hard as fuck.

She's writhing underneath him as he slides a hand under her shirt. I catch the outline of his hand cupping her breast as he breaks the kiss, strips off her shirt, pulls down her bra, and lets both fall to the floor.

"I knew you'd blush on more than just your cheeks." He stares down at her tits. "Fuck, these nipples are the exact shade of pink I imagined they'd be," he says, pulling one into his mouth.

"When were you picturing her nipples?" I ask, my voice raspier than I intended as I rub my erection over my shorts.

The smile on Bennett's face is infectious as he looks over at me, pulling off his shirt before he speaks. "That night I watched you two. She was riding you and I could only see her back. I watched you suck on these tits, and I was desperate to know what they looked like."

"She likes a lot of pressure," I tell him, still stroking my cock as he returns his focus to my wife's chest.

"Where?" he asks, nipping on the flesh of her breast.

"Everywhere. Her nipples. Her clit. Her ass."

"Oh, this is going to be fun," he says, a devious smile on his face.

"What's going to be f—AH!" Becka starts and then moans when Bennett pinches one nipple, before biting the other. Her moans get louder when his mouth moves to the other breast, and his hand snakes down her torso, stopping at the top of her leggings. He hesitates for a second, teasing a finger along her waistband, when she grabs his hand and moves it lower.

Becka's hand glides along his hips, and the moment it connects with Bennett's cock, he lets out a throaty groan.

"Take it out," Bennett demands between kisses to her chest.

I reach into my shorts and pull out my cock, fisting it in my hand when I realize he's talking to Becka. He shifts up her body and kisses along her shoulder and neck as she slips her hand inside his pants.

"Holy shit," Becka whispers. I assume she's impressed with the size of his dick. She's pulled it out and is playing with something on the tip. "Are you *pierced*?" she asks, her voice full of wonder.

"I am," he confirms, leaning back on his arm as he looks down at her. She's still playing with the head of his dick, fascinated with her discovery.

"I have questions. Sorry, I know this is a mood killer, but I've only ever read about this in books," she says, shifting down the couch to get a closer look.

He chuckles, reaching down to fist the base of his cock. "Ask away."

"Why did you get it? Is it for your pleasure or your partner's? Did it hurt? How long was the recovery? Does it actually feel good for your partner, or do the books exaggerate?"

"Wait, I didn't see a piercing," I interject.

"When did you see his dick?" I hear a hint of hurt in her tone. She hates being left out.

"I walked in on him in the shower after you left with the girls the other day," I explain. "Before basketball."

"Not sure how you missed it, but I had just come and it's on the underside."

"Hold on, I'm missing something. Holy fuck, is this how Bridget feels?" she mutters.

"I was relieving some tension in the shower when your husband walked in on me to deliver a towel. I had my back to him when I came, and I was somewhat soft when I turned around. It could be hard to see from that angle since it's a barbell," Bennett explains.

"Nothing happened without you," I assure her.

"But to answer your questions, I got it after my divorce. I figured it was a good time since I wasn't planning on being with anyone and I had nothing but time to kill. I haven't had the opportunity to use it with anyone yet, so I can't speak to who gets more pleasure from it, but it feels good when I'm playing with it. It hurt worse than my vasectomy did, and I couldn't use it for a few months during recovery. I was in a dark place when I got it and I needed the pain to remind me that I was alive, that I was still here."

"Shit, I didn't know things were that bad," Becka says, letting go of his dick and pulling back. "And we just abandoned you."

"You had to, or Miranda would've made sure of it. I don't blame you. And I wasn't upset about losing Miranda, I was more upset that I'd failed at something I wanted so badly. My parents have been happily married for almost fifty years, and my marriage only lasted two. And I missed you two so much. You were the best part of my marriage. Then there was the fact that I was thrust into parenthood. Finding out I had a daughter who didn't know who I was, trying to prove to her family that I wanted her, and fighting for custody of her. It was the loneliest time of my life. I know it's a ridiculous reason to get my dick pierced, considering all that was happening in my life, but that's my story."

Becka pulls him into a soft kiss, then pulls back and holds his face in her hands.

"We're not going anywhere," she says against his lips. "No matter what happens, we're not losing you again."

His hands tangle in her hair as they kiss, and he lowers his body over hers. My cock throbs as I shift in my seat.

"Please, Bex," he says, trailing a hand down her body and into her panties.

"Oh fuck," she moans as his hand wiggles against her pussy. I can only imagine what he's doing to her, but whatever it is, she's enjoying the hell out of it as she bucks against him, gripping his wrist to guide it to a spot that makes her moan louder.

"That's it? Right there? That's where you need my fingers?" he asks.

"Yes, yes, oh fuck yes."

"What about here?" he asks, shoving his hand deeper into her panties. "Can I play here with my fingers while my mouth sucks this perfect little clit?"

"Y–yes, please, yes!"

I've never seen a man move faster than Bennett does when he yanks down her leggings and panties in one swift movement and positions himself between her thighs. His hand moves rapidly back and forth as he crooks two fingers into her pussy. Taking his time, he kisses her inner thighs, licking and biting as his hand continues fucking her. "Hold your legs for me, Bex."

She quickly complies as he licks closer and closer to the apex of her thighs. "Fuck, this is so hot to watch," I say without thought.

Becka's head turns to me as she reaches out a hand in my direction. "Baby, please, I need you."

I can't deny my wife anything, especially when she says it like that. Immediately, I'm on my feet, closing the distance between us. Bennett is feasting on her cunt as she writhes and moans, pulling my face to hers as soon as I'm close enough. I pinch one of her nipples between my fingers as I kiss her deeply, letting her feel every ounce of love in me with the thrust of my tongue.

"Oh shit, oh fuck!" she moans, and I know that Bennett has locked on to that magic spot that always has her coming quickly. "I'm going to—oh fuck!" she cries as she throws her head back and wails out her orgasm. My eyes meet Bennett's right as Becka squirts, covering him with her release.

Bennett looks between us with amazement. "Fuck, B, you've got a squirter? Oh, we're going to have so much fun with this," he says as he licks around her pussy, eager to enjoy every drop. I've only made her squirt a few times, but I know he's in heaven right now, just like I was when I discovered she could do this.

It's surreal watching someone else lap at her cunt. All I want to do is taste her right now and see if I can taste him on her skin.

His rough hand grabs mine, pulling me closer to him.

As if reading my mind, Bennett asks, "Wanna taste our girl? See how good she tastes on me?" He clasps a hand on my neck and pulls my face to his.

The moment his lips touch mine, a bolt of electricity races through my veins, the same way it did when I first kissed Becka. His lips are covered in her cum. We're not gentle with each other—he's nipping and sucking my lips, thrusting his tongue against mine with force, and it spurs me on. The scruff of his facial hair feels strange against my skin, but I welcome the burn.

I pull him toward me, and he stumbles out from between Becka's legs until he's kneeling on the floor next to the couch with me. "Fuck, she tastes so good on your skin," I groan, pulling him closer to me until I can feel his cock against mine as he bites and sucks his way down my neck.

"I love that our first kiss includes your wife. She covered my face with her cum, and now I can cover you in her too."

156

"Fuck, that's hot," Becka says as I pull Bennett's mouth to mine again.

His hard cock presses against mine as we start thrusting against each other, our mouths battling for control. I can't deny how good this feels. How right this feels. "You were right," I pant, pulling back so I can look him in the eyes. "I want release. You've made me a needy mess with the way you're kissing and rubbing against me."

"Can I use my mouth?" he asks as his eyes fill with excitement.

"Yes," I say as Becka sits up and makes room for me beside her. I pull off my shorts and boxers then sit next to her as Bennett gets into position between my legs. His fingers lightly graze up my quads, tickling the hairs in his wake.

Becka turns my face to hers and pulls me into a kiss as Bennett's mouth covers the head of my dick. I jolt and let out a guttural groan against her lips as my cock slides deeper into his mouth.

"Fuuuck," I moan as he hollows his cheeks and sucks hard. "That feels so... mmmmm... fuck, that feels good," I say between kisses. "His mouth, your lips. Fuck, I need more of this."

"I loved both of your mouths on me," Becka says against my lips right as Bennett swirls his tongue around the head of my cock then takes me to the back of his throat.

Out of instinct, I reach for his head, guiding his movements as he bobs on my cock.

"Use me, B. Fuck my face till you come. Show me how you need it."

With my free hand, I reach down and cup my balls, tugging lightly when his hand pushes mine away and takes over the movement.

"Fuck, that's it," I rasp as I guide his rhythm on my cock. "Fist the base with one hand, and tug on my balls with the other. Fuck. Just like that."

He pulls off me. "I have an idea. Come here, Bex," he says. "I need you to ride his cock, get it nice and wet. B, can you hold on through her orgasm and pull her off before you come?"

"I'm so down to try," I say, my body shuddering at his words.

Becka straddles me and slowly sinks down. "Fuck, Daddy, your fat cock feels so good."

Right when she gets a good rhythm going, I feel Bennett's tongue gliding up the base of my dick. He tugs on my balls and continues licking and sucking me every time Becka lifts up. She must feel him too because her moans get louder. I reach down and pinch her clit, and within seconds she's clamping down on my cock like a vise and coming. When I can no longer hold off my own release, I lift her up and Bennett pulls me back into his mouth as he tugs on my balls. The sensation has me blowing my load so quickly, I don't have time to warn him. "Fuck, oh fuck, Bennett," I roar, throwing my head back.

When I come to, Becka is next to me while Bennett looks at me with reverence in his eyes as he gently licks me clean. "I've been wanting to do that since I saw you fucking."

CHAPTER 19

BENNETT

I f you told me five years ago that I'd be sucking Robert off while he fucked his wife, I'd have thought you were crazy. But here we are. After giving each of them release, Becka stares at me with wide eyes. I spent way too many afternoons stealing glances at those eyes, memorizing every shade within them. Her left one is a tone darker than her right, and the right has tiny little flecks of gold in it.

And now those eyes are locked on my cock, something I never thought I'd ever experience. My dick swells with pride as a drop of precum beads at the head. Her delicate fingers reach out to play with my piercing, gliding it back and forth through the precum before fingering the balls on the ends.

I'm thrusting into her touch and squirming on my knees in front of her as I suck in air through my teeth and speak. "Fuck, Bex. I like you touching my cock." My head falls back, euphoria lighting up every nerve in my body when a large hand wraps around the base of my shaft and my hips freeze. Holy fuck, now Robert's touching my cock. I see the vulnerability on his face, but there's also lust in his gaze.

"Is this okay?" he asks in the most timid voice I've ever heard him use. I've craved this man's touch on my skin since the first time he bodychecked me during our first pick-up game.

"More than fucking okay."

"I don't know what I'm doing."

"Yes, you do. Touch it like you touch yours. Use mine like it's yours, oh fuck, it's yours," I croak out right as Becka crawls off the couch and lowers her mouth onto me. Robert's hand firmly grips the base of my shaft as he guides it in and out of Becka's mouth.

"Get it wet, baby, that's it. Such an obedient little slut, aren't you?" Robert says to Bex.

Holy shit, this is every wet dream I've ever had come true. Praise and degradation are huge turn-ons for me. For Bex too, apparently—she's preening from Robert's words, her mouth coating me in her spit, and I watch one of her hands slip between her thighs.

I'm never letting them go. This is everything I never knew I wanted, and I'd be the biggest fool alive if I let them slip through my grasp.

Reaching out, I thread my hands through her hair and set a slow rhythm as I rut into her face. "Look at me, Bex. That's my good fucking girl. Keep those eyes on me. I'm going to use that perfect fucking mouth and you're going to take it like a dirty whore, do you hear me?"

"Mmmmph," she moans as she grinds against her hand.

"But if it gets too much, you tap my thigh twice and I'll stop. Got it? Do it for me now so I know I have your consent."

Removing her hand from her clit, she reaches up and taps my thigh twice.

"Put those filthy fucking fingers back on your clit and make yourself come while I fuck this perfect hole," I command.

Desire courses through me and I pick up my thrusts, fucking her face with more force. I turn my gaze on Robert, whose eyes have widened in concern for Becka. I suspect he isn't this rough with her. His hand is still gripped around my base, not stroking anymore, but he's not stopping this. Our good girl consented to this and she isn't tapping out, so I push her harder and get his attention.

"Look at me, B," I demand as his eyes flick to mine. "She feels so fucking good like this. I can hear how wet she is right now. But I need your eyes on *me*, not her. She'll let me know if it's too much."

Hesitantly his eyes lock with mine, and his grip twists on my cock. "You're doing such a good job, baby, taking his cock," he tells her, even though he's looking at me.

"That's it, B, talk her through this." My thrusting picks up pace and I place my free hand on his shoulder for balance.

Eyes still on me, hand still fisting and twisting on the base of my cock, Robert continues his praise. "You're so fucking good, baby. Taking it so well. I'm so proud of you."

The combination of having both of their eyes on me and his words of affirmation to her have my orgasm building hard and quick.

She pulls back while Robert pumps further up and down my cock. "Holy shit, yes, more of that. Fuck, you're going to make me come," I say, not sure which of them I'm talking to. "Oh fuck, that's it. I'm going to come so hard, pull off if you don't want it," I warn Bex, throwing my head back.

Her tongue plays with my piercing, moving it back and forth at a maddening pace, and between that and Robert's hand, that's all it takes. I fist her hair as I spill into her mouth.

"Swallow," Robert demands, and I watch as she obeys.

Once she's taken every ounce of me, she cries out, dropping to her hands. Holy shit, is she coming again?

"That's it, baby, ride my hand," Robert says. I didn't realize he was touching us both.

Once we're all sated and have collapsed onto the floor, I untangle myself and stand. "I need to get cleaned up, if anyone wants to join me in the shower," I say to them with a wink.

"Go without me, I need a minute," Bex says on an exhale.

"I don't think the three of us would fit in either of our showers anyway," Robert says.

"We'll fit in my new shower, once it's finished," I hint. "It's going to have two waterfall showerheads and a few other ones on the side that will target your whole body. It'll be big enough to fit at least six people, according to the specs."

"That sounds amazing," Becka says. "If only it was ready right now."

"You planning on having more than just us in there?" Robert asks, a hint of uneasiness in his voice.

"Fuck no. If it were up to me, it'd be just the three of us in there every day," I say without thinking.

Shit, was that too much too soon? I look at him for confirmation, and I swear I see a brief smile.

"We should talk about how this is going to work though," Becka starts, pushing up to sit. "I know we won't get a lot of kid-free nights while you're staying with us, but what happens now?"

Her reminder that this living arrangement is temporary stabs at my chest momentarily.

"I mean, I don't know about you two, but I really enjoyed that, and there are so many things that we didn't do that I'd love to try. That is, if you guys liked it. I think you did—I mean, we all came, so I'd call that a success. But if it was too much, we can talk about it. Sorry, feel free to stop me at any time, I'm just processing my thoughts," Becka says.

I pull her up against me and press my lips against hers, silencing her. The heat of her skin lights a fire in my body everywhere it touches as I wrap my arms around her, trying to get her as close as I can.

"That's one way to shut me up," she says breathlessly as she pulls back, and I kiss down her neck.

"I never thought I'd say this, but I really like watching you kiss my wife," Robert says, surprising us both as we break our connection and turn to him at the same time. "Fuck, I shouldn't have said that," he mutters, sitting back on the couch.

"It's okay," I assure him, sliding a palm over his knee, making small circles. "It's important for us to talk about this."

"Based on how much you two made me come, it's clear I'm on board with all of this. And if you want to keep exploring, I'm game," she says, then looks at Robert. "But if it's too much, we can pause or stop. I want to make sure we're all on the same page."

"It's unsettling how okay I am with all of this." Robert takes a deep inhale.

I can tell it's hard for him to gather his thoughts, but he's never shied away from sharing his feelings during our friendship. It just takes him time, and what we experienced tonight was a first for him—well, for all of us.

"Just keep talking to us," I say, my head bouncing between them. "We all need to be honest, and it might help if we know what limits everyone has too. I'm aware that we're juggling two kids, and nights like these might be hard to schedule often. But selfishly, I want to know if I get one-on-one time with either of you. I'm happy to keep running interference at bedtime if you want time together, but are you okay with time alone with me too, or is this an all-or-nothing situation?"

They look at each other, almost having a silent conversation, and then Becka squeezes his leg three times. Robert nods in response, and Becka begins. "I'm open to one-on-one time with each of you, and I'm okay with you two alone together as long as I don't feel left out. It's kind of a trigger for me. If I know it's happening first, or if it's understood that I'm allowed to join at any time, then it's fine by me."

"Baby, you'd always be open to join, and I'd tell you first," Robert affirms.

"It's cute that you think you could plan it, but I know how it feels to get swept up in a moment with you, Robert. You can't always plan ahead, but as long as I know that I could join you if I walk in on it, or you at least tell me after, that will help me."

"Bex, I will never turn you away, especially now that I know what you can do with that tongue," I promise, giving her a quick peck on the cheek as they pinken under my words. "Fuck me, that blush will be my undoing."

"How about I make us something to eat, and we can finish the film?" Robert says, reaching for his shorts.

"Are we up for round two later?" Becka asks, raising an eyebrow as she pulls her shirt on.

"Absofuckinglutely," I say as I head to the stairs without reaching for my clothes. "And I can feel both of your eyes on me, just so you know, and I don't hate it," I say with a laugh, reaching the steps before turning to throw them a wink on my way to the shower.

CHAPTER 20
BECKA

This is better than anything I've read in any book or seen in porn, and a million times hotter in person.

There's something so empowering about having two hot men on their knees for you. And when you have feelings for both of those men, and the sex is about more than a physical connection? Maybe that's why it feels so incredible.

I'm kind of in awe of my husband right now. I knew there was more to him than even he realized. Thank goodness he didn't push me away when I kept poorly articulating all this with him. I never dreamed that he'd give in to those thoughts, or that those fantasies could involve Bennett, but it makes sense. Robert feels safe with both of us. He didn't have much in the way of a sexual history because he didn't have an emotional connection to the people he was with, not like he does with us. Maybe this is the start of something bigger than all of us.

Robert whips up a light pasta dish as I prepare a salad. It reminds me of all the impromptu meals we shared back in the day when the guys would go play basketball and end up back here. There were signs that Bennett wasn't happy in his marriage, and it should've been obvious by the amount of time he spent over here that their relationship wouldn't last.

Shit. I'd nearly forgotten that he was with my sister. My sister who I so desperately want a better connection with.

She will never forgive me for this. Guilt hits me hard, and I gather my plates and head to the sink to scrub away my feelings like Lady Macbeth scrubbing away the evidence of her crime.

Bennett appears next to me. "I know that look. You okay?" He grabs a pan from my hands and starts drying it.

"What's going on?" Robert says from the table as he gets up to join us. "What did I miss?"

"Bex just had a freak-out and is taking it out on the dishes, and if I had to guess, it has to do with her sister."

"Fuck. Is that it, baby? It's okay, I can fix this," Robert says, placing a hand on my lower back. His words mean well, but this isn't something he can fix right now.

"I got this, B. How 'bout you go draw up a bath for her with lots of bubbles and her Kindle? I'll help her with the dishes and bring her up to you when we're done."

Robert hesitates for a minute, looking between us. "Would that help?"

Warmth blooms in my chest, and I nod.

"Sounds like a plan," Robert says, springing into action.

Once I hear water running upstairs, I let out a deep breath. Bracing my hands on the counter I drop my head and let go of the tears I was holding in. "I'm such a shitty sister. She's never going to forgive me."

Bennett pulls me into his arms, holding me against his chest, one hand in my hair, while the other strokes up and down my back. "It's okay, Bex. Let it out."

"I slept with her husband—"

"Ex-husband, but continue."

"And she's going to be so pissed. Fuck, what am I going to do? She's never going to speak to me again. Oh my God, she's never going to speak to me again. I don't know if I can handle that. She's the only blood relative I have left. What the fuck have I done? How could I be so selfish? She can't find out about this. Maybe this was a bad idea, maybe tonight is all we get. I don't know if I could handle losing my sister. I should've thought this through. Why didn't I think this through?" I ramble as I dissolve into sobs against his chest.

We stand there for a few minutes as he holds me, and I mumble out the last of my intrusive thoughts.

"Get it all out?"

I awkwardly nod against his chest.

"Good, now it's my turn," he says as he takes my cheeks in his hands. "I'm not hers. Do you hear me? We dated, we got married, but I was never hers and she was never mine. You're not a shitty person or sister. And she doesn't have to know what we're doing right now. You don't owe her that. I never felt a fraction of a spark for her like I feel for you and Robert. But no matter what happens, you'll have me. And if she has a problem with that, that's on her, not you. I spent several years watching you appease her. I saw how hard you tried. I saw you, even if she didn't, and I'm sure I'm not the first to tell you that you deserve better. So even if she does walk away, you wouldn't have lost anything because you'll have gained me," he says, pulling my face to his, sealing his breathtaking words with a kiss that steals the rest of the air from my lungs.

I didn't go into this evening thinking I was going to fall for someone. I thought we'd have some fun, a few orgasms, scratch an itch, and then we'd go back to our lives. But this is so much more than that. This man is meeting my needs in a way few have, not even Robert. I love my husband, and I'd never try to change who he is, but he's a fixer, a problem-solver. Bennett is a caretaker, healing wounds that have been plaguing my emotional health for years. And it hits me that I need both.

Is it possible to fall for someone this quickly when I'm

already so deeply in love with my husband? Bennett's only been back in our life for a few weeks. But he feels like the missing piece to our life, to our family—not just him, Lexie too. She's brought my girl so much joy. It just feels right, all of us together as a family.

There's nothing I can say in response to his words, so I let him kiss me, pouring every thought in my head and every feeling in my heart into his lips. I don't know how long we stand there holding each other, tangled up in one another, but the house is silent, the water no longer running upstairs. I groan when he pulls back, not wanting to break the spell we're under.

His brilliant blue eyes sparkle under my gaze. "Let's get you into that bath so you can relax, okay?"

I nod as he pulls me toward the stairs, and when I sink into the bubbles minutes later, my heart feels full and bursting. Several candles are lit, and my Kindle is propped on the bath tray in front of me as I get lost in a story about two friends who fall in love with the same girl.

When I emerge from the bathroom five chapters later—because Sara Cate's books always pull me in—I find my guys lying on the bed in their shorts, watching TV, a Becka-shaped hole between them.

"Are we actually having a sleepover? Because I'm so down for this," I say as a crawl across the bed and plop between them. "But not if we're going to watch sports highlights."

"I was going to head to my room once I knew you were okay," Bennett says, "but then you came out naked and changed my mind."

"Are you feeling better?" Robert asks, stroking a hand up my arm as he shifts in the bed to face me, turning the TV off. "Bennett filled me in."

"I'm good for now. I'm done worrying about things I can't do anything about at the moment. Let future Becka worry about that one," I say, stretching as I arch my back and push my breasts into the air.

Two mouths latch on to my nipples and pin me back against the mattress. Oh shit, this feels so good. This is something every woman should experience at least once in her life. Robert's mouth is sucking hard as the tip of his tongue flicks against my nipple, while Bennett's alternating between nibbling and sucking. It's strange feeling two different sensations on my breasts at the same time, but they're both equally stimulating and pleasureful.

A hand glides down my body and teases between my legs. I don't even know whose it is, and at this point, I don't care. I'm so close to coming that one quick swipe of my clit is all it would take. "Please, don't tease me," I beg as I hold their heads firmly in place. In seconds, I feel fingers press against my clit and my body detonates as pleasure courses through me, like waves at high tide, full and round, relentlessly crashing against the shore.

"She's ready for you," Robert says, pulling off my breast, catching Bennett's attention.

"Do you want this, Bex?" he asks, looking up at me, his eyes silently begging.

"Yes," I rush out, reaching for his face.

"I'm sterile. Haven't been with anyone since my divorce, and my last test was clear."

"I've only ever been with Becka," Robert tells him.

"My last test was at my yearly visit, and nothing to report," I add.

Bennett pulls off his athletic shorts, his dick bobbing free. "You ready to test out the jewelry?" he asks, moving down the bed and positioning himself between my thighs.

"Hell yes, give it to me," I beg as he lowers his mouth to my pussy.

"Not that I don't believe you, B, but I gotta make sure our girl is nice and wet. Plus, I need another taste," he says as he pushes two fingers into me, latching onto my clit in the process.

"Oh fuck!" I cry, my back bowing off the bed right as Robert's mouth swallows my moans. He's fully naked now too, his thick length pressing against my outer thigh. Bennett's talented tongue is playing with my clit, nearly bringing me to the brink again when he pulls back and looks up at me, my arousal glistening on his lips.

"You ready, Bex?"

Nodding, I reach down and grab his cock, lining it up with my entrance. "Need you inside me." I look down to watch him push the head inside.

"Oh fuck. Fuck! Bex, you're squeezing me so tight. I knew you'd feel fucking perfect."

Robert reaches down and plays with my clit, making small circles around it as he slowly increases the pressure and Bennett pushes in another couple inches. "Relax, baby, let us make you feel good."

"Such a good boy, talking your wife through it while I fill up her greedy cunt with this cock," Bennett rasps as he presses all the way in, and I let out a deep moan in response. "You like it when I talk to him like that, don't you? I felt the way you squeezed me when I called him a good boy."

"Yes!" I cry.

"And your husband's cock likes it too. Look at how it's dripping for me. Take him in your mouth while I fuck this pretty cunt," he demands as he starts thrusting in and out at a brutal pace, fucking me into the mattress as my legs wrap around him.

Reaching out, I grab Robert's cock, and he guides it to my mouth. Swirling my tongue around the crown, I lick and tease before taking him as deep as I can. Once he hits the back of my throat, I gag and he pulls out. I grip his cock and hold him in place. "Don't stop next time. You can be rough with me. I'm not going to break, if I need to stop, I'll tap out."

He nods but looks unsure when he slowly thrusts back in my mouth. I move closer to him as I start pulling him into my throat, tears filling my eyes. I'm not delicate, despite how my husband treats me sometimes. I need him to know that I can take it, and if it wasn't for Bennett and the way he fucked my face earlier, I don't think Robert ever would've tried. When I watched how he fucked Alyx's face in the club, I realized that he was holding back with me. And in one night, Bennett has broken down barriers for both of us, uniting us all.

My orgasm is short but intense as I moan around Robert's cock.

"Holy fuck, Bex, *that's* what you feel like when you come? I could live in this pussy every fucking day."

"I want to try something," Robert says meekly.

"Paris?" Bennett asks.

"How'd you know?"

"Great minds."

Holy shit, they're going to Eiffel Tower me. This is every why-choose fantasy I've ever had come to life. They flip me onto my hands and knees as Robert kneels in front of me and Bennett thrusts into me from behind. His movements are slow at first as he holds my hips and pulses, grinding against me.

"Take him in your mouth, and I'll get this party started," he says from behind me as I lower my mouth onto Robert's huge cock.

In all the years we've been married, I've never been able to get his whole dick in my mouth, but I give it my best effort and place his hand on the back of my head, encouraging him to set the pace he wants. He doesn't go easy on me, and I do my best to breathe through my nose, taking gulps of air every time I pop off and lick the head. Robert's breathing is labored as he fists the hair at my nape, claiming my mouth with every snap of his hips.

"That fucking mouth is magic," he groans as Bennett's thrusts get more intense. Each time he slams his hips against my ass, Robert's cock is forced a little deeper into my throat, and I love it.

"Fuck, I'm close," Bennett growls, squeezing my ass.

"Once you finish with her, I'm going to finish in her cunt," Robert grits out.

That's all it takes, just their words, and I'm coming hard, squeezing Bennett's cock as he stills inside me. Before I realize what's happening, Robert's sitting back against the headboard, pulling me up his body, and I'm still pulsing when he lowers me onto his cock. He grabs me by the throat and squeezes just the way I like it. The fluttering in my pussy ramps back up and I'm coming again as he fucks up into me.

"This cunt is ours. You hear me?" Robert says with a desperation I've rarely heard from him as I nod against the hand still holding my throat. "Fuck, I can feel the mess he made inside you."

Warmth pools at the place we connect, the sounds so obscene. He watches with rapt fascination as my orgasm builds again.

"That's it, Bex. Fuck your husband's cock. Squeeze him like you did me," Bennett's voice comes from behind me. "You like fucking my cum back into your wife, don't you, B? You can't look away. Think you can push it all back in?" Bennett challenges him.

Not one to back down, Robert's grip tightens on my neck, forcing me to look into his hazel eyes, but instead of my husband's usual gentle smile, I see a feral beast. "You need us both to fill you up like our dirty cumslut, huh? You want Daddy's cum too, don't you? Gonna make a mess of this filthy fucking cunt," he grunts, pounding into me at a brutal pace.

"Yes, Daddy. I'm...I'm..." For once I'm at a loss for words, unable to vocalize any of the thoughts in my head as I clench around him, my nails digging into his pecs. He lets out a guttural noise I've never heard him make as he comes, using his final thrusts to push into me as hard as he can.

We collapse back onto the mattress as my orgasm finally subsides and I struggle to catch my breath. I feel movement as the deep rumble of Robert's voice vibrates my cheek resting on his chest. "Where do you think you're going?" I feel a warm arm resting on my back and look over to see Bennett curled into Robert's side.

After another round of showers and a change of sheets—because romance books don't warn you about how messy group sex really is—the three of us are snuggled in bed together for the night with me in the middle.

"I wish we could do this every night," I say into Bennett's chest as Robert rolls over and wraps an arm around my waist.

"Might as well take advantage of it while the girls aren't here. As much as I'm enjoying this, I don't want to confuse them or have them walk in on this," Robert says sleepily.

Bennett stiffens under my hold, and I cup his face forcing him to look at me. "We can tell them when we're all ready. Until then, let's just enjoy this when we can. No one gets to break our bubble until we all agree."

His body relaxes, and he kisses the top of my head. And for the first time in a while, my thoughts don't hold sleep captive, and I drift off easily.

CHAPTER 21
BECKA

When I wake the next morning, I feel a warm body pressed behind me and wiggle my ass against it. I can tell by the smell of sandalwood that it's Bennett, but when I reach out for Robert, I find only sheets.

"He left about ten minutes ago to get Hallie," Bennett grumbles into my ear. "I'm need to get Lexie in a bit."

"So that gives us a little less than an hour before adult snuggles are interrupted," I croak, my voice still froggy from sleep.

"That's plenty of time," he says as he kisses my shoulder and glides a hand down my hips. "I know we talked about this last night, but is it okay if we do this without Robert?"

"He said he was fine with it," I say, arching my neck back as he peppers kisses along it.

"Good." He slips a hand into my sleep shorts while grinding his cock against my ass. "Fuck, Bex, you're already wet?" he groans as he slips a finger in my pussy, working my clit with the palm of his hand.

Together, we awkwardly maneuver my shorts down as he slips another thick finger in as I clench around it.

"I've never felt anyone squeeze like that before," he rasps as he nips along my collarbone.

"Kegels," I grit out right as my orgasm hits me and I moan his name.

"You and Robert ever play here?" he asks, gliding his fingers back further.

"Yes, we both enjoy ass play, and we have plenty of his and hers toys for that too," I inform him, still panting through my release as I roll onto my back.

"Fuck, that's going to be fun to explore with you two later." He pushes his boxers down, then pulls me on top of him. "But right now, I need you to ride me with that perfect pussy."

I hover over him, lining him up with my entrance before I slowly sink down on his length. "Holy shit, I can really feel your piercing at this angle."

"If you keep fucking squeezing me, this is going to be over in two pumps."

I flex around him a few times as his grip on my waist tightens. "You were saying?" I tease.

"Are you trying to kill me?"

"I'll take it easy on you," I say as I start moving back and forth, gyrating on his length as I grind my clit against his pelvis.

"Yes, that's it, Bex. Use me. Tell me what to do."

Alyx's words ring in my ear.

You have a little domme in you.

He starts to thrust his hips up into me, and I stop my movements. "Did I tell you to move? You're going to lie there and I'm going to use this cock to make myself come, do you hear me?"

"Yes, ma'am," he says, folding his hands behind his head.

I lean forward and slap his face with my breasts a few times as he grins up at me. "Open," I demand as he opens his mouth and sticks his tongue out. I hover my nipple right above his mouth, slightly out of his reach. It gently sways with my movements as I continue grinding on him.

"Such an obedient boy," I praise, and I swear I feel his dick jerk inside me. "Now, you're going to suck my nipple until I come."

I barely finish my sentence before his mouth shoots up, latching on to my nipple as he sucks and nibbles the flesh.

"That's a good… fuck, that's so good. Oh, fuck, right there. Yes. Yes, Bennett!" I cry, as a powerful orgasm washes over me.

He pops off my nipple, grabs the back of my neck, and pulls my mouth to his. I can feel the warmth of his breath against my lips. "I'll never get over the way your cunt squeezes me when you come, the little noises you make, the look of bliss on your face. But my favorite part is the way that pretty little blush travels all over your skin, I want to kiss every inch of it, you're so fucking perfect." He closes the distance between our mouths, pulling me firmly against him.

When he pulls back and looks at me, still rocking on top of him, I can see his feelings all over his face. He feels this too.

"So fucking beautiful. I don't know what thought just popped in your head, but the way you're blushing right now has me ready to blow. I want to paint your pretty pink blush with my cum," he growls, flipping me over and positioning himself between my legs. He grabs a pillow, placing it under my ass, and then pushes into me, setting a brutal rhythm as he fucks me hard, relentlessly, like it's something he's been dying to do for years. And I can tell from the look in his eyes that it's true. This man looks at me with so much longing that I can't turn away. I hold his gaze as his barbell rubs against that perfect spot on my inner wall and I can feel the wave building again.

"That's it, you keep those fucking eyes on me," he grits out between thrusts.

"I'm going to—I'm gonna—" I start, right as the orgasm crashes over me.

"I know. I can feel you squeezing my cock, fuck, Bex," he groans right as he pulls out, painting me with his cum. I swear this man comes for a full minute.

Once he finishes, he drops to his knees, hovering over me as he surveys his handiwork. "You look beautiful covered in me." He leans in and kisses me, pressing his full weight against me. When he pulls back, I'm breathless and panting. This man can wind me up into a frenzy with just a kiss.

His arms wrap around my waist as he lifts me, the evidence of his orgasm sticky between us as he sits on the edge of the bed, my legs locked firmly around his hips. "I meant to bring this up last night, but there wasn't a good time with everything that was going on."

"Tell me about it. I'm going to think about last night for years to come," I say, smiling against his lips as I lean in to kiss him. When he doesn't fully kiss me back, I pull back and look at him. "What is it?"

"I know how upset you got when B and I made plans without you. You said something last night about not wanting to be left out of the sexy stuff, and it made me realize that we left you out of the decision when Robert agreed to let us stay with you guys. I made a comment about needing a place to stay and he offered. I didn't realize that he didn't run it by you till you told me that first night, and after last night it makes more sense. So, I'm sorry."

"Thank you, that means a lot," I say, taken aback at how easily he was able to put all that together.

"So, I heard from my contractor, and it turns out I'm going to be out of my house for a little longer than I originally expected," he says with a grimace.

"How long?"

"Six more weeks?" he says sheepishly. "Apparently, I bought one of the worst houses in one of the best neighborhoods. But I don't want to put you out even more. I can find a hotel if it's too much."

"Is it bad that I was worried you were going to tell me that your contractor finished early and that you were leaving?" I laugh nervously. "Sorry, I should probably keep some of these thoughts in my head. Don't want to scare you off."

"There's nothing you could do that would scare me off," he says, pulling me into a kiss.

"Six more weeks of this, huh?" I say, breaking the kiss. "Not sure if I'm going to be able to manage."

He glides a hand up my side tickling me as I try to wiggle free from his hold.

"I'm fine with you guys extending your stay, and thank you for including me in the decision this time."

"We're gonna take a quick shower, and then I'm going eat this perfect pussy for breakfast before everyone gets home," he promises as he carries me to the bathroom. "And I'm looking forward to six more weekends of doing exactly this with both of you."

I feel like a shit best friend, so I text Bridget after our shower. I intended to pick up Hallie myself this morning, and while I'm thankful for the extra sleep and time with Bennett, I wanted to catch up with my best friend.

ME

Thank you for watching Hallie last night. It means more to us than you know.

BRIDGET

Tell me you broke a dry spell without telling me you broke a dry spell.

Let's just say, it was an epic night.

Do tell...

Nope, that's not how our dynamic works.
You're the one spilling all the spicy details of
your exploits, not me. I'm married and boring.

Why do I get the feeling that's not true?

You know what a fan I am of breadcrumbs.

Fuck you.

Oh, I meant to ask you, how are things with
Hank? Robert said he was there when he
dropped Hallie off.

It is what it is. He keeps standing Ethan up for
therapy. It's a shame, it'd help him.

Sounds like it's been helping you.

It has, thanks for the recommendation. Dr.
Hugh is great.

I'm glad you like her! Speaking of therapy,
wanna join me for the next book club
meeting?

Maybe the next one? I've got a lot going on
right now with work and planning Ethan's
birthday party next month. I don't have time
to read off my TBR, let alone assigned
reading.

No worries! Lemme know the date so I can
put it in my calendar.

I'm at Mina and Dre's mercy since it's their
restaurant, so it may not be on his actual
birthday, but I'll let you know!

That works! Love you!

Love you.

I set my phone down and let out a relieved sigh. Bridget is my best friend, and I feel crappy keeping this whole Bennett thing from her, but it's only temporary. Once we figure out what this is, she'll be the first one I talk to. Part of me wants to tell her everything right now. My texts to her have slowed down considerably, but that's how our friendship is. One minute I'm relentlessly pestering her, the next she's begging me to be her wing woman so she can find a hookup. Except this last hookup became her forever. And now between Hallie starting school, me going back to work, and Bennett coming back into our lives—in more ways than one—texting my bestie isn't the biggest priority. For now, I need to focus on the men in front of me and the little girls demanding my attention.

CHAPTER 22

BECKA

I'm twenty minutes into a phone call with a whiny customer when my phone lights up with a text from Bennett.

> Can you go pick up Lexie at school? I'm stuck at a listing and can't get away.

> > Sure, is everything okay?

> All they told me was that she was upset and they're having trouble calming her down. TBH, I kinda cut them off because a client was walking in but I added you to her pick-up list.

> > No problem, I'll take my lunch and go get her.

> Thanks, Bex.

My phone lights up with a call from the school right after I let my manager know that I'm logging off for my lunch break.

"Is this Mrs. Gardner?"

"Yes, is everything okay with Hallie?" I ask, worried.

"Well, that's what I'm calling about. Hallie is fine, but she's upset and wants to go home."

"I'm on my way," I say as I hop into the car and drive up to the school. When I walk into the office moments later, the principal ushers me back to her office where I find a sobbing Lexie sitting on a couch holding hands with Hallie. There's another woman in the room who introduces herself as the counselor. She stands and ushers Lexie to follow her before I stop her. "I'm here for them both. I'm on Lexie's pick-up list. She's staying with us at the moment." I take a seat on the couch next to Lexie and gently stroke her hair. She exhales a big breath and leans against me, looking up at me, her earnest eyes full of sadness. "It's okay, bug," I say, using the nickname I've heard Bennett use, hoping to instill a sense of peace and familiarity in her.

"Am I in trouble?" Hallie asks as she looks up at me with big eyes. "Marcus was making fun of Lexie, and I told him to stop but he didn't. He kept saying he'd only stop if Lexie told him to."

Lexie burrows into my side, small tremors wracking her body as her tears soak my shirt. Her sobs are silent, but her breathing is loud.

"We've already dealt with the other student," the principal assures me. "Hallie was a great friend. She stood up for her friend respectfully. You should be proud." I look over at Hallie, but her gaze is fixed on Lexie, worry etched in her features.

"I wanna go home, Mama. If Lexie's going home, I wanna go with her," she says, still clutching Lexie's hand.

"Can I speak with you out in the hall?" the principal asks. It's difficult to leave the girls, but Lexie looks up at me, her other hand gripping mine and squeezes it once for yes.

Once we're out of earshot, the principal speaks. "I tried explaining things to Lexie's dad on the phone, but I was hoping one of her parents could give us some advice."

"I'm not her parent, but I'm happy to help."

"Oh, my mistake. She's very comfortable with you."

I smile, thinking about how close I've grown to Lexie in the past couple weeks.

"It was difficult for us to understand what happened given Lexie's lack of speech," she starts.

"She lost her mom in a car accident, and her grandparents a couple years after that. From what I understand from her dad, she used to be able to speak, but given all the trauma she's been through, she struggles with it. It's a lot for her to be away from the people that understand her nonverbal cues. She is still learning to communicate with her dad and us and is in speech therapy," I explain.

"I'd like her dad to get in touch with us. I think we have some options we can explore that would help. But I just want to say, I was really impressed with the way Hallie stepped in and not only stood up for her but was able to help communicate what happened on behalf of Lexie."

My heart swells at her words and I'm thankful these two little girls found each other.

Bennett

Later that night at home, Bex relays today's events to us. "I'd like to teach that kid a lesson or two," Robert seethes. "Who treats someone that way? It's October, not the first week of school. I'm sure everyone is aware of Lexie's abilities by now, so to say that, at this point in the year, that was targeted bullying. I see it all the time at my school, but in elementary school? I wonder what that kid walked away with. Probably a slap on the wrist," he says, pacing the length of the kitchen. I haven't seen him this fired up before. Even Lexie and Hallie have moved on from the events of the day. I feel like there's more to this than he's letting on.

"The principal didn't mention his punishment, and I didn't ask," Bex adds.

"Yeah, they're not allowed to talk about another student with you. It's against policy," he says, and I smile. If anyone is aware of school rules, it's B.

"I trust that the school dealt with it appropriately. The important thing is that our girls had each other. You should be proud that you raised a fierce little warrior who will stand up against injustice."

Robert nods, still leaning against the counter, the veins in his biceps and forearms still popping, his shoulders bunched to his ears as he breathes loudly through his nose. Bex runs her hands up his back, and I'm overcome with the urge to join her, but my gaze flicks to the girls playing in the living room and I hold myself back, my hands clenching like Mr. Darcy as the urge to comfort him courses through me.

"I'm missing something," I say, my voice low, trying not to attract the girls' attention.

"My brother was bullied. It's a trigger for me," he says out of the side of his mouth, and a memory of us on the court, a brief conversation we shared about siblings, flashes through my mind. "I need a minute," he says as he stalks to the basement door, closing it behind him as he descends.

"Is he okay?" I ask Bex, her gaze fixed on the door.

"I think so. He carries a lot of guilt about what happened to his brother," she says, wrapping her arms around her body.

"Fuck, I wish I could hold you right now."

"But the girls."

"The girls," I agree, but quickly change my mind when I see a tear fall down her cheek. "Fuck it, friends hug. C'mere." I reach for her hand, pulling her against me. She burrows into me, her eyes still on the basement door as I rub my cheek on the crown of her head.

"He could really use a hug like this, and a friend like you in his life," she says, wiping her face.

"He will always have me. You both will," I say. I'll be damned if I lose them ever again. Even if this doesn't go any further than what we did the other night, I will never walk away from this friendship. Not when it's healed me in ways nothing could, and not when it's brought my daughter to life.

CHAPTER 23

ROBERT

"I hear you're into giving *and* receiving? Didn't have you *pegged* as anything other than a top, so I'm excited about this revelation," Bennett says, and I nearly spit out my beer.

I shoot a look at Becka. "You told him?"

It's been a week since our night of fun and we're all watching TV after the girls have gone to bed.

"I didn't mention the pegging specifically, but when we had some fun together last Sunday, I told him we both enjoyed some backdoor action and had our own toys."

"B, it's not like there are any secrets between us anymore. This just gives us more ways to scratch that itch next time," he says with a wink.

"Jesus," I groan, shaking my head.

"Are you mad that she told me?" Bennett asks hesitantly.

"Yes... no... I don't know." I pick at the label on my beer. It feels weird having this conversation, even though I know it's one that needs to happen.

"You gotta share more than that with me, B," he says, leaning against the armrest of the couch as he turns to face me.

"Is this something we really need to talk about?" I ask.

"Absolutely," Bennett says as he looks between me and

Becka where she's standing behind the recliner. "Consent is important to me, especially in this situation. I want to know what turns you on. But I'd still check with you before trying something new. And hearing that you're into both and might be vers like me, well, that gets me really fucking hard. It opens up so many different positions I can put you both in." He grins.

His words have my cock stirring, but I'm stuck on what he means by "vers." In my limited sexual history, it's not a word I've come across. When I look at Becka, she's smiling at him, that blush spreading on her neck and chest.

"Fuck, Bex, that's all it takes to make you blush like that?" he asks as I pull out my phone to look up what he's talking about. "Are we boring you over there, B?" he teases.

"No, I'm just—"

Bennett plucks the phone from my grasp. "What's so much more interesting than what we were talking about?" he asks, scrolling through the page I was on.

I'm mortified, wanting to sink into the couch and let it swallow me whole. I'll let this man suck my cock, apparently, but revealing how clueless I am about this stuff? Nope, that's where I draw the line. I set my beer on the coffee table, and I'm about to swing my legs off the couch when he grabs my foot and sits on my legs, pinning me in place.

"What the fuck?"

"I'm sorry, I was only fucking with you," he says gently, staring into my eyes as he hands me my phone back. "If you have questions, just ask. I was serious about communicating with us about all this."

I wait for him to say more, but it's clear he's waiting on me. "I didn't know what vers meant, and I was looking it up."

He inches up my legs so he's hovering over my thighs, "Vers means you can top or bottom. I was just surprised, because I figured you'd be a top, if anything. I shouldn't have judged the book by the cover."

I think about his words for a minute. "If we're both vers, does that mean you can fuck me, and I can fuck you?"

He groans. "You can't say shit like that to me when I'm sitting in your lap and not expect me to take you up on it."

"I've only ever done that with Becka," I say, looking up at him. "I've never let anyone put their actual…" I trail off, hoping he doesn't make me finish that sentence. This is humiliating enough. Not because we're talking about something my parents would shame me to hell for—at this point, fuck them and my Catholic guilt—I'm just mortified having to talk about my actual lack of experience and knowledge as a thirty-eight-year-old man. Even my wife knows more about this shit from all the books she reads.

"You can say cock, B. Say it, please, I'm begging you," he whines, wiggling in my lap. I can see the outline of his erection through his sweatpants, and mine twitches in response.

"I've never had an actual cock in my ass. Only toys." I look over at Becka for her input, but she's just rubbing her thighs together watching our exchange.

"Don't look at her, B, look at me," he demands, pulling my focus back to him as he grips my chin between two fingers. "Are you telling me I get to fuck this virgin ass?"

"I—I, uh…" I start, unsure of what to say. *Um, yes please, that sounds amazing?* Part of me wants him to pin my legs back and let him go to town. Another part is worried how things will change if I let him. Oral is one thing. But letting him inside me, that's something I've only experienced with Becka, and even then, it was a toy. He's fucked Becka, and that was really hot to watch, but I can't kick this feeling that if I let him fuck me, everything will be different. That I'll be breaking more of our vows.

I vow to always choose you above others, even when life is difficult.

Even though that was her promise to me, I feel like shit about the fact that she's letting me explore this with Bennett, choosing to put me over anyone else, while I let someone else get me off.

"It's just sex, B. Just the three of us making each other feel good. Don't overthink it," he says, leaning down and pressing a kiss to my neck.

"It's so sexy watching you pin my husband down while he tries not to let his intrusive thoughts win," Becka pipes up.

I don't know how she does it, but she always knows what I'm thinking, and not just that, my entire thought process, shame spiral and all. She's the only person I've ever been this vulnerable with, and letting Bennett in too is fucking with me in ways I never expected.

"Are you gonna share your husband with me, Bex?" Bennett says against the skin of my neck as his hot breath tickles me, causing goosebumps to break out. "Cuz there's nothing more I'd love to do right now than fuck him while he fucks you."

The way they're talking about me, like I'm not even here, is turning me the fuck on, and I decide to mess with him as I lift up my thighs, causing him to slide down my legs, closer to the erection tenting my pants.

"I'm right here, asshole. And if you want mine, you're going to need to beg." A surge of confidence washes over me as his eyes widen in surprise.

"Shit, don't tease me, B. I'm already a needy mess for you, and your words are going to make me embarrass myself in my pants."

"Beg me for it. Beg to fuck my ass. Tell me how badly you want it," I grit out as I move my hips in slow circles, teasing his cock with mine.

"Please, B," he moans as I thrust hard against him, my hands reaching down to grab his ass, holding him in place. His face hovers over mine as we lock eyes, our noses touching as he speaks against my lips, his fingers gripping the sides of my face and neck. "Oh fuck, I want it. I want it so fucking bad, you have no idea. Please let me take your ass. Please, I'll be such a good boy for you. You can top from the bottom, just tell me what to do, what you like, please. I want to live inside your perfect fucking ass. I'll do anything you want."

"Since you asked nicely…" I trail off, shrugging.

He closes the distance between our lips as he thrusts his tongue into my mouth at the same time he thrusts his hips against me, and the dual sensation has me moaning into his mouth as he swallows the sound. Every time we've kissed, it feels like this fight for control, similar to how we are on the court, fighting for the ball, fighting to see who's going to score more points. It's different than kissing Becka, and I'm starting to crave both experiences as they calm different beasts inside me.

"I'll give you two a minute and go patrol the hallway upstairs to make sure the girls don't sneak down here. And then maybe we can take this back to the bedroom?" Becka asks, her soft voice coming from across the room.

I nod against Bennett's lips, but I'm not sure if she sees it. I break the kiss and look over where I heard her voice, but she's gone. Bennett bites my neck and then licks at it, flicking it with the tip of his tongue. "Fuck, that feels good." I stretch my neck out more in offering.

He scrapes his teeth along the flesh, and my hips buck into him involuntarily.

"That's the spot, huh? Right here?" He drags his teeth along the same path, causing me to buck into him again.

"What are you doing to me?" I grunt. I swear this man can work me up into a frenzy faster than even Becka can. Is it because it's new and the novelty hasn't worn off? Guilt slams into me. I love my wife. I'm more attracted to her now than I've ever been. The novelty has *never* worn off with her. So why am I having these thoughts about Bennett? Shouldn't she be enough for me?

Bennett moves down my body, positioning himself

between my thighs as his quads force my legs open. "Stop thinking and just focus on how this feels. I want you to know how good I can make you feel, B," he says, grinding the base of his cock against my balls as his hand squeezes my length over my pants.

Before I can second-guess my actions, I swat his hand away and pull my pants down enough to let my cock spring free. "Need your mouth," I grit out, closing my eyes, trying to hide my eagerness.

His warm, perfect fucking mouth slides down my length seconds later. Holy shit, I'm going to blow way sooner than I want to. "Slow down, you're going to make me come."

He pulls off my dick and sits back on his heels between my thighs. "What if I want you to come? What if I got a taste of your cum the other night and it's all I've been thinking about since? Are you going to deny me? Or would you prefer to fill your wife's cunt so I can lick it clean after, then I can taste the mess I'm going to turn you both into?"

A bead of precum leaks from my tip at his filthy words. This man could give me lessons on dirty talk.

His eyes flick to the crown of my cock, eyeing the precum there. "Both it is," he says as he fists the base and pulls me back into his mouth. He works me furiously, sucking hard, saliva pooling out of his mouth, while lightly grazing his teeth on each upstroke, and squeezing his hand, twisting it as his mouth moves up and down. The motion makes it feel like his mouth never leaves my dick, and I thread my fingers through his hair guiding his movements as I piston up into his mouth simultaneously. It's not two pumps, but it might as well be with how fast this man has me coming.

The euphoria coursing through my body is unlike anything I've ever felt during a blow job—and Becka gives *really* good blow jobs. But there's something about this man and his mouth that unleashes a beast in me. I always worry about hurting my wife, and the other night with Bennett showed me she's capable of handling much more than I've given her.

If that alone didn't prove that he's supposed to be a part of this, then I don't know what would. He's already awakened parts of me that I either didn't know existed, or I've kept hidden. No wonder Becka felt like she wasn't enough for me. There are parts of me that only feel comfortable with Bennett. And while that makes me feel like a shitty husband, it also makes me crave my best friend more. I only hope that I'm not throwing away my marriage over really fucking good sex.

CHAPTER 24
BENNETT

I can't get enough of the way this man feels or tastes when he comes in my mouth. Robert's a mess on the couch, panting as he tries to collect his breath, one arm slung over his face while the other hand still grips my hair as I lick the last of his release off his cock.

Since he's distracted, I decide to slip a finger under his balls as I slide back to his opening.

"Upstairs," he commands, stopping my actions, as I put his pants back in place and offer him a hand, pulling him up.

I follow behind him as we ascend the stairs, playfully poking at his perfectly round ass as he climbs. He chuckles softly, shaking his head. "You're just as bad as Becka."

His words warm my heart more than they should. I love that he thinks of me the same way he thinks of her, and I secretly hope this will continue once renovations are done on my house. The desire to be picked, to have someone choose me, is the reason why I rushed into a marriage with a woman I shouldn't have. But I'm determined not to let my baggage ruin the fun we're about to have. They've picked me, for now, for fun, and I need to remind myself of that.

I don't think either of us are prepared for the sight before us when we walk in the room, closing and locking the door behind us. Becka is sprawled out on the bed, fully naked, one hand pushing against the headboard above her for balance, as she fucks herself with a realistic-looking vibrator. "Oh fuck, oh fuck," she moans as Robert and I practically push each other out of the way to get to her.

Robert reaches her first, batting the vibrator out of her hand as he shoves his face between her thighs. I pull my clothes off and stroke myself as I watch him bring her to orgasm.

"Yes, Daddy. Right there, oh fuck yes, Daddy," she cries out as I get closer to her, sealing my mouth over hers to quiet her cries of pleasure.

"Couldn't wait for us, huh?" Robert smirks as he wipes the sheen from his face with two fingers, before popping them into his mouth and sucking them clean, making eye contact with me the entire time.

"I figured I'd get ready for you guys. I knew where this was headed, so I pulled out some toys, and then you took so long, I figured I'd have a little fun on my own."

"Toys?" Robert asks, then Becka pulls her legs up to her chest, wiggling her ass a little.

"Fuck, I love that plug in you."

I grab her thigh, shifting her so I can see what he's looking at, and sure as fuck, there's a pretty little red heart-shaped ruby adorning her ass. I reach down, running my fingers along it.

"It's my birthstone," she explains as I play with it. "Robert's got a citrine one for November. We should get you one. What's the birthstone for August?"

"Peridot," I say, pulling out the plug all the way, before pushing it back in.

A shiver courses through her body as a blush spreads on her face and chest.

"Is this where you want to be fucked tonight, Bex? In this

perfect fucking ass?" I ask, continuing to tease her with the toy.

"I don't care," she says, breathless. "I need one or both of your cocks in me right now."

"Damn, Bex, don't tease me. I've got an early morning tomorrow, and if we're going to fuck you like that, I'm going to need more time, and fewer ears around that could wake up. We're going to make you scream so loud, you're not going to be able to speak tomorrow."

When I look over, Robert's tossing me a bottle of lube, and I catch it one-handed. I can tell he's nervous by the way he's chewing on his lip and picking at the skin on his thumb. Anxious to get his consent, I pat the space next to Becka, motioning him to come over.

Robert

"I want to do the… what we were… what we talked about downstairs," I admit nervously, standing next to the bed.

Bennett grabs my hand, stroking the back of it with his thumb. "Look, I really want this, but it's okay if you've changed your mind, B. I know how it is to be caught up in a moment and you can't control the dirty shit that comes out of your mouth. If you aren't ready to back it up with action yet, it's okay. We can try again later."

"I want this. I just don't want to fuck it up."

"You're not going to fuck it up," he reassures me. "And nothing has to change. We can keep doing what feels good, what feels right."

"Can I…can I say something first?"

"Okay." Bennett nods, and Becka sits up next to him.

I take a deep breath. "I owe you both an apology for all the shitty things I've said and done out of anger, when the voices in my head told me that this was wrong. Part of me has always wanted this, with both of you, and I felt guilty for wanting it, and then I felt selfish for wanting it with more than one person. I know I'm not as experienced in any of this, and I know I'm going to screw this up and say the wrong thing at times. But nothing has ever felt better than being with both of you, and I want to do this, even if that makes me selfish."

"It doesn't make you selfish," Becka says, green eyes shining. "I'm so proud of how far you've come."

"Come here," Bennett says, pulling my hand till I'm standing between his legs. His hands move in steady strokes up and down the backs of my thighs. "Do I need to prep you?"

"Yeah," I rasp as he pulls down my sweats and boxers. My cock juts out proud as he licks up my balls and continues all the way up the shaft. Becka moves over, making room for me to sit between them.

Shifting back toward the middle of the bed, I lie back, propping my knees up so my feet are flat. He pushes my thighs toward my torso, opening me up. I feel exposed and vulnerable and still somehow safe with this man.

"Is this okay?" he asks, running a finger between my cheeks.

A shudder barrels through me at his touch. "Yeah, that feels good."

He leans down and licks around my hole as Becka takes a hold of my cock, guiding it into her mouth. They work together, going to town on me, licking and sucking until I'm whimpering and moaning. "Please," I beg, unable to stand one more minute without this man inside me, needing to feel that connection to him.

"Please what?" he teases, popping his head up.

"Fuck me. I need to feel you inside me when I'm inside my wife."

He pops open the lube, coating his fingers with a generous amount before pushing one inside, working it in and out. "Ahhh, fuck. More," I cry as he slips another finger in. When he adds a third finger, I'm begging for his cock.

"Bex, baby, lie back on the bed so he can fuck you and I can fuck him," Bennett says, and she complies quickly, crawling under me once I flip over onto my knees.

Running a hand up my spine, he grabs my shoulder, pulling me against him, my back to his front. The smell of sandalwood and leather overwhelming me, his warm breath against my ear. "This ass is mine," he hisses, smacking it hard. "My cock is the only cock allowed to fuck you here. Is that clear?" There's a desperate edge to his voice as if he needs me to make this promise.

"Yes," I tell him as he pushes me forward onto my hands, working his lubed cock into me.

"So fucking tight," he groans, slowly easing himself in. "Give me a color, B. How are you doing?"

"Green," I say as a shudder rocks through me. "Oh fuck, I can feel your piercing. So fucking good," I moan as he presses in further.

"I knew this ass would be perfect. Knew it would feel this fucking good." His hips push against me, letting me know he's all the way in. Hovering over me, he presses gentle kisses along my shoulders. "You've been edging me all night, and I'm not going to last. You better fill her perfect cunt with your fat cock now."

Becka grips the base of my cock, a smirk on her face as she lines me up with her opening. I push inside her swiftly causing her to gasp, the sound music to my ears. Each thrust in feels so fucking good, and each time I pull out, Bennett's cock pushes deeper into me. I can't decide which sensation I enjoy more, but I'm already on the edge, willing my orgasm away so I can revel in this moment with them. I've never felt more grounded, more in control, as the realization washes over me.

After several minutes, Bennett grips my hips, driving into me harder, forcing me to fuck Becka at his pace.

Her delicate hand reaches up and grips my neck, surprising me at the role reversal. "That's it, fuck your best friend, Bennett. You should see what a mess he is for you. Every thrust lights up his face with a different emotion."

I've never felt this free before, as if each time he thrusts, he pushes pieces of himself inside me, filling up the broken cracks in my armor. I feel more whole, more like myself than I ever have.

"Oh fuck. Fuck. This feels—" I grit out, barely able to contain my release. There are no words to describe how incredible it feels to be buried to the hilt in my wife's cunt while Bennett fills my ass.

"Fuck me, I'm gonna come," he cries, pulling out of my ass. Briefly, I mourn the loss of our connection. "Gonna paint you with my cum, B. Mark you as mine," he groans spilling ropes of hot cum onto my back.

I continue fucking my wife, playing with her clit, loving how tight she feels with the plug still in her ass while I fill her cunt. When Bennett reaches down and tugs on my balls, that's all it takes to have me filling her with my cum as she spasms around my cock. Bennett collapses onto his back on the bed next to Bex and I land between them, covering them with my body.

"We're going to have to change the sheets again," Becka pants, a slight annoyance creeping into her tone.

"I'll pick up some extra sets," Bennett offers. "We're definitely doing more of that."

"I need to clean up," I say but remain unmoving as he strokes up my arm.

"I'm going to warm up the shower," Bex says as she scoots out from under me and saunters over to the en suite.

"You okay, B?"

I sigh against him. "This is going to sound nuts, but I feel empty without you inside me." It's all I'm able to admit right now.

He smiles and I feel his heart beating rapidly in his chest under my arm, the rhythm matching my own. "It felt okay? I didn't hurt you?" he asks, sounding uncharacteristically uncertain.

"It was perfect, both of you at the same time," I assure him, pulling him into a kiss, so I don't share the rest of my thoughts. No one has ever made me come like that before, and it feels illicit, dangerous. Like I'm breaking every vow I've ever made to my wife, because for the first time, I want someone else as much as I want her.

CHAPTER 25

ROBERT

After overhearing another frustrating conversation about Miles's lack of food options in his foster home, I decide I've had enough. While the girls are upstairs playing, I share my problem with Becka and Bennett. We've been working on communication when it comes to our feelings and adult time, but if this is going to work, I need to be able to unload my burdens on them too, as much as I might hate it.

"Miles is hungry," I blurt out.

Bennett chuckles. "Is that what you named that monster between your thighs? Do you call it that because it's a mile long? If this is how you want to ask for sexy time, I could totally get on board."

My cheeks heat and I shake my head in frustration as Becka bursts out laughing.

"Oh my gosh, stop! Miles is one of his students, not his dick!" she says as they both burst into laughter, and I can't help but join them.

Here I am brooding away, all stuck in my head, and my sunshines find a way to pull me out of the darkest part of myself.

"Alright, enough. Get your giggles out now. This is serious, and I need your help."

"You haven't come up with a plan to fix something? This must be serious." Becka places a hand on mine as she stands beside me in the kitchen.

"Miles is my student," I start, turning my attention to Bennett. "His foster family does the bare minimum the state requires to provide for him, and that includes food. I've been packing extra in my lunch for school, but he's a teenage boy and I'm worried he's not getting enough."

"I wondered where all the apples were going. I scolded Hallie for going through them too quickly."

"I can't put money in his lunch account, or he'll know something's up. And sneaking snacks isn't cutting it."

"Can you report the foster family?" Becka asks.

"They're not technically doing anything wrong, so there's little the state could do. Plus, this is his seventh home. I'm not sure moving again would be good for his mental health, and you never know if the next home will be worse."

"You've thought about every angle," Bennett says, scratching at the light stubble on his jaw.

"If the kid wasn't so fucking stubborn, I could bring him food. He tried to drop my class on the first day of school because he was worried his foster family wouldn't pay the fees."

"My mom has been begging us to come by for family dinner, but the timing's been off. What if we started our own family dinner here?" Bennett suggests. "We could all invite a few people. I could appease my mom, and you could invite Miles."

"I'd have to invite a few students so he doesn't get suspicious. Would you be okay with that?" I ask, looking at Becka.

She nods. "It sounds fun. We could do something cheap and easy, like hot dogs."

"Don't worry about the food, I've got it covered," Bennett

offers. Before we can protest, he holds up a hand. "You're letting me stay here and it was my idea. It's the least I can do."

A week later, tension is high as the three of us work together to clean the house for family dinner, but as soon as we make progress in one area, one of the girls makes a mess behind us, thwarting our efforts.

Lexie gives Becka an apple to cut, and I pull Bennett aside as my mind works through worst-case scenarios. "If any toilet paper goes missing, just be chill," I say as I sweep the last of the dirt into the dustpan.

"Okay, you can't say something like that and not expect a few follow-up questions," Bennett says, pausing his meal prep to open a string cheese for Hallie. "First, why would our toilet paper go missing? Are people going to be taking massive dumps while they're here? Also, it's toilet paper, why would I care if people use it? I can go to Costco and buy a bunch if you're that worried about it."

"That's not a bad idea, actually."

"Seriously, what is going on? Are you inviting a bunch of klepto students into your house?"

"Remember what I told you about Miles?" I ask.

"Yeah, what about him?"

"So, the stinginess doesn't only apply to food. I overheard him tell Hakim that they gave him a strike for using the wrong toilet paper. They bought him the cheap kind, and he used their good three-ply, which costs more. Three strikes, and he's out."

"That's really fucked up," Bennett says distractedly. To the outside observer it may look like he's not paying attention to me, but I've known him long enough to recognize his thinking face. I can tell he's formulating a plan in his mind, I'm just not sure what it could entail.

A few hours later, I'm in the kitchen when people start arriving. I've had students at my house before to film for class. You never know when you're going to need a backdrop for a scene, plus I have a shed full of flats and canvases for filming and a decent green screen setup in my basement.

"Mr. G! Bold of you to let me near your pantry. You worried I might raid it?" Miles calls out in a volume too loud for the small space we're in, with Hakim following behind him.

If only he knew. "I'm counting on it," I say, a small smile creasing my lips. "Hey, Hakim."

"Hey, Mr. Gardner. Dude, check out this spread," Hakim says to Miles, but when we look at him, he's shoved an entire sausage wrap in his mouth.

"What?" he says with pursed lips around the food.

"Help yourself, Miles," I say.

Owen comes up behind them, and I'm quickly forgotten in the shuffle of bro hugs as the teens greet each other, and I sneak out of the room right as Bennett's mom and dad walk through the door. We go through introductions, and Bennett corrals his parents into the living room to spend time with the girls.

All week, my anxiety's been through the roof, constantly worried that Miles wouldn't come, that he would come, that he'd figure out why he was invited, that someone would figure out something was going on with me, my wife, and Bennett. But as I look around the room at the different groups gathered, my shoulders relax. I head back into the kitchen to see what my students are up to.

"Shit, man, you tap that yet?" Hakim asks Owen, and I send him a stern look.

"Look, I've been your age, and I know that you spend most of the day thinking about one thing, but I don't want to hear you talk about women that way. Ever. Especially not about what I assume is another student in my film class."

Owen looks sheepish, and the boys all apologize in unison.

"That's not what I was talking about when you walked in, I swear," Owen says.

"Yeah, sorry, that was all me. He was telling us about his idea for their next project," Hakim adds.

"If I can convince her to write the script so I can shoot it. She has a great eye, and she's incredibly creative, but she's so—"

"Stubborn?" I interject.

"Frustrating," he says.

"Well, this next project has a tight deadline, so if you want to check out one of the good cameras, you better storyboard that thing quickly," I warn. This happens every year when we get to the horror unit. It's the genre I've seen make or break teams, and even though all the equipment is in working order, there are cameras that groups prefer over others, and those get snatched up quickly.

Miles laughs. "He's still trying to talk Reagan into working with him again."

"What are you and Tweedledee working on?" I ask Miles.

"What does that make me? Tweedledum?" Miles says, outraged.

"You are the one who ate cat food, no?"

"He's got you there!" Hakim chimes in.

"That's fair," Miles concedes, popping several crackers into his mouth.

I shake my head as I watch the crumbs rain down from his lips all over the counter and floor. Are all teenage boys this messy? I don't remember me or my siblings being this messy, but given the strict religious upbringing and shit we endured, my memories of that time of my life are foggy at best, and the ones that are crystal clear are the ones I wish I could forget.

"No ideas yet," Miles says with a mouthful of food. Lexie walks up and tugs on his shirt, pointing to the tray of crackers.

He points to several items until she nods her approval and hands her the snacks before she skips back to the tea party.

"If we can't think of anything, we can always do a documentary-style horror film of surviving life in your foster family's house," Hakim says, redrawing the focus as Miles smacks him in the stomach and his eyes dart to mine.

"What's going on over there?" I ask, crossing my arms as I lean against the counter. As a mandatory reporter, I have a duty to report anything I hear, and my stomach sinks knowing that I'm not going to like whatever comes out. Nothing I've overheard up to this point has been considered neglect or abuse, and I bristle as I wait for Miles to talk.

"Shut up, bro," he hisses to Hakim. "It's nothing. Just stupid shit that gets on my nerves, it could be worse."

"Language," I warn as my eyes flick to the girls in the living room still playing tea party with Bennett and his mom. "Let's go sit on the porch."

Once we're settled into our chairs on the deck, I kick my feet back. "Talk."

"It's nothing. I can handle it," Miles says, toeing a loose board on the deck.

We sit there in silence for several minutes in an awkward standoff. I haven't gotten this far with him by pushing him, but I'm not going to sit by and tolerate his foster family treating him like shit either.

Once it's clear that he's not budging, I turn to Owen. "Any thoughts about where you're applying next year?"

"My dad wants me to go to film school and offered to pay for it and everything, so I have a couple in mind out west. But my mom wants me to stay nearby and has been laying on the guilt trip, which pisses my dad off even more. They'd been mostly getting along after the divorce, but me going to college has opened old wounds. Mom thinks Dad is trying to buy my love with an expensive school, but she doesn't get it—he's supporting me pursuing my dreams. I love them both, but I'm tired of being in the middle of their drama. Getting out of Ohio seems better and better every day."

"Shit, man, that sucks," Hakim says.

"What about you?" I ask him. He's got another year before he applies, but it's good to have a plan.

"My moms don't care where I go, as long as I can get a scholarship. Ommi has a connection at Faith Union, so I could probably get in there and pay nothing, but that place isn't really friendly to my people, if you know what I mean."

"I know a film professor over there, if you change your mind," I offer.

He smiles in thanks. "I'll let you know, I got time."

"What about you, Miles, what are your plans?"

"Once I'm free and no longer a ward of the state?" He laughs but none of us join in. We're used to the way he makes light of his situation, and I'm thankful he has these guys to support him. "I dunno. I don't see college being my thing, so I'll probably look for a job doing whatever."

"You're such a talented filmmaker—all of you are—and I'd hate to see you waste your talent. I've got contacts at a lot of colleges and film schools, and I'd be happy to put in a good word for any of you."

"The Cobras have this summer internship that I'd like to do. I don't think it's paid, but I saw a posting on their social media about it. They have other paid ones, but those are during the school year," Miles tells me.

"You can do anything you set your mind to," I say and inwardly cringe at the cliché teacher speak escaping my mouth.

"Okay, enough of this sappy shit. No offense, Mr. G, but let's talk plot, cuz I'm going to be checking out one of the good cameras on Monday." Miles launches into an idea for a horror film that focuses on a simple minimalist plot, reminiscent of Hitchcock. And this is where this kid shines. I lean back in my chair, hands behind my head as Miles speaks animatedly about his idea, with Hakim and Owen occasionally chiming in.

CHAPTER 26

BECKA

My little girl is reveling in all the attention Bennett's parents are lavishing on her. She's pulled out all her Pajama Pigeon dolls and has made three costume changes. She's even got Bennett's dad in a fancy hat and boa as she pours him fake cups of tea.

Hallie doesn't get grandparent time like this with my mom since we've gone non-contact, but even before then, my mom wouldn't make time to see her new—and only—grandchild, insisting we come to her. And when I calmly explained why that wasn't possible, between feedings, pumping, nap schedules, and babyproofing, she let us know how she felt about it, yelling, ranting, and accusing us of denying her access to her granddaughter.

Robert's parents are only ever interested in taking Hallie to church to indoctrinate her, so we decided early on that we'd have limited contact with them, preferring them to come to us so we could monitor their visits.

Needless to say, Hallie has experienced a desert in the grandparent department, so this evening has been a welcome departure from what we've been used to.

Bennett's parents are just as lovely as when I first met them at his wedding. To my sister. Fuck, I'd nearly forgotten again.

"Hey, Bex, you okay over there?"

"Yeah." I force a smile. "Would anyone like a refill?" I offer as I collect glasses, and when no one takes me up on my offer, I head to the kitchen.

I begin filling up the sink with water. Even though we have a dishwasher, I often prefer to wash things by hand. It's quicker and it helps me get out my pent-up frustration when my emotions become too much.

"I see we're rage-washing again," Bennett says, coming up next to me as he grabs a dish towel, ready to dry after I scrub. He's definitely picked up that this is one of my tells. It took Robert years to figure this out, and he often makes himself scarce to avoid a fight. But Bennett seems to know exactly what to say to calm me down, unafraid of me lashing out. He'll let me vent without interruption or problem-solving, and I realize it's something I've always wanted.

I don't want to change my husband, I love him exactly the way he is, but I've always wanted someone to be able to read me without me even needing to share my thoughts, and Bennett does that. And I need them both, differences and all, to help me manage my thoughts and fix my problems.

"You don't have to talk about it if you don't want to, but just know, that if it was only me and you and Robert right now, my lips would be on you, and whatever's got you all up in your head would be the last thing on your mind," he teases.

"So, you two think you can solve all my problems with your magical dicks?" I snort.

"While my cock loves you calling it magical, no, our dicks aren't going to solve all of your problems—but I'd fuck those thoughts right out of your head until you're ready to share them."

A throat clears behind us as Bennett's mom walks into the

kitchen. She looks between us briefly before smiling. "You two look like you're up to no good."

"You know me," Bennett says, taking a glass from my hand and drying it.

"That I do, son, and I have to say while I'm disappointed you two didn't come stay with us during your renovation, I can tell you've got a good thing going on here." I shift nervously as I watch her eyes glance over at Robert, still on the deck with his students.

Does she know? Or at least suspect? Her tone is warm, not judgmental, as she looks between us again and raises an eyebrow. "I've never seen Lexie smile this much. And you look happier than I've ever seen you," she mentions, looking at her son.

"I'm happy. Really happy," he says, bumping my shoulder as he taps his hands on the sink to shake off the excess water.

"That's wonderful," she says as she looks back at the girls in the living room who are now riding Mr. Emerson like a pony. "His back is going to be sore tomorrow, but he'll say it was worth it." She chuckles. "Anyway, I was coming in here to ask if I could put the girls down for bed tonight. And if everything works out, I'd be happy to take them next weekend so you guys can have some grown-up time. I'd like to do a trial run while you're here in case it goes off the rails."

My eyes dart to Bennett in panic.

"I remember how exhausting it was having young kids," she adds. "The three of you need some time to relax."

"I'd love a kid-free trip to the bookstore, and I'm sure Robert and Bennett would love to shoot hoops," I say awkwardly, coming up with any possible reason why the three of us would need a weekend together, because she cannot be saying what I think she's saying? Surely, she can't approve of her son hopping from one sister to another?

"I'm sure the three of you can think of a better way to spend a kid-free night than that. Go have dinner, see a movie, do adult things," she says with a wink as she leaves the kitchen.

Bennett and I stand stock-still, then turn to each other at the same time and burst out laughing.

"She did not just suggest—" I start.

"That she take our girls so the three of us can have adult time? Yes, she did." Bennett says.

"Does that mean she's okay with the three of us… hanging out?"

"If she's offering to watch the girls, that means she approves."

"Well, I'm not going to turn down free childcare. But how did she know? And how can she approve? I know that polyamory isn't a new thing, but this is Ohio. It isn't exactly *that* common here."

"Mom's always been intuitive. She can pick up on people's energies. She'll have the girls building a rock and crystal collection before they leave her place."

"But how can she be okay with us?"

"Ah, you aren't talking about the throuple part?"

"I'm talking about the part where you swapped out one sister for another," I hiss under my breath.

"She never liked Miranda and always said how dark her aura was."

"I love how quickly she's taken to the girls. And they both love her. Hallie's never had someone like that in her life."

"Well, she does now, and we're not going anywhere. It feels nice to be picked, and I'm glad our girls picked each other," he says as he puts away the glasses. He changes the subject before I have a chance to delve deeper into that sentence. "Now the only question is, where are we going for adult time?"

"I know just the place."

CHAPTER 27

BECKA

I'm panicking a few days later when I finally get a text from Bridget and find out that Ethan's birthday party is the same night as our date night. So, I text the only person I can think of who will understand.

> Did you see that Ethan's party is Saturday night?

ALYX

Yup

> That's a whole week after his actual birthday, I know Bridget said she was at your moms' mercy, but they could've done it closer to the aotual day.

Yup

> I'm panicking over here. We've already made plans for dinner before we meet you at Pulse. Are we still good to use your room?

Yup, all the other private rooms are booked so you don't really have any options.

Shit

Yup

Can you please say something other
than yup?

[cat video of oh no oh no oh no no no no no
song]

Cute

Did that distract you from your panic spiral?

Kinda

I'm going to stop by the restaurant, make an
appearance, then I'll meet you at the club.

You are?!?!? Fuck! Now I'm going to be the
only asshole who doesn't go! I'd do the same,
but we already made dinner plans and it'd be
suspicious if we all left E's party at the same
time.

[video of don't be suspicious clip]

Chill, I got this. I'll tell him I'm meeting up with
friends. They won't know it's you guys.
Especially if they already think you're on a
date night.

Ugh, I hate lying to her. I usually tell her
everything.

Hate to break it to you, but they're all up each
other's asses in a love bubble and I doubt
she'll even notice.

Not that anyone wouldn't notice your fine ass

That makes me feel a little better.

———————

When we arrive at the club Saturday, Bennett gets the club rules spiel, and then Alyx escorts us back to his private room.

"Thanks for letting us use your room. Was Bridget mad?"

"She was surprised to learn that we text, but she was sucking face with E when I left, so I think she'll get over it." Alyx turns to give Bennett a once-over. "Who is this tall drink of water?"

"Alyx, this is Bennett, he's..." I trail off, looking between Robert and Bennett for permission to share more.

"I'm the itch they're scratching," Bennett says, offering Alyx his hand.

My heart sinks at his words. He must know that he's more than that to us? It may have started that way, but it's quickly become so much more.

"Well, once that itch is satisfied, hit me up if you need another back scratcher," Alyx says to Bennett with a wink. Bennett smiles awkwardly, and I fill with dread at the thought of this being only temporary. Is that what he wants?

Robert crosses his arms and scowls as he takes a step in front of Bennett.

Alyx holds his hands up. "Message received, hoss. More than an itch, got it."

"How do you all know each other?" Bennett asks.

"How do I explain this? Alyx is best friends with my best friend's boyfriend. And he's the one who first... scratched our itch. But you're our partner in this," I say to Bennett, wrapping an arm around his waist.

"So, he's the one who got a taste of B first," Bennett says, looking Alyx up and down with interest.

"Oh, I see why you picked this one," Alyx teases. "You traded one flirt for another."

"What can I say, we have a type," I say, never breaking eye

214

contact with Bennett as Robert puts a possessive arm around him.

"Okay, I'm digging this smile on your face, Becka, and while I'm disappointed not to be included in this party, I hope you're not retiring as my wing-woman."

"I'll have to check my schedule."

"Alright, kids, I'm off. Have fun, and no need to worry about cleaning up. The crew will come to hose it down once you're finished," Alyx tells us.

As soon as the door clicks closed behind him, Bennett cups my cheeks and pulls me into his lips as the breath whooshes from my lungs. Every kiss with this man is intense and soul-searching. His tongue teases along the seam of my lips until I open for him, and he pushes inside. I expected him to be rough and forceful, but he's taking his time, exploring my mouth tenderly as if he has all the time in the world.

"Partner," he rasps out between kisses. I can hear Robert kissing along Bennett's neck and shoulders as he continues cupping my face.

"I didn't know what to call you," I whisper breathlessly. "I wasn't sure if we were ready to take this public with anyone. But I choose you, we pick you. You're our partner, not a distraction. Not an itch."

"I told you both," Bennett says, pulling back as he holds my cheek in one hand and reaches back for Robert's with the other, "I'm in this for whatever you all want to call it, but I'd be lying if I said that this is just sex for me."

Robert pulls Bennett into a brutal kiss, and I stand in awe, watching them fight for control. It's so sexy watching my husband lose himself in his best friend. I'll admit that I'm equally excited and a little jealous of the way he's kissing Bennett. We've come a long way in our marriage sexually, but Robert is gentle with me for the most part. We've explored some kink, a little impact play, and BDSM, but I've never had to use a safe word. Robert pulls back way before my limit could ever be reached. He has no such problem with Bennett, however, and the rough way they handle each other is intense.

I step back out of Bennett's arms as the two of them pull each other closer, oblivious to me. And for once, I'm okay with it. We've all come so far in these past couple of months. The three of us feel right together, and even though I know it's still hard for Robert to be open about what's going on between the three of us, I'm confident he'll get there one day.

Placing my jacket on a chair near the door, I slide my dress over my head to reveal the skintight corset, tiny lace thong, and thigh-high boots I'm wearing underneath. I'm not confident enough to go full dominatrix in costume, but my outfit hints at it. I stride confidently over to my guys and clear my throat to get their attention.

"Holy fucking shit, baby," Robert says as his eyes rake up and down my form.

Bennett turns to me and does a double take. "You were wearing that under your dress this whole time?"

I nod as I walk past them to the bed. "Fucking perfection," Bennett croaks out as he follows me.

Now that I have them eating out of the palm of my hand, it's time for the real fun to begin. Channeling my inner domme. I've let her out in small doses, and those have been some of the most sexually gratifying experiences I've had. What could this hurt?

Robert reaches for my hip, and I grab his hand to stop him. "Not so fast, big guy. You two are playing by my rules tonight. No touching unless I tell you to, got it?"

He nods and goes to rest his hand on Bennett's hip when I get his attention again.

"And that goes for him too. You'll do as I say. You don't touch me, you don't touch each other, and you don't touch yourself unless I command it. Is that clear?"

"Yes, ma'am," they say in unison as they drop their hands.

"I feel like you need a whip, or a riding crop," Bennett says with a smirk. "You know, something that tells us you mean business."

"Maybe you could find me one," I suggest.

"Is that a question or a command, mistress?"

Ooh, I like that nickname. Lust courses through me as I order Robert to lie on the bed and Bennett to find me a toy. He crosses the room, looking through cupboards until he finds a riding crop, holding it up for my approval.

"That'll do," I say as he starts to move toward me, but I hold out a hand stopping him. "I didn't tell you to come back."

"Sorry, mistress."

"You can make it up to me by taking all those clothes off and crawling back over here."

He blinks once and swallows, his Adam's apple bobbing with the movement.

"Is that going to be a problem?" I ask.

"No, ma'am."

"Mistress," I correct.

"No, mistress, not a problem," he says as he pulls his shirt over his head and slides off his pants and boxers, kicking off his shoes and socks first. Then he drops to his hands and knees, putting the crop in his mouth as he crawls to me.

Once he's close enough, I press my boot against him, pushing him to sit back on his heels. His chest expands and contracts with each stuttered breath he takes. The look of desire on his face sends a bolt of lust through me, making my panties instantly flood. I'm in awe of his restraint.

"Such a good boy," I praise as he sits back on his knees, and I take the crop from his mouth. "Now get on the bed."

"Yes, mistress," he says, sitting and leaning back on his hands so his hard cock juts out proudly.

Robert's eyes flick to it, eyeing it hungrily.

"Do you want to play too?" I ask my husband as I trail the tip of the crop down his chest.

"Please, mistress," he begs, a hint of desperation I rarely hear in his voice.

"Go fetch me a toy."

Robert stalks across the room, an earned confidence in his swagger as he approaches the drawers. It doesn't take him long to find a realistic-looking vibrator, complete with veins along the shaft. He removes the toy from the box and then looks at me for instructions.

"Are you going to be a good boy and get naked for me too?" I ask, smacking the crop against my hand once. "Or am I going to need to punish that ass?"

"I'll do whatever you want me to do, mistress," he promises as he pulls his clothes off until he's fully naked and leaking precum from the tip of his fat cock.

"Such a good husband," I say, stalking toward him slowly before walking a circle around him, trailing the tip of the crop along his back and torso. "I want you to take as much of that cock in your mouth as you can, as you crawl to your best friend," I whisper near his ear before cracking the crop on his ass. "Give me a color."

"Green," he says, dropping to his hands and knees.

"Stay," I command, grabbing a packet of lube and setting it on his back. "Now crawl to him, and don't let that drop or you'll be punished."

"Yes, mistress," he says, and then sucks the vibrator into his mouth, crawling across the floor. He waits at the side of the bed looking up at Bennett who spreads his legs wider as Robert gets closer.

"Bennett, put the lube and toy on the nightstand. Then I want both of you to sit on the bed and keep your eyes on me as you fist each other's cocks," I say, lowering myself into the chair in the corner, balancing the crop on my thighs.

"Yes, mistress," they say in unison.

Once they're in position on the bed, I slowly slide my legs open and glide my fingers up toward my pussy. "Neither one of you are allowed to come," I say as I watch them work each other furiously. My guys are competitive. I know how they get when they're playing basketball, having heard the way the shit talk would follow them home. And they're no different in the bedroom, each one determined to bring the other as close to orgasm as they can while trying to hold off their own.

Their eyes never leave mine, and I revel in my power over them. A year ago, I was still learning to ask for what I wanted, but this scene feels like a huge step forward, and yet, not entirely out of my current comfort zone.

When I move my panties to the side, dipping one finger into my pussy, I let out a throaty moan. Once my finger is soaked in my arousal, I slide it up to my clit, making slow circles, applying firm pressure. Robert bites his lip as he pumps Bennett's cock harder, and Bennett growls in response, quickening his movements. Neither one is willing to back down. It's a sexy game of chicken, and I feel like the true winner.

I continue working my clit until I feel the first tingles of my orgasm build. It doesn't take long before I'm spasming on my hand, clenching my thighs as I ride out the pulses coursing through my body, legs shaking.

"Fucking beautiful," Bennett grits out, breaking the spell.

I walk across the room, their eyes watching every sway of my hips. When I get to the side of the bed, I hold my hand out. "Suck," I command, and they let go of each other's cocks as they crawl toward me. Since I only used one finger and they can't clean it at the same time, I smirk, an idea forming in my head. "Whoever cleans my finger gets my ass, while the other gets my pussy."

Robert shoots an arm out, holding Bennett back as he grabs my wrist. "Such a good husband," I say, stroking his head as he pulls my finger into his mouth, swirling his tongue around it as he sucks it clean.

Bennett's sitting back on his heels, smirking, and I wonder

if he let Robert win. "I need one more orgasm before you two stretch me with your fat cocks. Bennett, be a good boy and grab that vibrator. I want you to fuck my cunt with it until I come." Pushing Robert back, I move to the center of the bed on all fours and look at Bennett over my shoulder as he grabs the toy and gets in position.

"Permission to join, mistress," Robert begs, his voice cracking slightly near the end. I've never seen my husband so needy, and my clit throbs at his plea.

"What were you thinking?"

"I want you to fuck my face while he fucks you with that toy," he says. "Please, mistress," he tacks on.

Well, who the fuck is going to turn that down? "Permission granted," I say as he slides between my legs, forcing Bennett to straddle him as he moves into position with the toy.

Together they work me into a frenzy, Robert flicking and sucking my clit as Bennett plunges the toy in and out of my pussy and his finger rims my other hole. "I'm so close," I gasp as I grind myself against my husband's face. "Oh fuck, I'm… I'm coming," I cry, a powerful orgasm rolling through my body as I collapse forward on the bed, my ass in the air as I moan into the sheets.

"I need this fucking pussy," Bennett says, removing the toy and licking me from my clit to my ass. I buck against him, still sensitive from my orgasm. "Come here, Bex." An arm wraps around my torso, and I'm pulled onto his warm chest, too boneless to fight him or continue calling the shots, needing them to take over and use me until they're sated.

Bennett must read my thoughts when he says, "We've got you, Bex. We're going to make you feel so good." My chest fills with warmth as his hands glide down my body, lifting my hips until he's filling me with his cock. "Fuck, Bex, you're so wet for us." He continues guiding me up and down his length as I prop myself up on my arms, looking into his beautiful blue eyes. "There she is. Are you ready for us?"

I nod, but he continues, "Give me a color."

"Green," I rasp, trying to show him how much I feel for him, for both of them. My heart is full, bursting at the seams with affection for these men.

"I know, Bex. Me too," he says, reading me again.

Another hand kneads my ass as a finger slides between my cheeks, teasing my hole. "You ready for me, baby?" Robert's deep voice rumbles behind me, and I turn to see him lubing his cock as he straddles Bennett's legs.

"Please," I beg. His hand spreads my cheeks as he eases the head of his cock into me. Bennett pauses his thrusts as Robert slowly pushes in.

The feeling of fullness is intense. We've used a toy during anal before, so the feeling of being stuffed like this isn't entirely new. I clench around Bennett, and he groans as Robert slides a hand up my back.

"Breathe, baby. It'll fit, but I need you to relax," he soothes.

Tilting my head, I make eye contact with him. "Remember our anniversary this year?"

I see the moment it registers on his face. He knows what I'm asking for. He grabs the back of my neck, pulling me up and toward him in one quick movement as he speaks against my ear. "Are you going to be my dirty fucking whore? Or his good little girl?"

My pussy contracts around Bennett at Robert's words.

"Holy shit, Bex. You're such a good girl, squeezing this cock like that," Bennett groans, running a hand up to pinch my nipple before Robert releases my neck and I collapse onto Bennett's chest.

There's a slight burn as Robert pushes the rest of the way in with a grunt. "Fuuuck! This ass is mine to use, mine to defile with my cum. You're going to take it all like a good fucking wife." Robert lets out a hiss as Bennett thrusts up into me. "Goddamn it, I can feel you. Oh shit, I can feel your fucking piercing when you do that," he rasps as Bennett continues his thrusts.

"You like it?" he asks, arching his back as a smirk lights up his face, his cock rubbing my inner walls as the hard ball of his piercing traces a path up and down; Robert groaning with each slow thrust he makes as I mewl out my pleasure.

"Oh God, so full. You both feel so good." My nails dig into Bennett's chest as I try to find purchase.

"That's right, baby. Take your husband's cock in your tight little ass while you sit on my best friend's dick. Let us use this filthy body and fill you up," Robert rasps between thrusts.

"You feel so good fucking our girl, B. Imagine how good it would feel with both of us in this pussy together."

A growl emanates from Robert's chest as his thrusts pick up speed. They start with alternating rhythms but slowly work in tandem, matching each other's pace as Robert growls filthy things in my ear while Bennett praises me with his words and hands.

"Such a filthy fucking slut," Robert says, smacking my ass. "Are you gonna come from these two cocks filling up your holes? Dirty fucking girl, I bet you're loving this so much. So greedy to be filled."

"Fuck, yes. It's so good," I whimper. "Give me more."

"You're taking these big cocks so well, Bex. Look at you, that's my girl. You're his filthy little slut and my beautiful, perfect girl, aren't you?"

The combination of their words, their thrusts, their hands, their mouths—it's too much. I squeeze them both as my orgasm explodes in my core.

"That's it, Bex, choke this cock with your perfect cunt. So beautiful. You can take all of us," Bennett says as his thrusting gets erratic, his orgasm derailing his movements.

"Gonna fill this fucking perfect ass," Robert growls as he delivers one final thrust and fills me with his cum, collapsing against me as I lie limp against Bennett in a Becka sandwich.

"At least we don't have to clean these sheets. I'm tired of doing laundry," Robert grumbles as he flops down next to us.

"You're getting awfully sassy over there. Where's that riding crop when you need it?" I look over at him, as I lie on top of Bennett.

"I think you left it by the chair when you finger-fucked yourself," Bennett says between breaths.

We lie there for longer than we should, our breathing eventually syncing up as we cling to each other. With each rise of Bennett's chest, I ache to share my thoughts.

This is so much more than just sex.

These two were always meant to be my home.

My soulmates.

CHAPTER 28

BENNETT

"I want a nickname too. Lexie is bug, Mama is Bex, and Daddy is B. What am I? And make it something cool, cuz Daddy calls me silly names!"

"He does? Like what?"

"Halligator!" she exclaims. "And sometimes Hallie-peen."

Working to stifle the laugh building inside me, I smile and bite my lip as I look at her in the mirror. "Are you sure that's it?"

"It's something like that. He said it was a pepper and he calls me that when I'm being sassy."

"You mean jalapeno?" I ask.

"That's it!" she yells excitedly.

Laughing, I grab the comb from the dresser. Only Robert would call his kid Halapeno when she's being spicy, and this girl can sure be a spicy little ball of sass when she wants something. I love it.

"And Auntie Bridget calls me Halo. I think it's because she sometimes pronounces my name Haley instead of Hallie."

"Maybe it's because you're a perfect angel?" I suggest.

"I'm an angel, but that's not why she calls me that, and now Uncle Ethan calls me that too. I like him, he's fun. And I like Bridget. She's bossy like me, and Ethan makes yummy food."

I've heard Becka mention her best friend, but I've yet to meet her. While I'm enjoying our time together and the little family we've built, I'm starting to feel like their dirty little secret.

"Do you think Bridget will be at your birthday party?" I ask. It's still a little over six weeks away, but I can't stop my curiosity, especially when this kid will talk and talk, over-sharing every thought in her head, exactly like her mama. It's an easy way to get information, which is something I need because I'm not sure where I stand with her parents.

"I dunno, probably. So what nickname do I get? And it needs to start with a B like everyone else's," she says, quickly changing the subject again.

I think for a second as I comb her hair back and start braiding it. "What about Hallie-bear, or just Bear, because you're cuddly like a teddy bear, and you act like a grizzly if you don't get enough sleep." I do my best bear growl, pushing my face next to hers in the mirror as her soft giggle fills the room.

"Then you're my Benny-bear cuz you're grumpy too!"

"When am I grumpy?" I say, feigning indignation.

"Only before you drink coffee. But you're not grumpy like Daddy, just quiet. You don't talk as much as normal."

My eyes start welling with tears, and I look up and blink quickly, willing them away, amazed at how this little girl sees me.

"You're doing that thing when you cry, but you don't want me to know you're crying, aren't you? S'okay, Mama does it too."

Fuck, I love this girl. I love her like I love Lexie. I can't separate them now, but with the recent update from my contractor letting me know that their work will be finished in a little over a week, I know our time here is ending soon—unless I do something about that.

"Love you, Hallie-bear," I say, slipping the tiny rubber band on the end of her plait as I kiss the top of her head.

Infectious giggles spill out of her as she tries to squirm away. "Ew, you're getting tears all on me!" Laughter overtakes me at her ridiculousness as I intentionally rub my cheek on her head, pretending to wipe all my tears on her.

"Sorry, I didn't have a tissue," I tease.

"Benny-bear! Stop it!" She giggles before checking her reflection in the mirror. I reach for the hairspray and finish fixing her flyaways when I feel a tap on my arm and see Lexie over my shoulder in the mirror.

"Hey, bug, you want a braid too?"

"Yes!" Hallie exclaims as Lexie nods. "We can match!"

And I get to work giving my girls twin hairdos. If only every existential crisis could be solved by matching braids.

Once their hair is done, I follow the girls downstairs to the kitchen. We've become a well-oiled machine with Becka making breakfast, Robert packing lunches, and me getting the girls dressed. It feels completely natural, the five of us doing this every morning.

"Green grapes for Lexie, and red ones for Hallie." Robert says as he places the girls' Pajama Pigeon lunch bags into their backpacks. Hallie insisted they get matching ones, and I couldn't deny either of them. It warms my heart knowing he's learned all my daughter's food idiosyncrasies in the short time he's known her.

The scene reminds me of my house growing up, me and my siblings running around before my parents ushered us out the door for school. For the first time in my life, I feel like I'm where I'm supposed to be, one step closer to the love I've always craved.

CHAPTER 29

ROBERT

There are a million things I should be doing, grading student films among them, but I'm grateful we have family dinner this weekend. We ended up having a small group tonight, just three of my students since Bennett's family is busy getting ready for the upcoming Thanksgiving holiday. I've invited my brother and sister, but neither has been able to make it yet.

"Miles!" Hallie shouts as she and Lexie run to the door to hug him. He scoops them up and drops them onto the couch, ruffling their hair before joining us in the kitchen and shoving a fistful of chips into his mouth.

We're crowded around the counter as the girls play in the living room with Bennett and Becka.

"What's up with that dude?" Hakim asks.

My stomach sinks, worried that my students suspect something is going on and the possibility that they might out us. Swallowing down every nerve, I play it cool, keeping my voice even and casual. "Who? Bennett?"

"Yeah, does he live here or something?" Miles asks curiously.

"No, but he's been staying with us while his house is under

227

construction. He's my best friend and he and his daughter needed a place to stay, so I offered to help."

"You do that a lot, Mr. G," Miles says, stuffing another handful of chips in his mouth.

The comment catches me off guard, sounding way more meaningful than he probably intended it to be. I brush it off, opting to treat it like the tease it probably is. "Contrary to popular belief, I do not have a ton of people staying at my house. I already manage a classroom zoo full of wild animals at school all day, I'm not running a hotel out of my spare bedroom at night." My tone is dry, but there's a hint of a smile on my lips as I cross my arms and lean back against the counter.

"Shoot, he got you." Hakim laughs, and I'm relieved that the boys have toned down their language around the kids.

"Is this cuz you made me eat cat food? It was one time!" Miles whines.

"I didn't *make* you do anything. But if it has a tail, whiskers, and meows like a cat, it might be a cat. Just make sure you use the litter box."

The boys burst into laughter, causing Bennett and the girls to startle, looking over. I nod my head at them, and they go back to their tea party.

Because this kid can't stand to be one-upped, he stands up proudly, walks into the living room, and drops to his hands and knees, prowling around the room before letting out a loud "MEEEEOOOOWWWWW."

Hallie goes crazy, flapping her arms and squawking like a parrot. Lexie's delicately fluttering her wings, following close behind her.

"Benny-bear, save us! There's a cat at our tea party! He's going to eat us!" she wails, climbing onto the couch and then launching herself onto Bennett's back as Becka's melodic laugh permeates the space.

Miles stops his movements and pretend licks his paw

before smoothing down his hair with it. Lexie jumps off the couch and tentatively walks over to him, reaching her hand out to pet him, but looking like she's still afraid he'll bite. He leans into her hand and makes a purring sound, fully committing to the bit.

"Oh my God, please tell me someone is filming this." Owen wheezes with laughter, looking between Hakim and me.

Hakim shakes his head. "Total missed opportunity. This is blackmail gold."

"You think he'd be embarrassed by this? I wouldn't be surprised if he reenacted it in the lunchroom tomorrow." I say.

Miles joins the tea party, trying to balance a teacup on his paw.

Hallie is still bear-hugging Bennett's back when he walks into the kitchen to join us.

"Let me down! The tea party isn't over," Hallie cries between giggles.

"Are you sure that cat's not going to eat you? Maybe you should stay there, just to be safe."

"He isn't eating Lexie," she says hopefully.

"Maybe he doesn't like pigeons. I hear parrots are tastier," he taunts, pulling her over his shoulder and pretending to nibble her arms as she squirms, laughing. When he sets her down, she runs back into the living room and begins directing the scene, telling Miles how to sit and hold his cup, laughing each time he purposely does it wrong. My chest squeezes at the sight, and a memory of me my brothers playing with my sister flashes before my eyes.

Bennett reaches across me for a handful of chips, breaking my trance. "My brother mentioned that he has a few extra tickets for a game next week. I have a work thing that night, and I know Becka and the girls aren't into hockey. Do you know anyone that wants to go to a Cobras game?" he asks, saying the last sentence louder than the rest.

Miles shoots up, sprinting into the kitchen. "Did you say Cobras game?"

"I did," Bennett confirms, popping another chip in his mouth.

"Does your brother work for the Cobras or something?" Owen asks.

"He's on the team," Bennett says casually as the boys lose their minds. "But he doesn't get a lot of playing time since he's new."

"Holy sh—" Hakim starts as I give him a death glare. "I mean, crap, holy crap, is your brother Bryson Emerson?"

"You've heard of him?" I ask, kind of impressed.

"These two are obsessed with the Cobras. This one can tell you the stats on every player," Owen says, pointing to Hakim. "While Miles talks nonstop about wanting to work there. They're kind of insufferable sometimes."

Miles moves closer to Hakim, slapping him in the chest as he speaks. "Dude, we could check out a camera, and I could get some shots of the team and edit together a demo reel for them. Maybe that'll help me get a job there," he says excitedly.

"I'll let you figure out who you're taking," Bennett says close to my ear, electricity coursing through me at his touch as he squeezes my shoulder and struts back into the living room.

"I guess that dude's cool," Hakim says.

"Yeah, he's pretty cool," I agree.

"So, who are you taking to the game?" Miles says, flashing his teeth in a huge grin as I shake my head.

CHAPTER 30

BENNETT

I wanted to do something to surprise Robert for his birthday, and I was hoping to take him to the Cobras game, but the legal issues at work have been more time-consuming than I'd expected. I'm glad he was able to go with Miles, and Bryson was able to get another ticket so Hakim could join them. But it's been weeks since our grumpy Scorpio's birthday, and the last thing he's expecting is a night out without kids.

Becka's dropping the girls off at my parents for the night and is planning to meet us at the restaurant wearing another gift for Robert, a pair of vibrating panties.

We're standing in the lobby of the restaurant when Bex walks in wearing a hot little green dress that accents all her curves.

"Who's watching the girls?" Robert asks as she joins us.

"My parents. They said they'd watch them as long as we need," I say.

The hostess seats us at a table in the back of the restaurant. I slide into the circular booth first, then Bex, then Robert next to her.

Once the server takes our order and brings our drinks, I

place a small box on the table, pushing it toward Robert. "Happy belated birthday, B."

He pulls off the ribbon, popping open the box and scrunching his face. "Are these what I think they are? Whose is whose?" he asks, discreetly taking out the remotes and placing one in each pocket of his coat.

"That's part of the fun," Bex teases, running a hand down her neck, slowly tracing the outline of her cleavage.

"You know how I feel about public displays of affection," he warns, sitting back and crossing his arms.

"You don't have to touch anything other than the remotes," Becka tells him.

"I'm not a big fan of attention in public either," Robert hedges.

"We're giving you control. You can do with the remotes as you please. Use them, or don't. We're at your mercy," I say.

A slight blush creeps over his cheeks as he slides his hands in his coat pockets. Becka squirms as she reaches for her silverware, setting it out on the table and placing her napkin in her lap. I chuckle inwardly knowing he's figured out which remote belongs to each of us now. A small vibration shoots through me, pulsing at an erratic rhythm, as I clear my throat and reach for my water, taking a small sip. That asshole takes that moment to turn up the intensity, and I have trouble swallowing as I try to maintain my composure.

He smirks, looking between us. "I take back what I said earlier. I'm a big fan of this."

Robert ends up teasing us the entire dinner, never allowing either of us to come, no matter how much we beg. And it's really fucking hot listening to Bex say "Please, Daddy" every time he turns her intensity down.

"What do you say we take this party home? We've got the house all to ourselves and I can't wait for you to really enjoy your presents," I say, flagging the server down for the bill.

Becka

WE'RE A MESS OF LIPS AND TEETH AND TONGUES AS WE STUMBLE into the house and up toward the bedroom. "Fewer clothes," I pant between kisses. It's hard to breathe when these two beautiful men have their hands and mouths all over me.

I break my kiss with Bennett as Robert pulls my dress over my head and removes my bra while Bennett pulls my vibrating panties off. They quickly disrobe, and we fall onto the bed with Bennett in front of me while Robert grinds his thick cock against my ass.

Throwing my leg over Bennett's hip, I grind against him as I kiss down his chest. I can feel Robert pull Bennett into a kiss as they both continue grinding against me. How did I ever get this lucky to have two men who want me and each other? They both fit me in different ways and together we feel whole, feel like home.

"Does this greedy pussy need more?" Bennett teases as he trails a finger down my front before circling my clit with the lightest amount of pressure.

"More," I agree as I turn my head and capture Robert's lips in a searing kiss.

The pressure on my clit increases when a finger slips into me and starts stroking against my inner wall.

"Gimme a hand, will ya?" Bennett says, and I feel Robert slide a hand between my cheeks before slipping a finger in with Bennett's.

"Oh fuck, yes!"

"Can you take more?" a voice whispers against my ear, and I nod my consent.

There's some shifting around, and then I feel each of them slip another finger inside me, the stretch intense. They work together, pumping in and out, stroking and probing as a thumb continues rubbing on my clit. My orgasm builds quickly, and I snake an arm behind me, grabbing Robert's neck as my other hand clutches Bennett's jaw needing to feel them both as the euphoria crashes into me. I can't speak as the intensity consumes me.

"You're doing so well, Bex. Can you take more?"

"Yes," I plead and then feel them remove their fingers. My eyes flutter open in confusion before Robert's cock thrusts inside me. "Oh fuck! Yes, please, more," I whine as I watch Bennett untangle my leg from his hip and throw it back over Robert, opening me up so he can thrust deeper.

My eyes close as the sensation consumes me. Robert continues pistoning into me, his hand on my stomach holding me in place when I feel a mouth on my clit and my eyes fly open to find Bennett staring up at me. I hadn't even realized he'd shifted down the bed.

"Fuck, you both taste so good," he groans as I watch him lick along Robert's shaft and up my lips before latching onto my clit and pulling it into his mouth. It looks so dirty, but it feels divine, and I can't look away as he repeats the motion several times. Robert slows down his movements, and Bennett takes his time licking around the place we're joined before he spits on Robert's dick and pushes two fingers into my pussy alongside Robert's cock.

"Fuck!" I gasp as I adjust to the sensation.

"Shit, that feels good," Robert groans.

"I need you," I cry as another orgasm builds. Bennett's fingers crook against my G-spot as Robert continues pumping into me.

"You need my cock with his, Bex? Is this greedy pussy gonna be able to handle two cocks?"

"Please. Oh shit." My hand flies out to grab Bennett's hair as I hold his mouth against my clit and like the good boy he is, he licks me through my second orgasm.

I feel boneless as I hear them talking and Robert pulls out of me right as Bennett lies down next to me and pulls me on top of him.

"Are you still wearing the plug from earlier?" Robert asks Bennett.

"You know I am, B. You gonna play with this ass while I fuck your wife's cunt?" Bennett asks as Robert hops off the bed, grabbing a remote out of his discarded clothing.

"Can you sit up for me, Bex?" Bennett asks softly.

Nodding against his chest, I slowly push up to straddle him.

"You're doing so well, baby. I need you to ride his dick," Robert says.

"Oh fuck, stroke it just like that," Bennett moans to Robert as I lift my hips and feel them both guide me onto his cock. "Yes, that's it, Bex, ride me. I need you nice and wet for us. Oh shit, B!" Bennett groans when I feel the vibrations from his plug as Robert chuckles softly behind me.

"You look so good taking his cock. Can you handle both of us?" Robert asks.

"Yes," I cry out. "Need you both."

There's a slight burn and a lot of pressure as the head of Robert's cock pushes into me, and I squeeze Bennett's chest as the burn slowly eases and Robert sinks in a few more inches. "Shit, you're so tight, baby. So fucking perfect for us."

"That's it, relax into us. You're taking us so well, Bex," Bennett whispers as he gazes up at me, his eyes so full of love.

"Fuck, that plug is making your dick vibrate against mine," Robert grits out as he slowly pushes the rest of the way in while Bennett continues his thrusts. "I need to move, is that okay, baby?" Robert asks from behind me as his fingertips tighten on my hips, his grip possessive.

"Yes, I need you both to fuck me," I whimper, over-whelmed. Desire courses through me, and all I can think about is coming, squeezing them both until they fill me with their cum so we can become one.

Robert's hips shoot forward as he plunges in and out and I've never felt fuller in my life. I wasn't prepared for this feeling. When Robert fucked me and the toy at the same time, it felt good, but this is otherwise. There's something about two bodies holding me, their heat surrounding me, two sets of lips, four hands, as their cocks fill me.

"You're so wet, you're soaking us both. This cunt is dripping for us like such a good girl," a voice says from behind me, but it's hard to concentrate with the sparks lighting up my body. It feels like a live wire traveling down every nerve ending in me.

"*Our* good girl. You both feel incredible." Bennett looks over my shoulder at the man fucking us both.

"Oh fuck, I can't begin to explain how good you both feel," Robert grits out between thrusts. "Her soft walls, your hard length, that fucking piercing, it's all so good. I'm not gonna last."

"I'm right there with you, but I need to fuck you both." Right as I'm adjusting to the sensation, Bennett starts to thrust up into me as he cups one of my breasts, tweaking the nipple. Sparks shoot through me as he continues twisting and pinching the tight bud before cupping my neck with his other hand and pulling me in for a kiss. The shift in angle allows Robert to go deeper, hitting that magic spot as my walls begin to flutter.

"So full. I'm coming, oh God, it's so intense. Fuck!" I pinch my eyes shut as my pussy squeezes them both. It feels like I'm free-falling off a cliff with no fear about when or where I'll land because I know they'll catch me.

"Fuuuck" comes a voice from behind me as another one whispers in my ear.

"That's it, squeeze us, Bex. You take us so well, filling you with our cum, you're gonna take every last fucking drop, aren't you? Make a mess of our cunt. Fuck, I love this cunt," Bennett rasps as he cups my cheeks, his eyes pleading with mine as he fills me.

I feel so full as I drop my head against his chest, willing the tears away, determined not to let the intensity of my emotions ruin the moment. My heart is so full of love for these men.

Robert collapses onto my back, sandwiching me between them. We're a hot, sweaty, sticky pile of bodies as I feel Robert's scruff rub against my cheek and listen to the rapid rhythm of Bennett's heartbeat against my face. When I turn my head, I see my two men in a passionate kiss, their tongues thrusting as they pour every declaration their hearts aren't ready to confess into each other's mouths.

"So fucking hot," I whisper into Bennett's chest, not wanting to break the moment. Hands glide up my sides, but I'm not sure whose they are, and before I can register what's happening, they're kissing me. Robert cups my jaw and licks at the seam of my lips as Bennett nibbles along my jawline before lavishing open-mouthed kisses along my neck.

I've never felt more loved, more worshipped or adored than I do in this moment. It only lasts a few seconds, but it feels like hours the way they're licking and kissing me, whispering words of praise into my ears.

As Robert pulls out, he flips onto his back next to us as Bennett wraps his arms around me and sits us up on the bed, his impressive length softening inside me. He lays me back between his legs before scooting backward, pulling out of me. Instantly I feel empty, and I reach for him, propping myself up on my elbows.

"Don't worry, Bex. I'm going to clean you up," he reassures as he lowers his head to my pussy. "With my mouth."

His warm tongue licks up my center and I gasp as my hips thrust forward and my head falls back. "Bennett, fuck."

Robert shifts from his spot on the bed and leans over to kiss my knee. "Can I help?"

Before I realize what's happening, Robert's hand is pinning my thigh open as he crawls between my legs to join Bennett as they both lick and suck my pussy. I stare down as hazel and blue eyes return my gaze, each holding a look so reverent and hungry, I can't help but feel adored as they worship me. I'm not sure Bennett realizes how big this moment is. Not too long ago, I asked Robert to lick his cum from me and he worried the act might mean he was gay. Now here he is, embracing his love for me and his best friend while they lick up their cum from me together.

"You taste like ours," Robert says reverently as he looks between Bennett and me.

"We doing this? The three of us? For real? No more scratching itches?" Bennett asks, vulnerability evident in his features as he grips Robert's hand in his.

"The five of us," Robert offers as he pulls Bennett into a kiss.

A tear slips down my cheek. I stay silent letting the emotions float through my head with every inhale and exhale.

Love you.

Love this.

Love us.

The words repeat in my head until someone moves, breaking me from my meditation, and a small sob bursts from me. Both men turn and climb over me, pinning me between them. I can't help but feel overwhelmed with love as they hold me.

"Are you okay?"

"Did we hurt you, Bex?"

"Baby, what's wrong?"

"Happy tears," I say between hiccups and giggles as Robert leans in to kiss along my shoulder while his arm wraps around my waist.

"Fuck, you scared me for a second. I thought you didn't want this," Bennett says, propping up on his elbow to look at us.

"I want this more than anything," I proclaim, quickly grabbing his arm and placing it atop Robert's on my stomach.

"More than anything," Robert echoes.

"The past couple months have been amazing, but this is more than us sneaking off to scratch an itch. This means something to me. I want to be in this with both of you, and when you're ready, I want to share it with the world. No more hiding," Bennett declares, pressing a kiss to my forehead and then Robert's. Robert pulls him back by the neck and kisses his forehead three times. I'm overcome with emotion understanding the gesture.

"We'll have to tell the girls. They're going to have questions," I say as my voice cracks, the emotion in my words seeping through. Bennett's hand reaches up and caresses my cheek, my skin tingling at his touch.

"We'll do it together."

CHAPTER 31

BENNETT

Once all the Thanksgiving leftovers are eaten, and the girls and Robert are back in school, Bex and I get a rare morning alone together. She's sitting in the kitchen scrolling on her phone when I walk in to prepare my to-go mug.

Construction on my house finished right before the holiday and I debate bringing it up. I don't want to leave, worried it could change things.

"Ooh, I like the way you look in that suit," Bex says, pulling me from my thoughts as she sets down her phone and sips her coffee that has entirely too much cream and sugar in it for my liking.

I close the distance between us, leaning down to press a kiss to her lips. But my little vixen has other plans, and before I realize it, she's slipping a hand down my front, rubbing my growing erection over my pants. While I'd normally jump at the chance to let her take this further, or fuck her in the kitchen, I pull back and cup her cheeks, forcing her to look at me.

"I'm all for whatever is going on in that beautiful, horny brain of yours, but I need to talk to you."

"This sounds serious," she says, a small crease appearing between her brows.

"I've enjoyed all the… fun we've been having the past few months. I never knew sex could be that good." I say, slightly nervous of being this vulnerable with her. It's one thing to share post-orgasm, but it's something else to be this honest with someone fully clothed.

"Why do I feel like there's a but coming?"

"But I'm aware that I'm the guest star in this situation, and I meant what I said the other night. I want this, with both of you. I'm all in," I say, stroking her cheek.

"Me too," she says against my palm, covering it with hers.

"And if I'm being honest, this is something I've wanted for a long time. I was with someone for three years looking for this feeling and never finding it. All I kept thinking was that I was with the wrong sister. At first, I thought I was in love with what you represented—someone fiercely loyal and protective who loves with her whole heart. But the more time I spent around you, the more I realized it was *you*. You were the one I wanted. I was hopelessly in love with you, and there wasn't a damn thing I could do about it. I was with Miranda, and you had Robert. And there was part of me that wanted what you two had. What threw me was that I was never jealous of Robert. And the thought of hurting him was unfathomable to me. I wanted to be the person standing beside him, loving you. Supporting you both. It took a lot longer for me to realize that I wanted Robert too."

"He wants this too, I can tell. He just needs more time to process his feelings before he's ready to share them with the world. Be patient with him. But you're not alone in the way you're feeling," she says hesitantly.

"I'm not?"

"I love you too. And I love Robert. I love this family we've created, and I will do everything it takes to make sure it stays together. And I know Robert feels the same way, even if he can't voice it yet. I've never seen that man come alive the way he has the last few months. About a year ago, I worried we weren't going to make it, because it was starting to feel like love wasn't enough. I knew something was missing from our relationship, and I didn't realize what it was until you came back into our life. You're the missing piece. Our grump needs both of his sunshines to balance him out. And I need my fixer *and* my caretaker."

"I'm your caretaker?" I ask, smiling.

"There are things that Robert does for me that I love, but there are things that I need in a partner that he can't provide. And I'd never try to change him. But I've spent most of my life searching for the person who'd take care of me in the way I needed, the way I'd longed for and never had."

"Your parents never did that for you?"

She lets out a sad laugh, shaking her head. "No, between my narcissistic mom and my dad trying to survive her wrath, no one was doing that at home. And my mom only got worse after my dad died. Maybe part of me hoped I could find that in my sister, but you know that was never going to happen. I even tried to find that in Bridget, but it wasn't until last year when she met her soulmate that I knew she'd found that for herself. Most of me was thrilled for her, and she deserves everything that man could give her, but part of me was sad for myself, because even though I have an amazing husband and a loving marriage, I didn't have that person who'd take care of me like that."

"I'm thrilled to be that for you, but I know Robert would do that for you too. Have you talked to him about it?" I ask, tilting her face up to mine so I can stare into her beautiful green eyes, the golden flecks shimmering in the early morning sunlight.

"I've talked to him about it. But Robert's default is to fix problems. He listens to solve, it's the way he's wired, but sometimes I need someone to just listen to hear me. And that's how *you're* wired. That first night you were here, when you washed dishes with me, you didn't try to solve my problems, or fix my feelings. You just listened. You can read me in a way he can't. I'm not going to get everything I need from one person. Some people get that, but I get everything I need from both of you. And I don't care if that makes me selfish, or if the world doesn't understand our love, this is what I need. The three of us and our kids, that's the life I want." She stretches up on her tiptoes to press a kiss against my Adam's apple.

"Bex, baby, I'm happy to be your caretaker, because I see you. I've always seen you. Those years apart were torture, because I missed you, and I missed Robert. I never thought that being with you both could be a real possibility for me either, but I'm never giving this up, either of you. I love you both so fucking much." I press a kiss to her lips, wrapping her in my arms, letting my mouth make declarations to hers until my coffee gets cold.

CHAPTER 32

BENNETT

"There's something we want to talk about with you two," Robert says as he walks into the kitchen, carrying Lexie with Hallie following close behind them.

It took us a week to find time together as a family so we could have this conversation with the girls. I can barely contain my excitement as I bounce around the kitchen collecting all the leftover plates from breakfast and depositing them into the sink as I wink at Bex. This is what I've always wanted. Love like this. And a family. It's all within my reach.

"Are we getting a puppy?" Hallie asks hopefully, and I see Lexie's eyes light up beside her.

"We're not getting a puppy," Becka tells her.

"Aww man!" She slinks into a seat at the table.

Lexie looks at me, her big brown eyes full of curiosity as I kneel and take her hands in mine. "Would it be okay with you if Daddy had a girlfriend?" She looks confused for a second but nods. "Would it be okay with you if Daddy had a boyfriend?" She nods again as Hallie interrupts.

"People can have boyfriends or girlfriends because we're allowed to love because it's love."

Becka giggles at Hallie's turn of phrase. "That's right, Hallie-bear, love is love."

"And Benny-bear has a boyfriend and a girlfriend because love is love, right?"

"That's right, Hallie-bear, you're so smart." I chuckle as I think about how I want to word what I say next.

"Wait! Are Mommy and Daddy your boyfriend and girlfriend?" Hallie asks in a burst of excitement.

"Would that be okay with you?" I ask tentatively.

"Does that mean I have to call you Daddy too?" she asks curiously, not a hint of disappointment in her tone.

"You can call me whatever you want," I offer as I look back into my quiet little girl's eyes and grab her hand. "Are you okay with this?"

Lexie nods and squeezes my hand once for "yes."

"Does this mean Lexie can be my sister?"

The three of us look at each other. I don't want to get Hallie's hopes up, but I can't deny that I want scream "yes" from the rooftops.

"Kind of," Becka interjects. "This is still new for all of us, and we're figuring out how to navigate everything and how it'll impact you two."

"But Benny-bear and Lexie have been here forever already. Are we gonna keep living together? Can Lexie and I share a room? If we get a new house, can we get a dog too?"

Hallie continues asking questions as I look at Robert and Becka. We haven't talked about a living arrangement, but our three-weeks-turn-extended stay has been perfect for all of us.

Robert nods at me with an "I got this" before addressing Hallie. "We're still figuring that out, sweet girl, and right now we're taking it day by day. I just wanted you to know that sometimes I might kiss Benny-bear like I kiss your mom, and she might kiss him like she kisses me. We haven't talked about us all moving in together after their stay here is over."

"As long as there isn't too much kissing, because kissing is gross." Hallie makes a disgusted face.

"Do you have any questions?" I ask, because this has gone too smoothly, too easy, too good to be true.

"Um, yeah. Can I tell my friends I have two dads and a mom?" Hallie asks. "My friend Mason has two dads, and people are sometimes mean to him about it, which is stupid, because Asher has two mommies and two daddies, and no one teases him. So maybe if I could tell people about my dads and mom it would make people stop being mean to Mason."

Fuck, I love this little girl. Only she would use this to empathize with others and help stand up to a bully. How can I tell her no? I look at Robert and Bex, and the looks on their faces tell me they feel the same. It wouldn't be the worst thing in the world to let one of our girls out us, but I can tell by the sweat trickling down Robert's brow that he's not quite ready for that.

"You have such a big heart, Halligator, but I think—"

"I think," I say, cutting him off, "I think this is private family business for now. Do you know what that means?"

"Like a secret?"

"Kinda like a secret, but—"

"But my teacher says that we shouldn't keep secrets."

"And your teacher's right. This isn't a secret we want to hide, but it's something we only want family to know right now. Does that make sense?"

"I think so. So I can only talk about it with family?"

"Right. The same way that people are mean to Mason because of his daddies, we don't want people to be mean to you because of your family. So we aren't going to tell people that don't need to know right now. One day, we will tell everyone, but we want to make sure we don't hurt anyone's feelings when we do."

"Oh! Is it because our family is so awesome and they'll be jealous that they don't have what we have? Like when we go to Disney, but we aren't supposed to talk about it too much because that's bragging?"

"Yeah, kinda like that, sweet girl," Bex says, smiling at her, but I can see the tension in her shoulders.

"When do we get to move into one big house and be a big loud family to everyone?" Hallie asks.

"Well, the contractors are done, so we won't be here that much longer," I explain as Lexie squeezes my hand twice to indicate "no." I look down at her as she points to Hallie and does one long squeeze for "I love you." My heart breaks at the thought of keeping these two apart.

Becka gives me a quizzical look, aware that Lexie is communicating something. "Is she okay? Is this too much?"

"She doesn't want to leave Hallie because she loves her," I explain as Lexie leaps up to hug Hallie, tears spilling down her cheeks and into her light brown hair.

"I want her to stay too," Hallie declares as they continue hugging. "She's my best friend."

Shit. We should've talked about this before we told the girls. I figured they'd have more questions about their parents dating, but they've been more accepting of that than any adult will probably be. They only see the good in others. Panic claws at my chest at the thought of losing the two people I love and at the thought of separating these little girls who've found a home in each other.

"You could move to my house now that it's finished. There are more than enough bedrooms, and the kitchen renovation will make it twice the size to accommodate the whole crew."

"Yes!" Hallie declares as she throws a fist in the air and jumps around continuing to chant the word.

Lexie throws her fist up too and makes a noise that sounds almost like "Yes!"

I drop to my knees and grab her, pulling her little body to mine. "Say it again."

"Ye-yea-ye!" she stutters out.

I plant kisses all over her face. She's so close. My little girl almost spoke. The only other time I've heard her say anything remotely resembling a word was at the park with Hallie when they jumped off the swings.

"It's not a yes yet, Hallie. We have to talk about it," Robert says in his stern dad voice.

"But it's not a no," she counters sweetly, batting her eyelashes at him. "C'mon, Lexie, let's go start packing my room!" She tugs Lexie toward the stairs, and they disappear up them.

"I'm sorry, I shouldn't have said anything. We should've talked about that first. I expected them to have more questions about our relationship, not our living arrangement."

"Should I put a stop to her packing?" Robert questions.

"Have you met our daughter?" Becka rolls her eyes. "They're going to throw toys in one little suitcase until she discovers one she hasn't seen in months and then dump everything out and start playing with all of them."

"I feel like we got steamrolled by a five-year-old," I say. "But I'm sorry. I don't know if I handled that right, and I feel like shit for asking her not to out us to her friends." I plop into a chair at the table and Robert cleans off the plates and loads them into the dishwasher.

"You did what you thought was best in a difficult situation. That's what parenting is. None of us have the answers, I certainly don't in this situation. I'm not ashamed of what we're doing, and I'm proud of both of you. But not everyone is going to be as accepting as the girls, and this is new for all of us. I want to make sure that we're all on board with the timing and way we come out with our relationship," Becka says.

"You can say it. It's my fault," Robert says as he shuts the dishwasher a little harder than expected, his anger at himself bubbling out of him.

"It's not your fault," Becka and I say at the same time.

"Fuck, you really are the same person sometimes," Robert

grumbles, but I catch the hint of a smile on his face as he plops into the chair beside me.

I turn to him and place my hand on his on the table. "I think what Bex and I are saying is that we get it. You're not a fan of people in general, and announcing us to the world opens up the door for people to comment on what we're doing. Not everyone will understand it, and there may be a lot of shitty comments about it. I want to be respectful of opening you up to that. The minute we tell the world, the trolls will come out, and we should be on the same page about the timing."

"Are you sure this is what you want? This is a big step. The three of us coming out to all our friends and family as poly is going to be a big adjustment." Becka wrings her hands. "I love our little bubble, and I'm not sure I'm ready to share this with the world yet. Moving into your house would force us to do that."

I stand and close the distance between us, holding her face in my hands. "I want this with you. I'm all in, but I'm happy to handle this however you need me to," I say, looking over at Robert. "There's nothing saying we have to move into my house once it's ready. We can stay here, if you want. Or if you're not ready for that, Lexie and I can move out until we're all ready for cohabitation."

"You're not going anywhere." Robert grabs my wrist. "We already lost too much time with you. I don't want to lose any more."

"Fuck, that means we're going to have to tell Miranda," Becka bemoans. "She's not going to take this well. And there's no way I could spin this to make it easier. She'll think it's a personal attack on her that I'm sleeping with her ex-husband."

"I'm sleeping with him too," Robert counters. "I dare her to say something to me about it."

"Does she even know that you're bi?" Becka asks me tentatively, her voice full of concern and empathy.

"It's something I never felt comfortable sharing with her. I hooked up with men and women before we met, but I've never been in a serious relationship with a man until now. It's not really something I've ever vocalized, even to myself."

"Same," Robert starts, "but... I don't think I'm bisexual. I enjoyed my one other encounter with a man before you, but I didn't feel anything for him, and I think I was more turned on by Becka watching than I was by him. I've never felt the way I do about you both with anyone else. The connection we have, our shared history, that's what's important to me. Is there a name for that?"

"Demisexual. It's when you need to feel a connection to someone to be attracted to them. You can be bisexual and demisexual," I offer.

His features are a mix of relief and elation as he sits with the word. "I think that's what I am. Demi and bi, but only bi for you. I don't think I'm into men in general, just one man. And now that I think about it, I don't think I'm into women either, just one woman. That's probably why I had such a hard time sexually before we met," he says to Bex.

"Do you feel better, now that you have a name for it?" I ask, my heart beating wildly in my chest knowing he could be feeling exactly what I'm feeling.

"I do. It always felt like this unnamed part of me that I didn't understand. I wasn't sure why no one ever really did it for me. Becka and I didn't even have sex until much later into our relationship."

"You needed that connection first," she says knowingly.

He blows out a huge breath. "Yeah. This is going to sound dramatic, but it feels like a veil has been lifted. Like I was in the dark for most of my life, just trying to feel things out, but never having any luck, and someone finally turned the light on. And I've always been this dark, moody cloud, but both of you have been huge sources of light for me. I never thought I could have both of you like this."

I take a step toward him and cup his cheek. He leans into my touch, and I graze my thumb along his jawline, pressing against the short hairs of his beard. Fuck, what I wouldn't give to feel that mouth on mine right now. And to feel it on my dick. That's something that we haven't explored yet, and the mere thought of it has my cock thickening. I know he wants this, I'm sure he loves me, but the insecurities in my brain need him to say it.

Bex must sense the sexual tension building in the room as Robert and I stare at each other. His gaze keeps dipping to my lips and then back up to my eyes. We're inches away from combustion when Bex speaks. "I'm going to grab the girls and take them shopping. That'll be a good distraction for them. We have some things to get before the holidays, so we might be gone for a few hours. That'll give you two time to… talk."

CHAPTER 33
ROBERT

Why am I hiding in my office, editing a film project when I could be spending time with one of my favorite people? I wish I fucking knew. Bennett and I used to hang out alone all the time, but we haven't done a lot of that lately.

And I'm scared that the feelings I know he wants to express will come out of his mouth, and I don't know if I can say those words back yet. It's not that I don't reciprocate the feeling. I do love him. But saying it aloud to him feels like a betrayal to Becka. I know that's absurd, especially when I already feel it.

I vow to love you, and only you, for the rest of my life.

If I admit my feelings to him, I'll have broken the last, most important vow I made to my wife—but I don't only love my wife, I love him too, and I know I will for the rest of my life. Maybe Becka's right. Maybe our vows can evolve like our marriage has.

"Knock, knock," Bennett says leaning on the doorframe with his arms crossed as I look up from my screen. "I can hear you thinking from downstairs. Talk to me, B."

"I'm working on a project for school," I say, the lie slipping easily from my tongue.

"Bullshit," he says as he approaches the desk. "There's too much snow to shoot hoops right now, so start talking."

Pushing my chair away from the desk I sigh and drop my head. Bennett's face enters my vision as he drops to his knees between my legs and looks up at me.

I don't know how to articulate this to him without hurting his feelings, without making him think that I'm choosing Becka over him. That's not a decision I could ever make; I'd choose them both.

His hands slide up my thighs in a slow, teasing way, and I quickly stand and head to the bedroom, calling over my shoulder, "I need to take a shower." Once I close the door behind me, I let out a deep breath and turn on the faucet, turning the heat up high. The room quickly fogs, as I slip off my clothes and pull open the glass door. Throwing my head back into the hot water, I relax into the stream as I wet my hair. I hear the click of the door and a brief blast of cool air, and even with my eyes closed, I know that I'm no longer alone.

"You don't want to lose any more time with me, but you bolt the minute I want to talk. Make that make sense, cuz I don't get it," Bennett says, standing in front of me fully naked, and my eyes rake down his body as I take him in.

"Because shit's getting real, and I'm still processing how I feel about it. Not everyone can talk about their feelings on your time frame like you and Becka," I snap back.

Bennett pushes me against the tile, catching me by surprise and crowding my space as he presses his body against me, his face inches from mine. My body is instantly alight, radiating heat everywhere he's touching me. "What the fuck?" I say, trying to sound pissed that he shoved me, but deep down, I'm begging him to touch me. I need to feel him on every inch of my skin. I need him to kiss me so I can show him every ounce of love I have for him because I can't say it.

So I plead with my eyes. Begging him to drop it and kiss me. Demanding he make the first move because I don't know if I can. I'm fully aware how unfair that is, but fuck, I need this man's hands on me more than I need my next breath.

"We really need to talk," he says weakly, inches from my lips, "But fuck it."

His mouth crashes hard against mine, our teeth clacking together as he bites and sucks on my lips. There are no apologies, no attempts to be gentle, as we fight for control, each of us desperate to show the other our furious need for the other. My hands claw at his back and shoulders as his mouth sucks and bites at my neck, leaving what I know will be claiming marks. And I don't fucking care.

Our hips grind together as our cocks seek out friction against each other. The echoes of our grunts and groans bounce around the small space, neither one of us willing to be the first to speak.

He starts sucking my skin harder, his bites punishing. I know what he's doing. He wants me to break, wants me to speak. He tests different parts of my body, determined to find the spot that'll make me crack.

But I'm a stubborn motherfucker, and I can beat him at this game. I drop to my knees and run my hands up his thighs, grabbing his balls, and then make one slow languid lick up his shaft.

I don't know what the fuck I'm doing, but my pride won't let me ask for help or be the first to speak, so I grab the base of his cock and pull him toward my mouth. My tongue darts out as I connect with his head, licking around the crown, then flicking my tongue into his slit, pulsing slightly before connecting with his hardware. I gently tug on it with my teeth, pulling it away from his skin as I cram my tongue underneath it. I lick around the base of his piercing, then suck the head of his cock in my mouth and use my tongue to wiggle the barbell back and forth. My actions feel like something I'd like to feel on my cock, but I have no clue if this is pleasurable. I hesitate briefly, but Bennett's hand threads through my hair, stroking it and tugging.

"That's it, fuuuck, I knew I'd love your perfect fucking mouth," he groans.

It's all the encouragement I need to keep going, and I repeat the movements as he guides my head.

"I need this so fucking much. Need you. Suck it in, give me more of that greedy mouth."

Flattening my tongue, I slide it down his shaft as I take more of his length. Once my mouth is full, I stiffen the tip of my tongue that's extended past my lips, and pulse against the base of his cock, then swipe it back and forth several times before I pull it back in my mouth and suck hard as I slide back up toward the tip.

"Holy fuck, fuck, what the fuck was that?" Bennett gasps, and I panic. Did he not like that?

"Shit, did that not feel good?" I ask, looking up at him for assurance. "I've never done this before so I figured I'd try some of the tricks I use on Becka's clit."

"Holy shit, you gotta teach me how you eat her pussy, because that thing you just did with your tongue was other-worldly, and I definitely want to return the pleasure to both of you."

"So, it was good?" I ask, needing his praise to get me out of my head.

"So fucking good," he says as he grips my jaw roughly in his hand. "Such a good fucking boy, sucking this cock like a pro. Now open up and choke on it."

With earned confidence, I slide up and down his length, sucking and teasing with my tongue. Bennett's a whimpering mess as he guides my head, setting the pace.

"Oh fuck, I'm gonna come. That's it. Oh fuck, I love this mouth. Fucking love it. Fuck, I love it so much. I love you, fuck. That's it, swallow it. Fuck."

I'm overwhelmed with emotion as I swallow every drop.

It's salty and tart, yet distinctly masculine. It tastes like him. And I love every inch of him, even if I can't say it.

His upper body is leaning against the tile as his hips stick out at an angle. I lean over and pull his forehead against my lips, planting three kisses there, before I exit the shower ready to bury my head back in my school project.

CHAPTER 34
BECKA

M y husband can be the most stubborn person on the planet. I don't know why he won't admit that he's in love with Bennett, but I know he is. There's not a thought that crosses his mind that I can't read on his face. He's so hopelessly in love with his best friend. I just hope they're able to work things out while we're gone. Not that there's any risk of Bennett bailing on us if Robert can't admit how he feels, but I know how much it's hurting Bennett to not hear those words.

"Mommy, can we go to the tea party place?" Hallie calls out from the back seat. "Ooh, that's a good idea!" she says, talking to Lexie, before addressing me. "Lexie said she wants to go to the place that paints fingernails. Can we go there instead?"

"Lexie said that? Did you say that?" I ask, making eye contact with her briefly in the rearview mirror as she nods her head.

"She wants purple nail polish since that's her favorite color," Hallie explains.

It baffles me how Hallie always knows what Lexie is trying to communicate, understanding her better than Bennett can most times. Since they've moved in, we've all picked up on some basic sign language, but Hallie seems to have a secret language with her best friend that only they can understand.

"Mmmmm," Lexie hums from the back seat. She's made some sounds before, and Bennett said she's making a lot of progress in therapy, but we're still waiting for her first words.

"That's right, mmmmmaaaa, you can do it," Hallie coaxes her. She spends the rest of the ride pointing out objects and saying the names to Lexie, who does her best to get out the first sound of each word. It's the most noise I've heard her make, and it warms my heart in ways I cannot begin to describe.

When we get to the strip mall, Lexie insists on being carried and clings to my leg the few times I do set her down. I love how comfortable she is with me, and the longer she lives with us, the more she feels like mine. In fact, I'm pretty sure I fell in love with her even before I fell for her father.

I've noticed that she's only glued to people like this who make her feel safe, and I wonder if those are the people she considers family.

We go in and out of several shops, with Lexie pointing to things she likes, using signs to communicate who each item is for. Once the girls have shopped for everyone on their lists, we head to the nail salon, putting our bags in the trunk of my car on the way. As I'm shoving everything in, trying to make it fit, I look down and don't see Lexie. I panic briefly before Hallie's giggle catches my attention and I see the two of them holding hands on the sidewalk.

I blow out a deep breath. Even though she was only out of my sight for a split second, my mind raced with a dozen worst-case possibilities. The same way it does when Hallie wanders off.

Closing the trunk, I take Lexie's free hand, and together we walk into the salon. The girls look through the wall of nail polish as I explain to the technician what services we'd like, settling on manicures for all of us.

The salon is nice, one of those places that caters to mommy and me services, with several kid-themed pedicure spas next to grown-up ones. We're escorted to three nail stations that are side by side. I choose the middle seat and Hallie sits on my left, but when I look over at Lexie, she's hesitating. The nail tech waves her over, pushing the chair out with her foot so Lexie can sit, but she shakes her head.

"Do you want to sit in your mommy's lap?" the technician asks.

Lexie nods her head and climbs onto my lap as I sit there stunned. I don't correct the technician that she isn't actually my daughter, and Lexie doesn't either. And she didn't hesitate to claim me, sitting in my lap and holding her nails out for the woman to paint. I rest my cheek on her head, breathing in the sweet scent of her shampoo.

And just like it did with her father, a piece of my heart clicks into place, knowing this little girl is exactly where she needs to be.

CHAPTER 35

ROBERT

It's the last family dinner before the holiday break, and I almost considered not having one, since we'll see most of the attendees over the holidays, and the other students will probably be busy with their families, but I had to make sure Miles got a holiday dinner in case his foster family won't let him join theirs.

I ended up inviting my brother as well. Jack and I drifted apart after Michael died, but with all the shit going on with Becka and her sister, I thought it might be nice to extend an olive branch to him. We all went our separate ways even though we don't live that far from each other. He's also a teacher, but he went the higher education route. I know at one point he shared a lot of my parents' beliefs and did a lot of work with their church, but I have no clue if he's still into all that. Hell, I've never even met his wife. I wasn't invited to their wedding, but it was a quick ceremony that not even my parents attended. And until tonight, he'd never met his niece.

Jack and I are in the kitchen talking, and the girls are playing in the living room with Miles. They've convinced him to join their pigeon tea party, and he looks like he's enjoying himself. I wonder how different his life would've been if he'd found a good foster family who could've adopted him as their own. But then maybe our paths would have never crossed.

"Which one is my niece again?" Jack asks.

"Well, the big one over there is Miles, he's one of my students. There are usually more of them here, but I guess it's just him tonight. The little girl with the light brown hair that's currently wearing a tiara full of feathers, that's Hallie," I say, pointing her out to him. "The little blonde one is Lexie, her dad is our… partner," I say, shifting in my seat. Jack will be my test to see if I can admit out loud what Bennett is to me and Becka. I hope he's cool with it and not about to tell me I'm going to hell for it. "She and Bennett have been staying here since September. Their home renovation displaced them, and then it turned into…" I trail off, unsure of how much to share.

"More?" Jack asks.

"Yeah." I wait for him to comment, to tell me I'm disgusting like Michael, or to ask the inevitable question about our sex life, or our sleeping arrangement, or any myriad of questions one might have, but he doesn't.

"I'm happy for you. I think it's awesome that you're able to have a family like this, even if it isn't the conventional one Mom and Dad wanted for us. And I think Michael would be proud of you too," he says, a slight hitch in his voice near the end.

"You think?"

"Yeah, I do. Did you ever talk about this stuff with him back then?"

"About my sexuality? No, I didn't figure it out until Bennett came back into our lives a few months ago. I'm not sure I've fully figured it out, honestly, but I'm into two specific people. I'm not into men, and I'm not into women. I'm into that man, and that woman. I've never been sexually attracted to anyone else besides them," I explain, relieved to share this little bit of myself with him.

"That's really fucking awesome, man."

I change the subject. "So, how's your Mrs. Gardner? Do you think I'll ever meet her?"

"She's great, but I doubt you'll get to meet her any time soon. She works a lot in social justice movements and travels a lot. I barely see her," he says quickly, like he's ready to move on to the next subject. "And she didn't take my name, so technically you're the only one with a Mrs. Gardner."

"I never thought I'd see the day you got married," I say, shaking my head.

"Look at us. I'm married with my wife's last name, and you're married with a boyfriend. Our conservative parents must be so proud."

"They may not be, but Michael would be," I say, echoing his earlier feelings.

"Fuck yeah, he would," he agrees, taking a sip of his drink. "For what it's worth, I blame myself too. I knew what was happening, but I selfishly didn't want to get caught in their crosshairs either. I should've stood up for him."

"It's not your fault, you were just a kid too," I tell him. *It's my fault.*

The doorbell rings and I make eye contact with Becka in the living room, but she shrugs. I pull up the camera on my phone, but I can't tell who it is with all their winter clothing. When I open the door a few rings later, Ethan's standing on our porch, and I usher him inside.

"Sorry, man, I didn't know you were coming," I say, making eye contact with my wife.

"Oh shoot, I forgot I invited Bridget. Does she need help bringing something in from the car?" Becka asks.

"No, she's home working on some last-minute paperwork for a project she's helping my dad with. I offered to come in her place."

Becka lets out a throaty laugh, and my cock reacts. I love my wife's laughs.

"You don't have to cover for her, Ethan. I know this is too

people-y for her. I'll text her later and give her a hard time," Becka tells him.

"I'm the one you want at a dinner party anyway," Ethan says. "Don't get me wrong, her cooking skills have come a long way, especially since we've been practicing with my Nonna's recipes, but who wouldn't want a professional chef to cook for their holiday party?" He grins, a dimple appearing on his cheek.

"A professional chef?" Miles asks, popping his feather tiara-adorned head around the corner.

"Yeah, man. I'm a chef at Mangia Bene. I brought some of my favorite dishes that I make at the restaurant, and this new cannoli recipe I've been testing. Nice crown, by the way," Ethan says as he sets the food down on the kitchen counter, unpacking it and adding it to the spread.

Miles starts digging in as Ethan introduces himself to everyone. I'm thankful for that as my social battery is slowly draining with each new person that arrives. Luckily, this gathering is smaller than normal, and we're not expecting anyone else. At least I don't think we are.

Bennett makes eye contact with me across the room and motions for me to follow him. Ethan and my brother are deep in conversation, clearly bonding over something that has them both talking animatedly. Becka has joined the tea party with the girls, so I walk down the hall with Bennett. He grabs my hand and pulls me into the laundry room.

"What are you doing?" I hiss, worried that someone will catch us.

He presses a soft kiss to my lips. "You looked like you were getting overwhelmed for a minute, and I wanted to pull you off so you could have a break."

I arch an eyebrow at him and scowl. "Pull me off?"

"I didn't mean it like that, but if you're willing…" he trails off with a wink.

"I'm not letting you give me a handy when our family is mere feet away."

"That's fair. I just saw that look on your face. You're the only introvert here, and it looked like you needed an out for a minute."

It's unnerving how right he is, and I fist my hand through his locks, pulling him into me as I kiss him. "I don't know how you do that, but thank you," I say against his lips.

"Mr. G?" a voice calls out a little too close for comfort.

"Thanks for helping me get that stain out, B," Bennett says a little too loudly as he steps back from me and turns toward the hallway. "Oh, hey, Miles."

"My bad. I was gonna use the restroom," Miles starts looking a little too closely at Bennett's shirt for my liking. Does he know Bennett's lying about a stain? Did he see us kissing? "Actually, I was wondering if one of you could take me home. I took the bus here, but I only had enough cash to get here."

"I'll take you. Lexie and I are going to be headed home soon anyway," Bennett says. I look at him and arch a brow, when it suddenly clicks that he's covering for me, for us, so Miles doesn't figure out that he basically lives here.

"Right, well, before you guys head out, I have a Christmas gift for you, Miles," I say as I walk past them, down the hall-way, hoping he'll follow me away from this awkward encounter. "It's in the basement."

"I'm not following you into your basement, Mr. G. That's how every creepy horror movie starts."

"Jesus, Miles. It's down in the film studio near my green screen setup," I clarify. "I'll go grab it, wait in the living room."

"I'm only teasing, I'll go with you," he offers as I open the basement door. "But you go first."

Once I locate the gift bag, I hand it to him and cross my arms, fully expecting him to put up a fight. If he won't take food from me, I know he won't accept this.

Miles opens the bag, pulling the tissue out like a clown

pulling scarves during a magic trick. It's a lot more enthusiasm than I'm expecting, and it breaks my heart wondering if it's the only gift he'll get this year, or if it's the only gift he's ever gotten.

"Holy shit, this is a Panasonic Pro!" Miles exclaims, his eyes as big as saucers before a sadness washes over them. "This is so fucking cool, Mr. G, but I can't take this. It's like a seventeen-hundred-dollar camera. There's nowhere I could put it that I wouldn't worry about it getting stolen."

"You can store it here, or at school," I suggest.

"It's too much," he protests.

"Nonsense. Every good filmmaker needs a camera," I argue, furrowing my brow so he knows I'm not backing down.

"Make your angry face at me all you want, but I can't accept this. This is really fucking awesome. But I can't," he says.

"It's not the latest model, and I found it secondhand, but it's in good shape. The original owner got it for her daughter because she wanted to be an influencer. She made one video with it and then switched back to her phone. The lady said it was collecting dust in her daughter's old room, and she wanted it to go to a good home. I can't think of anyone that deserves it more. And now you don't have to fight for the good ones at school." I hand the bag back to him.

He takes it reluctantly, staring at the camera for several seconds, his mouth opening and closing as he thinks through what he's going to say. "Can I leave it here for now?" he asks.

"Of course. Now let's get you home before the snow starts moving in."

"Think I can snag some of the food that dude brought? It was really fucking good."

"Sure, and get your swears out now, or Hallie will be all over you once we get upstairs."

"Can I—" he starts as I begin climbing the stairs. I get three steps up before I turn back to him.

"Can you what?"

"Look, I know you said it was used, but that still had to cost some money. Can I shovel your driveway? Mow your yard in the summer? Oh, I know, I can watch your kids. They already love me, and I can help them with tea parties all night while you guys go have a date night."

I don't correct him that only one of the girls is mine, and I'm not sure if he suspects anything is going on with Bennett, but he has a genuine smile on his face, and I can't turn him down. "I'll talk to Mrs. G."

Once we get upstairs, I pull Bennett aside in the kitchen as he pulls on his winter coat.

"Are you sure you're okay to take him?" I ask.

"It's okay. I'll tell Lexie we're going to stop for ice cream, drop him off, get her and Hallie a cone, and come back home."

"Here," I clarify, it's more of a statement than a question. This is his home.

"Here," he confirms as he grabs Lexie's boots and jacket. Once they leave, I sit in the living room and join my brother and Ethan, though I feel like a passenger in their lively discussion. My mind wanders to Bennett, and my muscles don't unclench until he and Lexie return a while later, ice cream in hand.

CHAPTER 36

BENNETT

"Benny-bear, can we see the elephants?" Hallie asks through a mouthful of popcorn.

"You need to finish chewing before you ask a question," I say as I playfully boop her nose.

"Are you sure you don't want to see the Halligators?" Robert asks, leaning down to pick up Lexie who's making grabby hands at him.

"Elephants, Daddy!" she scolds.

"Yeah, Daddy," I playfully say, half-mocking Hallie's tone, half-teasing.

"Watch it," he mutters under his breath to me, but I can see the smile in his eyes that tells me he's only half serious.

"Elephants it is." He sighs as we head to that area of the zoo.

"How do all the animals stay warm in the winter?" Hallie asks.

"That's a great question, and thank you for asking it without a mouthful of popcorn," I say.

"I can answer that one," Robert volunteers. "Most animals have an inside area at the zoo that has a heater, and the outdoor enclosures have extra blankets or heated mats. Some animals have a separate inside area that's closed to the public, which is why you'll see some parts of the zoo closed for the winter. They move the animals into their winter habitat, or they hibernate and aren't active in the winter, so they close their exhibit."

"Like the bears?" Hallie asks.

"Exactly," I say, excited to chime in as Lexie taps Robert's arm, asking to be set down. "How do you know so much about this?" I ask Robert once the girls run over to the elephant enclosure.

"I had a student shoot a film here a few years back. We got our own personal zookeeper as a tour guide, and he was a talker. Shared all kinds of facts I never asked for."

Hallie's giggles catch my attention, and I look over to see Lexie hunched over, her arm up to her face like a trunk as she swings it around wildly while Hallie makes elephant trumpet sounds for her.

"I've always wanted her to have a sister," Robert says so quietly I almost miss it. "I was afraid to bring it up to Becka because I know she doesn't have the best relationship with hers, and I was also worried another kid would kill our sex life worse than the first."

"This is the best of both worlds," I say, throwing an arm around his shoulder as we watch the girls play. "Now she gets a sister, and you get your wife back."

"But I get you too," he says, turning to me, our faces inches apart.

"You'll always have me," I promise with my whole heart, desperate to convince my brain that the words are true. I want them to be, but I thought I had a good thing before, and it was gone in the blink of an eye due to something completely out of my control. "Sorry, I know how you feel about PDA," I say, taking a small step back and dropping my arm.

"I want you too, Bennett. We're in this together. I've only ever been in love with Becka, but I'm willing to try, so I need you to communicate with me. I need to know what to do, and if something isn't working, let me know, and I'll do my best to fix it."

"Did you just admit you're in love with me?" I ask, my words teasing as a blush creeps into his cheeks and his hazel eyes grow wide. His gaze turns to search out the girls so he can deflect the question, but I can hear Hallie's giggles and know they're nearby. Fuck, I hope I didn't push him too far.

I nudge his shoulder with mine as we watch the girls dance around, each one taking turns acting out different animals.

"I meant what I said the other night. It wasn't just a mid-blow job confession. I do love you. And it's not a 'hey, love ya, man' kind of thing you say to your best friend. I'm so fucking in love with my best friend, I can't even concentrate. But if you're not there yet, that's okay."

"I'm there," he says so softly I almost miss it.

"Love you too," I say, throwing my arm back over his shoulder. Fuck it, this moment calls for a little PDA, but I won't push my luck. To my surprise, Robert leans in and presses three kisses to my forehead, before pulling away to wrangle our little girls.

Becka

"How'd it go at the zoo?" I ask, setting down my Kindle as Bennett approaches my side of the bed.

"Good. Robert's putting them down now. Hallie was disappointed that there weren't any pigeons, but we saw a few animals before all the holiday lights turned on," he says, stripping down to his boxers and sliding under the covers. "Did you get all the presents wrapped?"

"All the ones for the girls, at least. I'm never this ahead with holiday stuff, so thank you." I snuggle up against him, hooking a leg over his thigh.

"He almost said it," Bennett says as I look up at him.

"Said what?"

"That he loves me. He talked around it, and he was so close to saying those three little words. I know he does. It feels like he does," he says quietly.

"He loves you, we both do. I promise he'll get there. I know what's going on in that head of his, even if he doesn't."

"It's uncanny how well you know his thought process."

"What do you want for Christmas?" I ask, stroking lazy circles on his abdomen as I trace the divots of his muscles there.

"I already have exactly what I want," he says, pressing a kiss to my forehead. "All my life, I've wanted a love like my parents'. Growing up, they loved each other so much—it was passionate, understanding, forgiving, supportive, and everything I wanted for myself. I thought I had a chance at that before, but my marriage ending was the best thing that could've happened, because I got Lexie. I just needed a partner to share all this love with."

"You got two partners. And we love you and that little girl so damn much," I say, leaning up on my elbow and pressing my lips to his. I smile against his lips thinking about his words. It may not be conventional, but this arrangement is starting to feel...

Like home.

"I know I should be jealous watching you kiss my wife like that, but it's the hottest fucking thing and I could watch it all night," Robert says from the door as he locks it behind him.

"So, we haven't figured out holiday plans," I say, changing the subject, knowing that if I don't bring this up now, I may not get the chance before everyone starts disrobing.

"My mom is going to want us to come over," Bennett says, swiveling his head between us. "All of us."

"What about the rest of your family?" I ask tentatively.

"The whole Emerson clan will be there," he confirms, and

my gaze shifts to Robert, who looks uncomfortable. "My mom knows about our situation, but she won't say anything. You all can come as my friends," he says, a hint of dejection in his voice as Robert stands there, arms crossed, biting his lip.

"I vow to always communicate with you, open up to you, and share my feelings with you, even when it's hard for me," I say, reciting his vow to me as I look at him, waiting for an answer.

He blows out a deep breath as he rubs his forehead. "I'm just not comfortable with the world knowing yet. I'm sorry if that makes me an asshole. And I think we did a decent job explaining to Hallie who she can talk about us with, but if she looks at your folks as family, we'll never get her to shut up about it."

"And you don't want to put her in that position," I add, understanding what he's trying to say.

"Fuck no, I want her to be able to tell anyone she wants. But I'm not able to shout about it yet. I want to. But I don't want their holiday plans to become all about us and our relationship and the millions of questions that'll come from that."

"Got it," Bennett says, an edge to his tone. I slide a hand over his torso and squeeze, willing him to understand what my husband is trying to say, hoping he'll know how loved and wanted he is with us, even if Robert's not ready to go public.

"What we have is special and important to me, and I worry that once the world knows, things will change," Robert says, shifting on the balls of his feet. "There'll be more pressure on us, and selfishly, I like how easy this feels right now."

"Get the fuck over here, you grumpy asshole. You can't say shit like that to me and not expect me to kiss you," Bennett says, patting the sliver of bed beside him as we scoot over to make room for him.

Once Robert's close enough, Bennett reaches out and kisses him roughly. A small grunt escapes from one of their throats, but I'm not sure which one.

"Do we need to worry about Miranda showing up for Christmas?" Bennett asks suddenly, pulling out of the kiss.

"Don't mention that name when my hand is on your dick," Robert growls, still holding Bennett's erection. Bennett sits up on the bed, and Robert moves back to face him.

"I understand why you're not ready for a big holiday with my family, but I don't want to spend time with my ex either, especially once she finds out about all of us. No offense," Bennett says, addressing me with the last part.

"None taken. And you don't have to worry about her showing up over here. Any time we've seen her on a holiday, we go to her place. Trust me, this is the last place she'd show up for the holidays."

"What if we stayed here? If you want to invite your parents to stop by, I think I could handle that. I'm just not ready for the whole circus yet," Robert says.

"Just a couple clowns, not the whole clown car?" Bennett teases, pushing against Robert's arm.

"I want to keep you all to myself for now. I'm not ready for all the attention that comes from sharing you with the world, but I'm trying to get there," he says, pulling Bennett to him and kissing his forehead three times.

CHAPTER 37

ROBERT

"Mr. G!" a voice calls out as my classroom door swings open and Miles comes rushing in.

"Miles, we've talked about this. My lunch period is the part of my day I get away from you idiots," I say without looking up as I shove another handful of pretzels into my mouth.

"I'm sorry—" he starts, his voice trembling. My stomach drops. This kid doesn't apologize to me, ever, and the vulnerability I hear in his tone has me on edge. Miles deflects with humor, and despite our history, he's never once opened up to me. I've learned what I know about him from the nuggets of truth I extract in our banter, things I overhear him tell others, or from what I've read in his file.

"What's wrong?"

"It's nothing. I shouldn't have bothered you."

"Bullshit. Talk. Now," I growl as I gesture to the chair near my desk. "You want this? I filled up on pretzels, and I don't want to waste it," I say as I shake the sandwich at him. I don't normally curse a lot around my students, but something tells me this isn't the time to worry about that.

"Yeah," he says meekly as he takes the sandwich and sits, devouring it in a few bites.

Fuck, this must be serious if he's complying with my demands without attitude or a joke.

We sit there in silence for a few minutes as I wait for him to share. "Where are you supposed to be right now?"

"Why?"

"I can't cover for you if I don't know who to email. I'll say I need your help with a project and you can hang in here. I have planning after this today so no one will bother us."

"I was in D lunch with Mr. Rizetti's class, but I have gym next."

"I got you," I say as I start typing out an email to those teachers.

"Thanks," he says in a small voice.

A few more minutes of silence pass as I clean off my desk and open my laptop to start editing a project while I wait for him to find his words. I'm not a talker either, so I'm not going to pressure him to share if he's not ready.

"Why are you using a laptop instead of your computer?"

"My school-issued desktop is probably older than you and doesn't have enough memory to support Adobe. I can't edit projects on there. Don't you listen to anything I say in class?"

"They were talking shit about you," he blurts out. "I couldn't take it, so I left. I knew if I stayed, I'd be punching people in the middle of lunch, and I don't have enough strikes left with this family."

"Your foster family?" I ask as I continue clicking my mouse.

"Yeah."

"Are they being good to you?" I tense, afraid I already know the answer.

"They leave me alone."

"That's not the same thing," I say, glancing at him as I will him to look at me.

"Don't you want to know what they were saying about you?"

"Not really," I say flatly.

"What? Why?"

"Because it doesn't matter. People are going to think what they want about me, and there's not much I can do about that. I can't make people like me, and I can't make people stop talking about me, but I can control the way I react to it. Just like you were able to control your reaction. Instead of using your fists to solve a problem, you walked away. That's good."

We sit there for several minutes, and I hope my words are sinking in.

"They called you a fa— I can't say it," he winces as a rock settles in my gut.

"I see," I say, trying to maintain my composure. Why the hell would students be talking about my sexuality? How would they even know? I pull up my email and search for my teaching contract. There was a morality clause in there when I signed it, but I can't remember the details. My nerves calm momentarily when I remember that we have openly gay teachers on staff, but I need to know the exact wording of the document I signed.

"Earth to Mr. G," Miles sings as I pause my search and look at him.

"It's true?" he asks in a curious tone. There's no judgement, but I don't want to have this conversation with a student, even Miles.

"A teacher's private life is private, Miles—"

"Cut the crap. You talk about your girls all the time, and I've been to family dinner at your house multiple times. It's not my business, I know, but don't lie to me, bruh. There are too many adults in my life that do that. You're one of the good ones. Please don't let me down now."

His eyes are misty and full of hurt and it breaks my heart. "Miles, I'm not comfortable talking about this with you." I fold my arms over my rapidly beating heart.

"I told them that it doesn't matter who you love, or who

275

anyone loves, and that anyone that cared that much about what other people were doing behind closed doors was jealous or insecure, and then I walked away. They're probably gonna call me gay now, but that'll be a step up from the things I'm usually called."

"Thank you—"

"A kid said he saw you with a dude over holiday break and that you guys hugged and kissed. Then he called you that word. Was he talkin' about you and Bennett?"

My mind races as I try to recall when anyone would've seen me and Bennett hugging. A flashback of us at the zoo with the girls hits me, but I don't recall seeing any students around. I don't remember us exhibiting a lot of PDA, but that's when Bennett told me he loved me so that must be what the student saw.

"I figured something was going on. He's been at your house the last several family dinners. He's good people."

"You know, I started those dinners for you."

"What?" His voice cracks as his eyes shoot up to mine.

"I wanted to make sure you were getting meals on the weekends. Anyone is invited, but I knew you wouldn't come if you knew it was all for you. I overheard you telling Hakim how your current family sometimes forgets to feed you. That's why I've been packing more in my lunch this semester. I tell you I'm full so you'll take it. Like that sandwich you just inhaled. I made two, and I already ate mine. You deserve more than being forgotten and eating my leftovers."

"And you always cook too much so I'll take family dinner leftovers," he says as he stands and starts to walk toward the door.

I stand and round the corner of my desk. "Miles, I'm sorry I wasn't honest about the meals." He stops near the front of the room, his back to me as I continue, "It was Bennett's idea. I told him I had this student with food insecurities who's had bad luck in life but has more potential than any student I've ever taught. His family used to do family dinners, and anyone was welcome. So we started it up."

Miles turns and crosses to me in a few strides, pulling me into a hug. I stand there, letting him hug me, patting his back awkwardly. "My handbook says I'm not supposed to hug students, but know if you were my kid, I'd be returning the gesture."

"Good people," he croaks in my ear. "You and Bennett and Mrs. G." He steps back and quickly swipes at his eyes, trying to hide the tears I can clearly see, but I don't acknowledge.

An idea starts to form in my head, and after getting Miles set up on a laptop, I start researching what it'll take for me to make it happen.

CHAPTER 38

BENNETT

"I want custody of Miles," Robert says as he enters the house.

"I take it work didn't go well?" I ask as he methodically unpacks his lunch bag.

"He needs a family who cares about him, and we can him that. We could foster to adopt, or just foster since he's so close to being eighteen. There are a few requirements, but it's not as hard to become a foster parent as I thought. But he will need his own room since he's a boy and we have girls. Opposite genders can't share rooms unless they're all under five."

"And we don't have the space here," Becka finishes his thought.

"We don't here, but you do," he says, turning to me. "He'd have his own room, so would the girls—even if they don't use them."

"I do," I begin as warmth spreads through my chest.

"But according to my research, it can take three to four months or longer to get approved and go through all the applications, training and home visits. Miles may not have that long. He told me he's on his last strike with this family."

"Are you saying you're ready for us to move in together?" I ask, wanting to be sure I understand him.

"I looked at my teaching contract, and there's a morality clause, but it mainly pertains to not drinking or doing drugs. There's no mention of sexuality and who I can be with. I wanted to be sure that coming out as a throuple wouldn't affect my job, because moving in with you would force us to come out. But even if it did cost me my job, I'd find another. The two of you and those three kids are more important to me than a job."

I love this man and his rule-following brain. "So, I did a thing…" I start, and Robert crosses his arms, a scowl on his face.

"What did you do, Bennett?"

"I'm guessing it's a good thing based on the shit-eating grin on your face," Becka says.

"When you first mentioned Miles to me back in the fall, it got me thinking. I could see how much you cared about him, and it was obvious at that first family dinner that he looked up to you. You're a father figure to that kid. And he desperately needs that. I talked with him that first dinner, and he shared a little about his birth parents and shitty foster home."

"Shitty? He told me they left him alone." Robert frowns. Fuck, does he look cute when he frowns.

"They do, for the most part, but they've also said some really shitty things to him. He didn't want to worry or disappoint you, and there's no proof of their emotional abuse so it'd be his word against theirs. But it got me thinking about how I could help."

"What did you do?" he repeats softer, his warm hazel eyes crinkling as he smiles.

"You can be single and become a foster parent in Ohio, so I started the process back in September. My home study was completed last week, and I'm available for placement."

"You can foster Miles?" Becka asks, gripping Robert's arm.

"I can, and you do know I'd take care of all of us financially, right? You wouldn't need to work if you didn't want to. Just in case you moving in with me did cause any issues with your job."

"What are you saying?" Becka asks shakily as she lays a hand on my forearm.

I look at Robert, his beautiful hazel eyes sparkle in the late afternoon light of the kitchen. "I've seen the sacrifices you've made for your family, both of you. I can help with that."

"Are you saying I've been calling the wrong man Daddy this whole time?" Becka laughs and instantly eases the tension. Robert shoots her a stern look, and she leans into him. "I'm only joking, Daddy," she says, leaning up to kiss his cheek. "But seriously, how much are we talking about here, cuz I'd love to stop working in customer service if that's an option."

"Anything's an option when you have millions." I can do this for them. "I want to do this for us, for our family."

"Bennett, you can't—" Robert starts, but I cut him off.

"You're as bad as Miles, B. I'm not talking about a handout or a loan. I want us to live together in my house and make that our home. Me, you, Bex, our girls, and Miles. If that's what you want."

"You're serious? I knew you were in real estate, but you bought a fixer-upper. I figured you just found a good deal," he says, confusion screwing up his handsome features.

"I did, but I've put a lot of money into the renovation," I counter.

"So, Miranda did marry rich?" Bex asks.

"Marry rich?" I ask.

"Our mom told us to marry for money. I was the disappointment who married for love," she explains as Robert wraps an arm around her waist, pulling her against him.

"That explains a lot about our relationship, now that I think about it, and why she was in such a hurry to get married," I say.

"How come she didn't get more in the divorce?"

"Our prenup didn't pay out until the three-year mark, and we didn't make it that far. We're getting off-track here. You have a problem, and for once, I can fix it. Please let me help."

My eyes linger on Becka before we look at Robert for an answer.

He clears his throat, reaching an arm to me as his hand clasps the back of my neck, pulling me close and sandwiching Bex between us. "There's nothing I want more in this world than to build a life with you two. You're my safe place to land. Both of you. I've felt like something was missing in my life for a while now. Becka forced me to acknowledge it, and this is what I was missing. This family."

A sob rattles my chest as his grip tightens on my neck and he pulls my forehead to his lips, planting three kisses on it.

"Why three kisses?" I ask, unable to contain my joy at the gesture.

"What?"

"You always do three kisses," I mumble, suddenly embarrassed.

He grabs both of my cheeks and pulls my face to his, punctuating each kiss with a word. "I love you."

Holy shit, has he been telling me he loves me all along? He's been kissing my forehead like that for months. Tears well in my eyes as his thumb swipes the ones that escape down my cheeks. "This whole time?" I croak out.

"This whole time," he confirms.

"I love you too, B," I say and then turn to Bex. "I love you, Bex. You two have brought me back to life, and I'll do everything I can to repay that favor."

Bex's hand slides up my chest and brushes the hair from my face as her soft voice comforts me. "There's nothing to repay. You're family. We love you, Bennett, and we'll do anything we can to make sure you know that we're not going anywhere."

CHAPTER 39

ROBERT

If I thought family dinners were overwhelming, those are nothing compared to the chaos currently unfolding in my house.

Of course, Hallie insisted on a Pajama Pigeon party. Becka had tried to persuade her into a birthday party at the tea house they like to go to, but Hallie wanted everyone here.

She also insisted we make slime.

She's currently flapping her arms with her feather tiara, running around the living room with said slime, acting like it's bird poop.

If I'm being honest, it's not the mess I'm worried about. It's the people—too many of them invading my sanctuary. Too many opportunities for my talkative birthday girl to slip up and share our secret with the wrong person. And it's not that I don't want anyone to know; I just want to be in control of when and how.

There are way too many unknown factors here. And way too many fucking people.

In addition to the five hundred children in my house, Bennett's parents are here, along with a handful of parents I don't recognize who decided to stay behind with their kids.

Ethan and Bridget came too. It's been a while since Becka's seen her best friend, so I know she's excited they came.

"Ethan, hey, can you help with the piñata?" I ask, letting out a frustrated breath as I thrust the giant pigeon-shaped object at him.

"Sure, happy to. Where are we doing this thing?" he asks with a smile, and I point him in the direction of Bennett so they can hang it.

"Yo, Mr. G!"

I turn back to the front door and see Miles's goofy grin. He's standing there, kicking off his shoes with his arms wide open like he's waiting for a hug, with a gift bag hanging off his arm.

"What are you doing here?" I ask, confused.

"Hallie invited me at family dinner back in December, and I saw you had it written on your calendar at school.

"How'd you know it'd be here?" When it's clear I'm not going to hug him, he closes the distance and pulls me into a hug, as my body remains stiff against him.

"Hallie told me it'd be at her house," he says, pulling back. "Now where's the birthday girl?" He walks past me toward the living room, calling out for Hallie.

That's why she insisted the party had to be at our house, because she told Miles that it would be. Something flutters in my chest at the gesture my daughter made to include him.

Bennett and Ethan are corralling all the kids toward the piñata as Miles and I step into the room to join them and I see Becka slip off into the kitchen with Bridget.

We make sure the kids are hopped up on candy, cake, and ice cream before forcing them to sit still and watch my newly six-year-old open presents at a painstakingly slow pace. Lexie sits on the couch next to Miles, leaning against him as he props his arm along the back.

When Hallie gets to the bag Miles brought, she lets out a high-pitched squeal and runs over to him, dancing in place as she holds up the Pajama Pigeon figurines. She pulls him into a hug, jumping up and down against him, before pushing him aside to steal his spot on the couch, showing off the dolls to Lexie.

"Miles, how did you afford that doll set? They've been sold out since December, and the few I've found online weren't cheap," I ask, sounding more suspicious than I probably should, as I pull him away from the noise.

He shrugs, putting his hands in his pockets. "It's not a big deal."

My gut tightens. "You didn't do anything illegal to get that, did you?"

He shoots me a murderous look, and I throw my hands up in placation.

"I had a pair of Jordans from my last family. I outgrew them before I ever got to wear them, so I sold them."

Those dolls were the big-ticket item this past holiday season. He had to have spent at least a hundred dollars on my little girl.

I throw an arm around his neck, pulling him into an awkward side hug.

"Jeez, Mr. G, you're so obsessed with me," he groans sarcastically as I playfully shove him away.

This kid could be anywhere else on a weekend, and he chose to keep his word to my daughter and celebrate her. I can't help but smile like a fool for the rest of the party at how much love I have in my heart for these kids, all three of them

CHAPTER 40

BECKA

I can hardly believe that I was able to, one, get Bridget out of the house and out of her love bubble, and two, out into the land of the living where there are actual people. She's not a fan, but she loves me, and I guilted her into it, so here we are, walking into The Spicy Shelf.

The owner Amanda greets us as we walk in, and we find seats in the circle. Bridget was the one who introduced me to romance novels, and she used to joke that she preferred book boyfriends over real men—until she met her real-life book boyfriend and now, they're stupidly cute together.

"This isn't like AA where we have to introduce ourselves, right? I'm not about to have to get up there and be all, 'Hi, I'm Bridget, and I'm addicted to smut,' am I?"

"Oh my gosh, that'd be amazing, we should totally do that!" I gush, knocking my knee against her leg.

"Fuck, forget I said anything. Ugh, I'm surrounded by extroverts," she groans, putting her head in her hands.

"At least you read the book."

"Yeah, but I don't want to get up in front of people and talk about it. We could've talked about it over boozy ice cream. Why did I let you drag me here?"

"Because you love me."

Amanda stands up, starting the meeting. "Welcome, everyone, to the Spicy Spine Sisters book club. I can't wait to hear your thoughts about this month's read. Who wants to start?"

Several hands shoot up as the discussion begins.

"Damn, she's just gonna jump right into it? No easing in slowly?" Bridget whispers under her breath.

"Kinda how you and Ethan started, huh?" I shoot back, chuckling as she kicks at my shin.

"Look, all I'm saying is that I'm not a fan of these kinds of books," an older woman says across the circle. "Who needs that many dicks? It seems selfish."

"Oh, I love why-choose books. Who doesn't want to be worshipped by that many men at once?" a woman chimes in.

"But what about when there are more dicks than she has holes? Someone is always left out," another woman says.

"Not if her boyfriends are also boyfriends, then there's plenty of holes to go around," Hannah counters.

I sit there uncharacteristically quiet as I listen to their back and forth. Why is the universe confronting me with this now? Bridget elbows me, whispering in my ear. "Why aren't you jumping into this one? I know you have opinions on why choose. I once heard you give a seven-minute speech on your love of them."

I shrug, hoping she'll back off, but I can feel her eyes on me. She doesn't know about my real life why-choose situation, and I feel like an asshole for not telling her, but I'm not going to reveal my story to her like this.

"Some of us can't find one decent fish in the sea, and these FMCs get a whole school of them?" says the older woman.

"Tell me you've never been double-dicked down without telling me," a twentysomething mutters a few seats down from me.

"And the men in these books are so one-dimensional. You've got your sunshine guy who is all smiles, and your broody alpha. There's a smart one and a hot one. They're always the same," the older woman continues.

"I don't think that's the case for all why choose. I've read several that have well-developed characters with rich backstories. I think it depends if it's one that's mostly erotica or a romance, where the story is more forefront," Amanda adds. "If you didn't like this one, I have a lot of others I can recommend."

The older woman crosses her arms, looking around the circle, probably waiting for someone to back her up, but everyone is silent. "Well, I think it's unrealistic to fall in love with that many people at once. It's selfish. If one man can't provide for all your needs, then you need to find another man."

"Just because you believe in monogamy doesn't mean it works for everyone," I say, shocking myself at how forceful my words come out. The people-pleaser in me is cringing, but I can't listen to this woman's ignorance any longer. "Some people need variety, and if everyone is on board, there's nothing wrong with that. Not all people can be everything for their partner, and that doesn't mean they aren't good enough. Sometimes people need multiple supports and get different things from different people. And I think that's beautiful, and it should be celebrated."

Bridget's arm slides along the back of my chair, resting there as she squeezes my shoulder. "Love doesn't always look the way you think it should. It can be between two people or a group. And there's an entire community of people that exist that are polyamorous. It's not a fictional scenario made up for a book or for your entertainment. And these stories celebrate that, and those that practice it deserve to be represented in books and media," Bridget adds.

Her words tug at my heart. She doesn't even know she's defending my relationship and my family.

"Besides, the fantasy part of those books isn't all the sex in them, it's the men doing all the chores. There's usually one that cooks, one that cleans, one that's always watching the kids. The real fantasy isn't all the dicks, it's the way these men ease the mental load of the FMC," I add, trying to bring levity to the mood of the room.

"Hear! Hear!" Several women chime in as I lean back in my seat.

"If I had multiple boyfriends, there'd just be more abandoned socks in my house," a woman says.

"And more pee around your toilets!" someone adds.

True. More adults in our house means more random piles of clothes left on the bathroom floor, and more toilet seats left up. It may not be true for everyone, but even though my guys pull their weight around the house, there's definitely more messes to clean.

"Ethan's working tonight. I'm taking you back to my place after this," Bridget says out of the side of her mouth as we put on our coats.

Normally, I'd be excited about my best friend wanting to spend more time with me, but I feel like I'm being summoned to the principal's office. Between me practically ghosting her over the past few months and this outburst, I know she knows that something's up with me.

When we walk into Bridget's apartment, she goes straight to the kitchen and fixes my favorite treat.

I've been looking for family in all the wrong places all these years. I put so much weight into my relationship with my sister because she's the only blood relative I'm still in contact with. But Bridget is more of a sister to me than Miranda is. Losing Miranda would hurt, but losing Bridget's friendship would be something I could never recover from.

This revelation lifts the weights off my chest, and I join Bridget in the kitchen, pulling out a stool to sit at the island. "The first rule of fight club..." I start.

"Wait, that's my line when I used to tell you about my hookups. Does this mean…"

I interrupt her before she can finish the thought. "Promise me you won't tell anyone, not even Ethan."

"We don't talk about fight club," she finishes hesitantly.

"You know that guy you met at Hallie's birthday party?" I ask nervously.

"Yeah, the one I was talking to who recognized me as Auntie Bridget?"

"That's the one. So about him…"

"I'm not in the mood to trail after your breadcrumbs, Becka. Just spit it out," she snaps.

"He's my boyfriend. And Robert's boyfriend. The three of us are in a relationship," I say quickly.

She freezes, locking eyes with me. "Holy shit, your speech at book club makes more sense now, but I thought you were about to tell me that you were cheating on Robert. And you know how I feel about cheating."

"There was no cheating, don't worry. I know that's a trigger for you." Bridget's ex cheated on her. It's why she didn't date, and it's also why it took a while for Ethan to win her over. "But that's not all. He's Miranda's ex."

Bridget is mid-sip when I deliver the final breadcrumb, and she chokes on her drink as she swallows.

"Okay, I did not expect you to say that," she says through a cough as she fists her chest before walking around the island to sit in the stool next to me.

We sit there for what feels like forever, and then the tears hit me out of nowhere. Bridget rubs my shoulder. "Is that why you've been ghosting me? I used to get daily texts from you."

I nod. "I'm a shitty friend."

"Then, according to that logic, I'm an asshole, because I text you way less than you text me. Life happens, Becka. I'm confident in our friendship, even if we don't talk every day. Tell me everything."

"Sorry, I don't even know why I'm crying," I say, wiping away the tears. "It feels good to talk about it. This has been going on for months, and it's been amazing, but part of me needed to talk to you and tell you everything, but I didn't want to burst your new love bubble with my drama. Not that it's drama, it's actually really great. Bennett is everything that both of us have always needed. At first, I was worried that adding another person to our marriage would change the way I feel about Robert, or the way he feels about me, but it only heightened everything. Like, I didn't know I was capable of loving this many people this much. It literally feels like I'm going to burst, there's so much love in me for Robert and Bennett, and Hallie and Lexie. Oh, and Miles too."

"Alright, Gretel, Imma need you to fill in some of these breadcrumbs. Lexie is Bennett's daughter, right? But who is Miles?"

"Yes, Lexie and Hallie are like sisters already, and Miles is a student from Robert's advanced film class at school. He's been coming to our family dinners, and the girls are obsessed with him. He's kind of become a staple at our house. His foster family isn't super involved in his life, and he's on his own a lot. Robert was worried about him, so Bennett suggested we do family dinners for some of his students. I think Miles looks at Robert like a father figure."

"It sounds like your family has doubled since our last hang out."

"It's more like a hodgepodge of people living under one roof."

"Becka, that's a family. It can be anything you make it. You've just been looking for it in the wrong places. Miranda and your mom aren't the family you were meant to have, they're just the one you were born into. But I've watched you build friendships and communities over the years. Hell, you've clung on to our relationship with fervor, and thank goodness you did, because I didn't have enough faith in people after what I went through in high school. I would've been content being alone the rest of my life if it weren't for you. And Ethan."

"How are things going with Ethan and his dad?"

"Better. I've been helping his dad with a work thing, so it's given us something different to focus on."

"I'm proud of you, Bridget," I say, leaning into her shoulder.

She reaches over and pats my head. It's awkward because of the way I'm leaning against her on the stool, but it means everything to me. Hugging just isn't her thing. "So, you're good? Problem solved?"

I chuckle as I sit up. "I really do have a type, don't I?"

"I'm not following."

"You and Robert are so much alike, and it's hilarious how I've never really noticed it before."

"Okay," she says, drawing out the word, probably waiting for me to elaborate.

"You're right, though. I've spent too much of my life chasing after a relationship that doesn't exist. And I've created this amazing family that I love more than anything, but I'm terrified of losing it."

"How would you lose it?"

"What if Miranda finds out?"

"And? So what? What's the worst that would happen?"

What is the worst that would happen? She'd tell my mom. I don't talk to her anyway. She'd stop speaking to me. At least then I wouldn't have to hear all the shitty things that come out of her mouth. Would I be okay if Hallie lost access to her aunt? Yeah, I think I would. There's nothing she could say to Bennett that he'd believe, nothing that would make him leave us. I can't think of a single thing she could do or say to destroy the family that we've built. But it does mean I'd lose her. Am I okay with that? I've spent my entire life chasing a relationship with her.

"Are you okay?" Bridget asks, pulling me out of my thoughts. "You keep tilting your head and nodding like you're having a whole-ass conversation with yourself but none of it is out loud."

"Sorry, I'm running through all of the worst-case scenarios in my head."

"I hear making a list helps," she says with a hint of snark.

"I love you, but that's more your thing."

"Well then, fill me in. What's the worst that you can come up with?"

"What if she tells everyone that I stole her man? I broke girl code—I'm literally dating her ex. You don't do that to friends. Or sisters."

"She's not your friend, and she's only your sister by blood. You have no loyalty to her. Besides, you're always going to be the villain in someone's story. And you've most likely been the villain in her eyes already. Hell, I'm sure everyone in her life is the villain since she can't ever seem to take responsibility for her own actions. That's not something you can control. And everyone that knows you will know the truth, and for those that don't, your actions will speak louder than her words. You're a good person, and nothing your sister says will ever change that in the eyes of those that matter."

"That's some deep shit, Bridget."

"Yeah, well, it comes from years of having to prove myself in the corporate world. Fuck the patriarchy," she says, raising her glass to mine. "But seriously, what would actually change if you cut her out too? You've already cut your mom out."

"Yeah, well, that was easy."

"So why is this so hard?"

"She's the last connection I have to the family I grew up with."

"Why are you still holding on to that? You gave me a hard time for holding on to the hurt and betrayal I felt from my ex. I believe you said that I let it make decisions it had no right making. How is this different? For years, I've watched you chase this idea of a relationship with your sister, and it's never made you happy. You're the most positive person I know, and she doesn't make you happy. Would you finally be happy if you had the kind of relationship with her you've always craved?"

"Probably not. We don't really have a lot in common, and all she does is complain."

"Or would you be happier if you finally let that go? I know I don't have any siblings, but what you and I have is a friendship that not many people find. Yes, life gets in the way sometimes, but the connection we share is real and sacred. I couldn't imagine having a better person in my corner than you. I'll be your sister."

Tears spill down my face, and I pull her into a hug. "I know you hate this touchy-feely crap, but you can't say shit like that to me and avoid it," I say through sobs and hiccups.

"It's kind of growing on me," she says into my hair, and I hug her tighter.

Bridget pulls back, her hands on my shoulders as she speaks, "What's the worst that would happen if she found out you're with Bennett? You wouldn't actually lose your sister, you'd lose the *idea* of a sister. You can't lose something you never had. She can't hurt you more than she already has. She can't take away anyone in your life that actually matters."

"I still think there's hope for Miranda. Sometimes I get glimpses of who we could be and the relationship we could have. I refuse to believe that she's irredeemable."

"Let her find redemption with someone else. That's her story, not yours."

"I know you're right." I sigh. "But why is letting go so hard?"

"Fucking tell me about it. But isn't it ironic that I'm giving you the same advice you gave me?"

"You were holding on to hurt and pain because of a shitty ex. This is different. You're asking me to let go of hope."

"The *hope* of a sister. The idea of a relationship you don't actually have," she corrects.

"Stop being so logical."

"Who knows, maybe she won't even care, and you'll have made this a bigger deal than it is."

We look at each other at the same time and break out into a fit of laughter.

"Yeah, this is going to be a shit show, but I'm here if you need backup," Bridget says, throwing her arm around my shoulder.

CHAPTER 41

BECKA

I answer a knock at the door to find the person I least want to see on the other side.

"Miranda? What are you doing here?" I ask as panic consumes me.

"I'm here to see my niece, of course! I got an invitation for a party. Did you let Hallie make them herself? It was cute," she asks as I stand awkwardly in the doorway.

"No, I made them," I say, stunned. Of course she would insult something I put a lot of work into crafting while also managing to miss the actual party. I reluctantly agreed to let Hallie invite her when she asked, knowing she wouldn't come. So why is she here now? "And the party was two weeks ago. You missed it."

"Like I was going to come to a kid's party. Eww, no thanks. I'd need a lot of booze and Lysol spray to deal with all those little brats running around. I don't know how you do it."

"So why are you here?" I ask again.

"Call me fashionably late. And don't worry, I brought the party with me," she says, holding up her arm with about ten gift bags hanging off of it. "I want to see the birthday girl."

Of course she would never randomly come to my house to see me. I should be happy that she's finally showing up for her niece, but it's still odd that she's here.

"It's not a good time right now. Hallie has a friend over." I attempt to close the door, but she pushes it open and shoves past me on her way into the house.

"No worries, I'm sure she'll be excited when she sees what I got her," she exclaims.

Fuck, where is Bennett right now? Maybe I can send him a text to tell him to not come downstairs. When I left our bedroom, the guys looked all snuggly so I offered to give them some alone time.

"The house is a mess, we're in the process of moving, and I'm not comfortable with you seeing it like this," I proclaim, already running through other excuses in case this one doesn't work.

"What else is new?" Her jab doesn't hurt as much as it normally would when anxiety overtakes my desire to impress her. "Hallie! Auntie Miranda is here!" she calls as she heads toward the kitchen.

"Miranda, stop," I plead as I follow behind her.

"There's my favorite niece!" she coos as she spots Hallie at the table playing dolls with Lexie.

"I'm your only niece!" Hallie giggles as she runs to my sister and is swept up in a big hug.

"I missed you so much, Hallie girl! I've got birthday presents!" Miranda says as she sets the bags on the table. More gifts than necessary for one little girl—but that's my sister. She disappears for months, then sweeps back in, love-bombing her way into my daughter's affections. It used to work, but my intuitive little empath has started putting pieces together.

"Can I share them with my sister?"

Miranda shoots me a confused look. Crap, how do I explain this? "Sister?" she asks me before turning back to

Hallie. "You don't have a sister, silly," she tells Hallie with a condescending tone.

"Yes, I do. This is my sister Lexie," Hallie declares, gesturing toward her friend.

"Well, she's not technically your sister, Hallie-bear," I say softly before meeting eyes with Miranda. "She's *like* a sister. They're best friends."

"But she lives here with us and we share a room and you said she could be my sister," Hallie says, her voice small and full of hurt.

"That's right, but she's not legally your sister which is why Auntie Miranda was confused," I offer, trying desperately not to cause any more trauma for these little girls.

"Hi, I'm Hallie's Aunt Miranda. It's nice to meet you."

Lexie stares up at my sister and offers her a small smile, one side of her mouth crooking up.

"What's the matter? No one ever taught you manners? You're supposed to say, 'It's nice to meet you' back to me," Miranda chides as she repeats the last part slowly like she's talking to someone who doesn't speak English.

Tears well up in Lexie's eyes as she gets up and runs into my arms. I bend down to scoop her up. "It's okay, Lexie-bug, she didn't know. You're okay, you don't have to do anything you don't want to do," I whisper in her ear as I rub circles on her back.

"Am I missing something here? She was rude."

"She's not rude," Hallie shouts. "She can't talk. *You're* rude."

"Excuse me?"

"I don't want these. You were mean to my sister, and that's not okay," Hallie says, pushing the gifts away from her and sitting back in her chair.

"She's not your sister," Miranda says. "Sisters have the same parents."

Another sob wracks Lexie's body as she squirms in my arms. I can tell she wants to run, but I'm determined to hold where I can keep her safe.

"Don't you dare," I say, pointing a finger at Miranda, summoning the courage I need to finally have his conversation with her. I channel my inner-Bridget. "Family comes in all forms, some blood, and some not. It doesn't matter how my daughters found each other, I won't let you come into my house and confuse them."

"But you said she had a *friend* over. Those were your words, were they not?"

I should've known she would try to gaslight me. It's what she does.

"I said that as an excuse because I didn't want you to come inside. And now you know why. You never listen, or if you do, you don't actually hear me."

"So, you lied?"

I laugh as I clutch at Lexie tighter, knowing she's only proving my point. "I didn't lie. They are friends and sisters, but you wouldn't know anything about that type of relationship."

Miranda contorts her face as if my words just struck her. "What is that supposed to mean?"

"It means that while we may be related by blood, we're not family. This is my family," I say, gesturing between my girls. "These little girls are my life, and I'd do anything for them."

"Don't forget about Daddy and Benny-bear!" Hallie exclaims.

"Benny-bear? Oh my God, Becka, did you have another kid? Some people don't even get one, and you have three?"

"Benny-bear is Daddy and Mommy's boyfriend," Hallie proudly corrects, and my heart bursts at the pride in her voice. Bless my sweet little girl and her conviction. I steel myself for the most difficult part of this impromptu confrontation.

"Did my little Hallie-bear call my name?" Bennett says as

he enters the kitchen, his hair tousled and face flush looking freshly fucked. "I thought I heard yelling, is everything o—?" He freezes as he takes in the full scene, Lexie crying in my arms as his ex-wife stands in place like a deer in headlights. My eyes roam over his chiseled features on display as he stands there shirtless in only a pair of athletic shorts. This is normal attire for him, and I wouldn't think anything of it if his ex-wife wasn't standing in our kitchen.

"William, what the fuck are you doing here?"

"No bad words!" Hallie scolds as she props her hands on her hips and scowls at her aunt.

"Oh my God, are you *sleeping* with him?"

It's at that moment that Robert walks in, also shirtless, and comes up behind Bennett wrapping him in a hug, one arm around his waist as the other rests on his collarbone. The gesture is claiming, making their physical connection clear.

"They sleep together every night," Hallie explains, still proud of herself as I inwardly cringe. She's too young to understand the real connotation of what she's saying, and in her innocent brain, she thinks we're literally talking about sleeping.

"What did you do, Becka, go scoop up my sloppy seconds as soon as you could? I knew you were jealous of our relationship, but I never expected you to do this to me."

Of course she's going to play the victim.

"To you? What exactly did I do to you, Miranda? Robert and I fell in love with Bennett. You don't have to understand it or accept it, and I get how this may be hard for you, but you will not come into our home and act like this. We didn't do any of this on purpose, and we didn't do it to hurt you. I understand how finding out like this could be upsetting, but it wasn't our intention to deceive or hurt you. This is still new for us, and we're navigating it as best we can, especially when there are kids involved." I don't dare mention Miles. There's no telling what Miranda might do, and I won't let her ruin his life or prevent us from fostering him.

"Is that the bastard you blew up our marriage for?" Miranda spits, pointing at the little girl burrowing into my chest.

"The fu—"

"Daddy, language!" Hallie shouts over the rest of Robert's curse.

"What did you just say about my daughter?" Robert starts again as Bennett looks at him with tears in his eyes. This is the first time Robert has referred to Lexie as his daughter, and while I'd love to revel in the significance of this moment, it's been tainted by Miranda's hateful spewing.

Bennett turns in Robert's arms until they are chest to chest and holds Robert's face in his palms, forcing him to make eye contact with him. "Her words hold no weight in our peace, do you understand? She wants a reaction. Don't give her one," he soothes as he plants a quick kiss on Robert's lips.

There's no hesitation in Bennett's steps as he walks over to me and strokes his daughter's back. "You good, baby girl?" he asks. Lexie nods, her cheek pressed to my chest as she looks up at him. His eyes meet mine, concern for us evident on his face. "You want me to take her?"

Lexie shakes her head against me, her big, pink lips puckering as she pushes air through them. "Mahhh–mmmm–muhh–mah-ma," she says as she hugs me tighter, making it clear she's seeking comfort from me at this moment.

"Did she say Mama?" Robert beams as he pulls all three of us into a hug.

"I've been helping her," Hallie proclaims as she runs over, and Bennett picks her up. "We practice every night. She can say a lot of sounds."

"I'm so proud of both of you," I say, tears filling my eyes. "You're the best sister, Hallie-bear. And you're amazing, Lexie-bug," I say, kissing the top of Lexie's head.

"Um, hello, I'm still here!" Miranda yells with a stomp of her foot, as if we could forget about her unwelcome presence, but we're too lost in the gravity of the moment with our girls to pay attention to her.

"We're not going to do this here. Not now, and not in front of our daughters," Robert demands as he takes a step toward Miranda.

"What are you going to do about it, big man? You going to intimidate me with your size and physically remove me?"

"Jesus, Miranda, he took one step toward you to put himself between us and you. He's not threatening you," I say, wanting to make it clear that I'm not going to put up with her gaslighting bullshit or allow my daughters to think that her behavior is normal.

"I think you should leave. We can have a discussion when everyone is calm, but we're done here," Robert says, gesturing toward the front door.

"What makes you think I want to talk to any of you ever again?" she says before zeroing in on me. "You stole my husband, you homewrecking whore!"

"I know you didn't just say that to my wife," Robert seethes. "That isn't remotely how any of this played out, but if that's the lie you need to tell yourself, then blame me too. I'm in love with that man as much as she is."

"Whatever you all have going on here is fucked up. You can't be happy enough with each other, you have to steal other people's men too?"

"Mommy and Daddy didn't steal anything. They all love each other because love is love. You should leave us alone and go love someone else!" my sweet girl snaps back at her from Bennett's arms.

"You heard her. I'll see you out," Robert says as he walks over to the front door and opens it. Miranda reluctantly follows him as she realizes she has no allies in this house, her little huffs of exasperation following her as she goes.

"I'm so freaking proud of you, baby girl," Robert says to Hallie as he walks back into the kitchen.

"She was so mean, and you always say we should stand up to bullies and she was being a bully."

Bennett pulls Hallie into his chest and kisses her cheek. "I love you, Hallie-bear. Don't ever change."

CHAPTER 42

ROBERT

I nod at students as they pass me in the hall walking to class. Miles rounds the corner headed for my room, and I immediately know something is wrong when I see the scrunch of his eyebrows and the way his hands are balled into fists at his side. He's walking quickly, too quickly, like he's on the verge of running.

"You're probably just like him!" a kid I don't recognize shouts from behind him.

The kid doesn't see me standing in the alcove by my door as he continues shouting taunts. Miles makes eye contact with me, and I silently urge him to ignore it with a slight shake of my head.

One minute Miles is walking toward me, and the next, I see his arms flailing out to break his fall as the kid trips him. His books fly across the floor as he hits the ground hard. Before I can get there, the kid is straddling him, delivering blow after blow as Miles moves his hands up to his face attempting to block the assault.

"Hey. Hey!" I shout in my scary dad voice as I weave through students. Fear grips me. I'm not allowed to put a hand on either student to break it up. All I can do is use my words and my size to try to intimidate the kid beating the life out of Miles. "Break it up. Now."

More students are gathering around, their phones out recording everything, and now I definitely can't do anything unless I want it being used as evidence against me. I glance around taking a mental picture of the students I see recording so I know who to call as witnesses when I see Owen round the corner. "Owen, go get Officer Brady now! And tell the front office we've got a fight."

"Please stop!" Miles begs as the kid lands a blow to his nose and blood sprays everywhere.

"Get off him now!" my voice booms, but it does nothing as the kid lands another brutal punch to Miles's ribs.

"I knew you were a pansy like your so-called hero." The kid spits in Miles's face, his words and saliva landing their blows.

"You're not worth losing my future over," Miles grits out as he tries to block another punch to his face.

"How does it feel knowing your hero can't do anything to stop me because he's as pathetic as you?"

"Break this up now, both of you!" I bellow, but the kid's right. I legally can't do anything to stop this fight.

"Would if I could, bruh, but I'm kinda being held captive here," Miles groans.

My stomach turns as my thoughts drift. Miles's face disappears, replaced by my brother Michael's. Suddenly I can't breathe.

The kid leans in, whispering something in Miles's ear. Something I'll never repeat. It's cruel, relentless, wrong.

Shame and guilt flood my brain, the emotions momentarily paralyzing me as I watch the fight, helpless. I know, logically, that Michael's death wasn't my fault, that there wasn't anything I could've done. But the what-ifs haunt me to this day.

What if I'd gotten an apartment off-campus and taken him with me?

What if I'd put off college for a year and stayed behind?

What if I'd stood up to my parents?

What if I'd told him he wasn't alone?

What if I'd told him that I knew how he felt?

I may not have figured out my sexuality until my late thirties, but deep down I've always known that something was different about me. There are so many things I would have done differently if I'd known that the day I left for college was going to be the last time I ever saw my brother. He was only a boy, barely thirteen. I should've stood up for him with our family, our community. Maybe it would've changed the outcome. Maybe he would've known how loved he was.

How many kids watched Michael when his bullies beat him to death? Did anyone say anything to stop it? Did he have anyone fighting for him that day? Was there a teacher nearby who couldn't intervene?

Help him. Do something.

I may not have been able to help my brother back then, but I can help Miles now.

"That's enough. I can't lay hands on either of you, but I can't help it if another student does." I glance around the crowd and look at the shocked faces of several kids and make my plea. "I'm sure there's someone here that wants to step in and stop this. All it'd take is some brave students to restrain him. I know I could explain this to Principal Morris, and there are enough people who are already filming who could prove you were helping stop a fight."

A few students step forward right as Officer Brady comes running down the hall. He's able to restrain the kid, and I drop down to look over Miles. His nose is gushing blood.

"Can you sit up?"

Miles rolls to his side but winces as he attempts it.

"Does anyone have a tissue? Or a tampon?" I ask the

remaining students. "I need to stop the bleeding, and either would be helpful."

A girl tosses me a tampon, and I remove it from its package and pull off my shirt to wipe the blood so I can assess which side is worse before I gently plug his left nostril.

"Did you just take your shirt off?" Miles asks.

"Is that what you're worried about right now? I have an undershirt on, and I didn't like this shirt anyway." I say as I dab at his other nostril with the sleeve.

"Oh good, both of you are wearing shirts," Miles slurs as his body goes slack.

"Miles? Miles!" I grab his wrist and feel for a pulse. It's strong, but I'm still concerned about a possible concussion when I hear the squawk of a radio as an EMT rolls a stretcher down the hallway.

"He's not responsive, but he's got a pulse," I relay to the EMT as they check his vitals and load him onto the stretcher.

I step back and let them work when I hear Principal Morris's voice. "Mr. Gardner, will you follow me to my office?"

"You can check the cameras, I didn't touch either of them. I know the handbook says we can't," I say as I take a seat in Principal Morris's office. Adrenaline is still coursing through my body as I fidget.

"Mr. Gardner, I'm Detective Ambrose. We'd like to collect a statement from you about what happened. Can you start at the beginning?" says the officer to the left of Principal Morris.

"Sure. I saw Miles coming down the hall and I knew something was wrong, and then I noticed this kid following him. I don't know that student's name, sorry. He was using homophobic slurs toward Miles, and then he tripped him and started pummeling him in the middle of the hallway. The kid had Miles pinned down and he was laying into him, and I know we can't stop an altercation between students by physical means, but I kept shouting at them to stop and he wouldn't. Michael was lying there, trying to block the blows, he wasn't fighting back. And there were tons of students filming it on their phones."

"Who's Michael?"

"What?" I look at him, confused.

"You said Michael, did you mean Miles?"

Shit, get it together, man. "Oh, yeah, I meant Miles."

"Got it. Continue," he urges.

"The kid kept punching, and there was nothing Miles could do with the way he was pinned. At one point the kid busted his nose and spit on him. And he kept saying the most vile things."

"Like what?"

I take a deep breath and blow it out slowly, nervous to share for fear of outing myself, but they're going to see it on someone's phone at some point, so I might as well. "He kept shouting slurs and implied that Miles was just like me and that I couldn't do anything to stop them."

"You?"

"Miles was standing up for me. He came to me a few weeks ago and let me know that there were students speculating about my sexuality. Miles told them off. On his own," I clarify. "I didn't ask him to say anything. Apparently, this kid has been running his mouth about me and trying to goad Miles into a reaction. That's what it looked like in the hallway today, and when the kid didn't get the reaction he wanted, he got physical. Miles was taking the high road. He told me he's walked away every time, and I can assure you, he was walking away from the kid today. That fight was one-sided."

"I see. Is that all?"

"I think so. Do you know what's going to happen to Miles? I know he's been in trouble in the past and has been moved around to a lot of different foster homes. He was worried that one more incident would result in him getting kicked out of his current home."

"I'm not sure, but there should be a social worker assigned to his case that you could follow up with," the officer responds.

"Thank you," I say as I stand and shake his hand.

"If you think of anything else, here's my card. Feel free to reach out."

"I will," I promise.

The officer leaves the room, and Principal Morris turns to me. "Robert, we still need to talk."

Returning to my seat, I look at him and have trouble deciphering his icy gaze. We sit there in a silent stare-off, and I'm determined not to speak first, aware that I don't owe him an explanation beyond what I shared with the officer.

"Are you okay?" he finally asks.

I lose it, sobs bursting from my chest as the tears spill down my cheeks. He walks over and rests a hand on my shoulder, patting it gently.

"My brother Michael was beaten to death by a bully at school. I wasn't there when it happened, but I think my mind disassociated for a minute there, because I swear, I was watching that kid beat up Michael. And I couldn't... I couldn't save him. And this time it was my fault. That kid went after Miles because of me. Miles was standing up for me. And I couldn't stop it. There was nothing I could do but watch. And I thought he was going to..." I break off, fighting for control of my emotions.

Once I take a few deep breaths, I look up at him and see concern etched on his features. "What's going to happen to him? Is he going to be okay?" I ask, wiping my face.

"Robert, there's something I need to talk to you about first," he says, his tone brooking no argument. Shit. Did I break a rule? The police are gone, so I'm not in that kind of trouble, but based on the look on his face, I may be risking losing my job here.

He walks around his desk and sits in his chair as he addresses me. "Right before the fight broke out, that student Tyler, the one that started the fight, was in the office between classes looking for something in the lost and found. He was in there when a woman walked in demanding to speak to the principal about you."

"Me?" I ask, trying to wrack my brain for who could possibly come up here wanting to talk about me.

"Yes, you. I was stepping out of my office because of all the commotion when she went on a profanity-filled, homophobic tirade about you. Said you were sleeping with her husband among a slew of other accusations."

That fucking bitch.

"What all did she say?" I ask, as my stomach does flips that would rival a gold medal gymnast.

"I don't care to repeat it, honestly. But Tyler was particularly interested, and he took off running. I suspect that's when he went after Miles and the fight broke out."

I pull out my phone and look up her social media profile for a picture. "Is this the woman?"

"That's her," he confirms.

"I'm not sleeping with her husband—well, that's not entirely true, but they're not married. I—"

"I don't need the details. What you do in your home is none of my business. I care about this school and my students, and keeping them safe, but when your personal life comes into my school causing one of my students to become severely injured, it *is* my business. I was able to coax her into my office and placate her until the police arrived. They asked her to leave the premises and attempted to escort her to her car, but she became belligerent. She ended up smacking the police officer and refused to comply when he placed her under arrest for assaulting an officer. She could be facing charges of some sort. And her earlier actions indirectly caused harm to a student. Either way, I spoke with the officer about a possible restraining order to keep her off school grounds."

"That's an excellent idea. I'm so sorry. I had no idea she'd do that, and I'll never forgive myself for what happened to Miles because of me."

"I want to be clear that this isn't your fault, Robert. You can't control what that woman did, any more than you could control Tyler's actions toward Miles. And I don't care who you love or what color you represent on a pride flag. You're one of our best teachers, and you've built an amazing program here. But I strongly advise you to do everything you can to make sure any personal drama you have doesn't end up in my building again."

"Yes, sir."

"I know you care deeply for your students, and I'm not sure if I'm supposed to share this or not, but if you're looking for Miles, he's at Nationwide Children's Hospital. And I think you should take some time off and check in with someone about your mental health. You went through a lot today, and it sounds like it triggered some underlying trauma you may have."

"Am I being suspended?" I ask, unsure what he's implying.

"Heavens, no. I can pull some paid time off for you to take a mental health break. Let me know if two weeks is enough. I just want you back healthy and ready to give your best to our students, and if you're worrying about Miles, you aren't going to be doing us any good here," he says warmly.

"Thank you," I say as we shake hands, and I leave his office determined to get home to let Becka know what's going on so I can check on my boy.

CHAPTER 43

BECKA

I'm wrapping up a phone call with a customer as Robert bursts through the front door three hours before he's due home. I know something's wrong the minute I see his face, and I send my manager a message letting her know I'm logging off for my lunch a little early.

"Robert, what is it, what's wrong?" I ask, running over to him at the door. He's still gripping the handle, seemingly frozen in place. I gingerly run my fingers along his arm, and he snaps out of his trance, pulling me forcefully against him.

"It's all my fucking fault. I pissed her off and she came to the school, probably trying to get revenge and get me fired, not realizing that Tyler would hear her and go after Miles."

"You pissed someone off? Who's Tyler, and what happened to Miles?"

"Miranda came to the school, shouting obscenities and homophobic slurs, demanding to speak to my principal."

I push back against his chest to look in his face, unsure I'm hearing him correctly. "Miranda did *what*?"

"I think she was mad about me getting in her face when she showed up here the other day."

"You did not get in her face. You took a step toward her and showed her to the front door so she would leave."

"But that has to be the reason why she went after me," he says weakly, a glassy look in his eyes.

"She went after you to hurt me. Because she thinks you're my weakness."

"He's hurt, baby. He's hurt, and it's my fault. And I couldn't do a fucking thing," he says through sobs as he breaks down in my arms.

"Who?"

"Miles," he croaks out.

"What? What happened?"

"This kid Tyler has been bullying Miles about me. Apparently, he saw me and Bennett at the zoo, and he started telling people I'm gay. Miles stood up to him, and the kid's been tormenting him since. He was in the office when Miranda showed up, heard her call me gay, and took off for Miles. I watched as he beat the shit out of Miles, and I couldn't lay a hand on either of them to stop it," he says through gritted teeth, his tone full of restrained rage.

"Holy shit. Is Miles okay?"

"He's at Children's. I need to go see him. I need to know he's okay."

Reaching up, I grab his face, holding on to his cheeks as I force him to look at me. "Baby, this isn't your fault. Do not blame yourself for this. I know Miles doesn't. That kid loves you."

He nods against my hand, sniffling as tears run down his face.

"For a split second, in the middle of the fight, I thought it was Michael."

"What?"

"I couldn't stop picturing Michael. That's where my brain went. And I kept thinking that I wasn't there for Michael and

312

because I couldn't stop the fight, I wasn't there for Miles either," he rasps, heartache evident in his words.

"You can be there for him now. Go be with our boy. Head there and let me know how he is, okay?"

He nods, pulling me into another tight hug before he turns and walks back out the door. I watch as he stalks toward his car. His normally imposing form seeming small and defeated. I've never seen him so broken, so crestfallen.

An hour after he leaves, my phone rings. The girls haven't gotten home from school yet, but I answer it without looking, hoping it's an update from Robert on Miles.

"Oh good, you answered. Look, I'm down at the station and I need someone to bail me out," a familiar voice says.

I pull the phone away from my ear to look at the number calling, but I don't recognize it.

"Hello!" the voice says in an annoyed tone.

"I'm sorry, who is this?" I say, squeezing my fist, willing my wildly beating heart to calm itself.

"Umm, who else would it be? It's your sister," Miranda shouts.

"I don't have a sister, you must have the wrong number," I say as calmly as I can.

"Becka, stop fucking around and come bail me out. It's your fault I'm here to begin with."

"I'll repeat, because clearly you aren't hearing me. I. Don't. Have. A. Sister. A sister is someone who loves you no matter what. Who doesn't try to destroy your life or blame you for everything that goes wrong in theirs. A sister doesn't say hurtful things to you every time you see her. A sister doesn't barge into your house calling your children vile names. And a sister doesn't go to your husband's job trying to out him and get him fired because that sister doesn't agree with who they love. I don't have a sister, but there is a person who did all those things, and I'm done wasting any more of my time on her. Now if you'll excuse me, a former family member of mine caused one of my children to be beaten within an inch of his life, and I'm waiting on a more important call with an update."

"Are you kidding me? This is my only fucking phone call, Becka. Get your ass down here and bail me out. What the hell am I supposed to do?" she wails as I end the call, not caring if those are the last words I ever hear her utter to me.

Bennett

"I GOT HERE AS FAST AS I COULD," I SAY, FINDING ROBERT IN THE waiting room and pulling him into a hug, before I remember we're in public and start to pull back. "Shit, sorry, no PDA."

Robert pulls me in tighter, one hand clasped around the back of my neck, the other resting on the small of my back. "I don't give a shit about that right now," he says as a shudder of relief passes through him and his woodsy scent washes over me.

"Becka filled me in. She's got the girls. What's going on with our boy?" I ask, my lips grazing the fabric on his shoulder as he holds me.

"I couldn't stop it," he says as a sob wracks his body. "This kid had him pinned, beating the shit out of him, and I couldn't do anything. I couldn't lay a hand on either of them. If I did, we could've lost the progress we've made to be his new family. Anyone could've pressed charges if I tried to pull them off each other. But there was blood everywhere and when the officer detained the kid, Miles was conscious, but I couldn't stop the bleeding and then he passed out. What if he isn't okay? He has to be okay." His breathing is erratic, and it feels like he's on the verge of a panic attack.

"He's going to be okay. You did everything you could in an impossible situation. You did so good, baby," I say, the nickname slipping out as I maneuver him into a chair. There's more to this than he's letting on, but I need him to calm down.

"He was talking to me one minute, and then he went limp. What if he has a concussion? What if there's brain damage or internal bleeding? What if there's too much blood loss? What blood type is he? I can give blood. He needs to be okay. I couldn't save Michael, but I will save Miles. I need to fix this. How do I fix this? I have to save him. I can't lose him," he babbles.

"B, you did everything in your power, I know you did," I say, taking his face in my hands. "I'm so fucking proud of you, and I know Michael would be too. Miles is going to be okay because of you." I will the words to be true.

"His foster family isn't even fucking here. Apparently, they've been out of town for the past week and he's been on his own. The school couldn't get a hold of them."

"What the fuck? How can they do that?" I ask incredulously.

"They can't. It means that Miles will no longer be in their placement. The social worker and I were talking when the nurse pulled her away. I don't know if it was about Miles or not, but I want to talk to her about getting him placed in our home. You've already done all the paperwork and training, and they've done a home visit and seen the new house. I've got to get him out of there."

"We will," I promise.

There's a flurry of movement behind us as a nurse approaches. "Mr. Emerson?"

"Yes, that's me," I say, standing as Robert clutches my hand tightly in his. I revel in the warmth of his palm and squeeze my strength into his as we brace for the update.

"I spoke with Miles's case worker. She got called away on another case with an infant, but she explained that Miles will be in your care once he's discharged. I'm sure she'll be by later to work out the details when she can."

We both let out sighs of relief as his grip on my hand tightens. I squeeze it three times to silently let him know I love him.

"Is he okay? Can we see him?" I ask.

"Miles has three broken ribs, a broken nose, and a concussion. He's going to need surgery on his nose to repair the nasal septum. The break was bad enough to affect his breathing. The surgery should only last about one to two hours. We'll keep him overnight to monitor him, but he should be able to go home tomorrow."

"Can he have surgery with a concussion?" Roberts asks, concern lacing his voice.

"It's a mild concussion, and it's safe for him to undergo surgery and anesthesia."

"Is there anything we need to know?" I ask.

"The case worker will share more details with you, but he won't be able to return to school for a few weeks or longer. He will need a lot of rest after the surgery and will need to limit physical activities, as well as activities that require concentration while he's healing from the concussion. No video games, watching TV, or reading."

"That's okay, one of us can stay home with him," Robert says.

"He's going to be in a bit of pain those first few days from the surgery and the broken ribs."

"His birth mother has a history of drug abuse. Is that in his chart? Is there anything we need to do for pain management? I know we can't make medical decisions and that he's just in our care, but I want to make sure he's okay," Robert adds.

"His case worker will follow up with Mr. Emerson with those details, but from what I can tell, he's going to be fine. I've seen a lot of kids in foster care come through here, and I've never seen foster parents this concerned or involved. That tells me that he's going to get everything he needs to have a successful recovery," the nurse says to me with a warm smile before she hurries off.

I tug on Robert's hand, sliding my other hand up his cheek. "He's going to be okay. We're going to make sure of it." He nods and pulls me toward him, resting his forehead against mine. At soon as he touches me, my breathing slows and my heartbeat calms. These people are imbedded so thoroughly in my heart, I can't wait to move them into my home.

CHAPTER 44
ROBERT

I t's another three hours before we're allowed back to see Miles. There's still a lot of red tape as we work with the social worker to make sure Bennett has everything he needs to allow Miles to go home with him tomorrow. I also reached out to Principal Morris to make sure it was okay for me to live with Miles and was thrilled to confirm that there wasn't anything in the code of conduct preventing it.

We let the girls know, and they're packing enough stuff for all of us to get through a week at Bennett's house before the moving company can bring the rest of our belongings. Luckily, most of the house is already fully furnished, and Miles will have his own room, which is the most important part.

Miles is sleeping when we walk in his hospital room, and I pull a chair next to his bed so I can sit closer to him.

"Hey, Miles. It's Mr. G and Bennett," I say, squeezing his hand.

He groans and shifts his head slightly.

"The entire starting line of the Cobras is here too," Bennett says from behind me as I shake my head.

"You're so full of shit, dude," Miles croaks out without

opening his eyes. His voice sounds different with all the tape and packing around his nose.

"Language," I warn.

"Why? The girls aren't here," Miles says softly.

"You didn't know that," I say.

"If Hallie was here, she'd be talking to every nurse about pigeons or trying to get them to have a tea party. And if Lexie was here, she'd be tucked against my side until she knew I was okay."

Well fuck, if that doesn't punch me right in the feels.

"The girls are with Bex, and they're packing," Bennett confirms.

"Why are they packing?" he asks, shifting around in the bed, wincing as he tries to get comfortable.

"That's what we wanted to talk to you about," I say. "You sustained some serious injuries. They had to do surgery to fix your nose, and you've got a few broken ribs and a concussion."

"You should see the other guy," Miles jokes, grimacing when he tries to laugh. "When's my warden getting here to haul me back to jail? I should probably swipe some toilet paper from here before I go."

"Miles, you aren't going back to that family. You're coming home with us," I say, squeezing his hand gently.

His eyes shoot open as they search around, finally connecting with mine. He must see the sincerity in my eyes as his fill with tears.

"Are you serious? I'm coming to your house?"

Bennett steps forward, clapping a hand on my shoulder as he addresses Miles. "Actually, all of us are moving into my house. It's in the same school district, but it's a little bigger and you'll have your own room."

"Bennett is going to be your new foster father, and since we're all together, that means you'll be part of our family," I say, looking between them. It feels so good to say out loud, to own it and claim it, not because of a rumor or fight, but because I choose to share it. Bennett runs his hand up and down my back, and I smile at him at the gesture.

"Robert told me what happened, not only today, but how you stood up for him, for us and our family. Even if you only had your suspicions, you were an ally for us, and it means a lot."

A small smile lights up Miles's face. "I knew it. Mr. G wasn't as grumpy this year, and as soon as I met you at family dinner, I knew it was because of you," he wheezes out.

I can tell he's in a bit of pain. "We can talk later, don't wear yourself out. Get some rest. I'm going to spend the night here, and Bennett and I will swap places in the morning."

———————

When Miles walks into his new bedroom the following day, there's a giant tower of toilet paper packages in the corner beside the door to his bathroom.

"That should last you till graduation," Bennett teases.

"Have you seen how this kid eats? That'll last him a week." I laugh as Miles turns to hug Bennett, who's careful not to squeeze him too hard.

"I don't know how to thank you," Miles says against Bennett's shoulder. "I'm going to make you proud. You won't regret this. I won't screw this up."

Bennett pulls back, looking him in the eyes, "Odds are, that's not true. You will screw up. That's part of growing up. But you're one of us now, part of this family, and we'll be here to help you and support you."

"And love you," I add. "You may be a real pain in my ass sometimes, but you're a son to me, Miles, and if you want us to make that official, we will."

He turns and looks at me, tears welling in his eyes, and I know the moment he sees it.

"Holy shit, is that a green screen setup?"

"Language," Hallie says, walking into the room.

"It is," I confirm. "There's a desk over there with everything you need to edit," I say, pointing to the corner of the room.

Bennett chuckles. "You only saw the toilet paper, huh?"

"We're going to make our own Pajama Pigeon movies, right?" Hallie asks him with big puppy dog eyes.

"I'll make any movies you want," Miles agrees as she hugs his waist.

"Careful, Halligator, he's got some ouchies in his body that will need a few weeks to heal, so we need to be gentle," I warn.

"Then we make the movies?" she asks, flashing her big eyes again.

"I promise," Miles says.

"C'mon, Hallie-bear, let's let big brother get his rest, okay?" Bennett says, scooping her up and leaving.

I help Miles to the bed, and once he's settled in, I turn to look at him from the door. "I'm serious about what I said before. If you want to make this official, either one of us will adopt you."

"Why are you so obsessed with me?" he teases before sobering. "It'd be kinda cool to share the same name."

"Anything for you, kid," I say, leaving the room to let him rest.

"Daddy, I have a question," Hallie says, catching me in the hall.

"What is it, baby girl?"

"Benny-bear said that Miles is my big brother, and Mommy said Lexie is my sister. But how will people know we're brothers and sisters if we have different last names?"

Her words and Miles's echo in my head as an idea begins to form. While a marriage between three people may not be legal in Ohio, we can make a commitment to prove that this is a permanent arrangement. And since Becka and I are already legally married, changing our last name to Bennett's would be the ultimate commitment to him, and would allow all our kids to have the same last name if Bennett adopts Miles.

I bend down and scoop her into my arms. "I have an idea, but we need to talk to Mommy first."

"So, I just got off the phone with my mom, and I'm thinking this non-contact thing you've got going with your mom is a good idea," I say, pinching the bridge of my nose as I blow out a frustrated breath.

"She didn't take it well, I'm guessing?" Bennett asks.

"We're an abomination in her eyes, or her church's eyes, I don't really give a fuck. Oh, and she kept talking about marriage vows and how sacred they are and how dare we break them when we made a commitment in front of God," I say, rolling my eyes.

"Now we know where you get it from," Bennett teases, slapping my ass as he passes me on the way to the fridge.

"I wasn't making a vow to God. I wrote vows for the love of my life, a set of rules that *we* created to live by. I made a commitment to put her first. And technically I did break a lot of the vows," I say.

"All our broken vows don't mean shit. We can make new ones. This is what matters. This. The three of us, Miles, and the girls. And I'll stand in front of anyone, legal or not, and make new vows to you both. You're the family I was meant to have. The family our kids deserve. They're thriving and living the life with each other they always wanted. They have the relationship I never had with my sister because they got to choose each other. Miles got to choose the father he always deserved. And I don't care what anyone outside of this house thinks about our relationship. Our kids deserve the best versions of us, and you both make me a better person. You bring out the best in each other. I've never seen either one of you more at peace than I have in the past few months. You deserve this. We deserve this, and so do our kids," Becka says fiercely as I pull her against me, kissing her forehead three times. "Do you remember what my last vow was to you?"

"I vow to love you, who you are, who you will become, and the family we build together," I say as she leans back to look at me.

"This is who you are, who we've become, and the family we've built. And I love you, both of you," she says, pulling Bennett into our embrace.

"We couldn't do this without you, Bex," Bennett says, wrapping his arms around us both.

"We love you, baby," I say, pulling her face to mine as I kiss her. When I pull back, Bennett swoops in and does the same. I watch as he slips his tongue in, kissing her harder. "Everything doesn't have to be a competition, Bennett," I grumble.

"Speak for yourself." Becka laughs. "I'll let you two duke it out over me once the kids go to bed." She winks as Bennett pulls my face toward his planting a wet, sloppy kiss on my cheek.

"Here you go, B. Now we're even," he teases, licking my cheek the same way he was kissing Becka's mouth a second ago.

I love these two people, and I'll happily spend the rest of my life shouting it to the world.

CHAPTER 45

BENNETT

It's been a few weeks since Miles was discharged, and his injuries are healing nicely, though it's been hard to keep a teenage boy still. It was worse the first week he was home when he couldn't read or play video games due to the concussion.

The house is unusually quiet for a Saturday morning as I walk into the kitchen to make my coffee, but instead of the full pot that's normally waiting for me, there's a note.

> *Bennett,*
> *At the park with the kids, meet me at the court when you see this. It's been too long since we've played hoops.*
> *-B*

What used to be a ten-minute drive from Robert's house is a five-minute walk from mine. I jog through the parking lot and smile to myself as I watch Robert taking shots at the basket.

He smiles as I approach, rebounding the ball before passing

it to me. But he overshoots and it bounces over my head as I run after it. I catch it before it hits the metal fence, and when I turn around, he's down on one knee with a ring pinched between his fingers.

"What are you doing?" I ask in shock, looking around, when Becka's hand grips my shoulder, and the girls walk up with Miles.

"William Bennett Emerson the third, you're my best friend, and one of the loves of my life. I love you, more than I know how to express with words. Will you become a permanent part of our family and marry us?" he asks, extending the ring.

"Yes. Yes, I'll marry you," I rasp as he stands and pulls me into a kiss. It's brief, but when he pulls away, I stand there in shock. "But you hate PDA."

"I don't mind it with the right people," he says, kissing my forehead three times.

A throat clears behind me, and when I turn, Hallie is on her knees. "Benny-bear, you're silly and make me laugh, and I want you to live with us and make my mommy and daddy happy forever," she says, holding up a friendship bracelet. Lexie grabs my hand, squeezing it once for yes, holding up another bracelet. Hers says "Lexie bug" and Hallie's says "Hallie bear." I take both bracelets, sliding them on my wrist.

"I promise to make Mommy and Daddy happy forever," I say as I bend down and hug them both.

"Mmmaaaah... mmmuh... daaaaah... daaaaah... buhh-hhh... beeeee," Lexie says.

Tears slip down my cheeks. "That's so good. You did so good, bug," I say, pulling her into a tight hug.

"I'm not good at this sappy sh— stuff, so thanks for making me part of this," Miles says, handing me a bracelet, and I chuckle, realizing they're all in on this.

I look at him, confused. "It says 'Ward' with a bunch of numbers after it."

"I'll change it once I get my own nickname," he says, flashing his signature smile.

"Got room for some more jewelry?" Becka's warm voice purrs near my ear as I turn to her. And my dick twitches a little in my joggers, thinking about her playing with some different jewelry on my body.

"I'll take any jewelry you want to give me," I say with a subtle wink.

"Bennett, you were the missing piece that was needed for us to feel whole as a family. Your warmth, your humor, your heart. You're everything we need, and if it weren't for you, the six of us wouldn't be standing here now asking you to marry us. And until the day comes when we can all legally marry, we want to write new vows and make a new commitment with you. Will you do that with us?"

"Yes, I will make any vow you need me to make," I say, looking around our little circle, "I love each and every one of you."

She slides the simple band onto my finger next to Robert's ring, and I pull her into a quick kiss.

"Can I say it now?" Hallie begs.

"Go ahead, Halligator," Robert says.

"And the best part is we're changing our names so we can all have the same one," Hallie squeals as she pulls Lexie into a hug.

"Just our last names," Bex says into my ear. "We're going to be the Emersons from now on."

Emotion clogs my throat, more tears spilling down my cheeks. "Really?"

"Really," Robert confirms.

Hallie hugs my waist, and I bend down to wrap her in a hug as she whispers in my ear, "It's like the Pajama Pigeon. We found our family, and I'm glad you're mine."

If you'd told me last year that my family would've tripled

in size and that I'd be part of a thriving throuple, I'd never have believed you. But these are my people, my home, and I'd do anything, make any vow, to keep them happy.

EPILOGUE

BENNETT

It took six months for us to plan a commitment ceremony. Becka was originally insistent that it had to be on the seventh of a month, since we were all born on the seventh and their original anniversary was on the seventh. When Robert pointed out that all the kids—even Miles—have birthdays on the eighth of the month, we agreed on the eighth of August, the day after my birthday. And a week before my adoption of Miles is official.

There aren't a lot of people gathered with us today. We kept it small on purpose. We decided not to have bridesmaids or groomsmen and opted to have my mother officiate. We didn't invite any of Becka's former family members, and Robert's parents didn't respond to our invitation, but his siblings showed up for us, along with my siblings and parents, and Bridget and Ethan. There's even a seat saved for Michael next to them.

We opted to get married in the park near our house and the guests' chairs are arranged in a circle around us. Once Lexie and Hallie finish running around the circle, spreading rose petals, they take their seats next to Miles, Lexie leaning into his side. The three of us stand in the center facing my mom, Bex between us with each of our arms wrapped around her waist, as Robert and I join our free hands in front of her, hers resting atop them. She looks gorgeous in a deep purple wrap dress, and I can't help but stare at her as the breeze whips around strands of her chestnut locks. The girls insisted we all wear purple since it's Lexie's favorite color, and Bex looks radiant in it.

I look over at Robert, and he breaks his gaze on Bex to hold mine, giving me a rare smile with teeth. Fuck, he's the most handsome man on the planet when he smiles at me like that.

"We're gathered here today to celebrate the love of these three beautiful people, Becka, Bennett, and Robert. And while the state of Ohio may not legally recognize it, these three are making a commitment today to each other, in front of their friends and family, to walk a path together, choosing each other daily, practicing forgiveness and devotion. I raised my kids to build communities, and that's exactly what these three have done. Just like birds build nests, and spiders weave webs, these three have created something bigger than themselves, creating a foundation for their family to thrive," my mom says as a tear rolls down my cheek and Robert reaches over to swipe at it.

"If you're here today, it's because these three chose you to bear witness to their vows as they make a commitment to each other. You're important to them and the journey they're embarking on. Love is a concept that lives in our hearts, and while marriage may be an outward expression of that love on paper, true joining and commitment comes from within. It draws upon the depths of our being, connecting our hearts and souls, born out of loving one another, caring for others before ourselves, and sharing who we are at our core. I've never witnessed a love like these three have. It's beautiful and powerful, blessed by each of you here today who support it.

At this time, I'd like to invite Becka, Bennett, and Robert to share the vows they've written for each other," Mom says, taking a small step back. She nods at me to go ahead.

I turn to my partners, holding each of their hands in mine as I speak. "I vow to share all of myself with you, all the sunshine your raincloud could ever need, and all the light and warmth you both deserve. I vow to be the best partner and father that I can, showing up for you all every day. And I vow to choose this family over everything else. You're the most important thing in my life, and I love each and every one of you more than my words could ever convey," I say, making eye contact with Robert and Becka, and each of our children on the last part.

"I'd like to go next," Robert says, as Bex and I both nod our agreement. "Everyone here knows how important these vows have been in my life. So, I vow to be more flexible with my vows, because I don't want to write any more ever again." There are a few chuckles around the circle as he continues. "I choose the two of you and your happiness over all others, and I choose our kids, the family we've made, and the future we create together. I vow to prioritize our family first. I vow to give you all of myself, my grumpiness, my humor, my truths, my sandwiches"—he directs the last part at Miles—"my complicated emotions, my love, everything that I am, every day for as long as any one of us is alive. I know that's dark, but that's who I am, your grumpy little storm cloud, keeping it real. And I know with certainty that I will love you both until my dying day."

"Great, now you both made me cry," Bex says with a smile as Robert and I each reach up to wipe her tears. "I vow to be honest with both of you, to share how I feel, and to honor your feelings. I vow to live fully, love boldly, and laugh loudly and often. Even if I'm getting double the dad jokes. I vow to cherish this life and this family we've built together. I vow to keep this family we've created at the center of my heart, protecting it, nurturing it, and loving it. To know that I'm enough, that I have a place in it, as do each of us, and know that we're stronger together as we each bring something unique to the table. I love you so much," she says as her voice cracks. She nods to my mom that she's done.

"With these vows, the three of you are committing to choose love. And since you've already exchanged rings, we'll move on to the declarations. Becka, do you take these men to be your lifelong partners?"

"I do," she says, her eyes bouncing between both of us.

"Robert, do you take this woman and this man to be your lifelong partners?"

"Fuck yeah, I do."

"Daddy, language," Hallie interrupts as everyone laughs.

"Sorry, Halapeno. I do," he corrects.

"And, Bennett, do you take this man and this woman to be your lifelong partners?"

"I do," I say, looking at each of them, seeing the love I have for them reflected in their eyes.

"And with that, and all the love in my heart, I now pronounce you husbands and wife. You may kiss your partners," she says as I hear our little girls cheer.

Robert and I nod at each other and grab Becka's face, each of us planting kisses on her cheeks before he pulls my lips to his. It's short, yet full of passion as he pulls back, and leans into Becka, kissing her fiercely, before she pulls back and presses her lips to mine.

"I can't wait to fuck my wife and my husband later," I say quietly so only they can hear and the responding blush on both of their cheeks makes my dick twitch in my suit.

It's been a few weeks since we got back from our honeymoon, and we're trying to soak in the last few bits of summer before the leaves turn and pumpkins start popping up everywhere.

"Dada! Dada! Wooka me!" Lexie yells at me from the swings, wanting my attention as she and Hallie compete to see who can swing higher. I never thought I'd ever see the day that my little girl screamed my name from across the playground, and it's a sound I'll never get tired of hearing. While she's still far behind her peers, her vocabulary is growing every day. And it tickles me pink to see our girls share the same competitive streak their daddies do.

"I'm so proud of you, bug!" I call as Robert stretches his arm around my shoulder.

I lean into his touch. "PDA on a random Sunday, Mr. Emerson? What did I do to deserve such royal treatment?" I say, snuggling into him. It's still surreal that we all share the last name, and that I get to call this man my husband.

"Yo, G, look at what I found!" Miles calls out as he runs toward us with a skateboard in hand.

"I told you to stop calling me that." Robert furrows his brow, trying to appear sterner than he is. "I can't keep up with all the letters, first I'm B, then I'm G, but not Mr. G anymore. And don't start calling me Mr. E. There's two of us now, and that'll get confusing."

"I told you I'm not calling you Daddy like the girls do," Miles teases. "What about Pops?"

He considers it. "It's not a letter, so I'll allow it. Now, what have you got there? I hope you're not trying to end up back in the hospital."

"I found it by the ramps. Someone must have left it. I figured I'd run home and grab my camera, and then I could use this like a makeshift dolly and get some cool B-roll shots."

"That's not a bad idea," Robert says.

Miles takes off in the direction of the house, and I turn to Robert.

"I found out today that he didn't get that internship with the Cobras," I tell him.

"I thought he wasn't supposed to find out until closer to graduation. He's gonna be so crushed," Robert says.

"Not when he finds out that he's being offered a job on their video production team. With the season starting soon, they're looking for another camera guy and were impressed with his demo reel."

Robert leaps off the bench, jumping in front of me as he grabs my arms. "Are you serious?"

"Yup. It'll be part time while he's in school, but come next season, he'll have a full-time position with them."

He pumps a fist in the air, and I chuckle at his excitement.

"And don't worry, Bryson can keep an eye on him and make sure he stays out of trouble."

"Maybe we don't have the puck bunny chaser acting as a role model for our son," Robert jokes.

"Good call. When is Becka done with book club?" I ask as Robert checks his phone.

"She's normally only gone for a couple hours, but Bridget was joining her along with some of Ethan's sisters. Emma and Ella, I think? She said that there was a girl crisis they needed to solve, and they were going to head back to Bridget's after for drinks, so I don't think we'll see her till late tonight. One of us may need to pick her up."

"Wanna shoot some hoops, maybe teach the girls how to play?" I ask.

"That's a great idea," he says, leaning over to kiss my fore-head three times. And that's exactly what we do, teach our girls how to play the sport that bonded us together as Miles scoots around us filming.

Our life is still chaotic, and some days it feels like we're all pulled in different directions, but there's nowhere else I'd rather be, than with this family we built.

THE END

Not ready to say goodbye to Becka, Robert, and Bennett?
Download the bonus scene here to find out what went down
on their honeymoon:
https://dl.bookfunnel.com/6kiszwc3z2

ACKNOWLEDGMENTS

Sarah, my amazing editor, my books wouldn't exist without you. Thank you for taking the lump of clay I plop in front of you and helping me shape it into something beautiful. I look forward to reading your thoughts each time I turn in a manuscript, and our zoom sessions give me life!

This book was a joy to write. I could live in this throuple's world forever! What made it easy was hearing your voice in my head, Rose. Every time Becka laughs, I hear your laugh. I am forever grateful that Romancelandia brought you back into my life. Your joy, your friendship, your smile brought me comfort during a difficult time and I cannot thank you enough. I look forward to all the magic we make together!

Amanda, thank you for being the first person to read my books. You see them at their rawest and messiest and still love them, and it means everything to me. I love how excited you get about these characters and this world, and your excitement keeps me going.

I love how much you love these characters, Bianca. Thank you for loving Robert so much, and for all the inspo pics and videos every time you find a new Robert! And I can't wait to read all the stories you create!

Layla, you can do it. I know you will get this far. Haha, I love you! Thank you for the laughs, the support, the reminders to keep my voice down when hot servers walk by our table. I'm at a ten!

Thank you to all of my beta readers. Amanda, Bianca, Hannah, Angelica, Stacey, and Hannah G. Your feedback and enthusiasm means the world to me. I appreciate every note, every comment, every reaction you share with me. You helped me shape this story into what it is and I appreciate you!

Indie publishing isn't easy. It's a complicated process and I constantly feel like I'm forgetting a step or doing it wrong. But there are several authors who have helped me as I navigate the journey, letting me pick their brains, pepper them with questions, or just vent about a character giving me trouble. Thank you Abby, Adrian, Berlin, Emme, Jenni, and Liz. You all write wonderful books and are incredible woman I admire!

Shell, thank you for being nothing like Miranda. We may live thousands of miles apart, and I know you hate talking on the phone, but I love you so much, seeeeeeester.

KT, I had to throw in a reference to our favorite movie and show. Thank you for letting me pick your brain for my next story. Our friendship has endured and I'm thankful you still put up with my perverted antics. Who can say they're still besties with their high school bff? We can!

Heather, I hope you made it this far and that I didn't traumatize you too much! I promise you'll enjoy the next one. And so will meatpie.

Sandy, I'm sorry there still weren't any dragons, but there were plenty of birds. And plenty of dicks! I think Jean needs more batteries; you should send her some.

Keep those cover models coming, Jean. You can send me hot guy pics all day. Maybe I'll do a writing retreat in Hawaii, and you can help me find some Hula men for inspiration. Make sure you send Sandy some batteries! Mahalo!

Because I promised him that I would give him credit, but refuse to put his name on a smutty novel, thank you to my youngest for your help with Pajama Pigeon. Little do you know your antics in kindergarten were the inspiration for that scene. Your ideas were very insightful, giving the reader a villain to root against and conflict for our heroes to overcome. And I will never get tired of doing all the voices and noises when I read you a story, even if you are into chapter books now.

To the love of my life, my ultimate book boyfriend and the grump to my sunshine. Thank you for holding down the fort, for feeding the gremlins, and making sure I eat as well. You are my best friend and I love you and the family we've built. There isn't another soul I'd want to be mated with for life. I love you, grumpy bear.

ALSO BY MYA MORE

The Broken Series

All Her Broken Pieces

Bridget and Ethan's story. An age gap (she's older), forced proximity, black cat/golden retriever spicy romance.

All Our Broken Vows

Becka, Robert, and Bennett's story. An MMF, bi-awakening romance with found family, a single dad, and friends that become so much more.

All His Broken Rules

Emma & John's story. A forbidden professor student romance.

All Their Broken Promises

Coming 2026

The Chestnut Mountain Series

The Santa Rules

A holiday rom com with a single mom, a single dad, two kids, and a whole lot of fun.

The Lucky List

A rom com with a tired single mom, 2 active little boys, an Irish firefighter, and a whole lot of luck.

The Summer Plans

A rom com about a single mom with 3 kids, a single dad firefighter, an unforgettable vacation, and a second chance to get it right.

Coming May 21st, 2026

ABOUT THE AUTHOR

Mya has always had a passion for storytelling and has a background in theatre, film, and education. She lives in the Midwest with her husband and children, working a nonromantic job by day while writing romance at night. Her books are contemporary romance with more love, more spice, and more HEAs. When she's not writing, she enjoys reading, singing karaoke, playing mermaids in the pool, and doing puzzles.

I love hearing from readers! Check out my socials below or email me at myamorewrites@gmail.com

www.authormyamore.com

www.ingramcontent.com/pod-product-compliance
Lightning Source LLC
Chambersburg PA
CBHW071917130726
47909CB00014B/2057